Evan Green is a well-known media personality and motoring journalist whose four previous novels, *Alice to Nowhere*, *Adam's Empire*, *Kalinda* and *Dust and Glory*, have all been best sellers. He is also the author of several successful works of non-fiction.

A former rally driver of international renown, he has driven around or across Australia thirty-five times, thus gaining priceless background material for his novel, *Bet Your Life*.

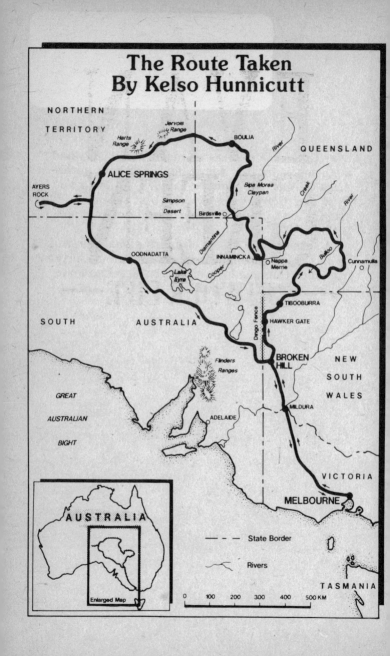

The Route Taken
By Kelso Hunnicutt

EVAN GREEN

GREEN

—BET YOUR LIFE—

PAN
AUSTRALIA

Also by Evan Green in Pan
DUST AND GLORY
HIT THE ROAD, JACK

First published 1992 by Pan Macmillan Publishers Australia
a division of Pan Macmillan Australia Pty Limited
63–71 Balfour Street, Chippendale, Sydney
A.C.N. 001 184 014

Reprinted 1992

National Library of Australia
cataloguing-in-publication data:

Green, Evan.
Bet your life.
ISBN0 330 27330 2.

I. Title.

A823.3

Typeset in 10/11 pt Century Book
by Post Typesetters
Printed in Australia by The Book Printer

1

Kelso Hunnicutt thought: any woman who was such an easy pick-up was bound to make a rotten wife.

He'd met Laura while sweeping leaves from his courtyard. He'd opened the gate and without looking, swept the leaves straight onto the footpath and onto the feet of this tall, good-looking woman who was walking by. They'd had dinner that night, got married two months later. And now she'd left him.

He said nothing all day, not even to his partner. He waited until they were at the pub that night, sitting in their usual corner. Gerry Montague seemed to think it was a joke. Hunnicutt had to repeat the story. Laura had gone.

'Gone? You mean as in gone to visit her sister?' Montague sipped his beer, mixing doubt with the froth. 'Or do you mean she's really left you, like she's never coming back again?'

'Gone for good. At least, that's what she said.'

They were silent for a while, each studying a different wall. There were a few other men in the lounge bar, regulars who drifted in after office hours. The television in the other corner was showing the evening news and someone called out for the barman to turn up the volume.

'Women are always leaving home,' Montague said, his eyes drawn to the screen. 'All my wives

1

did, many times.' Another sip. His mouth twitched, anxious to smile.

'You're not me, Gerry. And Laura's not one of your multitude of ex-wives.'

Montague frowned, matching Hunnicutt's mood. 'When did she leave?'

'Last night.' He lifted his glass but put it down again without drinking. 'I was stupid to marry her. She's a tart.'

Montague kept watching the TV. From somewhere in the world, a tall building was on fire. Not much of a story but good images.

'She's been seeing another man.'

'She told you that?'

Hunnicutt shook his head. 'But I know.' This time he drank deeply and rapidly. 'She's been seeing him for a while. You can sense these things. I should have woken up to it earlier.'

'You accused her of seeing another man?'

'Last night.'

'Which is why the lady left.'

'Lady!' Hunnicutt laughed bitterly, and the man who was trying to hear the news glanced at him. 'She turned on a fine show of outrage,' he continued, speaking softly. 'My wife's a great actress, Gerry. She was the picture of injured innocence.'

'You could be jumping to conclusions. A jealous husband can easily make a bloody fool of himself.'

'I've been a bloody fool for a long time. I've been blind. There've been signs. I was just too stupid to read them.'

'So.' Montague spread his fingers as though playing a chord on the table. 'Here's the story. You accuse her of seeing another man. She denies it and takes umbrage. She walks out.' He paused. 'First time, or has she done it before?'

Hunnicutt sighed. He was beginning to feel foolish. 'First time. Don't try and analyse me, Gerry.'

Montague raised both hands. 'Wouldn't think of it, old chum.'

'Let's just leave it at this: I've been a fool, she's gone and good riddance.'

The hands were still in the air. 'If you say so. Ready for another drink?'

Hunnicutt drank more beer. The news item was about Malakov. It had been a major story for three days. The man had disappeared from the Soviet Embassy in Canberra. So had a million dollars. Malakov, so the story went, was hiding somewhere in the outback.

'Still haven't caught him,' Montague said, grinning. The manhunt was a funny story, amusing to everyone but the Russians.

'The man's a fool,' Hunnicutt said.

'He got away with a million.'

'But he's gone bush. Where are they looking for him now?'

Montague squinted towards the television screen. 'This report's from Alice Springs. I guess they think he's somewhere in the Centre.'

'Crazy.'

'Why? There's a lot of country out there.'

'Yeah, and he doesn't know any of it. He'll stand out…'

'…Like an ant on an iceblock,' Montague suggested.

'Exactly. He should have stayed in one of the cities. Got himself lost in the crowd.'

Montague grunted. 'Malakov's probably already left the country. Had a false passport in his bag, a false beard on his chin, a genuine blonde on his arm, and was off on the first flight out of Sydney. Caught a plane to Bangkok or Jakarta before the Ambassador found that someone had emptied the safe.'

3

'He should have but he didn't.' Hunnicutt stretched his legs and rattled an adjoining chair. 'No, he's gone bush.'

The TV showed an aerial shot of a police Landcruiser stirring dust on a desert track. The track, no more than twin grooves of pale sand, neatly divided the screen into diagonal segments of desolation.

Montague knew nothing about the Australian bush and Hunnicutt was something of an expert, but he said, 'There seems to be an awful lot of empty space for him to hide in'.

'You've got to know the outback to hide in the outback.'

Montague shrugged. 'He's lasted three days.'

'They'll get him. Or he'll perish.' Slowly Hunnicutt turned the glass in his hands. 'He's not the man to do it but it could be done.'

Montague waited until the news item ended. He turned to his friend. 'What could?'

'You could hide out there and not be found.'

'Me?' He laughed.

Hunnicutt smiled kindly. No, not his business partner. Montague was a middle-aged pom, born and bred in London. Since he'd moved to Melbourne, he'd never been further from the centre of the city than the Healesville Sanctuary. He was addicted to money and Porsches. Great at spending but not so good at driving. Shame. The car was wasted on him. Hunnicutt closed his eyes, thinking of Malakov and the hunt. Thinking about the challenge. 'No, not you, Gerry. But it could be done. By someone who knew the bush, knew the tracks, knew what he was doing.'

'Like who?'

Hunnicutt took a deep breath. 'Me,' he said, and laughed.

He was called Kelso Hunnicutt but Kelso was too different, so most people knew him as Kelly.

He made films. Not big-screen films that smashed box-office records and had critics raving about the new wave of Australian movies; but small stuff like the documentary he had just finished for a Japanese car importer. It revealed in glittering detail the new grille, steering wheel and sixteen-valve engine on the latest range of four-cylinder family cars. It might be screened at the Motor Show, but mostly it would be shown on videos in scores of car dealerships. The customer would watch while the salesman slipped out for a cup of coffee. The film ran for eleven minutes, fifty-seven seconds — time for two cups. The audience would be ordinary people who had thought of buying a small Ford or Holden. This film, his film, was intended to make them change their minds.

Laura hated those films.

When they first met, on the day when he swept the leaves over her ankles, she thought he was a big-time movie producer. The sort of man who made *The Man from Snowy River* or *Crocodile Dundee*. She presumed they would go to Hollywood — after all, Peter Weir and Bruce Beresford had done it. She loved *Witness* (mainly because it had Harrison Ford in it), and hadn't *Driving Miss Daisy* won an Oscar? Weir, Beresford and Schepisi had paved the way. Why couldn't Kelly Hunnicutt follow? (It had to be Kelly; Kelso Hunnicutt was too ridiculous.) Why couldn't he be a genuine Hollywood director and live in a big house in Beverly Hills? Mix with the stars — even invite Harrison Ford across for drinks. But no, Kelly made films that explained why you should buy a car with overhead camshafts, or that showed you how to glue vinyl tiles to your kitchen floor, or tried to persuade you to fly to Alice Springs for your holidays.

5

He was late home that night. He felt bad. He'd had too much to drink and the rats of guilt were sniffing and nibbling at the walls of his conscience. Maybe he'd been wrong. Laura had been so out-raged. Correction — had *seemed* so outraged. He could never tell. She was a great actress.

'You bastard, Kelso Hunnicutt,' she had shouted. It was unusual for her to swear. Unusual to call him Kelso, too, unless she was really angry. 'You're the one who's never home. You're always tripping around the country, making those tacky little films of yours, driving along your awful bush tracks, sleep-ing with a new woman every night. And yet you have the hide to accuse me.'

He'd tried to assure her he didn't sleep with a new woman every night, but she'd gone off her head and hadn't given him a chance to say another word. He grinned. God, she'd been impressive.

Now he was lonely.

He checked the refrigerator for another beer. There was only milk and even then it was that wretched low-calorie, high-protein stuff she fan-cied. Always worried about her figure. It was a good figure. She'd been a model.

The South African was in town. He was a big man, with iron-grey hair and an old-fashioned crew cut. He looked like a hard man and he was — anyone who had spent years prospecting on his own in dry and remote country had to be tough. Kolven-bach was a typical Boer with a back-of-the-throat voice that emitted bent and strangled vowels; and when he stood too close, which was his habit, Kelly felt intimidated. It was not just the man's immense bulk. His eyes always seemed to be searching the other person's face and finding something lacking.

Despite all this, Kelly liked him. Kolvenbach was direct. And sharp. The man had a sense of humour,

6

and knowing his voice was the cause of some amusement — he could detect the slightest wrinkle of distaste in Montague's nostrils or the first flare of superiority in an eyebrow — he played upon the difference in accents. He was lavish in his praise of Montague. A fine English gentleman, he called him; a real toff with a command of English that humbled a rough old prospector like himself. 'Your English is cultured,' Kolvenbach would say. 'Mine is nonsense.' He pronounced it noon-since.

The irony eluded Montague by the most slender of margins. Gerry liked praise. Tickle his vanity and, if you were clever enough, he was as helpless as a dog having its belly scratched. So Kolvenbach tickled him. But with Kelly, the big Boer was rough. He was constantly shaking his head in bafflement. He was trying hard, he would say, but he just couldn't understand Kelly's true-blue Aussie nasal rasp. It was his way of saying he preferred to deal with Kelly and thought him the more genuine of the two. Kelly understood that. Gerry was a real bullshit artist. That was his role in the company — he did the selling and collected the money, Kelly made the films.

Kolvenbach was rough but he had good points. He knew his diamonds and he loved the outback. But best of all he had made a lot of money, and he wanted to spend some of it with them.

'Your film will have to show,' Kolvenbach was saying, 'that the mine will not only *not* be harmful to the environment, but it will be positively beneficial.' The last words, Kelly thought, sounded as though the syllables had been mixed with a mouth full of chaff.

'Of course,' Montague said.

Kolvenbach studied him with calculating eyes. 'It will be a tough job. The environmentalists are strong. Not always fair but they know how to touch politicians in their most sensitive places.'

'But you're doing a lot of replanting,' Kelly prompted.

'I'm putting in trees where trees have never grown before. Water, shrubs, everything.' He coughed to clear his throat. 'And then there is the Aboriginal question.'

'Oh God, this mine of yours isn't going to be on a sacred site?' Montague's English accent, always well-cultivated when Kolvenbach was around, was even more pronounced.

'Every site is sacred when there's money involved.' The South African winked at Kelly.

'You can get around it?' Kelly asked.

'The Aboriginal people I'm dealing with so far are reasonable.' He allowed himself a smile. 'No one has lived there or near there for a hundred years, I'd say. The traditional owners were harder to find than the diamonds.'

'So,' Montague said, striking the table with his fingers, 'our film has to convince people that there has been no damage to the environment and that the traditional owners, if there truly are such people, are happy.'

Kolvenbach tilted his chin in acknowledgment. 'What I'd like now would be for someone to come up north with me.' He nodded towards Kelly. 'You could see the place for yourself. No good just talking about it.'

'Fine,' said Kelly. He would enjoy the long flight in Kolvenbach's aircraft and there was no other work booked. They needed this film.

'When?' Montague asked.

'In three weeks' time.'

'Why so long?' Kelly asked and immediately regretted sounding anxious. Not good for business. The studio mustn't appear to be short of customers; no doubt Gerry would remind him of that later.

'Can't go before then. There's too much to do

8

in Melbourne.' The Boer locked fingers; his hands began to wrestle. 'I found me a nice buyer today.'

'Someone who will buy your diamonds?' Montague asked.

'Someone who already has.' The right hand had bent the other back. The right hand, Kelly guessed, was Kolvenbach, and the vanquished left was the diamond buyer. 'Just a sample I brought down,' Kolvenbach added and, with his hands now free, reached down to pat his briefcase. 'He paid well.'

Kelly's eyes widened. 'You're not carrying a lot of cash around the city in that bag?' Kolvenbach always seemed to have large sums on him. He'd discussed it with Gerry many times.

The South African grinned and his hard, sunburned skin cracked into fine wrinkles.

'What are you going to do with all this money you're making?' Montague was jovial, casual — one millionaire to another.

'Put it in the bank, I hope,' Kelly said and felt out of his class.

'I might buy a big, luxury yacht.' It was a joke. Kolvenbach only spent money on essentials. Some, like the aircraft, were expensive, but he only used his money to make money.

'The bank,' Kelly repeated.

Kolvenbach checked his watch. 'The bank has closed. Besides, banks have records and records are read by nosy people.'

'Put it somewhere safe.'

The South African winked. 'I have somewhere safe.'

A big map of Australia covered one wall of Kelly Hunnicutt's office. He was studying it when the telephone rang. It was Laura's sister.

'You haven't gone yet?' she began.

'No.' Instantly, Kelly thought of smarter answers

but said nothing. He liked Tricia. She was a bit slow and she talked too much, but she was genuine.

'I hear Laura's left home.'

'Who told you that?'

'Laura.'

He paused. 'How is she?'

'Same as always. Busy. Working on some secret scheme or another. You know what she's like.'

'Yes,' he said and wondered if he did.

'Do you want to know where she is?'

He hesitated.

'Kelly, I think you should do something about this. Go and see her and drag her back home.'

'By the hair?'

'If you have to.'

He laughed. 'I think I'd have to. She wouldn't come voluntarily. We had a pretty nasty argument.'

'I know. You said she had another man. She denied it.'

Another pause. 'Yes. I was pretty rough.'

'Well, I think you should go and see her and talk to her and take her back home.' She gave him an address in Carlton.

Kelly was surprised. 'I thought she might have been staying with you.'

'No way. Too many people where I live.' A pause. 'She's had this place just off Drummond Street for a while.'

He was silent, shocked. If she had a flat, she must have been planning to leave him. Before the argument.

'You didn't know, did you?'

Still stunned, he shook his head and then said, 'No'.

'She told me there's no one else, too. She was most emphatic. But she was lying.'

Silence. A numbness, as chilling as ice, rose up through his chest and paralysed his throat.

10

'I know who it is, Kelly. I've known for a while. I've seen them together.'

He didn't want to hear this. He didn't want Laura's sister ringing up and telling him he'd been right. He wanted to be told he'd been wrong; that there was no other man.

'It's that partner of yours.'

2

Kelly was sipping his first beer when Montague arrived. They had arranged to meet in the bar to talk further about Kolvenbach's film. Montague was short of breath. Just back from Carlton, or are you going later? Kelly thought, but smiled. He wouldn't let on that he knew. 'Thought you mightn't be coming,' he said.

Montague ordered a drink and sat down. 'Got caught in the traffic.'

'Pretty bad was it?' Kelly avoided the other man's eyes. 'Who was it you had to see?'

'Gibson from McCann's.' Montague's eyebrows rose in surprise. 'Bathrooms. Remember?' They've got the account for all this gear from Germany. Rip out your old bathtub and put in this magic German stuff, and you too can have your back scrubbed in a dream world.'

'Oh, yes.' He didn't remember but Montague was always chasing prospects. Kelly slowed his racing mind by taking a sip of beer. Bathrooms. Another of the trade films that Laura hated so much. 'Any luck?'

'They're still interested. Apparently there's a marketing meeting in a fortnight.'

'Does Gibson want us along when he makes his presentation?' He tried to sound interested.

'He's going to let me know.'

Kelly nodded. A nice safe answer. You could have been anywhere, you deceitful bastard, he thought. I'm going to play you like a fish, a fish that doesn't want to be landed and doesn't even know it's been hooked.

So he steered the conversation around to Kolvenbach's diamond mine and the film they would make for him. The South African was no piker when it came to budgets. He was prepared to spend 120,000 dollars on his documentary. Its audience would be small: just a few parliamentarians and a select group of influential people in Canberra and Western Australia. Kolvenbach knew that face-to-face meetings wouldn't work. If he went around explaining to these people what he intended doing up in the Kimberleys — telling them how many workers he would employ, how big a town he'd build, how he'd care for the environment and deal fairly with any Aborigines who claimed traditional ownership — they'd be hearing his voice but not listening to what he was saying. The accent would ruin things. South African, they'd think; and his case would need to be twice as strong as anyone else's. Prejudice built high hurdles, even when you were a sincere man like Kolvenbach.

One hundred and twenty thousand for a film and a narrator with a good Australian accent would be money well invested. For Kolvenbach it would be petty cash. He was planning to spend twelve million on the mine in the first year.

By the second round of drinks, Montague's voice was slurred. He confessed he'd had a few drinks in the agency boardroom. He scratched his nose a few times, always a sign that he had something on his mind, and wondered aloud if they could charge Kolvenbach more for his film. One hundred and fifty thousand was a nice round figure. Another 30,000 dollars would hardly be noticed if the big

13

man was budgeting to spend four hundred times that amount in twelve months.

Four hundred? Montague was quick with figures and Kelly always got confused when there were a lot of noughts in a sum. He shook his head. 'Don't be greedy, Gerry. We'll make good money if we charge 120,000 dollars.'

This fellow is so cool, Kelly thought. Here he is, pinching my wife, and he talks business as though nothing had happened. And he can still do his arithmetic. Kelly was so agitated he'd have had trouble with two plus two.

'One hundred and fifty would be nicer.' Montague smiled like an amiable pickpocket, caught with his hand on your wallet.

'We'd lose the job. Kolvenbach wouldn't stand for a hike in the price.'

'Shame.' Montague slouched forward, head hanging, shoulders loose. He must have had more than a few drinks with Gibson. He was drunk. Which meant that he *had* been at the agency, not with Laura, because she wasn't into heavy drinking. Or was it an act? Kelly had seen Montague turn on some amazing performances to impress people who might spend money with the company. He could be everything from a stand-up comic to the Duke of Edinburgh, depending on the client.

'It might be a shame,' Kelly said, eyeing his partner intently, 'but it'd be a disaster to lose the whole lot and that's what would happen if we tried to con the big bloke. He's not someone you can con.' Not like me, he thought.

Kelly ordered more drinks, even though Montague protested — not too vigorously — that he'd had enough. Get him really drunk and see what he has to say, Kelly thought. But after another two rounds, Montague hadn't said any more and Kelly was feeling woozy himself, and beginning to have doubts. He only had Tricia's word about Laura and Gerry. What if she *had* seen them together? What was wrong with that? They knew each other. It might have been perfectly innocent. It was his fortieth birthday in a month's time and they could have been planning something — a party or a special present. Oh God, imagine losing his wife and his best friend because he was just a jealous, suspicious bastard. He always had been. Rushed to conclusions — usually wrong.

Montague smiled happily at him. 'You're right, old chum,' he said. 'Absolutely right.' Kelly seemed not to follow. 'I mean about Cutting Back or Kolvenbach or Jumping Jack or whatever his name is.' A giggle turned into a hiccup. 'Absolutely right. As always. We must do the honourable thing. Stick to the quote. Be gentlemen.'

The television news came on. Malakov had been caught. The police had arrested him in a motel at Tennant Creek.

Kelly grinned in triumph. 'Told you so. He should have hidden himself in one of the big cities.'

'But you could have got away with it?' Montague said slowly. It was a challenge.

'In the outback?' Kelly considered. 'Yes. I'd know where to go.'

'Bullshit.' The insult was delivered amiably.

'Is not.' I sound drunk too, Kelly thought to himself. Can't even speak properly. He thought again. Not a bad idea. Pretend he'd had too much to drink and Montague might open up. 'I mean I could hide from the police. Very effectively.' He had trouble pronouncing the last word. 'I know every road in the outback.' That, he thought, truly is bullshit but it sounds like the sort of boast that a drunken man might make.

'They'd catch you in one day.' Montague emptied his glass and kept his eyes on the ceiling, as though something up there had inspired him. 'Well, maybe not in a day but certainly, *certainly*, in one week.'

'Certainly? As in absolutely positively?'

'Absolutely, old boy. One week, and they'd have you behind bars.'

'I know roads that aren't on the map. I have been to places where no white man has been.'

'Well what are *you*?' Montague looked around to see if anyone had heard the line and appreciated the wit, but the bar was almost empty.

'I mean before me.' Kelly leaned forward. 'I have made more films on the outback than any living man.'

Montague matched his angle. 'How about the Leyland brothers?'

Kelly raised his glass. 'I said man, not men. There are two of them.'

'You still haven't made half as many outback films as they have.'

'I've made a lot.'

Montague raised his empty glass. 'True. And some bloody good films, if I may be permitted to offer my congratulations to a fine film-maker.' Only then did he seem to notice that his glass was empty. He signalled the barman. 'But the police would still catch you within one week. You're having yourself on, Kelly old chum.'

'They wouldn't even find my tracks.' He smiled confidently, and then added, 'Unless they were very old'.

'The policemen?' Montague laughed.

'The tracks, Gerry, the tracks. I could get lost in the outback and never be found. One week did you say?'

Montague nodded.

Kelly shook his head. He was serious now. 'If I drove into the outback, intending to elude the police, they would not find me within seven days.'

16

'In your Landcruiser?'

'In anything.' He laughed. 'Except that Porsche of yours. That thing stands out like dogs' balls and would get stuck in the first sandy crossing.'

'But in that Landcruiser of yours, you say you could drive into the outback and hide from the police for a week?'

'Yes.' Kelly nodded vigorously. 'Guaranteed.'

'Bet you couldn't.'

Kelly leaned forward and took the other man's hand. 'You're on.'

The new drinks arrived. After the barman had left, Kelly said, 'What's the bet?'

Montague looked uncertain and said nothing.

'You were talking through your hat, weren't you, Gerry?'

'No.' Montague seemed to be calculating odds. He scratched his nose. 'Your car against mine.'

As light-hearted as a pair of schoolboys planning a practical joke, they worked out the details. Kelly must leave that night. At twelve. The bet would end at midnight on the following Thursday. Kelly would have to leave Melbourne and drive towards the outback. If the police found Kelly within the seven days, he would give his turbocharged diesel Landcruiser to Montague. If Kelly eluded the police, he would win Montague's Porsche Turbo.

Montague offered to help Kelly pack. He would be the official starter to make sure Kelly left precisely on time. He left his car in the car park. He'd had too much to drink, he said, and spent the ten minutes it took Kelly to drive home making disparaging remarks about the Toyota.

They pulled up in Kelly's driveway.

'How much did you pay for this truck?' Montague asked, gripping the passenger's panic handle.

'Sixty-five thousand.'

17

'You were robbed, old son.' He fingered the vinyl roof lining. 'I'd say it was worth about twenty-five.'

'Bullshit.'

Montague smiled happily. 'Which means I'm giving you odds of about ten to one.'

It took Kelly several seconds to do the sum. 'A quarter of a million for that overgrown Volkswagen of yours? You've got to be nuts.'

'You're not welshing on the bet?'

'Absolutely not.' And then two things occurred to him. The first was that Montague didn't sound drunk any more. Had the prospect of losing his car sobered him up, or was this all an act? A ploy to get him out of Melbourne for a week. Jesus Christ, he'd be out of town, sitting on the banks of some outback creek while Montague and Laura would be in the city, doing what they liked. He looked sideways at his partner.

Montague had twisted in the seat to examine the rear compartment of the Landcruiser. 'It could be handy,' he said grudgingly, as though he'd never thought about owning a four-wheel drive. 'If only I had a farm I could use it to carry pigs in.' He smiled broadly. 'I'll give you this: there's plenty of room.'

He didn't act like a man who was thinking deviously. Just a happy drunk. The slurred voice was back.

The second thought was practical. 'How the hell are you going to get the police to look for me?'

Montague gazed out the window. His mouth was open, sucking in ideas.

'You haven't thought about that, have you?' Kelly drummed the rim of the steering wheel. 'I don't want them thinking I robbed the company safe or something like that.'

'Of course not.'

'Well why would they bother looking for me? If

they don't mount some sort of search, like they did for Malakov, there's no point to the bet, is there?'

'I suppose not,' Montague said slowly.

Kelly felt relieved. Montague hadn't planned this. He wasn't scheming to spend a week with Laura. It had just been the drink talking. He laughed. 'Great bet. Your car's safe because there's no way we can make the thing work.'

'There's got to be some way,' Montague said, running one hand across the dashboard. 'I'd grown rather fond of the idea of taking this overpriced truck off your hands.'

'You weren't going to win and you know it.'

Montague scratched the tip of his nose. 'Let me think.'

'I'm not going to have the police coming after me with their guns drawn?'

'Of course not.'

'Good idea, Gerry, but it won't work.' He searched for the remote-control unit that would open the door of his garage. 'What we need is a reason for the search and there isn't one.'

'Unless...'

'Unless what?'

'Unless the police think they have to find you to help you. To save your life. Would that be acceptable?'

'What are you talking about, Gerry?'

Montague was animated now, bursting with ideas. 'Do you know Roger Simpson?'

'No.'

'He's a friend of mine. Chemist. Good man. He'd do anything I asked him.'

'Like what?'

'Well, supposing I went to the police tomorrow morning and told them you'd gone on a week's holiday. Headed for the bush. Destination unknown, but probably somewhere in the Northern Territory. Right?'

19

Kelly nodded.

'And I said you'd been sick. That's why you'd taken this sudden leave.' He waited for Kelly's approval. 'Well, sick men need medicine. Supposing I say you'd been to the chemist to get a prescription, and the chemist had given you the wrong pills. Something that could prove fatal.' He smiled triumphantly. 'So the police would have to find you to save your life.'

Kelly stroked his chin. 'This chemist friend of yours would go along with that?'

'Roger owes me a favour or two. He'd do it.'

'So the police wouldn't want to shoot me, they'd want to save me.'

'Absolutely. There's one thing though,' Montague added, suddenly looking doubtful. 'There could be a lot of publicity. It would be in all the papers. The public would be looking for you, too. It would make it harder for you.'

Kelly shrugged.

'Too tough for you?'

Kelly laughed. 'I can disappear for a week.'

'There could be a big search.'

'Good. The bigger, the better.'

'What do you say then?'

'I say you're on.'

They shook hands. Kelly felt happy. He was looking forward to the prospect of going bush and playing the game. And winning the Porsche. Best of all, he had just thought of a way to make sure Montague wouldn't see Laura in his absence. Just in case the bastard *was* tricking him and had planned all this.

He knew where Laura was staying. He'd take her with him. Whether she wanted to go or not.

3

It was the challenge. One man against the world. That was what excited Kelly. It wasn't only that he was angry because Gerry had been sleeping with Laura — or maybe hadn't been, which made him just as angry because that meant he'd been foolish enough to listen to Tricia and believe that his wife would run off with a slob like Gerry — and it wasn't that he'd like to own a Porsche or that he was three-quarters of the way to being drunk. It was the thought of being chased. Hunted. That was what excited him.

When he was a small boy, Kelly used to dream of being Robin Hood. Not because he wanted to use a bow and arrow, but because Robin Hood had been hunted. The wicked Sheriff of Nottingham and his men were after him, but Robin always eluded them because he knew Sherwood Forest so intimately.

Kelly liked the idea. One man, a good smart man who knew his territory, against the rest. Someone who could hide in the branches of a tree and laugh as the mounted hunters thundered by.

Later on, it had been Zorro. Same thing. A dashing swordsman with a white horse and a black mask, a rebel against the unjust state. Swish, swish, swish and his delicate trademark was inscribed on some villain's shirt. The soldiers searched and searched but they could never find him.

21

As a little kid he had longed to grow up so that he could hide among the oaks of Sherwood Forest or gallop his horse at night through the hills of southern California.

And here was Gerry inviting him to live out his boyhood fantasies; to be Robin Hood of the Mac-Donnell Ranges, Zorro in a four-wheel drive. He's risking a quarter-of-a-million-dollar motorcar, Kelly thought, and the fool doesn't realise I'd do it for nothing.

Kelly was wriggling into a pair of faded jeans that were a little tighter than they used to be. He stopped, embarrassed. A man who was almost forty and earned well over 100,000 dollars a year producing films about camshafts and floor tiles shouldn't be thinking of living out his childhood fantasies. Hiding from the police? He was nuts.

He grinned to himself. Hell, it would be fun. There was no work scheduled for next week and he wanted to get out of town. He threaded a belt through the pants, pulled it tighter than was comfortable to the notch he had used last year, and then started to pack. Two bush shirts for a week; another pair of pants, this time well-worn mole-skins; his bush boots; a jumper for the nights. Plus a weatherproof jacket — brown, so that he'd be hard to see from a distance — and his Akubra with its brim bent and stained just like a real bushie's hat.

He got his shaving gear and toothbrush but there was no toothpaste. He added it to the list of things he had jotted down, to buy at the first stop in the morning.

He'd never been to Sherwood Forest, although he'd flown to London a couple of times on business. He'd been to California, but driven a rented car along the freeway, not galloped a white horse at night back to a secret stable in a grand hacienda.

The bet was juvenile, stupid. Laura would say he was mad. He was. So what? She wouldn't understand. He *wanted* to do it. Be hunted. Elude the wicked sheriff, the Spanish soldiers, the Australian police.

He paused. He liked hiding. Not just from the police, but from many things. That was why he had never made any other sort of film. Just trade films. They were safe. No risk. No public to judge, no critics to condemn. He took a deep breath. Maybe one day.

He needed justification; something that made the bet seem logical or at least understandable to an outsider. He could always say he wanted the Porsche, but that was too mercenary. In any case, he was thinking that if he won the bet — *when* he won the bet — he wouldn't take the car. Let Gerry keep it. That would be a grand gesture. Humiliate the bastard.

It was the challenge, the affront to his honour. That was it.

Gerry was watching and smirking. Silly drunken prick, Kelly thought; he doesn't think I know the outback. That's why he has that stupid, provocative look on his face.

Well, thinking thoughts like that made the challenge an insult, a cause for a duel. Cars at dawn. He stifled a giggle. He knew the outback as well as... He tried to think of a comparison. He thought of the Birdsville mailman but that was out of date because these days the mail went to Birdsville by aircraft. Old Tom Kruse who used to drive up to Birdsville in a truck would have been a good bushman but he probably didn't know the Northern Territory. Just the Birdsville Track. Which was fair enough — the old Birdsville Track must have been a fearsome challenge. No problem these days.

He stopped packing for a moment. What had he been trying to think of? His head was fuzzy.

Gerry was still smirking.

Maybe I will take the Porsche, he said to himself, and felt a shiver of joyful anticipation.

He hiccupped and Gerry, watching, let his smirk become a grin.

Twenty-eight, he thought, smiling back. That's how many films he'd made in the outback. Admittedly some had been pretty bland, promoting tourism or someone's hotel; but there'd been a TV series on outback oddities, a sort of 'Believe It Or Not' down under and, while the presenter had been so stiff that the series had bombed, he'd seen a lot of the country. The scenery was great. Well filmed. Artistic. People had said that.

He'd also made some documentaries for an oil-exploration company. He'd gone with their geologists into the Kimberleys and west of Alice all through the Amadeus Basin. And in his own time, on holidays or when he had a week or two to spare, he'd roamed the outback. He was a nomad at heart, condemned to live in the city because of the need to make enough money to maintain the house in Armadale, and to keep Laura in expensive clothes and ensure she drove the latest model Mercedes.

Keep Laura? He'd lost her. He laughed ruefully and Gerry tilted his head. He didn't speak. Probably couldn't, Kelly thought. The poor bastard was as full as a boot.

Don't know the interior, eh? he said to himself, letting the smile linger. He'd driven along the water holes of Cooper's Creek, crossed the sand ridges around Birdsville, roamed the dry, lacerated ranges to the east and west of Alice Springs, been to Ayers Rock half a dozen times, ventured into the Petermann Ranges where the explorer Giles had roamed, and camped on his own in the Rawlinsons, with their crumbling, golden crowns of broken rock. He knew hidden gullies and quiet water holes where the sand was peppered with dingo tracks. Places no one else went to.

He was a good bushman. He mightn't have been the world's greatest film-maker although he made good money — which a lot of the arty fellows didn't — and there might have been dozens of things he did badly, as Laura was always reminding him; but he knew the outback.

He had the early stages of his route planned. He'd head for the Cooper. Go up through Mildura and Wentworth and stop at Broken Hill first thing in the morning. He'd fill his jerry cans with fuel, top up his water containers, and buy food and drinks. Purchase things at different shops so people would be less likely to remember him. Then off, north along the dingo fence to Cameron Corner, where the Queensland, South Australia and New South Wales borders met. All sand and stark trees. Lonely, beautiful country.

Then the Cooper. He'd decide later what to do after that. Maybe stay on the river. He knew a water hole where a colony of pelicans lived. He could camp in the bush, out of sight. No human went there; just the pelicans and him.

'What are you grinning at?' Montague asked.

'Just thinking of a place where the troopers will never find me.'

'Troopers? As in "Waltzing Matilda"? "Down came the troopers, one two three"?' Montague waited for Kelly to say something but his partner was silent. His face suggested he'd been found out. Montague grinned triumphantly. 'Is that where you're going to camp? You're going to be a jolly swagman and camp on a billabong?'

'I'm not saying.'

Montague prodded the bag that Kelly was carrying. 'I must say you look as though you're preparing for a long stay.'

'I am. For a whole week. I might even stay longer just to prove the point.' Kelly thrust out his chin. 'And I'm looking forward to having you present me with the keys of your car. You will fill the tank?'

Montague scratched his nose. 'Yours will probably have fallen apart by the time the cops bring you back. I hadn't thought of that. It'll be worth nothing. Wonder how much I'll get for it as junk?'

Kelly turned and put his bag in the Landcruiser. He frowned. Montague hadn't sounded drunk.

At a quarter to twelve they were in the kitchen drinking coffee. Kelly thought of taking the rifle that was in his closet. He brought it to the table, removed it from its leather case and sighted along the bore. Clean, even though he hadn't used it for more than a year. Montague shook his head vigorously. 'No gun,' he said, his voice a little slurred once more. 'That's not part of the bet.'

'You want me to starve?'

Montague laughed. 'Don't tell me you were thinking of living off the land?'

'Who knows?' He put the rifle back in the bag and checked that there was ammunition.

'No gun. I don't want you shooting those troopers, one, two, three.' Coffee cup in one hand, Montague went to the closet and handed Kelly a fishing rod. 'Take this. Fish is better for you than red meat anyhow. You'll live longer. Lower blood pressure, or something.' He took the gun from Kelly and put it back in the cupboard. 'You can take clothes, food, fishing rod, spares for the car, but no artillery.'

'That wasn't in the original bet.'

'It is now.'

Kelly toyed with the rod. There were fish in the water hole, which is why there were always so many pelicans. He looked up suddenly. 'Should we put all this in writing? I mean the bet and all the conditions.'

'A handshake will do me.'

He considered. He hated writing things down.
'Me too.'

Solemnly, they shook hands.

He got in the Toyota at two minutes to twelve. He
got out again immediately.

'What's up?' Montague asked. He was in the garage, near the light switch.

'I haven't locked the back door.'

'I'll do it for you. Get back in the car or you'll
be late.'

'You'll lock up?'

Montague dangled a key. 'You left it on the kitchen table.'

'Leave it under the big flower pot. That's where
I usually put it.'

'I know.' He grinned. 'If you don't stop talking,
you'll be late.'

Kelly remembered that Montague had no car.
'How are you getting home? Do you want a lift
somewhere?'

'I'll call a cab. Mind if I use your phone?'

'Go ahead.'

'Now, piss off.' Montague moved to the Toyota
and shook Kelly's hand. 'Have a good trip. I'll see
you in a day or so.'

'Like hell you will.' He started the motor and
then shouted above the clanking of the diesel.
'You're sure this chemist friend of yours will play
along?'

'No worries. Now, will you nick off.'

Kelly reversed out of the garage, flicked the lights
in salute, and used his remote control to close the
garage door.

Montague waited until the sound of the Toyota
had faded before going back to the house. From
his coat pocket he withdrew a pair of driving gloves

and put them on. He went to the closet and took out the rifle bag. Gently, hands shaking slightly, he put it on the table.

He picked up the phone and dialled a number. 'It's gone brilliantly.' A long pause while he listened. He nodded frequently. 'Yes,' he said, and hung up.

He went to the main bedroom and selected one of Kelly's jackets. He put it on. He fossicked among Kelly's shoes which were scattered untidily across the base of the wardrobe, and chose a brown pair with thick, patterned rubber soles. They were too big for him but he put them on. He left his own jacket on the bed and arranged his shoes neatly on the floor. He walked to the kitchen and got the rifle.

Montague left the house and walked to the next street, to the place where he had parked the rented Landcruiser late that afternoon. He drove to Kolvenbach's house.

Kelly parked opposite the address in Carlton. It was a small house, jammed in an untidy row of small houses. For a few minutes he sat in the Toyota, peering into the shadows masking the doorway, wondering who was inside. There was no light showing. Laura would be in bed. He tried to imagine what the house would be like inside. Narrow and cramped; a mean little house with tiny rooms. A small bedroom with a big double bed. At least Gerry wouldn't be in there with her. He'd still be waiting for a taxi. And then what would he do — come here? Kelly stroked the steering wheel. Let him come. She'd be gone by then.

Another thought was worrying him: were the sisters working together in all this? Had they played him for a fool? Was Gerry merely a diversion, a decoy, innocent and unaware of their scheme, a name to put Kelly off the track of the real lover?

Tricia could have lied. She'd help Laura. She'd do what her little sister asked.

Was there another man? Other men? Laura had had many boyfriends before they married. Was it one of them, living with Laura in this seedy little house? He closed his eyes and his imagination flared like a wildfire leaping through the treetops.

He got out of the Landcruiser and crossed to the other footpath. The road was rough and depressed, a drain of leaf stains and patched bitumen sunk beneath the shadowy serrations of gabled roofs. A few lights peeked through curtained windows, and rock music pulsed from a house only two doors from the place where Laura was staying. That house's front yard was filled with a jumble of cardboard boxes and old plastic bags. This wasn't a good part of Carlton. What the hell was Laura doing in an area like this? Her house had a verandah so small that it was almost filled by two bicycles. Laura on a bicycle? She had a Mercedes. Where was the car? There was no room for a garage. And who rode the second bike? He checked the house number. It was the right place.

He looked at his watch, straining to see its face in the light from the nearest street lamp. Twelve twenty-three. He knocked on the door.

No one answered.

He knocked again. If Laura were staying here, surely she'd be home now, at 12.23 on a Thursday night. Or Friday morning. He checked the date on his watch. It was Friday, first day of the bet. He spent a few moments inspecting the bicycles. They were both men's models. Built for touring. Lots of gears.

Then a terrible thought struck him. What if Laura had been sitting in her Mercedes at Armadale, just around the corner, waiting for him to leave the house? Supposing she and Gerry were there together, now, in his home. In his bed.

29

He knocked again. No one answered. He hammered at the door and the music blaring from the house two doors down stopped. He walked out on to the footpath. The lights in that house went out. They'd be watching through the window. He waved derisively and saw a curtain flutter.

He walked back to the Landcruiser and climbed into the driver's seat. He'd wait an hour. If she wasn't back by then, she could stay in Melbourne and she could go to hell.

Kolvenbach worked late, went to bed late, and was always up by six. He boasted about how little sleep he needed. Some men bragged about their drinking capacity or sexual prowess; the big South African was proud of his ability to stay awake. He could work harder and longer than any man he had ever met. He liked doing business at midnight. It gave him an advantage. He thought clearly late at night whereas the others — partners or rivals, it didn't matter — were usually drowsy or had had too much to drink.

He was expecting a visitor now. The gates were unlocked and the lights were on.

Montague left the rented Landcruiser in the street and looked around him. The building was set well back from the road, behind a high stone wall, and the garden was thick with shrubs and tall trees. Carrying the rifle in its leather bag under one arm, he walked up the gravel driveway until he was near the house. Then, using slow and measured steps, he turned and walked towards one of the windows. It meant crossing the garden, and his shoes, Kelly's rubber-soled casuals, left deep imprints in the soil. He turned to make sure the marks were clear, then trampled through a flower-bed beneath the window. Passing a rose bush, he brushed it with his shoulder several times until a thread caught on a thorn. Satisfied, he crossed the lawn to the front door and rang the bell.

Kolvenbach was surprised to see him. He leaned forward to glance into the night, searching for someone else. 'On your own?'

Montague nodded and walked in.

'I thought it was Kelly who had to see me.' Kolvenbach growled the words as he led the way into the study. 'That was the message I had on my machine. Kelly said he'd be here at midnight. He said it was urgent.' He rubbed one eye wearily, a sign that he hoped the meeting would be brief. 'Is he coming?'

'No.' Montague smiled. He was a good mimic and Kolvenbach had really thought it was Kelly on the telephone. Good. The message would still be on the recorder. 'Something happened at the last minute. I came instead.'

Kolvenbach nodded but did not look pleased. 'Want coffee?'

'No, thank you.' Montague put the long leather case on the table and unzipped it.

'What have you got there?'

Montague took out the rifle.

'What the hell's that for? Are you going hunting?'

'In a way.' Montague pointed the rifle at Kolvenbach's chest. 'I'm hunting for money. Diamonds too, if you've got them handy.'

The big man spread his hands on the table. 'I don't understand you, friend. What is this? A joke, a pommy joke?'

'No.' Montague smiled. 'It's a stick-up, a pommy stick-up.'

'You are joking.' Without taking his hands from the table, Kolvenbach sat down. 'It's not in good taste. It's late and I've got other things to do before I go to bed. Put that thing down.'

Montague was still smiling. 'I'm deadly serious.'

31

'You're holding me up?'

'Yes.'

Kolvenbach laughed. 'Where is Kelly? Filming all this with a hidden camera?'

'No.'

'Come on. I don't like playing games.'

'Open your safe.'

Kolvenbach clenched his fists. 'A hold-up?'

'Yes.'

'Why?'

'Because I want your money. And the diamonds.' He smiled pleasantly.

Kolvenbach shook his head. 'This is crazy. I know who you are. You can't get away with something like this.'

'Yes I can. Just open the safe.'

Kolvenbach tilted his head to one side. 'Why did Kelly ring me? Is he part of this?'

'Kelly didn't ring. I did.'

Kolvenbach nodded, slowly taking in the facts. 'So, you are robbing me and want me to open the safe. What if I say no?'

'Then I'll pull the trigger.'

'Then I won't be able to open the safe for you.'

'I know where to find the combination.' Montague enjoyed the look of doubt on Kolvenbach's face. 'It's in your book. The one you carry around with you.' He waggled a thumb towards the desk. 'In your briefcase.'

Kolvenbach stood up, unfolding his great body like a bear rising from its sleep. 'I should warn you,' he said, 'that this conversation has now reached the point where I am becoming annoyed. If you're drunk, why don't you just leave my house now, and you can ring me in the morning and make your apologies.'

'I'm not drunk.' Montague jerked the rifle so that the barrel pointed towards Kolvenbach's chin. 'And

32

if you don't do what I'm telling you to do, I'll just blow a hole in you and open the safe myself.'

The South African seemed about to laugh but suddenly lunged at him, his right hand grabbing for the end of the rifle. Montague stepped back and fired.

The bullet hit Kolvenbach in the middle of the chest. He fell against the chair and rolled with it on to the floor. He made one grunting sound, then a rattling wheeze.

Montague waited. There was no other movement, no sound except the hiss of air passing through his own clenched teeth. He covered his mouth to stifle the noise, and listened. Nothing; no dog barked, no neighbour shouted an alarm. He edged his way around the table. A bright red stain was spreading across Kolvenbach's shirt. He prodded the body with the rifle barrel and the man's head wobbled from one side to the other; the eyes were closed, the mouth open.

Montague went to a front room, turned off the solitary lamp and waited by the window. There were no cars passing the gateway, no sirens wailing in the distance, no torches flashing in the driveway. He went back to the study and put the rifle on the table. Bending down beside the body, he pressed the cuff of one coat sleeve against the bloodstain. Then he went to the desk, took the briefcase and, still wearing his gloves, extracted Kolvenbach's notebook.

He was on the telephone. He had poured himself a whisky and while he talked, held the glass up to the light. 'I've got everything,' he said, and took a sip. He could see Kolvenbach's legs beneath the table. The man had big feet. 'Yes, diamonds and enough cash to fill the rifle bag. God, the man was rolling in money.' He drank some more and listened.

33

'Yes I am,' he said, 'some of the big Boer's best Scotch.' Another pause. 'Don't worry, I needed it. Just to calm the nerves... Yes I will... Right.' He hung up.

It was nearly one o'clock when Montague returned to Kelly's house. He let himself in, put the rifle back in the cupboard and covered it with an old raincoat. He went to the bedroom, took off the coat and put it on its hanger in the wardrobe. He buried the shoes beneath the pile of footwear, put on his own shoes and jacket, then left. The last thing he did was hide the house key beneath a pot plant.

When he drove away, he accelerated harshly, spinning the wheels of the white Landcruiser.

4

Kelly had moved down the road to be well away from the house, and was parked between a florist's van and an old Valiant that had no wheels and was perched on four columns of bricks.

It was after one. He was about to leave when the Mercedes nosed into the street. It was travelling slowly, which surprised him because Laura was normally a tyre-squealer. She turned beneath the corner lamp and there was a flash of metallic silver. She'd wanted gold, he recalled, but wouldn't wait the extra three months for a gold Mercedes sports. He slid lower in his seat.

She had the top up. That was strange. Laura normally drove with the top down, even when rain was around. She'd park the car like that — open and exposed to the elements, and inviting some joyrider or professional car thief to jump in and drive away. It looked better as an open car, she said; and that was that. No argument. It was her car, even if he had paid for it. But tonight she had the top up. He peered towards the advancing lights. Why? Who was with her?

No one. Only Laura got out. She locked the car, rummaged in her handbag for something and then headed towards the house. He opened his door, slid down from the Landcruiser's high seat and hurried across the road. She spun around.

'Oh, Kelly,' she said, hand over her heart, 'you gave me such a fright.' She almost smiled but it was from relief, not from the pleasure of seeing him. She took a deep breath. 'What the hell are you doing here?'

'I came to see you.' He stayed at the gate.

Her hand was still on her chest. 'Who told you I was here?'

He shrugged. 'I found out. I've been waiting. Where have you been?'

She turned away and tried once more to put the key in the lock. Her hand shook and, frustrated, she lowered the key. 'We're back to that, are we? "Where do you go at nights? Who are you seeing?" Jesus Christ, Kelly, I can't even get away from you when I move out. What do I have to do?' She spun to face him again. 'I left you to get away from your constant harping, your suspicion about everything I do; and here you are, at some ungodly hour in the morning, following me around and asking me exactly the same questions. "Where have you been? Are you seeing some other man?" Don't you know any other words?'

'I didn't say you'd been with another man.'

'You meant it.'

'I've been waiting an hour.'

'Good. A pity it wasn't longer. I've been out all night.'

'Who with?'

'A friend.'

'A man?'

'A woman. Oh God, you're pathetic.'

He moved inside the gate and stepped up to the narrow verandah. 'Whose bikes are those?'

She brushed her hair back. 'What?'

'There are two bikes on the verandah.' He picked one up by the back wheel and let it drop. 'Who owns them?'

36

She took two deep breaths, not calming herself but stoking up her anger. 'Are you mad or something?'

'I just want to know who owns these bicycles, whose place this is, and where you've been.'

'Submit your questions in writing,' she said, 'and I'll fax you the answers. That's if you're in a hurry.' Her hands were steadier now and she turned to slide the key into the lock. He gripped her shoulder.

'I want to talk to you.'

'I don't want to talk to you. Go home, Kelly. I'll ring you in the morning.'

He pulled her around until she faced him. 'I won't be home in the morning. I'm going away.'

'Good. Stay away for a long time.'

'One week.' He grabbed the hand that held the key. 'I want you to come with me.'

'You *are* mad.' She peered to see his shadowed face. 'Have you been drinking? Your breath smells.'

'I've had a little. I'm not drunk though. I'm perfectly sober and I know what I'm doing.'

'That's a change.' She tried to shake herself loose. 'Would you kindly let me go?'

'You're coming with me, whether you want to or not.'

'Really?' It was the same mocking tone that annoyed him so much. It suggested his weakness, his uncertainty.

'Yes, damn you, really.' He took her by both wrists. 'Look, Laura, I don't want to hurt you but you are coming with me. There are things we've got to talk about.' He slowed his voice. He talked rapidly when excited and he'd been gabbling. 'I'm going bush for a week. You'll have a good time. We'll both have a good time.'

She struggled. 'You're crazy. If you don't let me go within ten seconds, I'm going to scream.'

'Who's inside? Who's going to come rushing to

your aid? The man who owns two bikes, or is it two men who own one bike each?'

'No one.' She tried to stamp on his foot. 'But the street is full of people. A lot of them are big men and not all of them are nice.' She stopped struggling. 'Will you let me go?'

'Have you been seeing Gerry?'

She went limp. 'What?' She started to laugh. 'Oh, you are nuts.'

'I want to know.'

'Gerry Montague?' And when he nodded, 'You mean have I been sleeping with Gerry Montague? Is that what you're asking me?'

'Have you?' It hurt to ask the question. Light from a street lamp was shining on her face. She looked pale and innocent. He felt rotten. He let her go.

'That's not only a stupid thing to ask,' she said, rubbing one wrist, 'it's insulting. Do you think I'd sleep with that fat slug?' She shook her head in revulsion.

'I was told you had been.'

She rubbed the other wrist, a little too dramatically, to make the point that he had hurt her. 'Who've you been talking to? Gerry? Is that what he says? Making drunken boasts about the women he's conquered?'

'Not Gerry.' He took the key and opened the door. 'Come on, you've got some packing to do. Enough for a week in the bush.'

'I am not coming with you.'

He pushed her through the door. 'You are, and you can either walk out or I'll carry you out. Unconscious if I have to.'

'You'd hit me?' she said. It was dark inside and he couldn't see her.

'You're damned right.' He found a switch and turned on a light. The house was tiny and clean, with worn floorboards and rooms running off the hallway. She was steadying herself against the wall. He reached out and she stepped away from him. She was frightened. Good, he thought. This is the new me you're dealing with, Laura. He waved one hand impatiently. 'Come on. We're in a hurry. I'm late already.'

She pushed back her hair. 'Late for what?'

'For getting out of town. I should have left an hour and a half ago.'

She tilted her head. 'Kelly, what have you done?'

'Nothing. Just decided to go bush for a week.'

'You haven't robbed a bank or done anything foolish like that?'

He lifted his left wrist and tapped his watch. 'You've got three minutes to pack.'

'I can't pack in three minutes. No woman can.'

'Try it. Go for the world record.'

He pushed her into the bedroom.

'Don't do that,' she shouted, and then calmed down. 'I'll pack. Just leave me alone.' She looked sideways at him. 'I've never seen you like this. What have you done, Kelly? Something really terrible?'

'Maybe something stupid.' He thought of the bet and then of the journey. 'But it'll be good. Maybe even profitable.'

He stood at the door, firing occasional questions. It was a friend's house, she explained as she flung a few clothes in a bag. The friend was in America for six months.

'Would you really hit me?'

'I might tie you up.' He'd found some cord and jerked it between his hands. He threw a pair of Reeboks on the bed. 'You'll need those. You won't need fancy shoes where we're going.'

'And where are we going?' She zipped the bag and picked it up. He thought for a moment she was going to throw it at him but she pulled it off the bed — a single bed — and let it swing at her side.

'Into the outback.' He grinned. She'd never been there but she hated it as a matter of principle, because it was his true love.

'Of course. The great outback. Where else?' That tone again. Humour the idiot.

He looked at his watch and gestured impatiently. 'Come on.'

She put the bag on the floor and thrust out her wrists.

'What's that for?'

'Don't you want to tie me up?'

She expected him to say no or to back away, knowing his bluff had been called. Instead, he stepped forward and spun a loop of the rope around her wrists.

'What the hell are you doing?' She pulled back suddenly and fell on the bed. She kicked at him. He grabbed her legs and wound the rope around her ankles.

'You are crazy, Kelso Hunnicutt. Mad as a mad dog.'

He had his hunting knife in his belt. He cut the rope, then knotted it tightly around her wrists and ankles. She screamed and he slapped her. She screamed again. He took out his handkerchief and stuffed it in her mouth. 'You spit that out,' he said, waving the knife at her, 'and I'll put it back in and shove it down your throat. Now shut up.'

With his wife over one shoulder and her bag in his other hand, he walked out to the Landcruiser.

5

The land was flat. No matter how far he drove, how fast he travelled, how much he peered into the night, the scenery was unchanging. Flat, dry and worn. There were fences and clusters of trees that scratched at the broad blob of white cast by his driving lights, but most of the time there was only the bitumen: straight, narrow, flanked by shadows and rushing towards him, to be devoured somewhere in the blackness beneath the Toyota.

He had passed through a few towns. They reminded Kelly of his aunt. Old and living in the past; but neat, even if the dress was to the fashions of forty or fifty years ago. They were small towns, always with a railway siding dominated by the concrete towers of wheat silos. This was the semidesert of northwestern Victoria; wheat country, where holdings were huge and life could be good if it rained and the Russians were buying wheat, and bad if times were tough, as they were now.

He drank more coffee, then resealed the top of the vacuum flask. He'd be glad when they crossed the Murray and got off the bitumen, away from the towns.

He glanced to his right. The sun would rise soon. Already the horizon was glowing a dull orange colour, and he imagined the scattered coals of a fire brushed by the last breath of night wind, and he thought of bush camps and the good feeling when he awoke before dawn and the last embers of his night fire were still burning.

The stars were fading. He would be sorry to see them go. He liked driving at night, when it was cool and the road was deserted. Darkness was a great insulator; it protected him from the world and let his imagination race as far as the faintest, most intriguing star in the heavens. He looked out again, bending forward to get a clearer view through the windscreen. The faint stars had gone, their pin-pricks of light mopped up by the glow spreading through the sky.

There were no clouds. It would be a warm day. Good. He relished the thought of the clear outback sun on his face.

Laura hadn't moved. She'd been asleep for the last three hours, almost from the time when he'd untied the ropes. He was feeling bad about that now. He'd threatened Laura; he'd pushed her around, tied her up and carried her, choking and kicking, out to the Landcruiser. She could have him up on a charge of kidnapping or abduction, or whatever it was you did when you took your wife by force. He shook his head in disbelief. He must have had too much to drink, been too wound up. That was it — he wasn't himself. It had been a terrible couple of days and he'd been under great emotional stress. He'd explain it all to her when she woke up. Those extraordinary things had happened because he loved her, because he needed her and because he wanted her to be with him. That was the reason, that was the thing that mattered. They should be together. Laura would understand.

He looked at the sleeping face. Would she? In recent months, Laura hadn't been too good at understanding. Maybe it had been his fault. Poor communication. He made good films, highly successful documentaries that got a commercial message across to the audience in simple, clear terms; why couldn't he do that with her?

Kelly yawned and rubbed his face. He checked the clock — they'd be through Red Cliffs soon, then Mildura. Then across the river into New South Wales. And on this new day, Friday, the police would be looking for him and the game would start in earnest. Important that he get to Broken Hill as early as possible, say around 8.30, buy what he needed and get out of town. Be away before the hunt started, before the police began searching for a Melbourne film-maker whose life was in danger.

What about Laura? He slumped a little, not knowing what to do. He couldn't tie her up again because she'd scream or throw herself out of the car at the first opportunity. He drummed the rim of the steering wheel. All right, she could go home. There was an air service from Broken Hill. He'd put her on a plane, send her back to Melbourne.

Back to Gerry?

What was all that about? Why had Tricia told him Laura was seeing Gerry? It couldn't be true. He'd watched Laura when he'd accused her. She was shocked, sure, but only because she thought the suggestion so outrageous, which it was. She was right — Gerry was a slug. Amiable, a good drinking companion, the sort of man that men liked, but not the type women fell in love with and definitely not the sort they ran away from home for. Why had Tricia told him such a story? Maybe she and Laura had argued. Women could be spiteful, an angry sister more so than anyone, or so he'd heard.

Laura was sleeping with her head bent at an awkward angle. He thought of reaching over and trying to move her, to make her more comfortable, but left her as she was. Let her sleep as long as possible. When she woke, she'd want coffee. Always did. Like a growling bear, she was, until she got her morning fix of caffeine. He grinned, thinking of good times. Then he thought of food. He hadn't eaten last night. He could taste bacon. He'd have it well done, nice and crispy, with grilled tomatoes, fried eggs, toast and coffee. There'd be a roadhouse at Broken Hill. They could risk having breakfast there before he put her on the plane.

There were lights up ahead. Red Cliffs. He'd be over the border soon. He checked the instruments, thought about turning on the radio to hear the news. What would they say? 'Police are searching for a leading Melbourne film-maker whose life is threatened by...' Something like that. He smiled to himself. Leading — would they really say that? Maybe they'd just call him a film-maker or, worse still, a Melbourne businessman. 'Police are searching for Melbourne businessman Kelso Hunnicutt...' sounded terrible. Or would they merely say 'man'? Oh God, that *would* be terrible. 'Police are searching for a man...' He winced. Please Gerry, he thought, concentrating hard on the message, make sure they call me 'a leading film-maker' or at least 'film-maker'. Get the name of the company in the story, he added, seizing on Gerry's weak spot: he'd do anything for publicity. The fact that the missing man, the man whose life was in danger, was the film-maker from Hunnicutt Montague Productions would be good for business. People would talk, ring the office, maybe even think of a commercial they needed. Gerry would think of that. Kelly relaxed. Gerry would be all right. He'd know what to do. He'd squeeze every commercial opportunity out of the story.

Should he turn on the radio? He looked at Laura, as though seeking guidance, but all he got from her was the rustle of a sleeper's deep breathing.

He checked his watch. It was far too early for the story to be on the radio. Gerry wouldn't be out of bed yet. He'd have to contact his chemist friend to get him to agree to the story about the wrong pills, then telephone the police. That would take... how long... three hours? After that, the press would have to be advised. He had until the midday news, and by then, he'd be well clear of Broken Hill, and travelling up the dingo fence.

Kelly was amazed by Laura's reaction. When he told her about the bet, she listened in silence. She sipped her coffee and rolled her head from side to side because her neck was stiff; but she said nothing. No questions, none of the biting sarcasm that he hated so much. She let him tell the story, which he did in a clumsy, halting way, getting out of sequence, having to go back and explain some things; but she didn't interrupt. Occasionally she glanced at him but there was no criticism in the look; just a kind of curiosity. It was a strange look, full of knowing and framed by unasked questions.

When he'd finished, she said Gerry Montague was a fool. That was all. She meant that Kelso Hunnicutt was a fool too, he knew, but she didn't say it. It was as though she understood how someone like Kelly — maybe *only* Kelly — would find such a challenge irresistible.

For the next twenty minutes they were silent. With no talk and just the tyres humming and the motor singing its constant note, he could feel a bond growing between them. The bond grew stronger, more real, with every kilometre they put between themselves and Melbourne. It was a good feeling; something he thought they'd lost months ago.

The first head frames projecting from the hills to the south of Broken Hill were in sight before he spoke again. 'I'm going to send you back to Melbourne.

45

I'll put you on the plane. There's a daily service. You could be back in Melbourne this afternoon.' He reached out to touch her hand but she kept her fingers clenched. 'I'm sorry for what I did... for everything I've done.'

She nodded without looking at him. Her mind seemed to be far away.

'Laura?' He waited until her head turned. 'You do want to go back?' He paused. 'You can, of course, but I'd like you to stay with me.'

A slight nod. No more.

'I'm sorry for the way I behaved. I'd like you to forget all that and stay with me. We could have a wonderful time.'

'I don't know.' She was still miles away.

They had breakfast at a roadhouse on the outskirts of the city. He talked about the route he planned to follow. She listened but her eyes had the vague look of someone who didn't understand. How could she? Brougham's Gate, Starvation Lake, Tibooburra, Cameron Corner, Bollard's Lagoon, Cooper's Creek — they were all meaningless names to a city woman. He reached across the table to grip her hand.

'If you come — if you choose to come — you'll have a great time. Laura, it will do you so much good to get away from Melbourne for a while. People go nuts in the city. They get sane again in the bush. We'll camp under the stars. We'll swim in lagoons. We'll be in places where the only other visitors will be the birds and the kangaroos.'

She nodded as people do when they're not listening. She had to make a phone call.

He leaned back in the chair. 'Who to?' Immediately he raised one hand in surrender. 'Sorry, none of my business.' He forced himself to smile cheerfully. 'Just don't tell anyone where I am. I'm in hiding, remember?'

46

'I have to ring.'

'Business call?' He said it brightly.

'Tricia. She'll be worried.'

Her sister? The two of them had argued, surely. 'Why do you have to ring her?'

'I was going to see her today. If I don't turn up she'll worry and if I'm still not home by tomorrow, the police won't be just looking for you, they'll be searching for me, too.'

He had to ask: 'How are you and Tricia getting on?'

'What a strange question.'

His shoulders and eyebrows rose to form arches of parallel innocence. 'It's just that you haven't seen her for a long time.'

'She's fine. I'm fine. We're both fine.'

'Well, that about covers everything.' He gave her his smile of complete satisfaction. But her face was blank. Emotions obscured, definitely not for public display. Something *had* happened. Now the sisters were getting together to patch things up.

He reached in his pocket for loose change for the phone call. 'Give her my love,' he said, and handed her the money.

She smiled and it was her warm smile, the first of the morning. The first for many mornings. 'I thought you didn't want people to know where you were? But if I give her your love...'

He waved a hand, dismissing the objection. He was thinking about something she'd said. 'If you're not back by tomorrow, the police will come looking for you. Isn't that what you said?'

'Yes.'

'That means you're not going back? You're staying with me?'

She twisted her mouth, as though having difficulty digesting the thought. 'Why don't you let me make my phone call and think about what I'm going

47

to do, and why don't you go off and fill up that truck of yours with smelly diesel.'

'I've got things to buy, too.'

'Buy them. I'll ring Tricia.'

'It could take me an hour.'

'Good. I'll be here, drinking my third cup of coffee and waiting for you.'

'You're really going to come on this trip, aren't you?'

'Go and do your shopping.'

He leaned forward and kissed her forehead. 'You're wonderful, Laura. I don't deserve you.'

She squeezed his hand. 'If you want to win this bet of yours, you'd better not waste another minute.'

He stood up. 'We'll have the best time.'

'I want you to promise me I can get an occasional drive of the Porsche, that's all.'

'You can *have* the Porsche,' he said and went outside. He was feeling wonderful.

6

Gerry Montague was expecting the call. This one came through the switchboard, not on his private line. Mary Calibrano, the woman who was the company's receptionist, secretary and office manager, said, 'The police,' and raised her eyebrows before adding ominously, 'They wanted to speak to Kelly'. Montague swung around in his chair so she couldn't see his face, took a deep breath and counted to three before speaking.

No, Mr Hunnicutt was not in. Yes, Mr Hunnicutt did work here. He was one of the partners. How could he help? His voice was steady. Like someone who has no idea that a dreadful thing has happened, he thought; and was impressed by his performance. Mary would be listening with growing fascination. She liked to mother Kelly, had a morbid fear of anyone in authority, and would be sick with worry. God, how he'd love her to hear what the detective was saying. This was wonderful. They must have found everything.

He buried the phone even deeper in the hollow formed by his head and shoulder, treasuring this conversation. It was, after all, his first test. He was silent for a long time, listening to what the detective had to say. Every now and then he nodded, mumbling an occasional word and letting his voice grow flatter, slower, and more shocked.

49

At the right time, he gasped, cleared his throat and turned briefly to stare at Mary. No, he didn't know where Mr Hunnicutt was. He should have been in the office by now. Of course he knew where his partner lived. He gave the detective Kelly's address.

It was 9.38 when Kelly rejoined Laura at the road-house. He apologised for having taken so long. 'Nothing in the local paper,' he said, flourishing a copy. When she gave him her 'what did you expect?' look, he smiled sheepishly and added, 'Too early, of course'.

'And not that big a news item, Kelly.' She said it gently. Normally, she would have dipped the barbs in acid.

'No.' He grinned. 'Of course.'

'It won't even be big in Melbourne.'

'Probably not.'

'I think Gerry Montague has made a stupid mistake. There'll be no search. You'll have a holiday and he'll lose his Porsche. Serves him right. Was he drunk when he made the bet?'

'A little.'

'About the same as you?'

He shrugged and produced a long supermarket docket. 'I bought a lot of food. Enough for two.'

She drank the last of the coffee.

He waited but she said nothing. 'The Land-cruiser's filled. So are all the jerry cans. There's enough for at least a thousand kilometres.' He took off his hat and toyed with the brim. 'How was Tricia?'

'Fine. I didn't say where we were but I said I was with you. She was *very* surprised. She sends her love.' Laura frowned. 'She's not very well. I'd like to ring back soon. Where will we be tonight?'

He hesitated before answering. 'Nowhere near a phone.'

'But there will be one somewhere along the way?'

He nodded, then sat beside her. 'Does all this mean what I think it means?'

She inclined her head. Rolled her eyes to one side. That meant yes. He knew the signs. She was indicating a certain reluctance, but she was saying yes.

'All the week?'

'Unless we get caught.' She leaned back. 'Which we won't. This should be fun.'

When the two detectives left, Mary Calibrano came into the office, but Gerry waved her away. 'Just leave me alone,' he said, holding his forehead. 'I'll tell you what happened later. Right now, I'm a little too upset to talk.'

She stayed at the door, as he knew she would. 'Are they looking for Kelly?'

He nodded.

'Why?'

'It's to do with that South African.'

'Mr Kolvenbach?'

He took his hand from his forehead and wiped his cheek. 'Mary, please.'

'What about Mr Kolvenbach?'

'Someone shot him last night.'

'Mr Kolvenbach? You mean shot dead?'

'Yes.'

She shook her head vigorously, trying to dislodge an unpleasant thought. 'Why are they looking for Kelly?'

'Apparently he was at Kolvenbach's place last night, very late. God knows why. The police think the two of them had a meeting.' He emitted a sigh that showed he didn't believe any of this. 'His name was in Kolvenbach's diary, one of his business cards was on the floor...' He looked up. 'Mary, do you know where the hell Kelly is?'

51

She shook her head.

'Did he say anything about going away?'

'Going away where?'

'Anywhere.'

'No. Didn't he meet you last night after work?'

'Only at the pub for the usual few drinks. He seemed pretty upset about something. He was rambling on about the outback again. You know how he is.'

She moved forward and put both hands on his desk. 'Do they think Kelly killed him? Is that why they were here?'

He covered his face. 'I don't know. I mean, I don't believe he would.' He looked up for an instant then shielded his eyes again. 'I don't know what to think. All I know is that the police want to talk to him.'

'I'll ring him.' When Montague looked surprised, she said, 'I'll call the house. To warn him'.

He hadn't thought she'd do that. He sat drumming his desk and fiddling with the drawer where he kept the list until she returned. 'A policeman answered the phone,' she said. She was ashen and looked sixty, not her true forty-five. You're going to be an ugly old woman, he thought, and showed great concern. 'The policeman wanted to know why I called. Gerry, I'm frightened.'

'What did you say?'

'That I wanted to talk to him. I told him I was his secretary.'

'That was all right, Mary. They won't be bothering you.' He waved a hand and let the fingers settle on his forehead. 'Do you think you could get me a cup of tea? I have the most incredible headache.' She left immediately, anxious to do something simple. As soon as she had gone, Montague opened the drawer, reached up for the taped envelope and took out the list to check what he had to do next.

They reached the dingo fence near Brougham's Gate and, at twelve, Kelly turned on the radio to hear the midday news. The reception was bad. Almost immediately, Laura switched the radio off.

'You know static gives me a headache,' she said. 'Besides, I've made a decision. This is going to be a holiday. We'll forget the rest of the world and that means no newspapers, no radio, and certainly no hourly news bulletins.'

'But I wanted to hear if they were looking for me.'

'It's too early and believe me, a story about a man taking the wrong tablets will be no big deal up here.'

He looked disappointed. 'I'd like to know.'

'And I'd like us to be on our own.'

Pointedly, he regarded the land around them; they were surrounded by sandy hills peppered with low scrub. They hadn't seen another vehicle in the two hours since they'd turned off the Silver City Highway. 'I don't think we could be more alone than this. This track's only used by the boundary riders who repair the fence.'

'I want to forget the rest of the world. That means doing without the radio. Okay?' She arched an eyebrow. Just one. He didn't know how she did that. 'Have you brought any tapes?'

'A box full.'

She found the box and began fossicking through his tapes. 'Classical, classical, classical... ah, Sinatra... I feel like something romantic.'

He was gazing ahead, along the wheel tracks which followed the tall netting fence through a ripple of sandy hills. He spoke softly, absent-mindedly. 'I might try to pick up an Adelaide station tonight, when the reception's better.'

'No,' she said, inserting the tape. 'I had other plans for tonight.' She shuffled towards him until

53

they touched. 'Now, where are you going to take me?'

The call came on his private line. Gerry Montague heard the voice and couldn't breathe. 'Who's speaking?' he managed to gasp and then felt he might be sick because a hot, sickly lump was filling his throat.

'The name's Kolvenbach. I want to see you. Urgently. Will half an hour from now be convenient?'

He made a noise. The other man waited a few seconds and then hung up.

'You knew my brother, I believe. I got your number from his little black book.'

Montague nodded. A few whiskies and thirty minutes of thinking time had calmed him. Magnus Kolvenbach was not as big as his brother but he was still a formidable man, at least 196 centimetres in height and unusually broad across the shoulders. He was younger, maybe in his late thirties. The sun had bleached his hair to the colour of ripe wheat and his skin had the grainy, glossy look of well-used leather. Some women would find him attractive, he thought, and immediately disliked the man.

'I won't beat around the bush. Have the police told you that Harald's safe was burgled?'

Montague shook his head. 'I don't know. I can't remember that. I'm sorry, it's been a bad day.'

'For me too.' Magnus Kolvenbach had arrived that morning on a plane from Singapore and gone straight to his brother's place only to be greeted by a house full of police. His face showed signs of weariness and worry, Montague noted, but none of sadness. This was a hard face.

'My brother and I were business partners.'

'I didn't know he had a brother. Or a partner.'

54

The younger Kolvenbach had the same unsettling eyes. Montague squirmed in his seat.

'There was a safe in the house. It was robbed. Everything taken. Money. Diamonds. Papers.' He lingered on the last word.

'Oh?' Montague hadn't had time to go through all the things he had stuffed in the bag. There were a few papers. He had thought of burning them.

'Why do you think your partner killed my brother?'

Montague managed to look horrified. 'We can't say that.'

'I can, Mr Montague. It's what the police believe. It's what I believe. They've found the rifle, even his shoes. The man left the sort of trail an elephant would make.' He grunted. 'He had an appointment with my brother last night. Do you know why?'

Montague displayed the palms of both hands. 'I have no idea.'

'I'm disappointed with that answer.' He lit a cigarette and then offered one to Montague. 'Surely one business partner would know what the other was doing?'

Montague took the cigarette and shook his head.

Kolvenbach looked around the office. The walls were lined with the titles of past films and photographs taken on location. 'Does your company make pictures?'

'Yes.'

'How come you knew my brother?'

'He asked us to make a film for him. We specialise in documentaries.' He concentrated on lighting his cigarette, to avoid those eyes. 'Your brother asked us to make a film about this new diamond venture of his.'

'You've completed the movie?'

'No. We hadn't started. We were only in the planning stages.'

'So your partner might have gone to see him about this movie?'

'No.' A short, derisive laugh. 'Not at that time of the night. Not Kelly.' Montague thought for a few moments and mumbled, as though talking to himself, 'He *was* short of money'.

'Your partner? How short?'

Montague looked up, his private thoughts disturbed. 'I'm not sure. We didn't discuss such things. We weren't that close, except in our business dealings. I looked after the commercial side of things; you know, money matters, marketing, finding clients and so on. He was the cameraman.' Another pause. 'He was always borrowing from me. He had wife trouble. Apparently she was extravagant. Drove a Mercedes sports car. He wasn't good at managing the income.'

'Things have been bad in this country, I believe.'

'Very bad. Money's tight. Those who've got it aren't spending it. Those who'd like to spend it, haven't got it.'

'And how are you for money, Mr Montague? Are you short, too?'

Montague's face sunk behind clasped hands. 'The business climate has not been good, Mr Kolvenbach, but the company is doing quite well. Not as well as we'd like, but adequately. The bank manager is still friendly. And as far as I personally am concerned, if that's what you're driving at, I manage my affairs quite well, thank you.'

Kolvenbach was silent for some time. He studied the pictures covering the walls. 'But Mr Hunnicutt was short of money?'

'Yes.'

Kolvenbach blew smoke towards a large black and white photograph of a group of Aborigines clustered around Kelly Hunnicutt and his camera. 'Is that the man who shot my brother?'

56

'Don't keep saying that.'

'Is that Mr Hunnicutt with the blacks?'

Montague cleared his throat. 'Yes. We made that picture three years ago.'

'When money was plentiful?'

He nodded.

Kolvenbach got up and studied the photograph. 'Did you think your partner was the type of man who would kill for money?'

Montague answered rapidly, decisively. 'No. Absolutely not. I'm sure he wouldn't. Hasn't. Not Kelly. Please stop saying that.'

'You're loyal, Mr Montague, but wrong.' Kolvenbach drew sharply on the cigarette. He sat down again and the leather chair squeaked under the weight. 'Anyhow, I won't beat around the bush. I have to find him.'

Montague laughed. 'I understand the police would like to do that too.'

Kolvenbach leaned forward. 'I have to find him before they do.'

Montague waited a long time before answering. 'Why?'

'Because of something your partner has taken.'

'Money?' The question begged to be contradicted.

'If the police find the money, they'll give it back to me. If the police find the diamonds, they'll give them back to me.' He had big hands. The fingers were square tipped, the skin pricked with scars. Kolvenbach rapped the table once. 'He has papers that I have to get back. I don't want anyone else to see them. Do you understand what I'm getting at?'

Montague was silent for a long time. 'No. I'm afraid you're talking in riddles.'

The South African grunted. 'Do you know where he is, this missing partner of yours?'

'No.'

57

'No idea?'

'I told you. I have no idea. He's just disappeared.'

Kolvenbach leaned back until the chair tilted. 'Do you know what I do for a living, Mr Montague?'

He pulled a long face. 'You said you were your brother's business partner. I assume you dig for diamonds or whatever else it was your brother did.'

'Oh, I was Harald's partner in this diamond venture all right. But I spend most of my time in Africa. I have another business there. I take people on big-game safaris. Just to look at animals and take their photographs. I used to be a hunter. One of the best, even if I say so myself. Excellent at stalking. A crack shot. Do you know what I'm going to do?'

Montague said nothing.

'I'm going to hunt your partner.'

The hairs at the back of Montague's neck tingled. He didn't understand what was happening but he knew instinctively that it could be good. 'You can't do that,' he said.

'Oh, believe me, I can. And with your help, I'm going to find him before the police do. He has something I need. There is something in those papers that would cause me intense embarrassment if it were ever seen by the wrong eyes. Do you understand me now?'

'I haven't got a clue what you're talking about.'

'But you understand what I'm saying?'

'I think so.'

'Good.' Kolvenbach searched for an ashtray, then dropped his cigarette to the floor and used the heel of his boot to grind it into the slate. 'Tell me, Mr Montague, where do you think your partner has hidden himself? Is he still in Melbourne?'

Montague thought for some time. 'No.'

'Ah. Why?'

'He loves the bush.'

'The bush.' Kolvenbach's eyes opened appreciatively. 'So he will have gone into the bush? He is a bushman?'

'He thinks he is. And it's possible that he's driven somewhere into the outback.'

'Driven.' Kolvenbach looked around the walls, as though one of the pictures might provide a clue that would lead him to the missing man. 'Mr Montague, I think you know more than you're telling me.' He leaned forward suddenly. 'In fact, I think you know a great deal more.' Kolvenbach made a pistol of his hand and aimed the finger at Montague's forehead. 'I'm staying at the Regent. We'll have dinner tonight. If you have another appointment, cancel it. This is serious, very serious, and I have little time to waste.' He stood up. 'Eight at the Regent. We'll talk.' He tapped his watch. 'Be there, or I'll come hunting for you before I start searching for your partner. And believe me, I am a very good hunter, Mr Montague.'

7

Montague sat on his own for a long time, thinking about what Kolvenbach had said and letting his thoughts flare into bright possibilities. Mary Calibrano waited outside. At last, unable to contain her curiosity, she walked into his office and asked about the visitor. He looked like a rugged version of Robert Redford, she suggested, trying to coax a smile from the man who was hunched so gloomily over his desk.

Montague remembered how she had prattled on about Redford after seeing *Out of Africa*, and glared at her. So many women judged men by their looks or their voices, not by their intellect or business acumen.

He dismissed the visitor as being someone involved with Kolvenbach's diamond mine; just a hireling trying to discover what commitments had been made regarding the film.

'The poor man's not even in his grave,' she murmured, all the while gazing at the doorway with the wistful look of one who hoped that the man with film-star looks might reappear. She turned and smoothed an eyebrow, a gesture that immediately restored her professional image. She coughed lightly to clear her voice. 'Any problems?'

'No.' Montague shuffled some papers.

She held a newspaper in her hand and shook

it to get his attention. 'I don't suppose Kelly has rung you?'

He looked up in surprise.

'Well, I thought he might. He must know you'd be sick with worry.' She spread the newspaper on his desk. 'His picture is on page one of the *Herald-Sun*.'

'I've seen the paper, Mary.'

'The story's on all the news bulletins. He must be aware the police are looking for him.'

Montague grunted. 'I'm sure he is.'

'Well, why doesn't he show up or at least ring?'

Montague smoothed the sheets of paper on his desk.

'Gerry, I'm frightened something's happened to him.' And when Montague seemed puzzled, she went on. 'Well, I know Kelly couldn't have done this thing, despite what they're saying about the police finding guns and muddy shoes and torn coats, and yet he's disappeared.' She waited for Montague to agree but he was concentrating on the papers on his desk. 'Gerry, I'm frightened that whoever killed Mr Kolvenbach might have done something terrible to Kelly. If Kelly was there, in Mr Kolvenbach's house at the same time as the killer...' Her voice became a whisper. 'I'm so worried.'

Montague sighed. 'We might have to face up to the fact that Kelly is involved.' He selected one sheet of paper and held it up. 'Kelly may not be the sweet little angel we think. I've been going over some figures. There seems to be some money missing.'

Her fingers spread across her chest. 'From here? Company money? That's not possible.'

'There are things you aren't aware of, Mary.' Another sigh, burdened with pain. 'It's quite serious. I have to go and see Harry Turner.'

Her lips twitched. She didn't like the accountant. Neither did Kelly. He always said Turner was a

61

devious old woman and not to be trusted, but he did nothing about it because he left the business side of things to Montague, and Montague got on well with Turner.

Montague checked his watch. 'I'm due at Harry's in fifteen minutes.'

'Are you saying Kelly has embezzled money?'

He rammed his briefcase under one arm. 'I'm not saying anything. I'm very confused. All I know, Mary, is that Kelly's gone and he's left us in one hell of a mess.'

Kelly had long been fascinated by the way Aborigines lived in the bush. Being supreme desert dwellers, they were the outback people he most respected, and most envied for their skills. He'd met a few and read about others from the old days. He knew how they hunted, what they ate, how they thrived in country where white men perished, how they used only what they needed. They were masters of conservation, preservers of scarce materials. They were true greenies, despite inhabiting a desperately brown country. They cherished the land, understood the plant life, respected the animals, and gathered or killed only what they could eat. When water was scarce, which was most of the time, they drank sparingly and saved what was left for others, never squandering the supply on something as trivial as washing. He could admire that, even if he could not bring himself to follow their example.

One thing he could emulate, however, was their technique with fire. They lit only small campfires, never burning more than was needed for the night. So when he went bush, Kelly normally lit a blackman's fire. He kept it small and prided himself on the way he created sufficient heat to boil water, roast meat or bake a damper without wasting precious wood. Just like the genuine desert nomads had done.

Tonight, however, he'd built a white-man's fire. It was big, it roared like a furnace and it consumed excessive amounts of timber. He didn't care. There were plenty of dead trees where they were camped, and each old tree had spent the last decade fencing itself behind a pile of dry, discarded branches. He kept throwing on wood and laughing as the flames sent sparks soaring into the night like volleys of shooting stars.

Kelly had built this extravagant fire because, for the first time, he had Laura with him in the bush, and because he wanted to please her and impress her. He was happier than he had been for months. They were together, they were in love again and there was no other living soul within a hundred kilometres.

He had stopped before dusk and chosen a site well off the track. It was in a shallow valley surrounded by sandhills. They'd eaten a meal which he had prepared and now they were sitting as close to the flames as the heat would allow.

The firelight danced on the ring of dead trees and sent long shadows flickering across the sandhills. Beyond the bright circle of light was a grey zone, where reality melted. Beyond that was a silent, intense darkness. It was perfect.

'It's spooky.' Laura shivered.

He put a blanket around her shoulders and wriggled closer. 'When the fire dies down a bit, we'll hear a few noises. Birds chattering, maybe a dingo coming close to see what's going on. Kangaroos thumping through the hills. It'll be great.' He paused to listen but heard only the spluttering and crackling of the fire. 'When we go to bed, we'll just lie quietly and gradually we'll hear all the sounds. A lot of these animals only come out at night.' He breathed deeply. 'It's wonderful.'

She leaned her head against his. 'You really like this sort of life, don't you?' She felt his head move up and down. 'Could you live out here?'

He picked up a twig and chewed it. 'No,' he said after a long pause. 'I like visiting these places, I like camping on my own — I mean, like this, with just the two of us — I like going where no one else goes, I like the long distances, I like the animals and birds, I like the sunrises and sunsets.' He removed the stick and examined its chewed end. 'I like all those things but I couldn't live here.' He laughed. 'Couldn't afford to.'

She kissed his cheek. God, she hadn't done that for so long.

'But if you could?'

More chewing. 'No. I'd probably go nuts after a few months.'

'A nice place to visit but you wouldn't want to live here?'

She was smiling. He knew that without seeing her face which was buried against his chest. 'I wouldn't want to live in one place. That's what it is, I think. I like to roam. There's so much to see and I want to see it all. I couldn't bear to stay in the one place.'

She lifted his hand and rubbed it against her cheek. 'Do you remember when we were first married we talked about going to live in America? You were going to be a big Hollywood director.'

You talked about it, he thought, but said, 'Yes'.

'I'd still like to do that.'

He pushed back an unruly lock of hair. 'Things are so tough these days. You can't just move camp and settle down in Hollywood and expect to make a living.'

'You could if you had the right film.' She turned, angling her body towards him. 'Why don't you get a really good script from some writer and take it

64

over there? It doesn't have to be another *Crocodile Dundee*. I couldn't stand it if you made a real ocker film. It should be just a good, general interest story that would appeal to audiences around the world. And one that could be made in Hollywood.'

She heard the tiny grunt that meant he disagreed but wasn't going to say anything.

'What about *Witness*, *Driving Miss Daisy*, *Lonesome Dove*, *Green Card*, *The Russia House*?' She delivered each title slowly, giving him time to think but not quite enough to interrupt. 'Not one of them's an Australian story but they were all made by Australian directors. People you know. Your contemporaries.'

He gave a tired laugh. This was an old argument, using names like Weir and Schepisi to shame him into uprooting himself and moving to Hollywood. It was a subject, he had to admit, that he'd dodged in the past. 'They're all established directors now,' he said softly, not wanting to sound petulant. 'Household names.'

'They weren't once.'

A long pause. They were good; that might be the difference. He wasn't too sure about his own abilities. Not with a major feature film. He might start shooting and, through force of habit, do a sequence on floor coverings or overhead camshafts.

'What are you laughing at?'

'I'm not laughing,' he said.

'I can feel your ribs shaking.'

'I was just thinking of something funny.'

'Tell me.' She elbowed him gently.

'No, it's private.' She persisted and he grabbed her. They rolled on the ground, away from the groundsheet, away from the fire.

When they stopped, they were both laughing. 'Where are you taking me?' She tried to rise but he had her pinned.

'Here,' he said. 'To this precise spot.'

'Is this where you attack all your women when you go into the outback? Is this Kelso Hunnicutt's sacred site?'

'Absolutely,' he said and kissed her.

Just how important were the documents? Montague had gone through them again but he had been forced to read them hastily and he still wasn't sure what they meant or referred to. Most were handwritten and he had trouble understanding the poor writing; probably Harald Kolvenbach's. One file in particular was mystifying. It consisted firstly of some notes which mentioned several names. Some sounded Aboriginal: Woolaru, Kalalpaninny, Mumpi. Each name had a sum of money alongside it. Men who'd worked at the South African's mine up in the Kimberleys? Payment for work? There was also a note written in a different hand. The person who'd sent it had used a thick-nibbed fountain pen, probably an expensive one, and signed it *Rob*. It said something had been arranged and mentioned a name. Not an Aboriginal name. That note was in an envelope that was postmarked Canberra. He would read the papers again when he went home.

'It is very important to me,' Magnus Kolvenbach repeated. 'Believe me, it is vital that I get to your friend before anyone else does.'

'By anyone else,' Montague suggested, 'you mean the police?'

'Of course. They will examine the material he stole from my brother's safe. There are things they must not read.'

Montague was well in control of himself now. He sat back, with his fingers locked across his waist. 'Naturally, I don't know what you're talking about and I think I should tell you that I don't care to

66

know. However,' he continued when he saw Kolvenbach was about to speak, 'there is something I should tell you about my own situation. Things have changed since we met this afternoon.'

The big man's eyes half closed. He reminded Montague of a lizard. All that was needed was the flicking tongue. 'What things?' Kolvenbach asked softly.

Montague unlocked his fingers and spread them across the tablecloth, taking care to avoid the silver knives and forks arranged so precisely in front of him. 'After I got over the shock of everything that happened today, I began to wonder why Kelly had disappeared. In other words, I began to wonder whether there could have been some sort of premeditation in all this. A plan. Do you know what I mean?'

The lizard eyes were unblinking. To avoid them, Montague lifted a glass and examined it. This man would drive him nuts. Kolvenbach didn't know, *couldn't* know what had happened, but those eyes seemed full of accusations. He held the glass higher, up to the light. 'I mean, if a man is planning to rob someone and even to murder that person, and works it all out very carefully and is planning to disappear, then there's no reason why that man shouldn't go the whole hog and rob someone else. Make off with as much loot as possible. Do you follow me?'

Kolvenbach drew slowly on his cigarette. 'Are you saying he robbed you too?'

'The company. Yes.'

'How much?'

'Are you going to tell me what's in those papers?'

Kolvenbach's lips curled in the beginnings of a smile. 'Fair enough. I presume he took a substantial amount.'

'A very large sum. One that imperils the future of my company.'

The cigarette was only partly smoked but Kolvenbach stubbed it in the ashtray. 'Your company? I thought you and Hunnicutt were partners.'

'I have the major investment.'

'Ah.' Kolvenbach spent some time dabbing his lips with a serviette. 'Let me see if I follow the gist of this conversation. Are you now saying that because you too have lost a large sum of money, you rather welcome the prospect of me finding your missing partner?'

'I'd like the money back. And I'd like no one else to know anything about it. It would be most embarrassing if the story got out.' Montague was part way through a Scotch and water. He sipped his drink, then took a long breath. 'The money was acquired, shall we say, under unusual circumstances. I would not like them revealed. And of course, embezzlement is not good for business.'

'Neither is murder, surely?'

'Embezzlement is worse.'

The waiter came for their order. When he had gone, Kolvenbach said, 'So, I have lost papers that no one else should see. You have lost money that no one else should know about.'

'You've summed it up rather well.'

'It would seem we have similar objectives. Does that make us partners?'

'In this one venture, possibly.' Another, quicker sip.

'All that remains then, Mr Montague, is for you to tell me where your missing friend is.'

Montague finished the last of his whisky. He didn't like this part. 'I don't know. However, I have some ideas.'

Kolvenbach blinked slowly. 'Good. Tell me.'

'Have you heard of Broken Hill?'

'No.'

'It's in western New South Wales. A big mining

town. I've never been there myself, but I believe it's surrounded by miles and miles of nothing.'

'Desert?'

'Very dry country. Quite rough, I understand.'

'And you believe Hunnicutt is in Broken Hill?'

He shook his head. 'I believe he's travelled through Broken Hill. He would have left there this morning. He's probably heading north.'

'For a man who knows nothing, you seem to know quite a lot.'

Montague waved the remark aside. 'There's a fence that separates New South Wales from South Australia.'

'A fence? You have fences along your State borders?'

'As I understand it, this one is to keep the wild dogs out.'

Kolvenbach scratched an eyebrow. 'Out of where?'

Montague fondled the empty glass. He desperately needed another drink. 'I'm not sure. The wild dogs are called dingoes. The fence is either to keep them out of South Australia or vice versa. Kelly would know. He's the outback expert.'

'And he's gone along this fence, where the wild dogs live?'

A waiter approached and Montague ordered another Scotch. 'I believe so,' he said and hoped the waiter would be quick.

Kolvenbach was not looking at him but scanning the room. This was even more disconcerting. When the man's eyes had finished their journey, he turned casually to Montague. 'He did tell you, then?'

'No.' Montague smiled even more casually, oozing confidence. 'Tell me, are you familiar with the story about that Russian diplomat, Malakov, who ran off with a bag of gold that he stole from the Soviet Embassy in Canberra?'

69

Kolvenbach frowned. 'What's a Russian diplomat got to do with it?'

Montague told him the story. 'The police were searching for Malakov for days. They thought he was hiding in the outback and Kelly was telling me one night that he could outrun the police if he had to. He said he'd go to Broken Hill and then up the dingo fence.'

Kolvenbach stroked his chin. 'He said this one night. That's all? You base all this on one conversation?'

'Not once, my dear fellow. He said it several times.' He was using the English accent that so impressed the older Kolvenbach. His drink arrived and Montague hurried to take the first sweet sip. 'If Kelly was planning to steal from me and to rob your brother, or even kill him, then he was also planning to go somewhere. He would have had it all worked out many days in advance. He was that sort of person. Right?'

The other man leaned forward. 'If he was going to steal from you, he wouldn't tell you where he was going.'

Montague hadn't thought of that. He took a longer drink, then managed a smile. 'He was, shall we say, a little under the influence. He gets very loose when he's had a few drinks. He becomes care-less and boastful.'

Kolvenbach seemed unconvinced. 'You think I should go to Broken Hill?'

'He will have been there.'

'You're certain?'

Montague paused, as though considering every option. 'Yes. You see, Kelly doesn't have that much imagination. If he was talking about Broken Hill and the dingo fence as being the best way to head in order to hide from the police, then that's where he'd go. I know him.' He smiled, amused at Kolvenbach's

70

doubt. 'How will you search for him? He's got a long start and he knows the bush.'

'He's driving by car?'

'Yes. He has a four-wheel drive. A diesel.'

'You can tell me the make, colour and registration number?'

'I can give you a photograph of the car.'

'And the man?'

'Yes. I have several pictures of him.'

'Do you know what he was wearing?'

Montague raised his shoulders in a gesture of helplessness. 'How would I know?' And then, after some thought, he added, 'He usually wears the same sort of gear when he goes bush. I could make an educated guess, if you like.'

The entrée arrived. Kolvenbach sampled the first oyster before speaking. 'You give me all that information then. And after we eat, you will come to my room and show me these places on the map. I will leave first thing in the morning.' He speared another oyster. 'Tell me, this road that runs along the fence where the wild dogs are, is it a much-used road?'

Montague busied himself with his smoked salmon. 'I've never been there or anywhere near it, but from what Kelly told me, there'll be nothing on it but the dogs and Kelly's four-wheel drive.'

'So I will find him easily?'

Montague smiled tolerantly. 'Maybe "easily" is not the right word. This is a very large country, Mr Kolvenbach.'

'I have been here before, Mr Montague.' Another oyster. 'Not to Broken Hill or to the country where they have to erect a fence to keep the wild dogs from raiding one State or the other, but I know this is a big country. I am used to big countries.'

'What will you drive?'

Kolvenbach arched an eyebrow. 'I will fly, Mr

Montague. I will take the plane Harald used to travel up to the Kimberleys. It is fast, it has a long range and it can land on rough airstrips. I can be wherever your friend has got to in half a day. With luck, I'll find him by lunchtime tomorrow.'

Montague coughed. He hadn't expected this. Carefully he laid a piece of salmon on a sliver of toast. 'And then what?'

'I will recover the things he has taken.' He wiped his lips. It was a remarkably delicate action for a man with such hard features. 'Tell me, are you concerned about what might happen to your murdering, thieving partner? Do you fear for his wellbeing?'

Montague had picked up the wine list. He spared Kolvenbach the briefest of glances. 'I don't know.'

Kolvenbach smiled. 'Oh, I think you do and I think we understand each other. Now,' he said, spreading the napkin across his lap, 'are we having white or red? I like your Australian wines.'

Late that night, when the fire had settled to a molten pile of golden embers, Laura raised herself on one elbow and, with her free hand, reached out and stroked Kelly's cheek. 'Can I ask you something?'

'Sure.' He tried to catch her hand but she rolled away suddenly. She lay on her back, gazing up at the stars.

'You won't be offended?'

He matched her pose. The sky was brilliant, all needle-point sparkles and ghostly swirls of galactic fog. 'It depends on what you want to ask me. Should I be offended?'

She reached for his hand so that her touch would reassure him. 'I can't help myself but I keep thinking about last night, when you came to that place in Carlton.' She felt his grip tighten. 'You were so strange, Kelly.' Now she used both her hands to hold his. 'You've never behaved like that before.'

'I told you, I'm sorry. I feel really ashamed of the way I behaved.'

'No, no, no. It was wonderful. I was a bit shocked at the time but you wanted me and you took me. A woman likes that. Especially if it's the man she loves who takes her. There's something wonderfully primitive about it.' She pulled his hand on to her chest. 'But I've been thinking and worrying. I don't want to, but I can't help it.'

He rolled towards her. 'Thinking about what?'

'Well, about that. What you did. The way you were... so strange. And about the crazy bet you say you've got with Gerry. And, Kelly, I get so frightened.'

He laughed but it was more in surprise than good humour. 'You think I'm going to lose the bet?'

She shook her head, desperate to expunge wild thoughts. 'This voice inside me keeps whispering that there is no bet. That you've done something wrong... something terrible... and that's why you were so strange... so violent, last night. And that's why you've run away like this.'

He was silent for a long time. She held his hand and pressed so hard she hurt him. 'There is a bet,' he said, emphasising each word, and her grip lessened. 'It may be crazy, it may seem stupid to other people, it certainly doesn't make any sense, but there is a bet.'

Her fingers ruffled the hairs on the back of his hand. 'And you haven't done anything terrible, like rob a bank?'

'Cross my heart.'

'You're not running away from the police? I mean, really and truly running away, like some desperado.'

'I'm just a little kid playing hide-and-seek, and betting my car against Gerry's.'

She kissed the palm of his hand. 'Good. We'll

73

play the game together. We'll have fun. And I won't worry again. Promise.' Another kiss. 'Kelly, I'm sorry.'

He held her in his arms until she was asleep. He could feel her breathing evenly, contentedly, and she curled into his body as though it were her rightful resting place. He stayed like that until his arm became numb and he had to slip it from beneath her shoulders. She rolled away from him but then moved back, murmuring a few garbled words and shaping her body to fit his.

But he could not sleep. He gazed up at the spangled sky, trying to remember the names of the major stars and constellations, but then drifting into doubt about whether the police were looking for him, or ever would. The police might have thought the whole thing was too silly. Or Gerry's chemist friend might have refused to go along with such a harebrained scheme. Surely it would damage the man professionally? Kelly hadn't thought of that. He became depressed. If the chemist refused to cooperate, if Gerry couldn't convince the police that Kelso Hunnicutt must be found urgently, there would be no search. He would have to call off the bet.

Were the police searching for him? He had to find out.

8

It was late when Montague returned to his apartment.
The first thing he did was to delve into the refrigerator
for a few cubes of ice. The second thing was to reach
even deeper into the freezer, remove the false backing
and retrieve an insulated bag. He poured himself a
whisky, added the ice cubes and opened the bag. He
put the diamonds to one side and counted the money.
Two hundred and seventy-six thousand US dollars,
mostly in crisp new bills. Forty-eight thousand Australian dollars, all in one-hundred-dollar notes with
the frosted face of Mawson staring accusingly at him.
At least a man who'd explored the Antarctic would
be at home in the freezer, Montague thought; and
let the whisky explore the limits of his mouth. He
did a quick calculation. The Australian currency was
worth about 36,500 American dollars. That made a
total of, say, 312,500 US dollars. They hadn't expected
so much. Kolvenbach was mad to have had that
amount of cash in his safe, he said to himself; and
toasted the man.

He left the diamonds in their little draw-string
pouches but caressed the swollen bags and tried
to estimate their worth. Millions. The man dealt
only in good stones.

He checked his watch. Eleven thirty-seven. Friday night. He was not to move the diamonds until
Monday. He took another sip from the glass. His

hand was shaking. Silly that. He'd been good with Kolvenbach but now he was shaking like a schoolboy about to face the headmaster. He took a deep breath and another drink. It would be a long and nerve-racking weekend. Damn it, why Monday? He wanted the diamonds out of the place now.

Magnus Kolvenbach worried him. If the man was as good as he said he was, he might catch Kelly tomorrow or on Sunday. And then what? Shoot first and ask questions afterwards? That would be perfect. Kolvenbach would find nothing but he'd assume Kelly had hidden the money and diamonds. The man could be digging holes in the outback for weeks. He liked that idea. They'd have the diamonds and the money out of the country while Kolvenbach was still shovelling away in the sandhills.

Montague finished the drink and put the money and the pouches back in the freezer. Then he looked at the papers. Rob. Who the devil was Rob and why was Kolvenbach so concerned about the papers? He examined the envelope with its Canberra post-mark. He turned it over. The flap was embossed. Montague moved closer to the light and adjusted his glasses. Parliament House.

He sat back in his chair and thought.

Kolvenbach was on the telephone. 'I know it's late but this is important. You've heard that my brother was killed?' He waved his hand, impatient for the other man to stop talking. 'Very nice of you but I didn't get you out of bed to hear such eloquent expressions of sympathy. I want you to know we have a problem... A big one... Believe me, it does involve you. The man who shot Harald also robbed the safe... Yes, quite a lot. Cash and diamonds. I don't know how much. Harald was a bit of a fool like that. Carried too much on him and let people know he didn't trust the banks.' Again the hand sliced through the air. 'That's not the point. I believe certain papers were in the safe.'

There was a long pause this time. Kolvenbach had time to light a fresh cigarette.

'Well, my brother was meticulous with things like that. He recorded everything, kept everything that was important... Yes it was, and it's gone. The man who shot Harald — Kelso Hunnicutt — took everything. The safe was empty, absolutely bare, and I have to assume that this Hunnicutt went off with the papers. And has read them.'

He let the man talk while his head rolled from side to side with growing impatience. 'I know all that. Here's what I'm doing. I'm going to find this Hunnicutt before the police do... Because I have certain information. First thing in the morning, I'm taking the company plane and flying up to Broken Hill... His business partner told me. He says he thinks the man's headed in that direction. Apparently this Hunnicutt's a bit of a bushman and he's likely to hide out in the outback... I have specific directions. I think I can find him.'

Another long pause. Kolvenbach checked his watch. He'd be lucky to get four hours' sleep. He nodded. 'Of course I want to get everything back... Yes, absolutely. He might have read everything and begun to put two and two together... I understand all that. I will be careful, believe me, but I can't afford a public outcry and neither can you. It would ruin everything — for both of us.'

Kolvenbach blew smoke towards the ceiling. 'Please, I haven't finished. There's something I want you to do. Have you got a pen and paper?' He waited a few seconds. 'Now, Hunnicutt's business partner is named Montague. He's English, I think, and the two of them operate a film company called Hunnicutt Montague Productions in South Melbourne. I don't trust this Montague.'

Kolvenbach gazed across the room to the sofa where the leather bag containing his rifles lay casually across the cushions. He was looking forward to the hunt. 'His first name is Gerald. He acts like Mr Righteous. Very pompous. Very British. I hate the type. He behaves as though the murder was a great shock to him. Tonight he told me a strange thing. He said Hunnicutt had been stealing money from the company. I don't know whether he's telling the truth or not but a gut feeling tells me the man is lying. I think it's quite possible he's in on the whole thing... That's right, they could have planned it together... What it means is that Montague could have seen the papers. He might even have them.'

Kolvenbach stubbed out his partly-smoked cigarette. 'I plan to go after Hunnicutt at first light. He must be our prime target. I have to get to him before the police do... You'd like the police to read that little note of yours?' Kolvenbach grunted. 'Look, if Montague is telling me the truth, then Hunnicutt is somewhere to the north of Broken Hill. I know that, but the police don't; so with a bit of luck, I can find him quickly and do whatever has to be done.'

He patted his pocket, searching for another cigarette. 'On the other hand, clever Mr Montague might be sending me on a wild goose chase. What I want you to do is to have someone keep an eye on him in my absence. You have contacts in Melbourne?... Good. Have them watch him. See where he goes, find out who he talks to. Search his house. It has to be done with discretion... I have no idea. Surely someone with as much influence as you can find out where the man lives? You might even get one of your best men,' he fumbled for the lighter and paused to let the irony take root, 'to look up his name in the Melbourne phone book.'

He let the other man talk for almost a minute

before interrupting. 'There's no point in blaming Harald. That was the way he was. Undoubtedly, he didn't expect to be murdered. Few people do.

'If Hunnicutt has the papers, I will get them back. I want your assurance that you will look after Montague... From tomorrow. You'll have to be quick... I'll try to call you again on Monday. Hopefully, I'll have good news.' Kolvenbach hung up and went to the couch.

Kelly was still awake. He lifted his wrist so that the glow from the fire shone on his watch. Almost one o'clock. Moving slowly so as not to disturb Laura, he wriggled out of the sleeping bag and went to the Landcruiser. He opened the door, turned the key and switched on the radio. Several South Australian stations were coming through clearly. With the volume down low, he turned from station to station, but none of them had a news bulletin. Then he remembered — South Australia was half an hour behind. He searched for a Melbourne station.

'... say Hunnicutt is thirty-nine years of age and 185 centimetres tall. He is believed to be driving a white Toyota Landcruiser. Anyone seeing either the man or...' The words faded as music from another station overwhelmed the signal. Kelly touched the knob. Another voice: '... one of the most intensive manhunts for years. Police say that Hunnicutt, an expert bushman, may have...' Yes, yes? Damn. The voice had disintegrated into a stream of static. Frantically, Kelly played with the tuning knob. Other stations drifted in, their signals blurred in a crossfire of music and chatter. He found the original station again but the newsreader was talking about the recession and the latest balance-of-payments figures.

He turned off the radio. The story had been a

main news item. Bigger than the recession. At one in the morning when the stations played only the most important news, the search for Kelly Hunnicutt was mentioned on at least two stations. Up front. It was a big story!

He went back to the sleeping bag, his face aglow from the twin stimulations of cold and excitement. So the police *were* searching for him. Good old Gerry. How had he done it? He lay down but couldn't sleep. He didn't care. He was looking forward to the next day, Saturday, when the chase would begin in earnest.

Important to plan now. He would head north, all the way along the fence to Cameron Corner. There'd be no police up there. Most likely, they wouldn't see anyone, not even one of the boundary riders who maintained the fence. He might take his time and show Laura the bird life on the lakes. They could see a really big mob of kangaroos. There were always roos around the fence. Then, in a day or so, they'd drive into Tibooburra to get fuel and maybe a little food. And to buy some newspapers. He desperately wanted to see what the papers were writing about him. Would they use his photograph? He'd never had his picture in the paper.

But if he waited a few days, the excitement might die down and there'd be nothing in the papers. Why not drive into town tomorrow? It would be safe. Tibooburra was a little place and the people there weren't worried about what went on in the rest of the world. He'd take care, of course, and possibly drive in at sunset. He'd travel quietly, just like a tourist, and come in from the north, as though he were driving down from Queensland. He might even ring Gerry. Yes, he would. He'd give the old fellow a surprise and find out what was going on.

9

Kolvenbach took off at dawn. He landed at Broken Hill, seeking fuel and information. He was lucky, getting what he needed from the one person — the refueller at the airport. The refueller was a young man who wore the obligatory white overalls and who seemed determined to reach old age without passing through the middle years. He had prematurely grey hair, a wrinkled brow that was raised in an attitude of permanent surprise and he was stooped, as though bearing a great weight on his shoulders. He was, however, a good, even anxious talker and before the hose had been coupled to the wing tank, Kolvenbach knew a great deal about him. He didn't care that the man was unmarried or that his younger brother had died in a motorbike accident only a few weeks before; but he was interested to learn that the man had originally come from around Tibooburra and was a keen shooter. The man chatted on. He belonged to the local gun club. Had a mantelpiece full of trophies. Before he took this job, he'd been a professional shooter. Spent years working the country between Tibooburra and Broken Hill, sometimes shooting kangaroos and foxes but mainly rabbits. He and his brother, the one who'd been killed on the motorbike, had a contract for an Adelaide pet-food company. Yes, he knew the dingo fence. He and his brother used

81

to work along it. Spent five years up there in the early eighties. Got as many as twenty-five hundred rabbits a night in a good season.

Airstrips? For the first time, the man seemed to take notice of Kolvenbach; he studied him intently, his compressed brow knotting itself into fresh patterns of curiosity. Why? Was he thinking of doing some shooting?

Kolvenbach lifted his hands noncommittally. Probably not, although he liked doing a spot of hunting.

Plenty of kangaroos about this year, the man said and nodded solemnly, as though bestowing the blessing needed for a stranger to commit mass slaughter. Back in the seventies, he and his brother had spent two weeks at a water hole near the Flinders Ranges and shot 9,000 roos. That was during the drought, of course, and there was no other water. The roos just came down to drink and got themselves shot. He smiled and looked younger.

Airstrips?

A few. It was pretty flat country. Plenty of places where you could land. The track rambled along the fence and through the sandhills, so it was no good, but there were dozens of salt pans and dry lakes. You had to be careful in putting down, though. Some of the saltpans had soft spots and sandy outcrops. Tibooburra had a proper strip, of course.

Kolvenbach nodded.

'What sort of rifle have you got?'

Kolvenbach gave an amateur's modest shrug. Only a cheap twenty-two.

The man smiled. There were plenty of rabbits.

Kelly had rebuilt the fire. This time he made it small and over breakfast, he confessed to having turned on the radio. He was still excited. He spoke rapidly. 'It was hard to hear anything clearly because there was so much interference and static, but I heard the story on two stations. It was a lead item.'

Laura looked at him with great curiosity. It could have been disbelief, Kelly noted, so he said, 'It must either have been the first or second story. I missed the beginning of the bulletin. On the first station I picked up, they followed my story with an item about the latest balance-of-payments disaster and how the recession's getting worse.' He paused, hoping she would be impressed, but she had the same look. Lamely, he added, 'I didn't hear it all. I heard my name and a bit of a description. That was all.'

She put down her coffee and spent a few moments removing any suggestion of doubt from her face. In fact, there was no expression at all. This was neutral Laura, prepared to let him have his say. He felt uneasy, even guilty. He didn't know why.

'Exactly what did they say?'

Exactly? She'd have made a good lawyer. His hands groped for the missing sentences. 'Well, it was a bit scrambled. They said I was thirty-nine and they said how tall I was.' He grinned triumphantly. 'I don't know what tale Gerry spun them but it must have been a beauty.'

She waited for his smile to subside. 'And they said you'd been given the wrong tablets?'

'No. I didn't hear the whole thing. The reception was bad and the signal kept on fading. That happened on both stations where I heard the story.' He poked the fire with a stick. 'Laura, you're not still worrying about whether I've robbed a bank or something, are you?'

She shook her head and smiled. 'No. That's all gone. It's just that . . .' She drank some coffee, needing time to think. 'It's just that it seems such a trivial thing for them to be making such a big deal of. A man has the wrong tablets?' She raised her

83

shoulders. 'Who cares? I mean, it's not world-shattering news, surely.'

Kelly felt compelled to defend the very foundation of the bet. 'It depends on the tablets. Maybe Gerry's friend, the chemist, said he'd given me something really lethal. Something so horrible the papers and radio stations just had to run the story.'

She was smiling again, doubting his words but anxious not to offend.

He prodded the fire once more. She was right. It didn't make sense. 'God knows what Gerry told them. It *was* at the front of the news bulletin, though. They *were* giving a description.'

She stood up and arched her back, stiff from having slept on Kelly's ultrafirm camping mattress. 'I've got an uneasy feeling about all this.' When he seemed about to protest, she waved a hand to stop him. 'It's not that silly dream I kept on having about you robbing the bank. It's Gerry Montague.'

'What about Gerry?' The old suspicions began to flare.

'Well, he's such a dill.'

He smiled, his jealousy wiped out by that one short salvo.

'I know he's your partner and I don't want to offend you, Kelly, but I've never really liked him. He's not... what's the word? Dependable. Or predictable. He's the sort of man who'd do something on the spur of the moment and think about the consequences later on. Like this bet. I mean, do you really want the police to be looking for you?'

He threw the stick on the fire and stood up. 'I don't mind. As long as they want to save my life, not put me in the cooler for a few months.'

She folded her arms tightly across her chest. 'I don't trust him. I'm worried about what he's told the police. He might have made up some entirely different story.'

84

He got the shovel and began scooping up the ashes. He not only made good fires; he covered them up. 'Do you know what I've decided?'

She raised an eyebrow. 'Tell me, please.'

'I thought we'd drive up the fence, not fast but without any long stops, and then we'd go into Tibooburra where I can buy a paper. That way, we can see what's going on.'

'Today?'

'Yes. We should be there by sundown. Good time to go in. No one'll notice us.'

'I thought we were going to take our time?'

'There's not that much to see,' he said slowly, conscious that he'd used a contrary argument only the previous day. 'We'll need some diesel, anyhow.'

'I thought we had enough for 1,000 kilometres?'

'After Tibooburra, we may have to go 1,000 kilometres to the next place.'

She confronted him, her hands on her hips. 'Kelly, why don't you admit it? You're just dying to see what's in the papers.'

'Yes.' He was pleased to be found out.

'Well, you're the boss. We'll do whatever you decide.' She meant it, he knew, and he hurried to pack the Landcruiser.

Montague was worried. There should have been another phone call. As soon as he returned to his apartment, he hurried to the answering machine but there was no message. He knew what to do, it was all on the list, but there should have been a call. He needed to discuss things. He needed reassurance. Cradling his forehead he sat down and forced himself to think of other things: the morning's meeting with the detective. Mallowes seemed a pleasant enough man. No sign of suspicion. Surprisingly, Montague had even detected a trace of compassion, good old-fashioned sympathy from a policeman for a decent citizen who had been let down badly by his business partner. Should he tell Mallowes about the missing money? It was a little early, surely. Better to wait, to give the subsequent impression of a loyal friend who had been reluctant to point the finger at a missing man, one who wasn't around to defend himself. Then make the revelation in a few days' time. Shock, horror — the monster had even stolen from his closest friend.

He thought of having a drink. No, mustn't drink too much. He needed a clear head. Again, the fear that something had been forgotten or would go wrong pricked at his gut. Calm down. Count to ten, take a couple of slow breaths. Think. The books had been carefully fixed. They would stand up to any scrutiny and they pointed to Kelly as the embezzler. A clever, devious embezzler, but without doubt the guilty man. Kelso Hunnicutt, the peripatetic cameraman with the ridiculous name, would be revealed as a sly and cunning thief. Not Gerald Montague, pillar of society, grieving partner in Hunnicutt Montague Productions, once so prominent in the field of documentary film-making and now facing ruin. Maybe he should ring Harry.

He looked up the number and then hesitated. His telephone had been moved. Nervously, he looked around. The cleaner hadn't been in, not on a Saturday morning; and in any case, she knew better than to move the phone. He was fastidious about that. The phone, the answering machine and his Teledex each had its special place on his desk. His silver Teledex with the ornate bear's head was always on the left side of the answering machine. The phone should be on the right. But now it was on the left. And at the wrong angle. Only slightly, but it was wrong. Montague had an engineer's fanaticism about things being parallel. He couldn't pass a tilted picture without adjusting it and he couldn't

86

bear to see the phone in the wrong place on the desk.

Someone had moved things. He touched the bear's head, flicking through the entries, not knowing what to do, then stood up suddenly. His flat had been broken into. While he was at the police station someone had forced his way in and moved the phone, gone through the directory, listened to the answering machine. Listened? Oh my God, what were they after? What was on the tape? He thought frantically. Nothing. He'd erased it. What else? He looked around him. The bookshelves. The encyclopaedias had been rearranged. They were normally lined up with their red leather spines neatly in a row, but two of the volumes stuck out slightly. Someone had pulled the books out and put them back hastily. Not stealing but searching. A wave of panic washed through him. Calm down. It might just have been a common thief. There'd been a wave of robberies in the last few months, mainly addicts after drug money. It could have been that. He went to the bedroom. No, the dollar coins, even a twenty-dollar note that he'd left there last night, were still next to the light.

He returned to the lounge and sat down. Oh Jesus, someone knew. They had come looking.

He went straight to the refrigerator, took out the ice cubes and was about to remove the false back when he stopped. They could be watching. He closed the freezer door, went to the windows and drew the curtains. After he had searched the apartment, he went back to the refrigerator. The panel was in place, the line of frost unbroken. He removed the panel. The diamonds were there. He made himself a drink, replaced the ice-cube tray and sat down to think.

Who?

When he finished his drink, he rang Harry Turner.

Kolvenbach had begun to have doubts, to think that searching for a single car in the immense sprawl of the Australian outback was a quest for only the most optimistic or self-opinionated of fools. But there it was — the car. Correction: a car. Mustn't jump to rash conclusions. It was the first vehicle he'd spotted in an hour's flying and it was still on the horizon. Too far away to be sure, but it looked like a car. Not bulky enough for a big truck. He grunted, partly in satisfaction, partly in sympathy for the quarry. A moving vehicle was so easy to see out here. This one trailed a telltale wisp of dust and, following the wheel tracks that lined the fence, it was as distinctive in this worn landscape as a lone yacht ploughing a creamy furrow through the sea. If this really was the man he was looking for, Kolvenbach thought, he'd have done better to have hidden among the three million inhabitants of Melbourne, instead of racing into empty country.

He banked to the right, to move away from the track so that he could have a better look at the driver. He lowered the flaps and descended until the aircraft was only thirty metres above the ground. He flew over a saltpan and stirred a pair of emus into galloping flight. He'd seen kangaroos earlier and even flown beneath a wedge-tailed eagle that was spiralling high on a thermal.

The car was much closer. It was crossing a low chain of sandhills, weaving constantly, several times passing beneath a low telephone line that ran parallel to the fence. He could see the vehicle clearly now and Kolvenbach whistled in triumph. It was a white four-wheel drive. He squinted. A Toyota. The broad roof was flashing reflected sunlight, as bright as a beacon, inviting him to close in on the target.

He looked ahead. Damn. He'd hoped to find Hunnicutt in flat country but there were hills here. Only

88

low hills, but continuous and covered in timber. No hope of landing.

He flew alongside the Landcruiser and saw a man stare up at him. It could have been Hunnicutt but it was hard to tell. And was that someone beside him? No one had said anything about Hunnicutt having someone with him.

He thought about turning and making another pass. No. If it were Hunnicutt, he would become suspicious, turn off the track and hide in the bush. Better for him to fly on, land somewhere and meet Hunnicutt on the track. Kolvenbach tipped the wings as though in greeting and flew on. He checked his map. Hawker Gate was nearby. There was a settlement of some sort there, possibly used by the boundary riders who patrolled the fence. The man at Broken Hill had told him about them. He would go to Hawker Gate.

10

Kolvenbach landed on a clearing rimmed by buckled plates of dried mud, and taxied the aircraft towards the buildings. He followed wheel tracks that led him safely through the mud and came to a gravelly clearing near the back of a house. It was hot and he stopped where shade from a broad tree dappled the cockpit. What had the man at Broken Hill called these places? Cottages. The South African smiled. Such an English term for so essentially an Australian building — the 'cottage' was a box of a house with timber walls and iron roof. It had tiny windows, made small to keep out light and therefore heat, and a minuscule verandah that was screened to keep out insects. The western wall was protected by shade trees; a desert species, he guessed, by their knotted bark and needlelike leaves. Behind the house were several sheds made of corrugated iron and roughly hewn timber posts that leaned with age. Fuel drums littered the yard, and pools of oil darkened the earth. Heaped against one corner of the fence was a mound of sand, out of which projected the remains of an old utility truck, exposed like the bones of a partly unearthed skeleton. Nearby was a little Suzuki four-wheel drive.

He switched off both motors and watched the propellers flicker to a halt. In the sudden quiet, he heard a dog barking. He got out of the plane and walked to the house. He called out, 'Anyone home?' but there was no answer. The dog appeared from one of the sheds. It was young and not sure of what welcome to offer. It began to circle him, barking and wagging its tail at the same time. Kolvenbach was good with animals. He held out his hand and the dog came closer, reluctant but willing, head angled, spine curled, tail constantly twitching. 'Where's your boss, boy?'

The dog let him stroke its ear. It followed Kolvenbach as he approached the back door, jumping back when he called out, 'Anyone about? Hello. Anyone there?' Kolvenbach had buzzed the house before landing. The man must be out, miles away, up along the fence.

The back door was open. Kolvenbach knocked, stood back and looked around, wondering if a frightened wife might be hiding inside. He walked into the house, calling as he went. No one. He walked around the house, peered into the distance for any sign of dust or movement, and then went to the Suzuki. It seemed relatively new although rough work had chewed much of the tread from the tyres. The key was in the ignition. Just like Africa. He went back to the aircraft, selected a rifle and got in the car. He started the motor and, with the dog barking furiously, drove off.

'I know you love the outback, Kelly,' Laura said slowly, building up to something, 'but don't you find this just a little bit boring? I mean, we've seen a lake with black swans and pelicans, and that was nice, even if the birds all went to the other end of the lake when we arrived; but otherwise, all we've seen is a big fence that looks as though it's about to be overwhelmed by sand, and we've seen a few hundred sandhills that all look the same, and we've seen the fence, and we've seen the telephone line that follows the fence, and we've seen trees, and we've seen the fence and we've seen the sandhills...' She laughed.

'You think I'm mad?'

'Completely.'

'You're right.' He laughed too. He'd never felt so good. 'The country's very different further to the north.'

'The fence changes?'

'We're going beyond the fence. After Tibooburra we'll go up to the Cooper. It's lovely along the river.'

'What's it like?'

'Big trees. Large water holes. Lots of birds. Very few fences.' He looked at her, testing her. 'It's very quiet.'

'Sounds good.' She'd been drinking mineral water and passed him the bottle. 'What are we going to see at Tibooburra? All I know about the town is that it's on the weather maps on the Sydney TV news and it always seems to be hot. You know, coldest place in the state, Kiandra; hottest place Tibooburra.'

Kelly hummed while he composed his thoughts. 'Well, it's small, naturally. We might go to Milparinka while we're up that way. It's even smaller, almost a ghost town. Some lovely old buildings. Much favoured by artists.' He passed back the bottle.

'You're sounding like one of your films.' She gripped his wrist to help guide him back on track. 'You started to tell me about Tibooburra.'

'Small. Hot. It's surrounded by boulders. Huge rocks, all rounded and polished. An extraordinary sight. The country's quite majestic, in a dry sort of way. There are a couple of pubs; one of them has a fabulous mural, painted by some famous artists. You know, people who stopped in for a drink on the way back from somewhere and ended up doing a piece for the pub wall. I think a few of them must have been well and truly soused because the mural's pretty ribald in places.'

'Sexy?'

'There are a few breasts and an occasional penis. It's very funny, though.'

'I must see it.'

He chewed at his lower lip. 'Mightn't be possible. There'll be people in the pub. Someone might recognise me.' He blushed. 'You know, it's possible my picture's been in the paper.'

'You hope.' They laughed. 'I'll go in the pub. You can stay outside. Would it have a phone?'

'The pub? Sure.'

'I'll ring Tricia.'

'You're still worried about her?'

'Desperately. She sounded really depressed.'

'Depressed? I thought you said she wasn't well.'

'Not well mentally. She's been having man trouble.'

'Again?'

'Afraid so. This last one was a beauty. Drugs, liquor, bisexuality, the lot. She's had a terrible few days.' She sighed, long enough for her distress to harden into frustration. 'Honestly, Kelly, I don't know where she finds these men.'

He was silent for a while, sorting through a jumble of thoughts. Tricia was depressed, unhappy in her latest love affair. A little unbalanced, perhaps... that could explain things. A few years ago, Tricia had been married to a Yugoslav who'd given her a tough time. He'd been a compulsive gambler; in the end, he sold the family car, made a killing at baccarat and used the money to nick off to the Philippines. Since then, she'd had a string of boyfriends. None of them was much good. So now she had mental problems.

'Kangaroo,' he shouted and pointed to the right. The animal bounded behind some trees before Laura saw it.

Back to his thoughts. If Tricia was not acting rationally it explained so much. After all, a temporarily unbalanced woman who was having unhappy and sordid love affairs was the sort of person who might invent stories about her sister; sort of transfer her own guilt to Laura.

'It was Tricia who told me you were seeing Gerry,' he said, and felt lighter for having made the confession.

Laura was still searching for the kangaroo. 'I thought it must have been.' She shook her head. 'Poor thing. She's really been off the planet for the last week or so.' She turned to Kelly. 'Me and Gerry? *Gerry!* I should be insulted.' And then, in a louder voice, 'How could you believe it? Kelly, you can be so stupid, so infuriatingly gullible.'

He shrugged, accepting the criticism. 'Anyhow, I'm glad you told me.'

'Told you what?'

'That Tricia's been depressed. That she's not herself. It explains why she invented such a story. You know, she's seeing a man, a rotten bastard of a bloke, and feels ashamed so she says *you're* seeing a man. It's very sad.'

'I should be angry with her.'

'If she hadn't said that, I wouldn't have gone crazy and come around to that house in Carlton and snatched you away.'

She made a small noise, as though laughing to herself, then kissed a fingertip and touched his forehead. 'In that case, I'm grateful to her.'

Kelly thought of stopping and kissing her, of telling her how ashamed he was ever to have doubted her. Instead, he grunted in surprise. A small four-wheel drive was cresting the next sandhill. It stopped in the middle of the track, blocking their way.

'Trouble?' Laura asked, gripping the panic

handle as the Landcruiser shuddered to a halt.

A man wearing a broadbrim hat, brown shirt, brown pants and boots got out of the vehicle. He seemed far too big for the small Suzuki.

Kelly tugged at the handbrake.

'Should you stop?'

'Not much choice.' He opened the door but left the engine idling. 'There's a badge on the side of the car so he's an official of some sort. I think he must be one of the boundary riders. You know — the men who fix the fence.' He raised a hand in greeting.

'Hello there.' The other man waved back and walked towards them. 'You're a long way from home, friend.'

Kelly was intrigued by the voice. The boundary riders he'd met on previous trips spoke slowly, rarely finished a sentence and had voices that rasped like barbed wire. This man spoke rapidly, linked his words and had an accent. Squeezed vowels. Southern African.

'Yes, we are,' Kelly said, aware that the man was examining his Victorian numberplate. He smiled. 'So are you.'

The man's eyes narrowed. He was perplexed.

'The voice,' Kelly said. 'South African?'

'Oh.' The man pushed back his hat. 'No, Rhodesian. Or these days I should say Zimbabwean, shouldn't I?'

Kelly smiled, intrigued by a thought. The man talked like Harald Kolvenbach, even had his stance. 'Been in the country long?'

'Ten years.' Kolvenbach was forced to produce a figure. He wasn't sure when Zimbabwe had gained its independence or when the great outflow of white settlers to Australia had occurred. He stared through the windscreen at Laura and gave the briefest of nods. 'Where are you two from? Melbourne?'

95

Kelly had spent days thinking about hiding from people but hadn't considered what to say when he met someone. 'Yes,' he said and thought, I'd make a great spy. The first time I'm asked a leading question I tell the truth. 'You work on the fence?' Kelly nodded towards the Suzuki.

'Yes.' There was silence and Kolvenbach felt compelled to add something. 'Not a bad job. Just have to drive up and down and keep the wild dogs out.'

'Are they bad this year?' Kelly hadn't seen any tracks.

'Oh yes. We're having a bad year. The last few days have been very busy.'

Kelly frowned. 'But isn't this the breeding season?' He'd been told this was the time when the dingoes went off into the dunes near the Stony Desert to have their litters.

'They're still bad.' Kolvenbach coughed. The man was Hunnicutt. No doubt. The registration on the vehicle was his and the face matched the photograph. But who was the woman? 'Anyhow, my friend, what are you doing up here? We don't see too many Melbourne drivers in this part of the world.'

'Just taking a trip.'

'Oh. A trip. A little holiday.' Kolvenbach walked to the side, as though examining the vehicle. 'And is everything in first-class condition? You need good tyres and a reliable engine when you come up into this country.' He stopped outside Laura's window. 'Good morning, madam.'

Madam? Kelly would have expected a boundary rider to have said 'missus' or just plain 'g'day'; not 'good morning, madam'. This was a land where 'no worries' was a major contribution to a conversation. Good morning, madam? He scratched his neck and stared quizzically at the other man. 'You remind me of someone.'

I'm sure I do, Kolvenbach thought, and you're very cool considering you shot my brother only two days ago. 'Oh? Who?'

'Someone I know back in Melbourne. He's South African. He's into diamonds.'

Kolvenbach adjusted his hat. He was watching the woman. She was avoiding his eyes and seemed nervous. 'What do you mean, *into* diamonds?'

'He explores for them, mines them, sells them. He's South African. Nice bloke.' Kelly grinned and Kolvenbach turned towards him, his face suddenly hard. 'Huge man.' Kelly lifted a hand to indicate height. 'Must be nearly seven feet tall.'

'That's very tall.' He ambled towards Kelly. 'Why do I remind you of him? I'm not seven feet tall.'

'You're still pretty big.' Kelly rubbed his chin. He was anxious to get moving. The man unsettled him. He was strange, not a normal bush type and too interested in Laura. He'd heard of couples being attacked in the outback; the man would be shot, the woman raped. This man had the look of an attacker. Nervously, Kelly cleared his throat; the man was waiting to hear more reasons. 'Well, you talk like my friend and you even look a bit like him. Same sort of face.' And eyes, he thought. This man had Harald Kolvenbach's disturbing habit of staring at you, of penetrating your thoughts.

'Your wife?' Kolvenbach inclined his head towards Laura.

'Yes.'

'You've got enough fuel, plenty of water and food?'

'Yes, thanks.' Short answers from now on. The man might merely be lonely and longing for conversation but Kelly was anxious to be under way.

'Where are you heading for?'

'Tibooburra.' Oops, done it again, Kelly thought. Ask me a question and I can't help blurting out the truth. Should finish with a lie. 'Then we're turning south and going down to Bourke and back to Melbourne.'

Kolvenbach indicated the fence. 'Strange place to come to, the back of nowhere.'

'I like the country.'

'Have you been here before?'

'Several times.'

'When was the last time?'

'Oh, a few years ago. I didn't run into you then.'

'No. So you're familiar with the country. You know where to go? You know the turn-offs, the hazards, and you're a good driver?'

Kelly nodded impatiently. 'Well, we'll be on our way.'

Kolvenbach looked at Laura once more. 'When will you and your wife get to Tibooburra?' He had trouble pronouncing the name, like someone new to the word.

Kelly hesitated. 'Possibly tomorrow or the day after. We're not in a hurry.'

Kolvenbach touched the brim of his hat. 'Good. Take your time. Have a good trip.' He held out his hand. 'By the way, my name's Williams. What's yours?'

I'm not a good liar, Kelly thought, licking his lips. He hadn't thought of another name. Stupid of him. 'Kelly, Peter Kelly.' He took Kolvenbach's hand. The grip hurt.

'Been nice meeting you, Mr Kelly.' He faced Laura, touched his hat and walked back to the Suzuki.

'See you later,' Kelly called out the traditional, meaningless farewell.

Kolvenbach turned and smiled. 'Yes.'

Kolvenbach pulled off the track and waited for ten minutes before following the Landcruiser. He was confused. He had found Hunnicutt but he'd also found a woman. He hadn't expected that. Hunnicutt said the woman was his wife. More likely his girl-friend. That made sense — killers carrying a fortune in diamonds and cash tended not to run away with their wives.

Hunnicutt had become a little nervous towards the end of their conversation but otherwise he'd behaved like an ordinary traveller. He'd even had the nerve to refer to his brother. That was incred-ible. Why would a man who'd recently shot someone talk about his victim like that? Call him a good bloke, joke about his height, speak as though he were still alive, as though nothing had happened to him.

Kolvenbach thought about that for a long time but got no answers that made sense. As he approached the cottage, he slowed. If the inspector had returned, there'd be trouble. No matter; he could handle it.

The dog ran out barking but no one was there. He parked the Suzuki where he had found it, took his rifle, coaxed the dog within tickling range and then walked to the plane. He would fly to Tibooburra and wait for Hunnicutt and his girlfriend to arrive. And ring Canberra.

George McCarthy ran a private investigation agency. He should have been playing golf, he said, and repeated the lament many times while he examined Montague's apartment. He was slow but thorough. When he finished, he sat down, refused Montague's offer of Scotch and poured himself a beer.

'Someone's been in here. You did well to pick up the signs.' He was wheezing from exertion, like a person who is greatly overweight, which he was.

'I'm meticulous about certain things. You should know that.'

'Except paying on time.' He laughed and wheezed

some more. 'Any idea who might have done this?'
He gave Montague a glance which was angled to
chip away secrets. 'Or why?'

'None at all. I'm mystified.'

'And nothing's missing?'

'Not that I can see.'

'Anything worth taking in here?' The same look.
Come on, tell me what's going on here, he was saying
but Montague maintained his mystified, innocent
expression and managed to look hurt.

'For Christ's sake, George, the place is full of
valuable things. The latest big-screen TV, Danish
hi-fi, a couple of VCRs. There was loose cash in
the bedroom.' He grunted, the sound a perplexed
man might make. 'There still *is* cash in the bloody
bedroom. Untouched. The wardrobe's full of two-
thousand-dollar suits, silk shirts, Italian shoes.
They, he, whoever it was, walked past thousands
of dollars' worth of goods.'

The fat man nodded and reached for some
cashews that Montague had placed on the table.
'Only the best, eh, Gerry?'

'You know me, George. And quit farting around.
What do you reckon?'

McCarthy filled his mouth with cashews and
chewed and nodded. I have a theory, he was saying.
Just give me a minute. And don't hustle me because
I know this job's being performed under the old
chums' act, so you're not going to pay me. He swallowed. 'Level with me, Gerry. What have you got
here? Or what did you have here that was so valuable someone sent a real pro in to do the place
over?'

Montague spread his hands. 'You can see what
I've got.'

'Did he knock off that fancy car of yours?'

'I was out in it.'

McCarthy swallowed some beer and reached for

more nuts. 'Do you think there was a chance the intruder was still here, inside the apartment, when you got home?'

Montague considered. 'No. I searched the place. Went through every room.'

'This bloke might be the next best thing to the invisible man.' He flicked cashews, single fire, into his mouth. 'He might have been checking what you had in here and been disturbed.'

'No.' Montague shook his head vigorously. 'There was no one here.'

McCarthy leaned back against the leather lounge. 'Doesn't make a lot of sense, does it?' He fiddled with a cushion. 'You don't think there's any connection between this break-in and what happened the other night?'

Montague frowned. They'd already discussed the murder. 'There's one thing I should tell you.' He coughed, clearing the way for an unpleasant delivery. 'My accountant tells me that Kelly had been cooking the books.'

The other man stopped chewing and waited for Montague to continue. He had been a top detective. He looked it now. Tough. Shrewd. The kind who made you blurt out things you didn't mean to say.

'There's quite a bit missing.'

The chewing resumed. 'How much?'

'Around forty thousand.'

'How badly will that affect the company?'

'It could send us to the wall. Things are pretty tough at the moment. No films being commissioned. No one wants to spend any money. We're sailing close to the wind, like everyone else, I suppose. The bank's howling. You know the story.'

McCarthy turned the glass in his hand. 'Are you saying your partner might have had something to do with this break-in?'

Montague raised his eyebrows, his hands, his

shoulders, even the level of his voice. 'I'm not implying anything. I'm just confused. This business with
Kelly is bad enough but the idea that someone can
just walk in here and go around moving things and
then leave without taking anything, really makes
my skin crawl.'

McCarthy put down his glass. 'But you think
there might be a connection between the break-
in and the thing Hunnicutt is alleged to have done
the other night.'

Montague's eyebrows were still up. 'I don't know.
It just seemed that whoever broke in knew his way
around.' He shook his head, noting the scowl on
his friend's face. 'No. I don't think Kelly had anything
to do with it.'

The fat man puffed out his cheeks, then spoke.
'I'd say one person entered the apartment. He came
through that window.' He pointed. 'There are faint
marks. Now, I didn't see how far the phone had
been moved or how the books had been shoved
out of line. I'll have to take your word for that but
you've definitely had someone in here.' He held up
a coin-sized object. 'Your telephone's been bugged.
Any idea why?'

Montague sank back into his chair. A bug. Any
calls today? Ones that really mattered. No. Thank
God for that. 'The police?' he suggested in a thin
voice. 'You know, in case Kelly rang here?'

McCarthy toyed with the bug. 'Not the police,
Gerry. Someone who's a highly experienced, highly
skilled and very careful break-and-enter artist has
been in here this morning. My guess is that he was
engaged by someone to look for something specific.'

'But the telephone bug?'

'If he didn't find what he was after, he might
have been hoping to hear you give him a few clues.'
More cashews. 'You are levelling with me?'

'Absolutely.'

102

He nodded slowly. 'What do you want me to do?'

'To tell the truth, George, I don't know, but I feel pretty bloody nervous.'

'Understandable.'

'What if he comes back? To put the bug back in place, for instance.'

McCarthy smiled. 'He knows we've found it. He's not going to put it back again.'

'Jesus.' Montague poured himself another drink. 'Maybe you should have left it where it was.'

'Talk sense, Gerry.'

Montague took several quick breaths. 'They'll be watching me. Should I go and live somewhere else?'

'You've got another home?'

'No.'

'Well, let's just talk about things that are possible. Do you want me to assign some good men to watch this place?'

That was exactly what Montague wanted but he felt he should hesitate before answering. 'What would that entail?'

'Someone living in here with you.'

Montague was shaking his head before the sentence was finished. 'Definitely not.'

'Watching from outside, then. Twenty-four hours if you want. Four men watching in six-hour shifts.'

'Expensive?'

'Gerry, I've seen your big-screen TV, your whizz-bang Danish hi-fi, your two-thousand-dollar suits. You've got millions. You can afford it.'

If only you knew, Montague thought, but managed to smile modestly. 'Maybe for a day or so. How good will they be?'

'I'll get the best. Whoever broke in was good. It took a nit-picking fanatic like you to notice something was disturbed, so my men will have to be of an equivalent calibre.'

'Better.'

'We'll try. I'll tell them to keep well out of sight. If the other man's watching you, they'll be watching him.' He juggled two nuts. 'How about your office?'

'Oh God, I hadn't thought of that.' Montague stroked his nose. Let them look. There was nothing in the premises of HMP that would incriminate him. After an appropriate time spent in contemplation, he shook his head. 'No. No need. I just want you to watch this place.'

McCarthy grinned. 'It *is* here then, isn't it?'

Montague looked exhausted. He shook his head. 'What are you talking about, George?'

'Okay.' He raised a hand in surrender. 'I'll have the first man on duty across the road in one hour. Ring me if anything happens.'

Montague nodded. 'Is it safe to use the phone?'

'I didn't find any other bugs. Mind you, there are a dozen other ways for these people to eavesdrop, but I don't think the room's bugged.' He played with his glass to emphasise its near emptiness. 'If the conversation is important, one you'd like to keep private, play music. Fill the room with sound. Turn on your stereophonic television and your Danish hi-fi. Remind them of all the goodies they left behind.' He winked and leaned forward to refill his glass.

Laura was dozing, put to sleep by the afternoon sun, the gentle pace, and the monotony of the country. Kelly was driving with his mind in automatic; following the wheel tracks up the fence but thinking of the meeting with the big man in the Suzuki. The man was out of place. He didn't belong along the fence. Kelly tried to think of all the worrying things he'd noticed during their brief meeting.

To start with, the man had been too well-dressed. Not a warp in the brim of his hat, not a rip in his trousers, not a stain on his shirt.

104

Amazing, considering the sort of work he had to do and the country he worked in. Next, the vehicle had been empty. The other boundary riders he'd met were always carrying rolls of fencing wire and tools; after all, their job was to fix or rebuild the fence. This man carried nothing. Kelly thought about that, and it worried him. The boundary riders didn't go for social drives along the fence. Where the hell was he off to? And then he remembered: it was Saturday. Maybe he was going south to visit the man in the next cottage. He relaxed a little; he'd forgotten it was the weekend.

Then he began to worry again. The man was too well spoken. He thought about that while he drove across a sandhill that was taller than any they had crossed so far. On the other side, a few kangaroos were lazing in the shade of low acacias. He thought of waking Laura but the roos hopped away and he drove on. Back to the man and his voice. That wasn't too much of a worry; a man could retain his African mannerisms for ten years, he supposed, although his accent and his calling Laura 'madam' made him a real rarity out here. But then there was the man's curiosity. Kelly didn't like that. The man was too interested in them. He'd had a good look at Laura, examined the Landcruiser with the keen eye of a traffic policeman. What the hell was he up to?

He was big enough to be a policeman. Kelly shook his head; the Suzuki wasn't a police vehicle and, in any case, if he had been a cop he'd have recognised Kelly and delivered an impassioned warning that his life was in danger. He grinned, thinking again of the hunt, and looking forward to reaching Tibooburra and seeing a paper.

But he was still puzzled about the man. Laura didn't like him. She formed instant opinions about people and she said he frightened her. What was her word? Sinister. It was, she said, as though he had come looking for them. But if he had, why didn't he say something? Warn him about the tablets or whatever the story was that Gerry had told the police?

He'd ring Gerry from Tibooburra. He drove a little faster.

11

When Kolvenbach walked into the bar, a few heads turned to see if the newcomer was stranger or friend. They stayed turned. This was a stranger and a big one. Kolvenbach took off his hat, used his fingers to rake his hair into place and straddled a stool. He looked at all the faces, one by one. Most turned away. A few mumbled greetings, then looked elsewhere.

The man behind the bar was polishing a glass. 'Pretty hot for this time of the year,' he said, reaching up to put the glass on a shelf above the bar. He slung the cloth over his shoulder. 'Now, what can I get you?'

'A beer will do, thanks.'

'No worries.' He filled a glass and passed it to Kolvenbach. 'Just arrived in town?'

The man had a heavy accent. European, Kolvenbach thought, peasant stock, not well educated, probably from somewhere around the eastern Mediterranean. Southern Italy, Greece, Turkey, Lebanon; he wasn't sure. It intrigued him. He liked putting people in a niche: it made him feel comfortable.

'Just arrived,' he said.

'Come far?'

'Yes.'

'Just passing through?'

'Maybe.' Kolvenbach wiped froth from his upper

lip. 'Haven't decided. Where would I find the manager?'

'Right here.' The man glanced around the room to make sure no one else wanted a drink. He put the cloth on the counter, changing from barman to manager, and leaned forward. 'What can I do for you?'

'Can you give me a room?'

'Depends what you want to do with it.'

'Sleep in it.' Neither was smiling.

'Then you've got it.' He might not be Mediterranean. He could come from further north. Hungarian. Ukrainian. Maybe Bulgarian. 'How long do you want to stay? One night? Two? A week? You'll need a month if you want to see all of the town.'

'A month?'

'This is a big place.' He smiled but quickly pulled his face back under control. 'On your own?'

'Only me.'

'Just staying the night?'

'Maybe a couple of days.'

'That's okay. Where are you from, mate?'

'Melbourne,' Kolvenbach said, and gave his name as Dennis Williams. The man at Tibooburra airport knew his real name because it was on all the documents and his credit card; but the fewer who knew, the better. People might still be talking about his brother and they'd remember the name. Not good, if something unpleasant happened to Hunnicutt. He said he was waiting for a friend who was due in a couple of days. No, he didn't need another hotel room. The man was driving up and towing a caravan.

After serving some other people, the manager showed Kolvenbach to his room at the back of the building, then led him to the telephone in his office. When the man had left, Kolvenbach rang Canberra.

It was a short conversation. Montague's apartment had been searched. Nothing had been found. His phone had been bugged, but the bug had been discovered and removed. Now, why would an innocent man search for a listening device? Montague was being watched. Any luck with Hunnicutt?

Kolvenbach reported having seen Hunnicutt, who was travelling with a woman. He expected them to reach Tibooburra in a day or two. He would intercept them and search the vehicle.

Conversation finished, Kolvenbach went back to his room, showered and returned to the bar. He asked the manager where he had come from.

'Adelaide.'

'Before that.'

'Nairobi.'

Kolvenbach was astonished. 'You're not African.'

'I am.' The man crossed his heart.

'Born in Kenya?'

'No. Born in Egypt. Alexandria.'

'You said you were African.'

The man was enjoying this. He liked Kolvenbach; every conversation could be a game of chess. 'And where the hell do you think Egypt is if it's not in Africa?'

Kolvenbach nodded. 'I thought you meant the real Africa. Not *North* Africa.' He frowned into his beer. At least he'd been on the correct sea, if on the wrong side. 'So you're Egyptian, eh?'

'Not strictly,' the man conceded. 'Born in Egypt but with a Greek mother and a Hungarian father.'

'Ah.' Kolvenbach felt a twinge of triumph.

The Greek-Hungarian-Egyptian was leaning closer. 'How about you, Dennis? You don't sound like a dinkum Aussie to me.'

'American.'

'You're not.'

It was Kolvenbach's turn to put his hand over his heart. 'From Kansas. Born and bred.'

'You don't sound American.'

'America is a big land, full of dozens of different accents. Mine's a Kansas accent. I'm from west Kansas. They speak differently in the east.'

'Is that so?' Scratching his neck, the man went off to serve a woman at the other end of the bar. She had just arrived and was looking around, as though searching for something.

Kolvenbach glanced at his watch. An hour before dinner. He wondered how many days he'd have to wait before Hunnicutt reached town. When the manager came back, he'd ask him about the chances of hiring a car. With a car, he could spend the morning scouting the area. It would be good to be familiar with the territory.

He leaned forward, burying his chin in his hands as a better idea came to him. He could try to borrow the manager's car. A borrowed car would be ideal. No records to fill in for the car rental — if there was such a thing in Tibooburra.

Kolvenbach wasn't concerned about what was happening at the other end of the room where the manager was being dazzled by Laura Hunnicutt's smile.

Just like a small boy who saves the best, the thing he really wants to do, until last, Kelly went to a service station before buying a paper. He had to get fuel but he wanted desperately to see a newspaper. It was not just the game: it was vanity. He knew that. Couldn't help it. He wanted to see his picture, his story, in the paper.

While the man at the service station began filling the tank, he wondered what he'd find when he drove around to the newsagent — a story on the front page? No. He chuckled and realised that the man filling the tank was staring at him. It would only be a small article, probably buried on page seven

110

or later. There *could* be a small picture. People would need to know what he looked like.

What if there was nothing? The car radio hadn't been able to pick up any station all day so he'd heard nothing more. There were only those tantalising reports from the late-night news. Were the police still looking for him? Or had they filed the Hunnicutt affair away under silly stories and got on with something important?

The man was looking at him intently. Every time Kelly glanced across, the man seemed to be staring at him with the quizzical expression of someone who was trying to place a face. Kelly was wearing his hat and his sunglasses, was affecting a limp, and hadn't shaved since leaving Melbourne; but still he felt uneasy. The man was behaving in the strangest way. He would turn away the instant their eyes met but stare at him at other times. He could see the reflection in the service station window. Weird. Then again, he reminded himself, the tall man at the dingo fence had been weird too. Maybe the people up here just stared at strangers. He paid and hurried away, as fast as the limp would allow.

He parked opposite the paper shop. Halfway across the road, he stopped. They sold the Sydney papers. He could see the posters. Both the *Herald* and the *Telegraph-Mirror* had the same story about a murder. SEARCH FOR DIAMOND KILLER GROWS. KILLER HUNT HEADS FOR BUSH. He grunted in disappointment. He'd been hoping, deep down where dreams are nurtured, that his story might be on a poster. It would make a great souvenir.

A wave of cynicism and doubt, those rough riding companions of truth, swept through him, weakening him as suddenly as some potent virus. If there had been a seat nearby, he'd have sat down. He felt exhausted. Laura was right. His story was no big deal. It was a joke. That's what it was and that's all it was: a stupid joke. Who cared about some obscure documentary film-maker who'd been given the wrong tablets? That's if anyone had ever believed such a story. What if the police had grown suspicious, put pressure on Gerry and made him confess it was just a prank, something done for a bet? Gerry could even be under arrest. The police wouldn't like having their time wasted, being made to look like fools, searching for a man who was playing a game of hide-and-seek with them just to win a bet. They could even be billed for the cost of a search; maybe hundreds of thousands of dollars.

He needed a couple of deep breaths to get him across the road. A sleeping dog was curled up on the gutter and he had to step around it. Outside the newsagency, where the posters leaned against the wall, he paused to examine his own image in the window. He looked ridiculous, an extra on a filmset or someone striving to be noticed. He took off his hat, removed the sunglasses, straightened his back and entered the shop.

The Sydney newspapers were on the floor. His own face stared up at him.

The hair at the back of his neck bristled. He was on the front page of both newspapers. Unbelievable. Both papers. He looked around. There was only an elderly woman in the shop. She was behind the counter, adding up figures on a piece of paper. He wanted to shout, 'That's me,' and have someone share his excitement but she was writing and besides, he mustn't let her know. He bent down beside the pile of papers.

The broadsheet *Sydney Morning Herald*, folded in half and with its front page rumpled and torn from the thousand-kilometre journey from Sydney, had his photograph up high, on the right side where the paper was badly creased. His face covered five columns. Under the picture and difficult to read because of the fold was the headline: DIAMOND KILLER STILL LOOSE. POLICE SAY HAUL WORTH $4 MILLION. Diamond Killer? Wrong item. Where was the story about him? He looked for a line beneath the picture, something that said this man's life is in danger; story page four, page six, page ten. But there was nothing. Just his name and that terrible headline.

He began to shake. Gripped by a nauseous panic, he picked up the tabloid *Telegraph-Mirror*. His face, stippled and ink smudged, stared up at him. It was a good picture, taken on location in the Gulf country. What was the shoot, who was the client? He couldn't remember because his mind was in turmoil, but he knew the picture used to hang on the wall of his office.

And beside his face, in huge type: HUNT MOVES TO BUSH. DIAMOND KILLER HIDING IN OUTBACK.

'Still hot,' said the woman behind the counter.

Somehow he managed to say yes and thrust both papers under his arm, just like a normal buyer would. *Diamond Killer?* Must get out, back to the car. Have to read the stories. Must ring Gerry. He tried to smile. The woman was saying they could do with rain. He offered five dollars An old man bent over a walking stick entered the shop and he and the woman began to talk.

Kelly hurried out of the shop. He heard the woman call that he'd forgotten his change but he quickened his pace, jumped in the car and drove off as fast as he could.

Laura had trouble reaching the number she wanted. When she got through, she could hear loud music in the background and when the man spoke, it was a whisper.

'Where the devil have you been?' Gerry Montague said.

12

Laura Hunnicutt sat in the manager's office, trying to take in the information. First, Montague's apartment had been broken into. Second, Kolvenbach's brother had turned up. Montague sounded as though he'd been drinking. He was dangerous when he drank — talked too much, became impulsive. And now he was panicking, convinced that someone knew he had the diamonds and was watching him.

Somehow, she had to get back to Melbourne. It had seemed a good idea to stay with Kelly, to guide him along the path that most suited their purposes, but now it was imperative that she return. Montague needed help.

She'd be safer in Melbourne, too, if the dead man's brother really was hunting Kelly. That must have been Magnus Kolvenbach they'd met along the fence. Montague had said he was flying his own aircraft and they'd seen a plane, and the description matched the man precisely. So Kolvenbach had found them.

Time to go home. Let fate and the big-game hunter take care of Kelly.

She was still thinking when the manager returned to the office. 'Bad news?' he said, wrinkling his brow to match hers.

'No.' She made a brave attempt to smile. 'It's just that my sister hasn't been well.'

Kolvenbach was driving the hotel manager's Holden Premier. Borrowing the car had been easy. He had been only halfway through his tale of need when the manager had fished in his pocket for the keys and told him the car was parked in a garage at the back of the hotel. 'Take it,' he said. 'Wipers don't work but it won't rain. Just put some gas in it.' He said gas so that Kolvenbach, being from Kansas, would understand.

The car was twenty years old. The bronze paint was fading, one window winder was missing and the front floor was covered in hardened mud chips that had fallen from the soles of many boots; but it started easily and seemed to run well. There was a rattle at the back; nothing more than a loose exhaust pipe, Kolvenbach guessed. A front brake squeaked. The windscreen was scratched. It was perfect. No one would look at him in a car like this. He planned to rise at dawn and drive along the road that ran towards the South Australian border and the dingo fence. All he needed was fuel and a good road map.

He was on his way to the service station when he saw Laura. She was crossing the road about a hundred metres ahead of him. He braked and pulled into the kerb, stopping only a few car lengths from her. He slumped in the seat to give the impression of being a smaller man, and put on his hat. She was glancing up and down the road, hands on her hips, mouth set in an angry line. Not hiding, but wanting to be seen. To be picked up. Of course. She was waiting for Hunnicutt. As she glanced up and down the street, she had the disapproving look of a woman whose man was late.

So they were in town — and at least a day ahead of schedule. Kolvenbach cursed himself for being so unprepared. He'd taken Hunnicutt at his word but the bastard must have been suspicious and raced up the fence to try to get here ahead of him. Ahead of him? He reconsidered. No, Hunnicutt didn't know that much. More likely, he took fright when a curious stranger appeared and drove as hard as he could to get to town. He probably needed fuel. Then he'd be on his way, to hide out in the bush country he knew so well. Kolvenbach grunted. First round to Hunnicutt. Never mind; he'd win the next. He knew they were in town; they didn't know he was here. Nor did they know who he was or what he intended doing.

He studied the woman. Angry or nervous? Hard to tell. Extremely agitated, though. She couldn't keep still, looking this way and that, constantly checking her watch. Suddenly, she became interested in something behind him. In his mirror he could see a Landcruiser approaching but it was grey and a utility. Wrong colour, wrong model. He twisted to examine both footpaths. Outside a shop, two men were talking. Neither of them was Hunnicutt.

The woman began walking towards him. He tilted his hat to cover his forehead and bent forward as if fiddling with the ignition key. She walked past, not interested in him or his car.

He let her pass, counted to ten and then pulled out from the kerb. He swung the car in a U-turn and drove slowly down the street. Once more he cursed himself. He'd come without any of his rifles or his gear, and the Holden was almost out of fuel; but he had to follow her. And when she rejoined Hunnicutt, he'd have to track the two of them or they'd disappear, and this time Hunnicutt wouldn't be doing something stupid like following a border fence. He could waste days, weeks, searching for them from the air. Where had Hunnicutt said they were going after this town? South, towards Melbourne, which probably meant they would head north. How far could he travel in the Holden? Ten

116

kilometres, maybe twenty. The needle of the fuel gauge was fluttering on the empty mark.

He saw the service station at the end of the street and took a risk. Increasing his speed, he passed the woman and drove up to a petrol pump. He jumped out and started to fill the tank.

'I'll do that.' The garage man, who had been turning on the station's lights, shuffled out to take the hose from Kolvenbach. 'We still give service here,' he said, making it sound as though Kolvenbach was to be last of the lucky ones. 'How much?'

'This much.' Kolvenbach showed a twenty-dollar note, but he was looking for the woman. She should be walking past soon. At that moment, a white Landcruiser drove past and braked suddenly. Hunnicutt. He'd stopped to pick up the woman.

'That'll do,' Kolvenbach said, frantically waving the note. 'Stop. That's enough.'

'Only put ten in,' the man said without stopping, but then noticed the Toyota. He used his free hand to grip Kolvenbach's shoulder and tried to turn him around, to face the road. 'Have you been reading about that shooting in Melbourne?' The speech accelerated and rose in pitch. 'The one where that South African bloke got murdered for all those diamonds?'

'What about it?' Kolvenbach could see the Toyota rocking slightly as the woman climbed aboard.

'That's him.'

'Who is?'

The man jabbed a finger towards the tail of the stationary Landcruiser. 'The bloke who shot the South African. He's in that four-wheel drive. He was in here earlier. Filled the tank and a drum. Took nearly ninety dollars' worth. I thought I recognised him. Wasn't sure at first but then I went and checked. His picture's in all the papers. Funny name. Helso...Belso. Something like that. I phoned the

117

police. They should be here any minute.' He squeezed Kolvenbach's shoulder and cackled nervously. 'The stupid bugger's come back... and here comes Roger.' He pointed up the road. A Falcon was racing towards the garage.

'Who's Roger?'

'The sergeant. Tough bastard but fair.' Another cackle. 'This'll be worth watching.'

Kolvenbach took the hose and put it back on the pump. He thrust the twenty dollars into the man's hand and jumped in the Holden. The man had lost interest in him. Eyes darting from the approaching police car to the Landcruiser, he was bouncing with excitement, rising up and down as though on springs.

With a squeal of tyres, the police Falcon drove onto the driveway. Much more quietly, Kolvenbach swung onto the road, just in time to see the Landcruiser drive away. He tucked in behind it.

Hunnicutt reached an intersection and turned right. Behind him, Kolvenbach could see the lights of the police car bouncing as the car careered off the service station driveway back onto the road, its roof light flashing brilliant blue. He stopped and waved the Falcon down.

'Are you after that four-wheel drive?' he shouted.

'Too right. Where'd he go?'

'Left. He was flying.'

The cry of thanks was lost in the whirr of a siren as the Falcon spun to the left. Kolvenbach watched it race down the road before he turned to the right.

Kelly parked on the outskirts of town beside the remains of a shed. Here, close to a wall of decaying wooden planks, the evening shadows were darkest. 'Did you hear a siren?'

'No.' She turned to face him. She was crying. 'Kelly, why did you do it? *How* could you do it?'

118

'I didn't.' He waved a crumpled newspaper. 'I don't know what this is all about.'

'Tricia was telling me. It's on all the news, day and night. Do you know what they're calling you? The Diamond Killer.' She covered her face.

He seized her wrists, trying to remove the barrier to her eyes. 'Laura, I didn't do it.'

She pulled away. 'I knew there was something wrong. I knew it.'

They were silent, looking away from each other. 'This is madness,' he said. 'I'm going to the police. I'll explain everything, I'll tell them this is some ghastly mistake.'

Wiping her eyes, she turned. 'Look at me, Kelly.' He did. 'Now tell me, did you or did you not do this thing? Did you shoot this man?'

'How could you even ask that question?'

'Please answer me.'

He took a deep breath and cradled his forehead. 'No, Laura, I did not. I have no idea what this is all about but I did not kill Harald Kolvenbach. I liked the man. We were friends. I was going to make a film for him. I was looking forward to it. Why the hell would I kill him?' He wiped his eyes. 'He's dead. I hadn't even thought about that. Jesus Christ.'

Now she was examining him, with some pity but little belief. He knew the expression and covered his face. 'You were like a madman when you came to my place that night,' she said, her voice soft but doubting, an adult coaxing the truth from a child.

He sat up straight and nodded, glad to agree on something. 'Yes. I thought you'd left me for another man. That can make a man mad.' He sniffed and wiped his nose. 'But I had not murdered a man, a man I liked, and stolen ... what was it? ... a couple of million dollars' worth of diamonds.' He

119

wiped his nose more vigorously. 'A sick woman — your sister — had told me a bizarre tale about you and my best friend, and I got mad. That was all. I'm sorry. I've apologised before. But this...' He slumped against the steering wheel. 'There's been a terrible mistake and I don't know what to do.'

A long silence. She was not looking at him. 'But you didn't do it? You swear to me?'

'I didn't do it. I swear.' A breeze was stirring and the old shed creaked.

'Then who did?'

He thumped the dashboard. 'I don't know. How would I know? You don't believe me, do you?' The faint wail of a siren drifted from the centre of town. 'That's a police car. They're looking for me.'

'It could be a fire engine. No one's looking for you.'

'Then who was that following us?'

'Oh for heaven's sake, Kelly, if you're going to have a nervous breakdown I'm getting out of this car.'

He tried to laugh but produced a braying sound. 'You don't think I've got good reasons for having a nervous breakdown?'

'Excellent. But it wouldn't help.'

'Dear Laura. Always the practical one.'

'One of us has to be. Now listen.' She prodded him. 'Sit up and listen.'

He sat back sullenly and folded his arms.

'First, you don't go to the police.' His eyes flickered in doubt and she shook a finger at him. 'You don't go, Kelly, because you don't know how they'll react. We have no idea what the police think about you or what you're supposed to have done.'

He laughed. 'I know what they think. It's in the paper. I'm supposed to have put a bullet through Harald Kolvenbach and then taken four million dollars' worth of diamonds.' Again he covered his eyes. 'They say he was shot with my rifle and they found my footprints in his garden and there's something about my clothes. I don't understand that. I didn't go anywhere near his house.'

'How could he have been shot with your rifle?'

He shook his head sadly. 'A mistake. They must have made a mistake.'

'Well, let's not worry about that,' she said, instantly signifying that it was worth a great deal of worry. 'What matters is that the police *think* you did all those things and so, if they find you, they'll be rough on you. Violent.'

'So what do I do?'

'Stay out of sight.'

'How do I do that?'

'Kelly, you prize idiot, that's what you've been doing for the past couple of days. That's what you were looking forward to, remember? Your little game of hide-and-seek with the police? Well, just keep going.'

'But they want me for murder.'

'It doesn't matter.' She reached over and took his hand. 'You're good enough to throw them off the track. You know the country so well you could stay out of sight for a month, not just a week.'

The tilt of his head meant he agreed. He took several deep breaths. He could hear the siren again, as mournful as the distant wailing of a cat.

She touched his chin to make him look at her. 'The longer you keep out of sight, the better. That'll give the police time to find the real killer.'

He nodded. 'What about you?'

'I don't know.' There was a long pause. She stroked his hand. 'I want to be with you. The last couple of days have been wonderful.'

'Then you do believe me?'

She covered her eyes with one hand. 'I think so.' Off came the hand and she leaned close. 'What

am I saying? Of course I believe you. Yes, of course.'
She kissed his cheek. 'You taste salty. Have you been
crying?'

He shook his head but wiped an eye. 'I don't
know what I've been doing.'

'I'd love to stay with you but I can't.'

His head lolled forward.

'And I can't, Kelly my love, because we're going
to need someone in Melbourne to find out what
the devil has been going on.'

His head still drooped. He'd wanted her to stay
with him. 'What do you mean?'

'Well, the whole business sounds fishy to me.
From all that Tricia told me — you know, your
gun, your clothes, your shoes — I'd say you'd been
set up.'

'I still don't follow you.'

'I'm saying that someone has tried to make it
look as though you murdered Harald Kolvenbach.'

'They've done a good job.' He laughed mirthlessly.
'At least I've got my picture in the paper.'

'Indeed you have.' She took both his hands. 'You
say there's a plane service from here?'

'I think so.'

'I'll catch a plane. I'm of more use to you in
Melbourne than I am out here, hiding away on the
edge of some billabong.'

'Why don't I ring Gerry?'

'I'll get in touch with him. I don't think you should
go near another town unless it's absolutely necessary. You just drop me off at the hotel and keep
going. Where did you say you were heading?'

'Up to the Cooper.' He brightened, recalling
earlier dreams.

'Go there. Keep out of sight.'

'You'll be all right?'

'I've got my love.' She kissed him again. 'And my
credit cards. What more could a girl want?'

'I don't want you to go.'

'I have to.' She squeezed his hand. 'Come on, get me to the hotel.'

When they were close to town, she said, 'By the way, did Kolvenbach have any family? A brother, perhaps?'

'A brother, yes, but I never met him. Why?'

'Oh, it was just something Tricia said. Nothing important.'

He shook his head. 'He was coming to Australia sometime soon. Poor bloke. What a welcome.' He pointed ahead. 'Here's the pub.'

She was already leaning over the seat, reaching for her bag. She grabbed it, kissed him and got out. 'Don't waste a minute. Go.'

'We have to keep in touch. I'll try to phone you.'

'Ring me at home. Whenever you can.'

'At nights.'

'I'll be waiting.'

'I don't know when I can get to a phone.' He was speaking slowly, more in control of himself now. 'There aren't many phone boxes along the Cooper.'

'Just call me when you can.'

With a wave that was almost a military salute, he drove off.

One block down the road, Kolvenbach slumped in dismay. He had hoped both the man and the woman would enter the hotel, to give him the chance to collect his gear. No time now. With the Holden's lights still turned off, he followed the Land-cruiser out of Tibooburra.

13

Montague was feeling pleased. This was the day he'd made 200,000 US dollars, which he wouldn't have to share with anyone. Certainly not Laura. There was no point showering money on her when there was no need, and there'd been no need to tell her how much cash he'd taken from Kolvenbach's safe. They hadn't expected much.

'How much?' she'd asked.

'Around 76,000 US dollars,' he'd said, very cool because he'd been rehearsing this bit, 'plus more than 40,000 in Australian money.' She'd been very impressed. Delighted, in fact. Why bother to mention the other 200,000 American dollars? She was happy and he had some money to put aside for his old age.

He finished his drink. The 200,000 was safe, wrapped in two big supermarket plastic bags and hidden in the ceiling.

Kolvenbach's heart was racing. The police car had damn near sideswiped him. It had come bursting from a side road or an alley — he couldn't tell which — and set off in pursuit of Hunnicutt. It must have been parked with all lights off. Now everything was on: headlights, spotlights, blue flashing light, siren.

He watched the chase. Hunnicutt accelerated, attempting to outrun the Falcon, but the police car gobbled up the distance between them. Then Hunnicutt did a clever thing — he swung off the road and charged across a rough paddock.

The policeman followed. At first, he tried to match pace with the Toyota but after a couple of nose dives which sent dirt and rocks showering into the air, he was forced to slow. The four-wheel drive constantly changed direction as Hunnicutt dodged piles of rock and solitary boulders. Move for move, the police car followed in his tracks, but lost ground.

'Go, you bastard,' Kolvenbach shouted. Hunnicutt was his prize, not the policeman's. Kolvenbach kept his car on the road, watching the chase, preparing to join in when the Landcruiser reached smoother terrain. If it did. He hadn't expected this. He'd thought Hunnicutt would stick to the road but if he continued to drive across country, he'd not only outrun the police car, he'd leave the old Holden far behind. In that case it would be goodbye Hunnicutt.

At that moment, the Landcruiser's headlights swept across a ridge of large boulders. The vehicle stopped, its way blocked. Hunnicutt waited only a few seconds before turning, intent on returning to the road.

The policeman tried a short cut to intercept the Toyota but became bogged in sand. Kolvenbach could hear the Falcon's motor roaring as the back wheels spun. Then he realised that Hunnicutt was not heading for the road but had speared off in another direction, confused by the darkness.

Hunnicutt needed a lighthouse, a beacon to guide him to the roadway. Kolvenbach turned on the Holden's lights and flicked high beam. Immediately, the Toyota swung towards him. Its big spotlights flashed up and down, dazzling him one moment, spearing into the sky the next, as the Landcruiser bounded across the rough ground.

'Not too fast,' Kolvenbach muttered as the big vehicle clattered through a batch of small stones. It hit larger rocks and the noise was like the clanging of a dozen gongs. 'Slower,' Kolvenbach screamed and as if obeying, Hunnicutt slowed. Still porpoising across the folds of land but travelling at a saner pace, the Toyota headed for the Holden's lights.

Kolvenbach continued driving out of town, moving slowly, showing Hunnicutt the way. He glanced towards the distant Falcon. It was moving again. Blast. Coming quickly, too.

The Toyota bounded on to the road behind Kolvenbach. With a blaring of horns and a shower of stones, it passed him on the wrong side. The driver waved. It was a gesture of thanks and Kolvenbach laughed. The man was polite. Here he was, running for his life and yet he was thanking a stranger for moving over. A worm of doubt twitched within Kolvenbach's brain. This was an unorthodox murderer.

The Falcon was close now. Kolvenbach watched, fascinated. The car was leaping from one bump to the next, leaving a trail of sparks like an out-of-control, ground-hugging skyrocket. The flashing blue light went out. There was another sparkling shower and the terrible sound of rock gouging steel, but not once did the engine note lessen. The policeman was driving that car flat out, prepared to destroy it if that was the only way to catch his man. The Falcon soared from the last bump like a surfboard leaving a breaker, flew across a row of low saltbushes, and struck the road. It bounced to the other side, slewed up a graded bank and, with its back end fishtailing and spitting stones, set off in pursuit.

Hunnicutt tried to turn off the road once more but he chose the wrong place. There was a ditch and he put the Toyota's nose into it. He was trying to reverse out when the police car slid to a halt beside him. The policeman jumped out, almost falling in his haste. He drew his gun. Running to the Landcruiser, he wrenched open the door and grabbed Hunnicutt by the arm. He dragged him out. Hunnicutt fell and the policeman pulled him to his feet, shoving him against the front of the vehicle.

Very Hollywood, thought Kolvenbach. He stopped behind the Falcon, found a suitable rock, and walked up to thë policeman.

'Can I help, officer?'

The policeman half turned. 'Please keep out of this, sir.'

'Trouble?'

'Just keep back.'

'What do you want him for? Is he drunk?'

The policeman was groping for his handcuffs. 'Will you just piss off.'

Kolvenbach was close now. He lifted the stone and struck the policeman on the head. The man fell against Kelly's back and slumped to the ground. He went down slowly, like an inflated toy losing air.

Kelly turned and squinted into the bright lights. He shaded his eyes. 'Who the hell are you?'

'We met earlier today. Don't you remember?' Kolvenbach moved so that Kelly could see him more clearly. 'What was your name ... ah, Mr Kelly wasn't it?'

'You're the man from the fence.'

'Yes.'

Kelly was shaking. He rubbed a knee, which hurt. 'What are you doing here?'

'I drove here.' He bent to pick up the policeman's gun.

'Why did you do that?' With distaste, Kelly glanced down at the policeman, who was sprawled across his feet. He shuffled clear.

'I did it because I didn't want him to arrest you.'

For the first time, Kelly sensed the menace in the man's voice. 'What do you want? What's all this about?'

Kolvenbach put the pistol in his pocket. 'You're Mr Kelso Hunnicutt, aren't you?'

Kelly said nothing. He wiped his lips. 'I'm stuck in the ditch. I have to get out.' It sounded idiotic but he couldn't think of anything else to say.

'Really?' Kolvenbach walked to one side so that the police car's blinding lights were behind him. 'We'll have to get a tow truck then, won't we?'

'I can get it out.' We're sparring, Kelly thought, trying to see the man clearly. He was all shadows and bright outlines.

'You are Kelso Hunnicutt, aren't you?'

'Who are you?' There must be a reward, Kelly thought, and this man was a modern version of a bounty hunter.

Kolvenbach was using the toe of his boot to prod the ribs of the policeman. He rolled him on his side. 'They don't build policemen's skulls like they used to. This poor fellow will be out for another ten minutes or more.' He smiled. At least, Kelly thought he smiled — the outline of the shadowed face had changed and he could see wrinkles near the mouth. 'Who am I? Let's just say I'm someone who's very interested in what you're carrying in that wagon of yours. You give it to me, and you can be on your way.'

Kelly pressed himself against the Landcruiser's door. The engine was idling, causing the vehicle to shake in a series of pulsing vibrations. 'What are you talking about?'

'Come, come, let's not waste time.'

'I didn't shoot anyone.'

There was no smile now. The outline was severe, unspoiled by any hint of mirth. 'Of course not. Get the bag.'

128

This man wasn't a bounty hunter. He was after the diamonds; a thief robbing a thief. He could deal with such a man, Kelly thought, and spread his hands in a suppliant gesture. 'I didn't steal any diamonds, if that's what you're after.'

'Just give me the bag, Mr Hunnicutt. I want everything that was in the safe.'

Kelly spread his hands wider. His voice was awash with sincerity. 'Look, I haven't got a thing. I didn't shoot anyone. I didn't steal anything.'

'The bag.' He held out his hand. The palm shone in the bright lights.

This man is unbalanced, Kelly thought and was surprised to find that he could think clearly. The chase had unsettled him but he was calm now. He made himself laugh. It was a friendly sound, one mate confiding to another. 'I haven't got it. Truly. I don't know what all this is about.' He hunched his shoulders, determined to make this man believe him. 'I only found out a little while ago that the police were looking for me.' He hesitated, feeling compelled to be truthful. 'Well, I already thought the police were looking for me but for something else. You see, there was this bet...' He shouldn't have said that. The man reached out and shoved him hard on the shoulder. He was exceptionally strong and his hand hit like a piece of hardwood.

'I don't want to hear any more of this nonsense.' He said 'noon-since' just like Harald Kolvenbach used to.

Kelly frowned, confused by vague recollections. 'Who are you, friend?'

'Not a friend.' Kolvenbach withdrew the gun. 'We haven't much time. Get the bag.'

When he finds nothing, he'll shoot me, Kelly thought. And then he'll probably shoot the policeman. Time to get away. He sighed, the prelude to confession. 'Okay.'

'Okay what?'

Kelly's body sagged in defeat. 'It's taped inside the winch and the winch is jammed in the ditch. I've got to try and reverse out.'

With mounting impatience, Kolvenbach waved the gun. The policeman was trying to raise an arm. 'Get in then. Be quick.' He moved to the front of the Landcruiser.

Kelly climbed into the cabin. He'd been working it out: it was difficult to reverse out of the ditch but, in low range, he might be able to go forward. His captor wouldn't expect that. With the advantage of surprise, he might gain a few seconds and be on his way before the man could fire. He slammed the door. The man was right in front of the Toyota, brightly lit by its four lights and holding the gun up high, like someone who knew how to use it.

Kelly took a deep breath. He put the lever into low range, selected first gear and turned to look behind him, as though about to reverse. 'Here goes.'

'Hurry up then, and remember, if you try...'

The Landcruiser lunged forward. Engine roaring, tyres clawing for grip, it rode up the other side of the ditch. Kolvenbach tried to jump clear but the kangaroo guard caught him on the hip and sent him flying to one side. Kelly snatched second gear, swung to the left to follow the line of the ditch and, with the vehicle bounding over ruts and rocks and with its load of fuel cans and camping gear jangling in the back, headed away from the road. He heard the back window shatter, heard the snarl of another bullet ricocheting off metal, then turned hard right. The ground was smooth. He was away.

Montague was asleep. He felt a cold touch on his forehead and tried to brush it away. His fingers bumped something solid and he opened his eyes. No dream. The cold thing was still there. His hand fanned the air and touched an arm. He cried out and sat up and then in quick succession, the bedside light was switched on, the mattress squeaked and a man settled himself on the side of the bed. He wore a raincoat, a hat and a clown's mask. He held a pistol in one hand and a large plastic supermarket bag in the other. He threw the bag against Montague's chest.

'Where's the rest of it?'

Montague clutched the bag.

'Where are the diamonds and the papers?'

Montague shook his head.

'I hope you're not going to be difficult.' He had a pleasant voice, deep and not at all in keeping with the clown's face. He nursed the pistol on his lap.

'Who are you?' Montague said.

'Because if you are going to be difficult and uncooperative, I'll be forced to make things unpleasant for you. We wouldn't like that, would we?' He was wearing thin cotton gloves and he pulled them up his wrists, like a fighter adjusting his boxing gloves before the bell.

'I said, who are you?'

It was a brave effort to appear unafraid but again the man ignored him. 'You weren't very imaginative when you tried to hide that package, Mr Montague. In the ceiling.' He clucked admonition. 'Really. Very amateurish.'

Montague pulled the plastic bag closer to his body.

'I haven't counted it yet,' the man said, 'but there appears to be a lot of money in there. But only money. Where's the rest?'

One bag. He hadn't found the other one. Montague held out the plastic bag. 'Do you want money? You can have half.' He thrust it closer to the man. 'Here. There's a lot. Thousands.'

131

The gunman adjusted the mask. It was too small for his face and left a crease on his chin. 'I can have the *lot*, Mr Montague.' He let the mask settle back in place and stretched his jaw. 'But I want more. I want the diamonds and I want the papers. Give them to me. Now.'

He was about to lift the pistol when George McCarthy entered the room. He came in quietly, out of sight of the gunman. He had a Smith and Wesson which he held in both hands, well clear of his body, and he advanced in a series of sideways steps, like a Spanish dancer moving to the slow rustle of castanets.

'If you value your life...' McCarthy said softly and then paused, expecting a jolt of fright to pass through the other man's body. It did. 'Don't move. You will raise both hands but not turn around.'

Slowly the man lifted his hands and held them in front of him. Montague slumped back into the bed. 'Oh my God, George.' He covered his forehead with a limp arm.

'Are you all right, Gerry?'

Montague nodded.

'Then get out of bed and get over here. Be careful. Keep clear of our friend. Has he got a gun?'

'Yes. In his lap.'

'Leave it there.' To the man: 'Raise your hands so that I can see them'. The man did. Then to Montague: 'Now, keeping well clear of the bed, come over to the doorway'.

As Montague got out of one side of the bed, McCarthy circled to the other until he could see the man's profile. 'Oh, we have a comedian here, have we?' He reached out and touched the man's shoulder with the barrel of his gun. 'Why don't we remember our good manners and take off our hat and our funny mask, eh?'

The man obeyed.

'Recognise him, Gerry?'

Montague shook his head. He was holding the plastic bag as a naked man holds a towel to his body.

McCarthy moved to the wall and faced the man. 'I have someone outside, in case you're thinking you might try something fancy with a fat old ex-cop.'

The man looked up. 'You're not a policeman?'

'Not at the moment. I remember the tricks, though.' He glanced at Montague. 'What's in the bag?'

Montague cleared his throat. 'Some cash. He found it.'

The tip of McCarthy's tongue did a slow lap of his lips. 'Is that what this is all about?'

Montague shook his head. 'I don't know.'

'I'd say it's a fair guess.'

The man on the bed swung his head from one side to the other. He flexed his shoulders, relaxing. 'If you're not a cop, who the hell are you?'

McCarthy winked at him. 'I'm the man with a gun big enough to blow your face off.' He turned briefly to Montague. 'You're sure you don't know him?'

'Never seen him before. Christ, do you want a drink, George?'

'No, and neither do you. Not yet. I think we should ask our friend a few questions, don't you?' He waved the gun at the man. 'First, put that little toy pistol of yours on the floor. Pick it up by the barrel.' Delicately, the man put his gun on the carpet. 'Now lie on the bed. Face down, arms out on either side.'

The man attempted to laugh. 'This is new. What's next? Madame Lash?'

'I told you we had a comedian.' McCarthy moved away from the wall. 'All right. It's question time. First question. Who are you?'

The man was silent.

'You're allowed one miss, and that was it. Second question. Who sent you here?'

McCarthy moved forward and ground the Smith and Wesson in the small of the man's back. The man twitched but didn't speak. 'A bullet there mightn't kill you but I guarantee you'd never walk again.' He stepped back and turned to Montague. 'I think we have two choices. Either we hand this clown over to the police or we do our own little bit of investigation. Do you mind, Gerry, if we spill a bit of blood on your carpet?'

He winked and Montague said, 'Go ahead'.

'I'm going to start by breaking a finger every time our friend refuses to answer a question. Then I might start cutting him. I haven't done that for a long time. I used to enjoy it.'

The man's arms moved but he said nothing.

McCarthy beckoned to Montague. 'First, a little break. You and I are going outside.' He whistled and another man appeared. He was shorter than McCarthy but even broader.

'Watch him,' McCarthy said. 'If he moves, do something unpleasant.' He raised his voice. 'You on the bed. My man here has a gun and he's stronger and fitter than me. He used to play rugby league but he was disqualified for life for biting a man's ear off. He's very good at it so don't make him angry.' He left the room. A trembling Montague followed.

'Thank you,' Montague said when they were in the lounge. 'Where in the name of heaven did you come from?'

'Spiro was watching your place. He called me when he saw that character slip inside.' McCarthy rearranged the cushions on the couch. 'Now you'd better level with me. Where'd that money come from? How'd that man know it was here?'

Montague had put the plastic bag on the floor.

He covered his face with both hands. An idea was developing. 'I'm being blackmailed, George.'

McCarthy went to the bar and got himself a can of beer. 'Who by?'

'I don't know.'

McCarthy stopped, his hand poised on the can's ring-pull. 'What do you mean, you don't know?'

'All I know is the man's first name. It's Rob.'

'You're being blackmailed by someone called Rob.' He returned to the couch. 'And that bundle of cash, I presume, is the money to pay him.'

Montague nodded.

"Okay. What did you do?' He took a few wheezing breaths and moved the pillows again but his eyes never left Montague. 'Something worthwhile like screw his wife, or is it more sordid than that?'

Montague was thinking at a furious pace but he managed to shake his head sadly. What story could he invent; what would McCarthy believe? All he knew about Rob was that he was from Canberra. A politician? Why not? A deep breath to indicate he was about to tell the truth, painful though it was... 'Nothing like that. It's to do with politics.' Montague let his hands fall to his lap. 'They say politics is a dirty business but I never realised...'

They talked for another ten minutes. McCarthy seemed fascinated by the plastic bag. He didn't want to know too much and didn't press Montague about the reason for the blackmail. All they agreed on in those ten minutes was that McCarthy would try to track down the mysterious Rob and that Montague would pay him half the 'ransom' money — 50,000 dollars — for his services.

The manager of the Tibooburra hotel had been delighted to welcome Laura back to his pub. He was not suspicious, because he knew she was worried about her sister. He thought it proper that

135

she had decided to abandon her holiday and return to Melbourne. Of course he had a room. And yes, he would wake her early and even cook breakfast himself so that she could be away in time to catch the flight.

The bedroom was small and stuffy, and she was having a bad dream. She was on a boat and it was rocking gently. She was about to dive over the side. There were people in the water with masks on and they were calling to her and so she put on her mask but she couldn't breathe. *She couldn't breathe.* The mask, something, was pressed tight against her mouth and nose.

She woke up, desperate for air. She tried to scream and swing her arms. She couldn't. Her arms were pinned to her sides.

'Be quiet,' a man whispered, his lips so close she could feel his breath on her ear. 'I won't hurt you.'

She struggled then stopped as the hand, a hard, rough hand, moved away from her nose and she was able to draw in air.

'You won't get hurt if you do what I tell you. Understand?' That voice. She knew it. 'Now, I'm going to turn on the light. If you make a noise, I will hit you. Understand?'

She nodded and he switched on the bedside lamp, still keeping one hand across her mouth. Kolvenbach. He took his hand away. 'I know who you are,' she said, blinking.

'Good. Then you know that your boyfriend murdered my brother.'

She clutched her throat. 'What are you doing here?'

He stood up. My God, he was big, she thought, and, shivering, pulled the sheet up to her chin. She was not going to let him know that she was scared, but she was — very scared.

'You and I are going on a little trip. We're going to catch your boyfriend.'

'Kelly?'

'He got away from me earlier tonight. You know where he's going. You'll show me.'

'I will not.'

He reached down, grabbed her arm and pulled her out of bed. It was effortless. She'd never felt such strength. He jiggled her from one foot to the other, then dropped her on to the bed.

'You have one minute to get dressed and pack what you want. Things are likely to be very busy around here in another ten minutes or so and I want to be well away before that happens.'

She was about to say she couldn't get ready in one minute but stopped. She covered her forehead.

'Hurry.'

She shook her head and faced him. He had incredible eyes. 'I'm getting sick of being kidnapped like this.'

The eyes narrowed.

'My husband kidnapped me the other night in Melbourne.' She hesitated. 'After the shooting. He forced me to go with him.'

'Hunnicutt? He really is your husband?'

'Oh, yes.' She had time for several deep breaths. 'We don't live together. We're separated. Or we were, before he abducted me and brought me up here.'

He walked a few paces. 'He has the diamonds?'

Another deep breath. 'I don't know. I think so, but he hasn't shown them to me.'

'You know where he's going?'

She nodded.

There was a noise downstairs. Someone had bumped into a chair. Kolvenbach looked at his watch. 'You have thirty seconds. Hurry.'

137

14

Another dust storm inside the cabin sent Kelly into a paroxysm of coughing. The Toyota was ploughing through a deep patch of bulldust and once more the shattered rear window sucked in a swirling cloud of the talcum-fine, pungent dust. He covered his nose with a handkerchief, sneezed and produced mud, then checked the outside mirror. There was still no sign of pursuing lights.

Since escaping from Kolvenbach, Kelly had avoided the main road. For the last four hours, he had driven along old station tracks, passing derelict windmills, following broken fences, opening and closing a score of gates, and stopping at least a dozen times to check faint intersections against the compass and his map. He had seen lights only once, and they had been dim lanterns shining from a distant outstation. He had not seen another car.

He stopped, got out, stretched, rubbed his sore knee and coughed again. He was covered in dust and shook a cloud of it from his hair. When he had drunk some water and washed his face, he went to the back of the vehicle, searched for a sheet of plastic and a roll of heavy-duty tape, and covered the gap in the tailgate.

Now what? He would soon have to sleep but he had stopped on a plain of unembellished monotony. A parked car would be visible for ten kilometres.

How would Gerry have described it? Standing out like an elephant on an iceberg. Something like that. He grinned. Right now, he'd love to be able to phone Gerry and tell him what had happened. He was enjoying himself. Getting away from that weird man who was after the diamonds had excited him. He'd outsmarted the bastard. He yawned. First things first. He had to get off this plain and find a hiding place where he could spend the night, or what was left of it.

He took out his Queensland map. He had crossed the border at Wompah Gate, passed the ruins of Old Tickalara and was now fairly close to the Bulloo River. He might camp there. It wasn't directly on his route to the Cooper, but that didn't matter. All he needed was somewhere to keep out of sight, and there'd be trees on the Bulloo.

For another thirty minutes he drove to the north, following an old track which became increasingly rough as it crossed a region of rocky outcrops. Eventually the track intersected fresh tyre marks that ran east. He turned along the new tracks and saw, faint in the remotest reach of his driving lights, a thin band of green-grey that was a row of trees. He stopped and took out his spotlight. He fanned the horizon. The line was constant. They were the trees bordering a river. The Bulloo.

He reached the trees and found a clear area protected by squat eucalypts and a tangle of bushes. There was water in the river. How much, he couldn't tell, but his lights flashed on a placid surface and sent bright reflections wavering across the trunks of trees on the far side. He parked where the Toyota would be most hidden, turned off the motor and listened. Silence; then the air began to pulse with the rhythmic chirp of insects. A few at first, then a bushland chorus as the river bank settled into its night-time routine of challenge and conversation. He walked away from the trees to get a clearer view of the sky. He gazed up at the stars and felt great contentment. He searched for satellites. There'd been a time when the outback sky seemed to be full of them but he hadn't noticed any in recent years. Was the space program slowing down or were his eyes getting weaker? He could see none now but the stars were dazzling and his eyes were so tired he had difficulty focusing. He walked back to the vehicle, took out his bed and lay in an open spot near the river bank.

The air was sharp with the hint of frost. He pulled his sleeping bag around his ears and gazed up at the sky, determined to see at least one satellite. He was asleep within a minute.

Something was touching his shoulder, prodding him. He was awake instantly. The half light of pre-dawn had bleached the sky to a dull grey and the eucalypts around him formed a cage of silhouettes. Another prod. Someone was behind him. His hands, clasped across his chest in the warmth of the sleeping bag, began shaking. Wild thoughts of violent policemen and tall men wanting diamonds rushed into the space vacated by sleep. He rolled over. A figure with a crumpled hat and a big coat was bending over him.

'Sorry to wake you.' It was a woman's voice. 'But you happen to have camped right on the spot where I want to do some work.' She squatted beside him. 'Do you mind?'

Kelly shivered as the fright passed from him. He unzipped the top half of his sleeping bag and sat up. About four hundred metres down the river, the back of a small truck projected from behind a tree. Smoke curled from a camp fire. There was no one else in sight. He had been looking, not listening, and he said, 'Sorry. What did you say?'

'I said do you mind?'

140

'No, I guess not.' He shook his head to clear his thoughts. This was an ordinary woman, saying ordinary things. He took a deep breath and rubbed his hands together. 'What do you want me to do?'

'Move. Please.' The second word came late, as though unaccustomed to being used in ordinary conversations.

'Move?' He stretched. 'Sure. Excuse me. I'm still half asleep. I only got here a few hours ago.'

'I know. Your lights woke me.'

He scratched his scalp. 'Did you say you had to do some work?'

'Yes.' She stood up and stuffed both hands deep into her jacket pockets. 'I'm an artist. I paint birds.' She removed one hand and pointed to a knot shadowing the trunk of a broad eucalypt. 'There are some birds nesting up there that I want to photograph. They'll come out at dawn. I need to be set up and ready.'

'Oh.' He examined the tree and yawned again. 'Did you say you were an artist or a photographer?'

'Artist. I take photographs and do some sketches but then I paint when I get back to my studio.'

Kelly had been bitten by some insect and he reached into the bag to scratch a leg. 'And what do you want me to do?'

'Move your car.'

He looked around. 'It's on the spot where you want to set up your tripod, is that it?'

'Exactly.' She did a little jiggle to keep warm. 'Look, I'm terribly sorry about this but I've been up and down this river for ten days and this is the best pair I've found.' She smiled. 'Parrots. A distinctive species.' It was her concession to an amateur. 'This is an awful thing to do to someone, isn't it?'

'Yes.'

'But you don't mind.' She smiled, sure that if

he did mind he would still move the car. This was a woman, Kelly thought, who was used to getting her own way and who would be astonished if he said 'get stuffed' and rolled over, which is what seventy-five per cent of red-blooded males would say.

'It's going to be a lovely day and dawn is the best part of the day.'

Now she was making him feel guilty about sleeping in. 'Undoubtedly,' he said, and got up. He'd gone to sleep fully clothed and tucked his shirt into his trousers as he rose. 'I suppose I can't object, not as one professional to another.'

She tilted her head. Her face expressed interest in him as a man, not as an object occupying a vital space. 'What do you do for a living?'

'I'm a cinematographer.' He pushed his hair into place. 'A cameraman.'

'You make films?'

'Yes.'

She took off her hat and shook her hair. It was straight and cut short. She ruffled the ends and jammed the hat back in place. This was a woman who didn't care about her appearance, Kelly guessed, but then a woman concerned about her looks wouldn't camp for ten days along the Bulloo. And on her own.

'You'd understand then,' she said and turned. 'I'll go and get my gear. And try not to make too much noise. Oh, would you like to join me for breakfast?'

'When?'

'After I take my pictures.'

'How did you get so dirty?' They were eating bacon, baked beans and toast. The beans were hers, the bacon and bread his. She pointed her knife at his face. 'You look as though you've driven through a dust storm.'

'I have. My own private one. The back window got broken during the night. Every dust heap did its best to choke me.'

'What broke the window? A stone?'

He nodded.

She matched him, nod for nod. 'The roads are terrible up here. I've punctured two tyres in three days.'

'That's tough,' he said, studying her as she stretched for the coffee pot. Bet she could fix a puncture, he thought, not just change a wheel. Independent. Capable. Bossy. She'd be a nightmare to live with; the sort of woman who wanted to do everything herself, whether she knew how to do it or not. Make him feel like a real dodo. He examined her more intently. Not good-looking in the way Laura was, but not bad. Nose a little too large, chin a little too firm. Good eyes; light blue and very bright, as though a light was shining inside. She seemed full of energy, the sort of woman who'd be impossible to keep up with. No wonder she worked on her own.

She poured the coffee. 'Any damage to your gear?' When he looked puzzled she added, 'From the dust. You said you were a cinematographer. I presume you're laden with expensive movie cameras and lenses and filters and lights and all the other things you people carry around with you.' She waited, managing to sip from her enamel mug and show interest at the same time.

He took longer to sample his coffee. She was no danger to him; just an eccentric young woman camping on her own. And she'd been on the Bulloo for ten days which meant that, almost certainly, she hadn't seen a newspaper about the Kolvenbach killing. Even so, he shouldn't have told her he made films.

'Not on this trip.'

'Not filming?'

'No.' She was eager for more and he said, 'Just looking. Planning a film. You know, selecting locations, things like that.'

She blew across her coffee. 'You must be very good or very rich. Or both.' She smiled. She had a large mouth and her face changed when she smiled. Very warm. Better-looking, too. It was the eyes. They glowed more brightly. This is a person people could trust, he told himself and then stopped; he was analysing her as though she were auditioning for a role in one of his documentaries. 'Hello, ladies. I want to talk to you about floor tiles . . .'

'Why are you smiling like that? Did I say something funny?'

He shook his head. 'I was amused by your question. Why did you say that?'

'Because only a very highly regarded film-maker or a fabulously rich person could afford the time to come out to a remote place like this just to have a look around. Most people would have to work. Use the time to earn a living.'

He shrugged, hoping to appear modest. 'I've made a lot of films. I can afford to be a bit selective.'

She held the mug in both hands and crossed her knees, like a child settling down for a long story. 'What sort of films do you make?'

Christ, he was getting in too deep.

Then she came to his rescue. 'I'm sorry, I should have asked you your name. I might have heard of you.' She moved her chin closer to the mug. 'You're not Bruce Beresford?'

'Not today.'

'Peter Weir?'

Sadly, he shook his head. She's playing with me, he thought. Not mocking, just having fun. And showing off a bit, too. It was nice, though.

'I know,' she said, compressing her lips in certainty.

'You're that cameraman who won an Academy Award for *Dances With Wolves*.'

'No.'

'Fred what's his name?' A smile was playing at one edge of her lips. 'You know, the director who did *Picnic at Hanging Rock* and then — what was it?... the one with that lovely Sean Connery... *The Russia House*.'

'You mean Fred Schepisi. No. I'm not him and he didn't do *Picnic at Hanging Rock*.'

'Oh.' She made the face of a schoolgirl who'd failed an exam question.

'Look, obviously you're very knowledgeable about films and that means you could think of a hundred names. And that means we'll be here all day because you'll never guess *my* name.' He sipped coffee to prepare for the lie. 'It's Kelly. David Kelly.'

Her mouth stretched into a variety of shapes as she sought the correct expression. 'Would you be terribly offended if I said I don't think I've ever heard of you?'

'Yes.'

'Oh.' She put down the coffee. 'What should I do then?'

'Tell me your name. I might have heard of you.'

She laughed. 'No one's heard of me, except a few publishers.' She hesitated, eyelids fluttering as she mentally checked a small list. 'And a few gallery owners.'

'So you've had books published and you exhibit in galleries?'

'Two books. Three exhibitions.'

'All about birds?'

'Yes. Oh, I draw animals too and I do an occasional landscape just for fun, but I'm best at birds.'

'I still don't know your name.'

She looked back towards the tree where she had photographed the nesting parrots.

145

'You're not going to tell me?'

She drank some coffee. 'I'm a very private person. Don't you think giving someone your name is a bit like drawing a veil away from your inner self?'

He scratched his chin. 'I've never thought of it like that. Perhaps I shouldn't have rushed out and given you my name. Now I feel naked.'

She laughed. Laughing was something she did easily and it drew him to her, as though the laugh generated some sort of magnetism. 'It doesn't matter much,' she said, 'because I can't remember what you said. I am the world's worst when it comes to introductions. In one ear, out the other, as they say. Was it David?'

'Correct.' He reached for the coffee pot and topped up both mugs. 'Let's just keep it on first name terms. In that way, you don't have to lift the veil completely.'

She smiled. 'Monica.'

'Nice name.'

The smile vanished. 'You didn't have to say that.'

'I know, but it is a nice name.'

'I thought you sounded a little ingratiating.'

'I was merely being truthful.'

She frowned. Different face. Interesting but with hard, deep lines. 'I don't like people who try to flatter you or who say obvious things, do you?'

He lifted his coffee. 'I don't mind the occasional bit of flattery. The trouble is, people rarely say nice things about me.' He sipped thoughtfully. 'It could become boring, I suppose. Too much of anything can.'

She stood up suddenly and bounced from one foot to the other, anxious to get moving.

'I have a flat tyre to fix.'

'Why don't I help you?'

She rubbed her hands together. 'Aren't you in a hurry to go somewhere?'

146

'No.'

'You don't have a tight schedule?'

'No.'

'Oh.' Hands on hips, she looked around at the gnarled gums lining the river bank. 'But you do have a destination?'

'Not really.'

She seemed to be searching for birds. 'Well, where are you going? I mean, eventually.'

He got to his feet slowly; his knee still hurt and it was stiffening. 'Wherever there's a quiet river, some big trees, and not many people. In fact, no people. I'm searching for a beautiful, typically Australian but absolutely uninhabited, isolated location.'

'How wonderful.'

'I think so.'

'Do a few birds matter?'

'No. Birds are good. Very welcome.'

She spread her hands. 'This is not bad. The trees have some wonderful shapes. Sunset last night was magnificent. And the parrots are superb.'

'Are you suggesting I should stay?'

'It's up to you. The water's good and deep enough to swim in. You could do with a wash.' She clapped her hands. 'But after we fix this tyre, eh?'

She was off and he followed.

15

Gerry Montague didn't get to sleep until an hour before dawn, and he woke up late. McCarthy was due at noon. He checked the clock — still time for a shower, some coffee and a quick think. He opened the bedside drawer and took out the notes he'd made before going to bed. The game was now divided into four parts and he'd drawn four columns on the page.

The first was headed *Laura and Me*. In it, he'd written: *(a) Diamonds. To be divided 50–50. (b) Ditto cash of $US76,000 and $A40,000. (c) Make contact re disposal of diamonds. Follow Laura's original plan in this regard.*

The second column was headed *Me*. He'd written *(a) Sum of extra cash was originally $US200,000. (b) Now $US150,000. (c) $50,000 for George who's unaware of second bag. (d) No one knows how much was in Kolvenbach's safe. Except me.*

The third was titled. *McCarthy. (a) Greedy. Thinks he's screwed me for half the money. (b) But good enough to track down Rob so that I can (i) find out who the devil Rob is and (ii) possibly make some money. (c) Will grow more curious. Must work out story to keep him happy.*

He'd underlined the last two sentences.

The fourth column was headed *Rob*. In it, he'd written: *(a) Who is he? (b) Why is K so desperate to recover papers? (c) K or Rob might pay to get papers back. (d) Work out way to return papers to K and get paid for it, but not give back diamonds or cash.*

He read his notes several times, underlined some words, and then lay back on the pillow, tapping his teeth with a pencil, his eyes fixed on the ceiling. He thought of Kelly and Kolvenbach. If the South African was as good as he thought he was, he should track Kelly down within a day or so. And that would be sensational. He could see the newspaper headline: *Diamond Killer Slain by Mystery Man.* Kelly would be disposed of, and the police would assume that the mystery man had taken the diamonds. Kolvenbach, of course, wouldn't find the diamonds but he could be persuaded that Kelly had hidden them somewhere in the outback. He wouldn't waste much time searching for them. As Kelly's killer, he'd be anxious to get out of the country as quickly as possible. Wonderful. It would be the perfect scenario.

Laura should be back today. Good. There were too many complications for him to handle. She was the one who understood how to dispose of the diamonds. Let her do that, so that he could concentrate on other things.

He'd have to keep her away from George, who knew nothing of her involvement. Nor should she learn about Kolvenbach's papers and the mysterious Rob. First, she'd become angry because he hadn't mentioned the papers on the phone and she was the sort of person who wanted to know everything. Then she'd either want her share of whatever money he could extort from Kolvenbach or Rob or, more likely, she'd order him to destroy the papers and forget about them. No way. There was money to be made from those papers and he had no intention of sharing it with anyone.

Still thinking, he went to the shower.

The woman puzzled Kolvenbach. She didn't behave as he'd expected. She'd gone quietly when they'd driven from the hotel and waited while he'd written the note to the publican explaining why he had to leave so early (and attaching two fifty-dollar notes to cover the cost of his accommodation and the inconvenience of leaving the Holden at the airport). Several times she could have tried to run away. He was ready for that but she made no attempt. She'd answered his questions on the flight up to the Cooper and now she was standing placidly in the shade cast by the tail while the man at Innamincka airstrip finished refuelling the plane.

Kolvenbach paid the man and walked to the motel. She followed him there, standing discreetly in the background, content to be observed but not heard.

The man at the motel assured them that any visitor to the Cooper would stop at Innamincka to buy fuel. There was no alternative. And no, no traveller answering Hunnicutt's description and driving a white Landcruiser had called in that morning. His friend was due that day, Kolvenbach said with an anxious frown, and returned to the aircraft.

'So he hasn't been here,' he said.

'It's a long way. Give him time.' The wind was ruffling her hair and she tried to hold it in place.

'This man of yours definitely said he was coming here. You're certain about that?'

'I told you he said he was going to the Cooper. That's all. He didn't mention any town.'

'There aren't any other towns. Just this.'

'Well, there we are. He'll have to come here.'

Kolvenbach scanned the horizon. The country reminded him of Africa, especially the parts he knew so well in Botswana and around the Kalahari.

The river was near. Even though it was called

150

Cooper's Creek it was a river and a long one by the standards of the outback. He knew that from studying his charts. Here at Innamincka, the Cooper was lined with big eucalypts, trees of great character, delicately mottled but grotesquely shaped. A few hundred years of droughts and floods had left their trunks gnarled and contorted and their limbs as knobble-jointed as roughly welded lumps of iron. But they were here to stay, to take all that fate and a cantankerous nature could hand out. He admired those qualities in men; why not in trees?

He shielded his eyes from the sun. This country was as paradoxical as southern Africa. While the landscape was dry, near-desert, it was marked by the faded brushstrokes of great floods. Even the ruins of the mission hospital and the old pub had been swept into reefs of washed and worn stones. A vast pile of sand-blasted and sun-darkened bottles, left over from the camel days when it was worth carting liquor from the south but not worth taking the empties back, had been scattered into acres of glassy rubbish. And along the river banks, skeins of weeds and grass, the high watermarks of past inundations, were knotted around the limbs of most trees.

Far from the river, sandhills shimmered in the heat haze.

Nasty country, he thought, but good for flying over. He moved closer to the woman. 'We should spot him from the air easily enough.' The wind had left a fine coating of grit on his skin and he wiped his face.

She turned. 'So what are we going to do?'

'Do a little flying. See what we can see. First, we'll head south again and follow that other road we saw on the way up.'

'And if he doesn't turn up?' There was genuine concern in her voice. Kolvenbach wondered

151

whether it was for her man, because she wanted him to get away, or whether it was for herself because she was frightened. He didn't believe her story about being kidnapped, but he was a suspicious man by nature; so suspicious, he had learned to mistrust his own intuitive feelings. He would wait.

'Get in the plane,' he ordered, and she got in.

'I believe my brother had a lot of cash in the safe.' Kolvenbach had to shout to be heard above the roar of the motors. He didn't look at her; he was examining the country to his left while following the thin strip of white that was the track to Orientos cattle station.

'I wouldn't know.'

'He didn't say anything?'

'No.' She thought for a while. What was it Gerry had told her? Seventy-something thousand in US dollars and about half that again in local currency. 'Well, he didn't say how much.'

He turned sharply. 'But there was money?'

'I think so. The newspapers said so.'

'I wasn't asking you what the newspapers said. I was asking what Hunnicutt said.'

'I don't remember.'

He banked to the right, so steeply that she grabbed the wheel in front of her. 'In the Ethiopian war,' Kolvenbach said, gradually straightening the aircraft, 'the Italians used to take captured chieftains up in planes and throw them out, on top of their tribe. It was a very effective way of demoralising the opposition.'

'And you're going to do that to me?' She glared defiantly. She was still holding on. 'What a shame I don't have a tribe.'

He smiled pleasantly. 'Well, you're not much use to me, you know.'

She turned her head away.

'All you've told me is that Hunnicutt, your alleged husband, is coming to the Cooper.'

'Don't call him alleged.'

He ignored her. 'I find out that it's a very long river and I also find out that you have no idea what part of the Cooper he's going to. Not very helpful.' He banked once more, laughed, then just as suddenly levelled the plane. 'It'd be so easy. I have a button I can press and your door would fly open.'

She folded her arms tightly. 'You've been seeing too many James Bond movies. That's a lot of crap and you know it.'

There was a hint of admiration in his grin. 'Tough lady. All right, there's no button. But I could still toss you out. Might get a few scratches on my face but you'd go.' He checked his map, then searched the road once more for a dust trail. There was none. 'Tell me, how big is the bag that your husband stole from my brother's safe?'

She let her head tilt backwards. 'I've told you. I haven't seen it.'

'Would it fit in the winch? That's where Hunnicutt told me it was.'

'How would I know?'

'Did you read the papers?'

'The newspapers?'

'No.' He leaned forward, looking past her towards the western horizon as he spoke. The country was the same: flat, scarred and splotched. The scars were dry creek beds and the splotches small salt lakes. Like Namibia. His eyes settled on her. 'I was referring to the papers that were in my brother's safe.'

'I didn't know there were any papers.' That was true. Gerry hadn't mentioned any papers. 'What sort of papers?'

'Business papers. Very important ones.'

She shook her head. 'Kelly didn't show me anything.'

He rolled on one hip to gain access to a trouser pocket. He removed a handkerchief and wiped his face. 'Yet you're certain he has everything with him in the car.'

'Look, I'm not certain of anything. I said I thought Kelly had the diamonds with him. That's what you asked me. That's what I told you.'

He wobbled the wings. 'Then you're not of much use to me, are you?'

He flew on, continually searching the horizon. Laura sat in silence, thinking that Kolvenbach might never find Kelly, not in this wilderness of dunes and salt lakes and gravelly plains. Not if Kelly was as good in the bush as he said he was. Therefore this hunt might end only if Kelly came looking for Kolvenbach. To rescue her. Kelly would try something as foolhardy as that.

She would be the bait, the irresistible attraction that would draw the quarry to the hunter. And once the two men met, Kolvenbach, with the armoury of weapons he carried in the plane, would quickly dispose of the troublesome Kelso Hunnicutt.

Kelly was examining some of Monica's sketches. They were good. Simple drawings with firm, sure lines. Some were done in pencil or charcoal, but mostly she used a fine nylon-tipped pen. The pages of her sketchbook were a mixture of drawings and notes. One page would have a parrot's head surrounded by notes about the beak or the plumage or where that bird had been seen, and another would be of a hawk on a branch with details of the way it gripped the branch and used its wings for balance. Two pages were devoted to a brolga's dance, done in a step-by-step sequence. There were

154

semitechnical drawings of birds in flight with encircled close-ups of the wing structure, and there were evocative drawings of a flock of cockatoos grazing in a field studded with anthills. Always copious notes. Memory joggers, she called them.

She had been driving through Queensland and the Northern Territory for three months. Her last camp had been up on the Gulf. She showed him some finished drawings of black cockatoos. He read the signature: M. Tate.

'You're very good.'

'Thank you.' She put the drawings back in a dust-proof bag and tightened the strap.

'And what's the next step?'

'I might go out to the Cooper. To Nappa Merrie.' She looked to see if the name meant anything. 'You know, where the Burke and Wills Dig Tree is. Around there.'

He nodded, lips tightly pursed, not to indicate he knew the place — it was just to the east of Innamincka — but to stop himself saying he was heading that way too. 'And then?'

'Home, I suppose. Back to the studio. Back to work.'

'Where's the studio?' He'd seen the Victorian plates on her Ford. 'Melbourne?'

'Just out of Melbourne.'

Up in the Dandenongs, he guessed, or maybe out Warburton way. She'd be a person who lived among trees. 'And what do you do back in the studio? Paint what you've seen?'

'Yes.' She put the bag in the back of her truck and slammed the tailgate. 'I want twenty paintings out of this trip. Plus a few drawings.'

'Like the ones of those black cockatoos?'

'Did you like them?'

He was about to say they were wonderful, but stopped himself, remembering she didn't trust flatterers. 'They were good.'

155

She looked doubtful but nodded agreement. She wiped her hands on her hips. 'I have to go somewhere for a few hours. Anything I can get you?'

He was surprised. 'You sound as though you're off to the corner store.'

'Not quite. There's a homestead up the river. They've promised me some meat. I have to collect it. Would you like some? I'm sure they'd give me extra.'

He shook his head. Their camping site seemed so remote he hadn't thought of people living nearby. 'This homestead, how far is it?'

'About twenty kilometres.' She ruffled her hair. 'Want to come? They're nice people.'

Eyes tight against the glare, he peered into the haze that blurred the horizon. Only the vapours moved, shuffling vague shapes in layers of gaseous grey. 'No, I don't think I will. I might just have a look at some of the scenery further down the river.'

'The water dries up downstream.'

'Ah.' He gazed up at the branches of a particularly large eucalypt, wanting to avoid her eyes. 'I might still have a bit of a look around. You know, for a location. A dry riverbed might be just what I'm looking for.'

'Suit yourself. Thanks for helping with the tyre. I'll be back in about three hours.'

He watched her leave. The homestead would have radio and possibly a TV dish. Almost certainly, they would have heard about the policeman being attacked at Tibooburra. Immediately her truck was out of sight, Kelly began repacking the Landcruiser.

16

Monica Tate led the two men in the battered old Land Rover to the camp. She was still in shock. They said David, or whatever his name was, was a murderer. Her intuition told her that was not possible, but the men had said there was no doubt. Fearfully, she followed the tracks to the place where they had camped. He was gone. A surge of relief made her giddy and she sat in the truck for a few moments, clasping her head.

The grazier and his tall son got out and looked around. The father was a pleasant old man but the son, a man in his mid-twenties, worried her. He had a lean face that was overwhelmed by a moustache of walrus proportions. He reminded her of illustrations she'd seen of gunfighters from the Wild West. He behaved like one too. He was strutting across the sand, his arms cradling a rifle that looked as though it would stop a scrub bull. His face twitched in disappointment. 'He's gone.'

The old grazier nodded agreement. He puffed out his chest, more sure than ever that he could have brought the man to justice but relieved that he would not be tested.

'You think it was him, Dad?'

'Certain. He's gone, run off.'

'Might of seen us coming.' The son squinted into the distance, searching for dust.

Nervously rubbing her hands on her jeans, Monica joined them. 'He did say he was going down the river to have a look around. Just for an hour or two.'

'No.' The old man walked to the spot where Monica indicated the Landcruiser had been parked. He squatted and touched the sand, as though to confirm that the four-wheel drive had gone. 'He's taken everything and shot through. You said it was a white Toyota?'

She nodded.

'Everything fits. The vehicle, the description of the bloke. Even what he does for a living. They fit exactly. It must have been this Hunnicutt.'

'He seemed nice.' It seemed inadequate but she was confused.

He grunted. 'You were lucky.'

The son, who had been scouting the river bank, returned and said, 'The radio reckoned there were two of them. The copper at Tibooburra stopped one — this Hunnicutt — and the second bloke came up behind the copper and flattened him.'

'There was definitely only one man here,' Monica said and conscious that Hunnicutt was supposed to have shot someone, shook her head vigorously. 'And he didn't have a gun.'

The father looked doubtful. 'How do you know?'

'Because I looked. Before I woke him up, I looked in his Landcruiser to see what he was carrying.'

'He could have had it hidden.'

The son was restless. He had never shot a man. 'Shouldn't we try and pick up his tracks and follow him?'

The old man patted the air, urging patience. 'We'll go down the river a bit, just in case he went that way. We'll look for tracks but only to get a direction. Then we'll head home and radio the police. Let them catch him. It's their job.' He turned to Monica. 'You're not staying here?'

She wiped her hands across her thighs. 'I guess not.'

'No guessing, miss. You've got to get out of here, just in case this Hunnicutt comes back.' He turned to walk to the old Land Rover, then stopped. 'Do you know what we forgot?'

She shook her head.

'Your meat.' He laughed and so did she.

'It doesn't matter.'

'Too right it does. A man needs his meat and so does a woman. You go straight back to the homestead and ask the missus for it. It's all ready for you in the freezer.'

'Thanks.' She smiled acceptance but had no intention of returning to the house. She was confused and frightened — the man almost certainly was the murderer the police were searching for and yet her mind swirled with guilt because she had started a hunt which could end in Hunnicutt being shot. All she wanted to do was get away from the Bulloo.

The son, anxious to resume the chase, was already in the Land Rover. The father touched the brim of his hat in farewell. 'Go straight back to the house now, and we'll see you up there.'

He got in and drove off. The barrel of the son's rifle projected through the open window.

'Poor David or Kelso or whatever your name is,' Monica said, and began gathering her things.

George McCarthy settled himself into the corner of Montague's sofa and spent some time staring up at the ceiling.

McCarthy's silences made Montague nervous. He walked to the hi-fi, turned down the volume and then flopped in a chair. He coughed to make sure the fat man was listening. 'What have you done with that character you caught last night?'

159

'Still got him.' The eyes came down from the ceiling. 'Why? Do you want him back?'

'No.' Montague made himself laugh. 'How long are you going to keep him?'

'Until we find out what this is all about.'

Montague played with a fingernail. 'Isn't that dangerous? I mean illegal. Keeping someone like that...'

McCarthy leaned forward to grasp Montague's knee. 'Gerry, old mate, what that man was doing was not exactly legal. The people he works for did not engage him for lawful employment, if you get my meaning.'

'I do, George, I do.'

'So, if you don't mind, I'll have my men just hang on to him until he either talks or we get to the bottom of this business. I don't think it would be wise to hand him over to the police or turn him loose.'

Montague shifted nervously. 'What if someone comes looking for him?'

'Here?'

'Yes.'

'That's a possibility.' He smiled as if relishing the thought. 'If people come searching for their missing friend, we'll nab them too.'

'You've got someone outside?'

'Of course. More than one. A veritable army guards you now, my friend.'

Montague squeezed his fingers. 'Isn't all this getting expensive?'

McCarthy gazed up at the ceiling once more. 'Very expensive. But there's a lot of money involved, isn't there, Gerry?' When Montague didn't answer, he took a deep, noisy breath and said, 'I've had a busy morning investigating this mysterious character, Rob'.

'And?'

160

'Well, I worked on a simple premise: that Rob was an important man.' Another pause. A wheezing cough to clear the throat and set the stage. 'If, as you say, this Rob lives in Canberra and if he wants a hundred grand from you and if, as we might reasonably suspect, he's involved with the business that happened here last night, then he's a man who thinks in large sums when he thinks of money, and he's a man who has considerable influence. What he's done so far takes connections, believe me.' McCarthy shuffled into a new position. 'Now, who are the people in Canberra with the most devious minds, the most money and the most influence?' He smiled cheekily.

Montague let his hands wander to the ends of the armrests. 'You mean he's a politician?'

McCarthy made the sign of a dart striking the target. 'Or a bureaucrat. Either way a very senior person.' Unable to remain still, he swung one leg over the other. 'Mind you, all this is hypothesis. Just possibilities. Anyhow, this morning I ran through the list of departmental heads and government ministers. I thought, why not start at the top? Well, I discovered there are two Robs. One Robert and one Robin. The Robert is a bureaucrat. He runs the Department of Foreign Affairs. The Robin is the minister in charge of Aboriginal affairs.'

Montague went to the drinks cabinet.

'A beer for me,' McCarthy called after him. 'Now, what I need to know is whether you've been having a foreign affair or an Aboriginal affair.'

Montague turned. McCarthy appeared to be laughing but made no noise.

'Merely a hypothesis, Gerry. I'm playing a game of supposings. To start with, I'm supposing you're telling me the truth. I've thought a lot about that and, frankly, the strongest likelihood is that you've been bullshitting me. On a one-to-ten scale of possibilities, I'd make that an eight.' He was still smiling. 'I can't see the head of the Department of Foreign Affairs or the Minister of Aboriginal Affairs having cause to blackmail someone like you.'

Montague returned with the drinks. 'You don't know, George, so just keep digging. That's your job. Find out what you can. You're making a lot of money out of this.'

McCarthy sighed. 'But I'm an ambitious fellow, Gerry. Never made much money in the police force. Not an honest cop, of course, but I was never one of the lucky ones who stumbled upon a pot of gold, if you get my meaning.' He paused to open the bottle. 'Therefore, when some real money appears on the horizon, I'm interested. All my old dreams, lusts and evil desires are rekindled. In other words...' he sampled the beer, '...there's no such thing as enough. I want to make as much as I can.'

Montague blanched. 'You're getting fifty thousand.'

'Compared to what I think you're making, that's chicken feed.'

'Jesus, George, it's half of what I have.'

With thespian gravity, McCarthy turned his head to avoid the embarrassment of catching his friend in a lie. 'Come, come, Gerry. I think I might reasonably expect to get more.'

'Where the hell from?'

McCarthy lifted his glass in a toast. 'From you. From Rob. From someone.' He leaned closer. 'What I'm suggesting is that you level with me. Cut out all the crap. If you're mixed up in some deal and there's money in it, I want a share of it. A big share.' He raised his free hand to silence Montague's protest. 'Look, Gerry, if you were prepared to cut me in for fifty grand without a quibble — which you did last night — there's got to be a lot more around. Follow me?'

Montague's eyes glazed.

'Hey, Gerry, mate, I don't care if it's shady. I've been dealing with dirt all my working life. I'm at the stage in my life where I want money. Lots of it. Enough to retire and lead a comfortable life. Understand?' He sipped from his glass but his eyes never left Montague. 'And believe me, I'm a valuable partner. Indispensable. I can find out things you can't. More important, I can protect you from whoever it is out there who wants to do you a gross mischief. In other words, you need me. You need me so much you can't say no.' He spent much time straightening the seam on one trouser leg. 'Now, let's start from the beginning and let's have none of this blackmail crap. Who the hell is Rob?'

Kelly travelled slowly, choosing his route with care and stopping regularly to search the horizon for danger signals that suggested humans: the lazy turning of a windmill, the glint of sunlight on an iron roof, thick dust stirred by moving cattle, the thin trail left by another vehicle. He had decided on a roundabout way to the Cooper. No one must see him. Not in the early stages, not until his true course was set, when he would be required to pass through a town.

He had to assume Monica would hear the news at the homestead and tell the people there about the stranger camped on the river. There would be a search and whoever came looking would find a clear, deep set of tracks pointing in the wrong direction.

The Cooper was to the west, so initially, Kelly went the other way. He'd crossed the Bulloo just south of the water hole where he and Monica had camped, at a place where there was much soft mud and where his tyres left impressions like plaster casts. He headed east for several kilometres, spinning the

wheels occasionally to make sure he could be followed. Then he drove south on a road unmarked
by any fresh tracks other than his own. A few
kilometres further on, he swung to the east but
this time left no trail. With great care, he turned
off the road, stopped to sweep away his tyre marks
and then headed slowly across a rock-encrusted
plain.

The nearest policeman was at Thargomindah.
Kelly imagined what would happen. The policeman
would get a message from the homestead, rush
there and then drive down to the campsite. He
would find the place deserted, scout around for
tracks, find the place where the Landcruiser had
crossed and, hopefully, follow the carefully laid false
trail. Because the policeman would be out of town,
Kelly would loop north, then west, to travel through
Thargomindah.

Going into the town was risky but there were
reasons. It would put him on a road that would
take him to the Cooper and it would get him to
a telephone. He had to ring Laura. There were no
phones on the Cooper — except at Innamincka
and down at the Moomba gas fields, and he dared
not visit either of those places.

He turned on the radio and to his relief picked
up Charleville. When the news came on, the story
about the search for Kelso Hunnicutt was the main
item. Only now the search was for two men.

Ten kilometres from the Cunnamulla–Thargomindah road, a big truck blocked the track. At first
it seemed abandoned and Kelly drove up, intending
to detour around it. But as he approached, a young
man with the bowed legs of a stockman climbed
from the cabin and waved him down. Kelly stopped.

They exchanged soft 'g'days'.

'Not going to Yakara, are you?'

164

Kelly shook his head.

'The bastard done its diff.'

Kelly nodded in sympathy.

The young man removed his hat and scratched his scalp, leaving his hair as dishevelled as trampled weeds. 'Wouldn't be heading for town, would you?'

'Thargomindah? No. Sorry.'

'Going as far as the main road?'

He had to say yes. There was nowhere else.

The young man adjusted his trouser belt. 'Couldn't drop me off there, could you? Then I could get a lift into town.'

He was harmless. 'Why not?'

The young man attempted to slam the truck door but it bounced open again. He left it like that and climbed in beside Kelly. 'Going to Cunnamulla, are you?'

'Going through Cunnamulla. Then up to Charleville.'

'Ah.' The young man's eyebrows rose as though Charleville was at the limit of settled territory. He let the Toyota bounce through three deep ruts before speaking again. 'Where you from?'

He might have noticed the Victorian number-plates so Kelly said, 'Mildura'.

The young man smiled. 'I was born in Balranald.' Almost made them neighbours, his expression implied. He braced himself while the vehicle dropped into, then reared out of, a deep hole. 'Been up here twenty years.' He settled back in the seat and tilted his hat so that it covered his forehead. 'I been stuck on this track since eight this morning. Lucky, I suppose. Thought no other bastard ever used it.' Kelly said nothing and the young man closed his eyes.

He opened them again when the helicopter flew overhead.

Kelly hadn't seen it approaching. It flew in low from behind the Landcruiser, travelling at little more than their pace and instantly encircling them in a cyclone of grit. The dust was blinding, the whoofling noise deafening. Then the helicopter was beyond them and turning side on. Hovering like some gigantic, menacing insect, it sank closer to the ground, forming an aerial barrier. Kelly saw two men staring down at him. They wore baseball caps and uniforms.

The young man grabbed his hat and put it on. 'Where'd that bastard come from?' He looked at Kelly, seeking a clue as to whether he should laugh or be alarmed.

'Don't know,' Kelly said and accelerated. He closed his eyes, fearing a collision, but the helicopter lifted at the last moment. He drove through the storm of dust and noise.

'Jesus, what are they doing?' Hand holding his hat in place, Kelly's passenger thrust his head out the window. 'They're coming after us again.'

Kelly swerved off the track but immediately realised the futility of that manoeuvre. The helicopter could follow wherever he went. He swung back into the wheel ruts. He could no longer see the aircraft. It was somewhere above him.

'You down there.' The voice was magnified and distorted. 'Stop immediately.'

'Are they the cops or something?' The young man was twisting the brim of his hat in distress.

Kelly recalled the radio bulletin. Police were searching for two men. Two. He glanced at his passenger and saw a decoy.

'They're crazy men,' he said, slowing the vehicle. 'But they're after me, not you. When I stop, you get out and run for your life.'

'Where?'

'Anywhere. Back down the track. Across there.' He pointed to a distant tree.

Again the mechanical voice. 'Stop immediately or we'll open fire.'

He grabbed the young man's arm. 'If they get you, tell them I'm carrying a machine gun and tell them the back of this wagon's full of dynamite. If they come near me, I'll blow it up.'

'What!'

'Tell them I'll blow it up and them with me. Now run.'

The young man scrambled from the cabin and began to run across the plain. He stopped briefly, looked back at Kelly, looked up at the hovering helicopter, and changed direction. Hat in hand, he galloped for the tree. Kelly drove off. He felt the vehicle rock. One of the helicopter's runners had bumped the roof.

'Stop at once.'

He drove faster, sending the Toyota into a series of buckjumping plunges as it crashed through a row of ruts and rocky ridges. The storm of dust abated. The helicopter had swung away to pursue the young man.

Kelly slowed and rubbed the sore spot where his head had hit the roof. Off to one side, the young man was still running, legs bowed and stumbling frequently on the rough ground. He covered his head as the helicopter raced past him and banked in a steep turn. The young man stopped and, as Kelly watched, flung down his hat and put up his hands. In a whirlwind of dust, the aircraft landed.

Kelly's mind raced, trying to match the energy boiling within his body. A police helicopter. He hadn't thought they'd use a chopper. Where had it flown from? Brisbane, Charleville? No matter; wherever it had come from, its appearance meant a search was in progress. A big search, probably what the papers would call a mammoth search. They loved words like mammoth.

He bent to look in a side mirror. The helicopter was on the ground, its rotor lazily flogging the air. The two policemen spilled from it and ran, bent in the crouch of helicopter people. Kelly thought that by now every police car within five hundred kilometres would be racing to the Bulloo, and squads of extra police would be flying out from Brisbane. There'd be roadblocks, cordons around towns and scores of policemen, all armed to the teeth, all looking for him. He laughed. Jesus, and he'd wanted his picture in the papers!

He let out a wild yell and swung a fist in the air. Let them try and catch him. He'd get away. He'd outwit them.

For a few moments, he was boosted by a strange elation, but then a rush of escaping energy burst from him like air from a balloon and he sagged with exhaustion. A helicopter. He hadn't expected that. How could he get away from a helicopter?

He glanced back. It was hard to see through the swirl of dust but the chopper was still grounded. The young man appeared to be on his knees with the policemen on either side of him.

His eyes swept across the land around him, desperately seeking somewhere to hide before the helicopter became airborne again. The long shadows of late afternoon were striping the ground but there was nowhere to hide. No dense clump of bushes he could drive into, no spread of trees to offer shelter within their gloomy fold. He was caught in open country. There was only patchy scrub, little taller than the Landcruiser. Hopeless.

He forced himself to slow down and to think. What could the men in the helicopter do? What were the points in their favour? They could fly over any terrain. Hover. Go as fast or as slow as he could. Okay, what couldn't they do? Fly without fuel. See him in the dark. He glanced to the west. Sunset was about half an hour away, so they could track him for no longer than that. Say thirty or forty kilometres maximum over this sort of terrain. How much fuel did they have? Helicopters didn't have a long range. No matter where it had come from, this one's destination was almost certainly Thargomindah; that was where the pilot would have planned to refuel, before joining in the scheduled search. That meant the aircraft was likely to be low on fuel. It couldn't follow him for long.

Then he thought about his story of the machine gun and the dynamite. He tittered; not a sensible sound but a sliver of noise slipping through the cracks of a desperate mind. He thought about it some more and laughed aloud. The story was crazy but brilliant. He hadn't planned it; he'd just said it, and it was perfect. They'd have to take the threat seriously, which meant they wouldn't shoot at him or land and try to stop him. They'd follow him but keep their distance.

All right, what should he do? He concentrated on driving over a bad stretch of rock and then came back to the problem. The answer was simple — slow down. The slower he went, the better for him, the worse for the police. The helicopter would have to hover to stay with him and thus use more fuel. And the fewer kilometres he covered in daylight, the less likely he was to give away the course he now intended to follow.

When he got to the main road, he would turn right, away from the Cooper. The police in the chopper would still be able to see him. Good. They would radio that he was heading east and summon assistance, probably from Cunnamulla. The police there would either race out to meet him or form a roadblock, probably the latter if they thought he was laden with explosives. Only he wouldn't arrive at any roadblock. Once the sun set, he'd be turning north towards a small opal field he knew.

Kelly had a new plan and it meant getting rid of the Toyota.

17

By the time Kelly reached the road, the helicopter was on his tail, flying just above the corkscrewing trail of dust, and staying a constant two hundred metres behind him. Which meant, Kelly reasoned, that the pilot was taking seriously his story about dynamite and a machine gun. The young truck driver would be on board, handcuffed. Kelly grinned in sympathy. Poor bloke — the police would think he was the second man, the one who had attacked the policeman at Tibooburra. He'd spend a day in gaol and be bombarded by questions from a dozen detectives before people believed what he'd been telling them: that he was a local whose truck had broken down on the way to Yakara.

It was nearly dark.

Kelly spent the next ten minutes thinking of all the flaws in his plan. The helicopter's tanks might be awash with fuel. It could be fitted with a search-light that would enable it to track him through the night. There might be other helicopters. Even now, police cars from Cunnamulla might be racing towards him, their arrival only minutes away. He could find himself sandwiched between the chopper and a thundering squad of cars.

Suddenly, the helicopter speeded up and drew alongside him. He caught a glimpse of a capped man wearing sunglasses and nursing a rifle. Then, abruptly, the helicopter swung across the top of the Landcruiser and flew wide to the other flank. There it spun in a slow circle, all the time keeping pace with the vehicle. It was the pilot's way of displaying superiority; of saying he could have stopped the Landcruiser if he wanted to, and that the only reason he hadn't done so was because, unlike Kelly, he wasn't prepared to blow himself up. Kelly knew what it meant. The pilot was departing, short of fuel, reluctantly leaving the arrest to others.

Kelly waved.

The pilot glared at him and, with a showy display of rapid banking, swung to the west. Kelly glimpsed a figure in the back. The truck driver. The helicopter climbed and gradually disappeared in the darkening sky.

Kelly stopped, gripped his hands to stop them from shaking, then drank some water. He checked either end of the road for the first glow of approaching headlights. Nothing. He turned off the engine. The distinctive pumping beat of the helicopter had faded. There was no distant roar of powerful motors. Nothing but the chirping of insects. Calmer now, he checked his map. The track he was seeking was on his left and he should reach it within the next five kilometres. With lights off and cranking the diesel up to top speed, he drove east.

She was an extraordinarily attractive woman. Not just good-looking. The world was full of good-looking women. Kolvenbach had known a few, even loved a couple briefly. No, she was strong. He'd been watching her closely all day and this woman possessed amazing self-control, a great inner strength. What a partner she'd be; the sort of woman he could leave to run his safari business while he travelled overseas to attend to his other affairs. She could

171

cope with anything from finicky American clients to bad-tempered bull elephants.

He didn't know her name and he wouldn't ask. Instead, he said, 'How long have you been married to this Hunnicutt fellow?'

'Why?'

A bad start. He shrugged. 'You don't seem the sort of woman who'd marry a man like that.'

'A man like what?'

'A man who's done what he's done. Terrible things.' He undid the second button of his shirt and scratched his chest. 'In my country, he'd be hanged. No argument.' He sat on the double bed in the motel room and it squeaked under his weight. 'I could understand it if he'd just stolen the diamonds. But killing my brother... There was no need for that. Harald was a good man.'

'Harald. I didn't know your brother's name.'

'Harald,' he repeated. 'With two a's. Not the way you'd spell it.'

She was sitting in the corner, beside the single bed. She gazed down at her crossed ankles. 'What's your name?'

'Magnus.'

'What a strange name.' She didn't look up but she smiled. 'What did your mother call you when you were a kid?'

'Magnus. Always Magnus. She was very proper. My father called me Gus. My brother called me Gussie.' He seemed embarrassed to have passed on such intimate information.

She examined him with frank eyes. He was a softer man when tired. She'd remember that. 'Gussie is such a little boy's name. It wouldn't suit you now.'

He crossed one leg over the other, preparing to remove his boots. 'We all grow up.'

'And change.' Her face grew wistful.

'Ah.' His eyes brightened. 'So Hunnicutt changed,

that's what happened? He became a different man after you married?' There was no need for an answer. He was convinced. 'I presume you were very young when you got married?'

If you call nearly thirty young, she thought, but shrugged.

'We all do things when we're young and regret them later.' He bent to untie a shoelace. 'I almost got married when I was twenty-three. To an English girl, would you believe. Her parents lived out of Nairobi.'

'But you didn't marry her.'

He shook his head.

'Why not?'

'I had a sudden and violent attack of good sense.'

'What was she like?'

'Pretty. Fair. Stuffy. She would have wanted to live in England. She was that type, you know? Very keen on the theatre.' He said 'thee-ah-tah', mimicking the English.

Laura tapped her feet on the lino. 'I can't imagine you as a married man.'

He dropped a boot on the floor and kicked it under the bed. 'Why not?'

'You don't seem the marrying type.'

He shoved the second boot out of sight. 'And why not?'

'You just don't. Too much of a man's man. You'd be set in your ways and demanding. Impossibly demanding.'

'Very true, Mrs Hunnicutt.'

'Laura. If you're going to continue to hold me prisoner...' she gave him a sugary smile, 'then you should know who it is you're imprisoning.'

'Laura.' He nodded approval. 'You've reminded me,' he said, trying to sound gruff, 'should I tie you to your bed tonight?'

He had booked them in as husband and wife

173

and they had already been through the business of which bed was his and which was hers.

'What if I wanted to get up during the night?' She was teasing him.

'If you called out, I'd undo the rope.'

'A gentleman to the end.'

He made a vestigial bow. 'On the other hand, if you gave me your word, I would merely lock the door and let you sleep in peace.'

'You mean without a rope around me?' Again, the sweet smile.

'Of course.'

'I had expected to be tied by the ankles and wrists to the bedposts. Spread-eagled for the night.'

He stood up, ducking to avoid the central light. 'I am not a barbarian. I will hunt Hunnicutt and do what must be done when I catch him, but I'm after him because of what he did to my brother.'

'And what he took.' She angled her head, wondering if she had gone too far.

Kolvenbach took a deep breath. 'I intend getting back what belongs — belonged — to my brother, and to me. That is fair. That is my way.' He stood in front of her and she felt overwhelmed by his presence. 'But there is no reason for me to treat you badly. Remember, I took you only because I thought you were in league with your husband.'

Slowly, she raised her eyes. 'And now you don't? Are you saying that at last you believe what I've been telling you?'

'Maybe. I'm prepared to believe you. I didn't at first. I thought you were in it up to your neck.'

'But not now?'

'Maybe.'

'Thank God for small mercies.' She sighed. 'So when are you going to turn me loose?'

'I didn't say I was.' He glanced around the motel room. 'But there's not much point in my turning

174

you loose, as you call it, here in Innamincka. You couldn't go anywhere. So I think I'll just hang on to you until we find that husband of yours.'

'Hang on to me?'

'Look after you. Keep you with me.'

'And then?'

'It depends on what happens when we find Hunnicutt. On what he does. What he tells me. That could be interesting.' He saw a flash of alarm colour her face. That was fear. She was frightened of her husband. 'I will protect you, don't worry. And I guarantee I will not harm you as long as you behave. I give you my most solemn word on that.' He paused to make sure she understood. 'I just want you to continue acting as you have been: making no fuss, keeping quiet, staying in the background.'

'Playing the loyal, silent wife.'

'If that's what you call it.' He folded his arms, splaying his great biceps. 'Tell me, Laura, do you want to see Hunnicutt caught or do you want him to get away?'

She lowered her eyes, the picture of a woman torn between past loyalties and present desires.

'Because I will catch him and depending on what he does, I might shoot him. I have no sympathy for the man.'

'You'd shoot him?' she said as though surprised.

'Yes. It would depend on whether he is helpful or not. Whether he resists or whether he gives me the things I'm seeking. But I would have no hesitation in killing him. I wanted you to know, to be very clear on that.'

Their eyes met. She turned away quickly. 'I have no love for him, if that's what you're asking me.'

He unfolded his arms and locked his fingers, leaning forward earnestly. 'I was asking if you wanted him caught.'

She whispered, 'He's done terrible things'.

175

Outside, a car door slammed. Kolvenbach went to the window and parted the curtains. A black man was walking from a station wagon. 'Fair enough. All I ask of you is a promise that you'll cause me no trouble. I don't want you passing notes to someone saying, *Help, I've been kidnapped...*' He slipped into a falsetto: '...*by this dreadful man.*'

She moved to her bed and prodded the mattress. 'I wouldn't call you dreadful. I think you're amusing.'

'Amusing.' He rubbed the stubble on his chin. 'I've never been called that.'

'Interesting, then. You're quite a fascinating man to observe, Mr Kolvenbach.'

'Magnus.'

She grimaced. 'Such a mouthful. Not Gus or Gussie?'

He puffed out his chest. Just like a pigeon. 'I'm sorry I told you.'

'No, I'm pleased you did. Gus doesn't suit you and Gussie is ridiculous. Magnus is much more appropriate. I could always call you Big K but then you'd sound like a breakfast cereal.' She smiled impishly. 'Magnus. I like it.'

He walked to his bed and sat down. The springs squeaked. 'Are you treating this business as some kind of game? Are you enjoying all this?'

She arched an eyebrow, in the way that had entranced Kelly. 'No, Magnus. I'm just relaxed. You see, I'm relieved to learn that, *finally*, you may believe what I've been telling you.' She lay on her pillow. 'I'm tired. Do you mind if we stop talking?'

He turned off the room light and went to the bathroom. 'You won't do anything silly? You won't try to crawl through the window and force me to bring you back?'

'I'll be here in the morning, don't worry.' There was no need for her to do anything. If Kelly came during the night, the motel owner would tell him that two friends were looking for him: a tall man with a South African accent and a woman whom the man could describe in great detail. Laura was certain of that, because the man had spent so much time leering at her.

Montague decided to leave the apartment and call Laura. She should have been back in Melbourne but she hadn't rung him, which was strange but fortunate because there was still a possibility that his telephone line was tapped. By George. It was just the sort of thing George would do — assure him the phone was clear and then bug it himself.

Montague ordered a taxi and waited until he heard the horn at the front door. He hurried out. The driver was a small Vietnamese wearing a sailor's cap. One of the boat people, Montague thought, and asked to be driven to the city. Halfway there, he had the taxi stop at a phone booth.

Laura didn't answer. He tried both the Carlton number and Kelly's house.

When Montague came out of the box, the taxi was empty.

A man approached. 'Finished with the phone?'

'Sure.' Montague began searching the chequer-board of bright lights and dark shadows marking the footpath. Where the devil had the driver got to?

He was gripped from behind. Strong hands held his arms and forced them behind his back. He was pushed into an alley. The driver was there, sitting against a wall and holding his head. Another man stood over him.

Montague was thrust against a wall.

'Where's Carlos, eh?'

The jab in the back hurt and he grunted with pain.

'What have you done with him?' The hands grabbed Montague's shoulders and spun him around. The man's face was in shadow. 'Where is Carlos? We'd like him back.' Now a jab in the belly. Montague doubled forward. Fingers seized his hair and pulled him upright.

'Look at me. I want some answers.'

Montague shook his head.

Another punch. He bent forward and was immediately straightened. 'I said look at me.'

'I don't know.' It hurt to breathe.

'Who were you calling, eh?' A punch was threatened but the man held back. Instead he used a finger to flick Montague's nose. 'The person who's got Carlos?'

Montague shook his head vigorously.

'Want to go for a little ride in a car? There's someone who'd like to know the answers to a few questions.'

The other man spoke. 'What do I do with the driver?'

'Take that silly-looking cap off his head and hit him over the skull.' The second man obeyed instantly. 'Now go to the taxi and take his money. Make it look like a robbery. He won't know what's been going on.'

The second man went to the cab. He didn't come back.

The man with Montague thrust him towards the street. He was about to peer around the corner of the building when a short man of exceptional width charged, ramming him with his shoulder. Montague was thrown to the ground. The man fell, got up and ran off.

The short man pulled Montague to his feet and began dusting his clothes. 'Sorry about that. Are you all right, Mr Montague?'

'You're George's man?'

'Spiro. Are you okay?'

Montague nodded but held his stomach.

'Sorry I was a bit slow but there were two of them.' He looked around and saw an approaching van. 'Here come the others. Get in, quickly.'

Several hands helped Montague to board through the central door. Spiro went to the back of the cab where the second assailant was lying, face down and unconscious. He picked him up and tossed him into the van.

McCarthy seemed relaxed. He offered Montague a whisky and sat on the arm of his chair. 'You shouldn't have done that, Gerry. That was a very foolish thing to do.' He waited but Montague said nothing so he got up and walked to the other side of the room. 'Who were you so desperate to talk to that you had to leave the apartment and go to a phone booth in a seedy part of town?'

Montague touched his forehead. 'I was going out for food. I wanted some takeaway. Chinese.'

'You don't buy Chinese takeaway in a phone booth.'

'I decided to order it by phone.'

'Ah.' McCarthy made an excessive show of being satisfied. 'The taxi driver had an uncle who owned a restaurant, is that it? He gave you the phone number?'

'I looked it up in the phone book.'

'Spiro tells me you didn't look up any number. You dialled two numbers.'

Montague took a long sip of his drink. 'Spiro was wrong.' He put down the glass as a thought struck him. 'Do you mean he was watching me all the time and he didn't try to stop that thug from thumping me?'

'Yes.'

'What do you mean — yes?'

'Yes he was watching you all the time, and yes he could have stopped that thug from thumping you. But I told him that if you got into trouble, wait a while.'

'Jesus Christ, George, that man was punching me and pulling my hair.'

'Hurts, doesn't it?'

'What the hell are you on about, George? What game do you think you're playing?'

McCarthy moved to a corner and admired an original painting. With his back to Montague, he said, 'It's a game called let the man know he needs me. Let him know we're dealing with dangerous people. That he's got to do exactly what he's told. Let him know I don't believe any of this bullshit he's been feeding me. Let him know that if he doesn't level with me and cut me in on this deal as an equal partner — after he pays all the expenses — that I'm going to let him wander the streets of Melbourne without any protection. No Spiro, no van full of bodyguards. And then let him see how long he's going to survive. That's what the game's called, Gerry.'

'You're a bastard, George,' he whispered.

'Yes.'

Montague held his drink in both hands and spent several moments contemplating it. 'You'd take your men away?'

'Every last one of them. You won't be able to walk out of this place. You won't even be safe *in* this place. My guess is you'd be lucky to last a couple of days. These are very unpleasant people who've come calling on you in recent times, Gerry. You can't handle them. I can.'

'You bastard.'

'We've been through all that. Look, mate,' he said, lowering himself once more on to the arm of Montague's chair, 'you've got yourself involved in something very big and if you want to know what I think,

I think you don't realise just how big it is or how big and nasty these people are that you're trifling with. In other words, you're out of your depth. My guess is that you think there may be a million in it but you don't know how to go about getting it. Am I right?'

Sadly, Montague shook his head. 'I didn't expect this sort of thing from you, George.'

'And I thought an old mate would come clean with me. You haven't. You've been lying your head off from day one.'

'Why do you say that?' He seemed tired and immensely disappointed.

'For Christ's sake, Gerry, every time you talk to me I get the impression you're going for an Academy Award. Just cut out the crap, will you?' McCarthy took several deep, noisy breaths to purge himself of all exasperation. 'Okay, the question was why do I say that. There are two reasons. One, I know you. Two, I've been making a lot of enquiries these last few days and I've learned a lot of things.' He wriggled to make himself more comfortable. 'You got me involved and you tried to feed me some schoolboy tale about being blackmailed. That, I presume, was to cover the fact that you had a hundred grand in American dollars wrapped up in a plastic bag. Very quaint. But I'm a smart cookie, George. Not a nice one, but gutter smart and good to have on your side, if you follow me. So what's the situation? To put it simply, things have got so bad that you can't do without me. I'm the only thing keeping you alive, old mate. Without me you're dead. And poor. With me, you'll stay alive and maybe the two of us'll make a few dollars from whatever this deal is that you've got going.'

Montague sighed. 'Sit down, George.' He pointed to another chair. 'Over there, please. You're squashing me.'

18

Kelly waited until nine o'clock before entering the little settlement at the opal fields. To his astonishment, he found a telephone box there. It was one of the new solar-powered devices that Telecom had been installing in unlikely places — a glassy booth stuck on a stony plain. It was a headlight's sweep away from the nearest building, a tin-and-wood shack that served as the miners' store.

Light fanned from the store's doorway. There were other buildings, sharp-edged shadows in the night. A few displayed rectangles of dull yellow where light leaked through hessian curtains. Kelly counted five lights. He waited. Outside the buildings, nothing moved.

He peered through the windscreen. All around him, he could distinguish the silhouettes of odd pieces of machinery and big and small vehicles. Slowly he turned the Toyota in a tight circle. Its lights flitted past the jib of a crane and an abandoned bulldozer bucket, to settle on an old truck with empty sockets where its headlamps had been. Behind it stood a front-end loader with its scoop poised like a praying mantis. He continued to circle. The lights swept across stained oil drums, a shed, a derrick lying on its side and two four-wheel drives. He stopped. Both were utilities, shabby from hard work. Near them was a semitrailer partly laden with

182

drums, then a heap of vehicles: a couple of old Holden utilities, a Pontiac minus its front wheels, a Falcon station wagon with one black door on its white body, and two more four-wheel drives. One was a wagon like his, but much older. The other was a nearly-new Toyota ute. He examined the latter with great interest, then turned off the lights and drove towards the telephone box.

None of the buildings had disgorged any curious residents. He switched off the engine and listened. From one of the shacks came the sound of a radio or tape player. A man was singing, a guitar twanging. Someone laughed. A woman. It was a high, shrill voice. From somewhere in the distance, a dog barked.

He sipped some water and looked around him once more. He'd worked out what he had to do but he hadn't expected that ridiculous phone box. He could call Laura.

He got out and with his hat pulled low to shade his face from the light, entered the booth and inserted his coins. He rang home. No one answered. He let it ring a long time, then decided to try again, wincing when the bell rang as his coins were refunded. Had she gone back to that place in Carlton? He didn't know that number. No, she said she was going home. He rang again. He checked his watch. She said she'd be waiting for his call.

Worried for her safety, he left the booth and walked slowly back to the Landcruiser. The dog barked again. Another responded and a distant voice snarled a command to shut up.

He could ring Gerry. Kelly went back to the booth.

Gerry Montague sounded like a tired old man.

'Gerry, what's wrong? Are you sick?'

'Who is it?' The line's awful. I can hardly hear you.'

'Me. Kelly.' He laughed, still astonished to be ringing from a solar box in the middle of a remote opal field.

Montague was silent for several seconds. 'Kelly. My God. Where are you?'

'You've never heard of the place. A little settlement near Cunnamulla.' Like a dog settling for the night, Kelly turned in a circle, peering into the darkness surrounding the glow of light in which he was centred. 'In western Queensland,' he added, remembering Montague's poor understanding of Australian geography. 'I'm in western Queensland.'

Kelly imagined the look on Montague's face. By now he'd be recovering from the shock but he'd still be gaping. Gerry would have been worried sick.

'I'm okay,' Kelly said, anticipating the question.

There was a long pause, so long that Kelly thought the line had been disconnected. Then, 'Jesus, it's good to hear from you. You've no idea how worried I've been.'

'Gerry, have you heard from Laura?' Another pause. Kelly shouted a series of hellos.

'I'm here, old son. I haven't heard a word from Laura. Didn't you say she'd left you and gone away somewhere?'

'She's been with me.'

Again the delay. Must be the line. 'What?'

'Laura was with me. I left her in Tibooburra. It's a long story. I'll tell you later. But she should be back in Melbourne by now. I tried to ring her at home and she didn't answer. I'm worried.'

'What do you want me to do?'

'Try and get in touch with her. Let her know that I'm all right. Let her know that I'll try and call again.'

Kelly thought he could hear Montague talking to someone but the line was alive with noises.

'Okay. I'll try.' A cough. 'Jesus, Kelly, what's been going on?'

'I was hoping you could tell me.'

'I've had the police in the office every hour of the day since this business started. Phone calls all night. It's been a nightmare.'

'Gerry, what happened to Kolvenbach?'

'Someone shot him.'

'So I heard.' He laughed bitterly and opened the door, to get a better view outside. A figure had emerged from one of the buildings and was heading towards the store. 'Do you know who?'

'The police are blaming you, old son.'

'Why? For God's sake, Gerry, why me?'

'Kelly, I have to ask this and I'm sorry, but did you shoot him?'

'Of course not.' It was a man. He was coming closer.

'That's what I've been telling them. I said they'd made a mistake. I said...'

'Look, Gerry, I've got to go. Someone's coming. I'll try and call you in a day or two. Don't forget about Laura.' He hung up without waiting for Montague's reply.

The man was close. He was old and had a limp. He peered towards the light and lifted a hand to shade his eyes. Kelly walked slowly to the Landcruiser. The man waved as though he should know him so Kelly waved back. The man went into the store and Kelly drove out of town.

Montague wiped his lips several times. So, Kelly didn't know where Laura was either. What the hell had happened to her? What was she up to? Working on some little deal of her own?

'He said he was in western Queensland. At some little town near a place called Cunnamulla.'

McCarthy lifted his glass. 'Ring the police, Gerry. Tell them he's just phoned. Tell them he's near Cunnamulla. They'll get him. We don't want him

185

driving back into Melbourne, asking awkward questions and getting in the way, do we?'

It was midnight. In bed at last, Gerry Montague began making another list. In the first column, he wrote: *LAURA. 1. Where is she? 2. What game is she playing? 3. Check contact re diamonds first thing tomorrow to see if she has made independent approach.*

In the second column, he wrote: *GEORGE. 1. Now believes me, I think.* (He underlined the last two words.) *2. Told him 100,000 was money Kelly made blackmailing a man called Rob. 3. Said I found cash hidden in Kelly's office, at the time I discovered Kelly had been stealing from the company. 4. Said I'd only seen a note from Rob postmarked Canberra. Which is why I know so little about our mysterious friend. 5. Said I didn't know the reason Kelly blackmailed him. 6. Said I thought there might be a few hundred thousand dollars more, but didn't know ... which is true. 7. George suggested we take over the blackmail which is what I said I'd been trying to do. 8. Said I believed possibility Kolvenbach was involved and blackmail business could be linked to the murder. 9. George is going to investigate K and see if there's a link with Rob. 10. I'm stuck with George but he's right, I do need him — for the time being.*

He took some aspirin and went over the list once more. He underlined some words. He always thought more clearly when he made written notes and he lay there for several minutes, rereading some paragraphs, trying to decide what he should do. He thought of keeping the list, just like he did with all his business notes, but these were too dangerous with George sniffing around. He could put them in the special hiding place with the plan Laura had prepared but that would have meant leaving the

186

house, and someone might see him. So he crumpled up the paper, put it in the ashtray next to the bed and used his lighter to set fire to it.

Laura was thirsty. She had no idea of the time but she could see the moon through a gap in the curtain and it looked cold and frosty — an after-midnight moon. She swung her legs out of the bed, sat on the edge for a few moments and then walked to the bathroom.

Kelly had said never to drink the local water but she was thirsty and to hell with Kelly. She turned on the tap.

'There's some soda water in the refrigerator.' She jumped as Kolvenbach turned on the light.

'Better not to drink from the tap.' He rubbed his chin. 'It might be full of frogs.'

'I didn't mean to wake you.' She stood awkwardly pulling her silk chemise down to hip level. Her panties were cut high to reveal her buttocks, and she was conscious of his stare. 'I was thirsty,' she said softly.

He took a deep breath. 'I'm a light sleeper. All those years in hunting camps.'

He turned away to find the soda water and two glasses.

'You were a hunter?'

'Yes. Big game.'

'Were?'

'Big-game hunters are an extinct species. Nowadays I take wealthy tourists on safari so they can take photographs. The more dangerous the animal, the more prized the photograph and the more money I make.'

She sat on her bed and examined him by the light streaming from the bathroom. 'You'd be a good hunter.'

'Yes.'

'But not a modest one.'

'I *am* a good hunter. Why deny it?'

She tilted her head, agreeing with the logic. 'Tell me, Magnus, what are you doing here?'

He looked puzzled. 'You already know. I'm searching for the man who killed my brother.'

'I mean in Australia.'

'I have business interests in many parts of the world. This is one of them.' He finished his glass and opened another bottle. 'Why do they make these things so damned small? More?' He topped up her glass without waiting for the answer. 'My brother was starting a diamond venture up in the northwest. A big mine. He'd made quite a discovery.' He reached under his bed for a small bag, felt inside and threw something to her. It landed on the sheet.

'That's a diamond?' In awe, she held it up to the light. It sparkled a faint pink. 'It's beautiful.'

'From the Kimberleys. High quality.'

She passed the diamond back to him. He caught her wrist. 'When you got out of bed, I thought maybe you were trying to escape.'

'You still don't trust me, then?'

'A man survives by keeping the fires of suspicion aglow.' He let her go. 'I'm glad you weren't trying to get away.'

'I gave you my word.'

'It takes time to learn whose word you can trust.'

She sat on the bed with her hands in her lap. 'You're not going to hurt me, are you?'

'No. Unless you do something very foolish.'

'Which I won't. And you're not going to try to take advantage of me? I mean, while we're like this. In the same room.'

He shook his head.

'Most men would.'

'I am not like most men.'

She wriggled her feet until they were beneath the sheet. 'Not interested in women?'

He looked away, disappointed by the question. 'Are you being provocative?'

'Merely curious.'

He looked up. 'I like to do one thing at a time. Right now, my mission is to find Hunnicutt and take back what is mine. I will allow nothing to distract me.'

She pulled the sheet up to her shoulders. 'And afterwards? Back to Africa? Off to the Kimberleys? Something else? Someone else?'

Kolvenbach shrugged.

'Magnus, have you stopped to think what you're going to do after you find Kelly?'

He went to the bathroom and turned off the light. 'I've already told you.'

'I didn't say when. I said after. Tonight you were saying you might shoot him.'

The bed groaned under his weight. 'Yes, I did.'

'In this country, you are not allowed to shoot people and then simply resume your normal affairs.'

More noise. He had rolled on to his side. 'You're asking how will I make my getaway?' He seemed amused. She wished she could see his face. 'If I do have to dispose of Hunnicutt, I will do it in such a way that no one will know what happened to him or who did it.'

She was silent for a long time. 'You'd hide the body? Bury him somewhere?'

'And the car. Believe me, if it comes to that sort of situation, the authorities will still be searching for Kelso Hunnicutt long after I've left the country.'

'You're cold-blooded.'

'Yes.'

'Aren't you frightened someone will find out?'

'The only person who will know is you. Are you going to tell on me, Laura?'

189

She said nothing.

'I don't think you will. I have a feeling you would not be unhappy to see your ex-husband disposed of. Correct?'

'That's a terrible thing to say.'

'Not so terrible. Look,' he said, shifting in bed once more and setting in motion a chain reaction of squeaks, 'it's not such a wicked thing. Your former husband is an evil man. He must have done terrible things to you. Lied, cheated, even beaten you. True?' Kolvenbach lay back on the pillow, tired by the speech. 'So I don't think it's terrible for you to want him dead.'

She whispered, 'How did you know all those things about Kelly?'

'I know what he's done. I know what such men do to their women. I think I know what sort of person you are, and I believe I understand how much you must have suffered. I am good at judging such things.'

She moved her legs restlessly. 'And you expect me to keep quiet if you kill Kelly?'

'Yes.'

She hesitated before speaking again. 'Dare I ask what would happen if I did tell someone?'

'You shouldn't ask.' He took a deep breath. 'Look, I think you want him dead. It's natural to protest and to say all the nice conventional things, but I think I know what you really want. He'd be better dead. Out of the way. It makes sense. I admire you for thinking that. Now, if you've had enough to drink, would you mind going to sleep? I want to make an early start.'

She could no longer see the moon through the curtain. She lay on the bed for several minutes, thinking and feeling confused. Kolvenbach was like some figure from a Nordic myth: terrible but just. 'Magnus?'

'Yes.' His voice was weary, a man desperately trying to be patient.

'You're the strangest man I've ever met.'

A little grunt. 'You said I was amusing.'

'You're a mixture. Interesting, amusing, terrible in your intensity, but just. Not compassionate but fair, in an old-fashioned sort of way. You have a very severe set of principles. I think you try to do what you think is proper.'

She thought she heard him muffle a laugh. 'This is a very late hour to be conducting psychoanalysis. But thank you, I appreciate the sentiment and I agree with the conclusion.'

She laughed to herself. The man even spoke like some Nordic god. 'What will you do after all this is over?'

'You will be the first to know, I promise you.'

She lay awake for a long time, thinking about the implications of that remark, grappling with confused thoughts. She was reasonably sure Kolvenbach did believe her. He certainly had no idea of her role in the murder of his brother; in fact, he was beginning to like her. So, what to do? Not much. Merely let herself be seen with Kolvenbach. When Kelly reached the Cooper, as he most certainly would (she knew her husband; if he said he was going somewhere, he went there), he would learn that she was with Kolvenbach. No matter how impossible the prospect, he'd try to rescue her. He was like that — guided by emotion, not sense.

What else was important?

Trying to ward off sleep, she sifted through details. Kolvenbach genuinely believed she was frightened of Kelly. She hadn't tried to convey that impression but he believed it and that was good. The more she could play the wronged, innocent woman, the better. Kolvenbach, she suspected,

preferred women to be that way. He was that ana-
chronism, an old-fashioned gentleman; hard on
men, a protector of women. If convinced of her
innocence, he would not contemplate using her as
bait. Which appealed to her sense of the absurd
because as soon as Kelly learned she was with
Kolvenbach, he would come rushing to her aid. The
weak chasing the mighty.

She thought about Kelly and Kolvenbach and
for a few semi-sleeping moments, saw them in some
sort of western shoot-out. Kolvenbach with his big-
game guns, Kelly with his maps.

She tossed restlessly for almost an hour before
falling asleep.

It was after two in the morning when Kelly returned
to the opal settlement. He came on foot, carrying
his torch, a length of plastic tubing and a few tools.
A single light shone from a house about fifty metres
from the store. He could make out a lantern slung
on the edge of a verandah. Someone might be out,
drinking or playing cards, and expected home late.
Or the lamp might have been forgotten. He waited,
searching the night for movement, listening for
sounds. He counted to one hundred, then moved.

Taking the phone box as his reference point,
he headed towards the place where the two most
promising four-wheel drives had been parked. First,
he went to the new utility. It was locked. Blast.
It must be very new; after the first few weeks of
ownership, no one ever locked his vehicle up here.

In frustration, he walked around the utility.
Good tyres, an electric winch. In the back were a
couple of twenty-litre drums, a length of rope, plus
a pick and shovel. Back to the driver's door. He
could break a window and try to short-circuit the
ignition but that was difficult with modern steering
column locks and he'd make too much noise. Using

his hands to hood the torch's beam, he walked to the older Landcruiser. It was brown, with its sides raked by scratches as though often driven through scrub. He'd had the same model; reliable but a bit of a truck to drive. The windows were down, doors unlocked, the key in the ignition. Thank God for a normal owner. It was a petrol model. And he had all that diesel in the back of his wagon. Never mind. There was petrol on the back of the semitrailer.

He slid behind the wheel, turned on the ignition and shone his torch on the instruments. The fuel gauge showed the tank was half full. He leaned across, brushing aside several boxes of matches, and opened the glovebox. Papers spilled out. He sifted through them. Bills, bank statements, a catalogue from a Charleville store, then bingo: not only registration papers but the owner's driving licence. Harold Hassemer. Born July 25, 1941. A little old, but he'd do. Kelso Hunnicutt would become Harold Hassemer.

He went back to the new utility and lifted the four drums from its tray. Three were full of kerosene. One contained gear oil. First he poured out the thick oil and rinsed the drum with kerosene, then he emptied the others and carried all four to the semitrailer.

In the distance a dog barked. He waited for it to stop and then climbed on the back of the truck. He uncapped a drum of super grade petrol and, using the plastic tubing, siphoned fuel into the four drums.

The dog barked again, but its yapping was desultory. No torch flashed. No angry voice yelled from a disturbed sleep.

One at a time, Kelly carried the drums to the old wagon. Eighty litres, plus thirty or so in the vehicle's tank. It would have to do. It should get

193

him to the Cooper. He put the drums in the back, then went to the utility. He took the shovel, pick and rope and put them in with the drums.

I'm a car thief, he thought. And a very unusual one. I'm taking an old Landcruiser and leaving a new one. Abandoning 60,000 dollars worth of vehicle for a heap worth ten, maybe fifteen. Not a very clever thief.

He started the engine, heard a chorus of dogs and with the lights off and keeping his foot away from the brake pedal, drove slowly to the place where he had hidden his Toyota.

19

Monica Tate planned staying at Nappa Merrie but she had to travel to Innamincka for fuel. She thought of staying a night at the motel, mainly for the hot shower, but she was operating on a tight budget and, still upset by the Hunnicutt affair, wanted to be apart from other people. So she camped on the river, isolated yet within reach of the town, and drove to the pumps early in the morning.

A tall man approached her. His deep suntan contrasted with straw-coloured, slightly unkempt hair. He had intense eyes. Quite hypnotic, she thought, and wondered if she could paint a face like that.

'Good morning.'

She nodded greetings.

'I see you've just arrived at Innamincka.'

Strange accent. Impressive man. 'Yes,' she said, curious.

'I was wondering if you'd seen a friend of mine. He's supposed to be travelling up here but he seems to be behind schedule.' A woman joined the man but stood deferentially to one side. She returned Monica's smile.

'I haven't seen many people. Not where I've come from.' She raised inquisitive eyebrows. 'Where is your friend travelling from?'

'The south. He was supposed to pass through Tibooburra the other day.'

'Sorry. I've come from the east.'

'Oh.' Kolvenbach shook his head and the woman turned, ready to return to the motel. The woman was interesting. Elegant looks. Good stance. Moved with grace, like a trained model.

The man had not moved. He rubbed his chin, as if intrigued by a possibility. 'My friend might have wandered off course. He's inclined to do that. He could have gone to the east, I suppose.' He moved closer and spoke earnestly. 'He's travelling on his own in a white Toyota Landcruiser. In his late thirties. About this tall.' He indicated with his hand. 'He's from Melbourne so the car has Victorian plates.'

Monica gasped. Only slightly, but Kolvenbach noticed. 'No,' she said. 'I haven't seen him.' She scratched her hair into place. 'But the roads are bad. He could be delayed.'

Kolvenbach leaned against the pump, his hair glowing in the backlight of early morning. 'Where were you in the east?'

This was ridiculous. A coincidence. There could be dozens of men travelling on their own in white Landcruisers. 'I'm a painter,' she said, fluttering a hand as though that covered a host of missing words. 'I've been roaming around. Camping on my own.'

'A painter.' He seemed extremely interested. 'What do you paint?'

She was about to say 'birds' but the lights of caution were flashing in her brain and she said, 'Anything'. Could he be looking for David — or Kelso Hunnicutt, as others called him?

'And where have you been painting?'

'All across western Queensland. How late's your friend?' She was the aggressive one now, asking him the questions.

196

Kolvenbach shrugged. 'A couple of days. I'm starting to worry.'

'Does he know the area?'

'Very well. He wouldn't be lost.'

'How did you get here?'

'By plane. I have my own aircraft.'

'Well, you could fly around and look for him. In case he's broken down.'

'I have been.' Kolvenbach had been studying his charts and knew the towns of western Queensland. 'Where have you been painting? Around Charleville, Cunnamulla, Quilpie?'

'Around there.'

'All those places?' He straightened and, noticing her untidy hair, ran his fingers through his own.

'I've been travelling. I like to keep moving.'

'On your own?'

'Always.'

'And where was the last place?'

This was too much. She was becoming flustered. 'Excuse me but I have to fill my tank and get back to the camp. I have work to do.' She busied herself with the pump.

'Of course. Thank you. Good painting.' He took the woman's arm and guided her, more like an escort than a husband, back to the motel.

Monica lifted a hand in acknowledgment and was pleased he'd gone. She was sure. He was looking for Kelso Hunnicutt.

Having safely crossed the Thargomindah-Quilpie road at dawn, Kelly approached the Bulloo. He slowed, dismayed by what he saw. Two vehicles formed a blockade across the bridge. He prepared to turn, presuming it was a police barrier, but then saw they were private vehicles: a car and a small truck. The car had its bonnet up.

He stopped, a little too far away, and a man

approached, walking slowly and smiling a good-neighbour smile but carrying a rifle in the crook of one arm.

'Sorry, mate,' he said when he reached Kelly's door. 'We're looking for a Melbourne bloke. Huddlebutt or something. In a white Landcruiser.' He examined the brown wagon. 'Haven't been through a lot of mud, have you?' He laughed. 'No, the copper asked us to block the bridge in case this Huddlebutt came along, and we bloody well have. Completely. The Falcon's gone and flattened its battery and we can't move the bastard. Haven't got a tow rope between the lot of us.' He moved the rifle to his other arm and with his free hand lifted his hat to scratch his forehead. 'But if you're carrying a tow rope and you'd like to pull the bloody thing out of the way, we can get the bugger started and you can get through at the same time. What do you reckon?'

'Sure.' Kelly smiled with relief.

'Mind giving me a lift back? Got a crook foot and every step saved is a bloody blessing.'

'Hop in.' Kelly glanced rapidly around the cabin. The maps; they were unusual. He threw them on to the back seat.

'Where are you heading for?' the man said when he had hauled himself up to the seat.

'Longreach.'

'Live up there?'

'Got friends.'

The man extended his hand. 'Anyhow, me name is Boris Lancaster.'

'Glad to know you.' Kelly hesitated. A name was expected. 'Harry Hassemer.'

The man didn't take Kelly's hand. 'Who?'

Kelly swallowed, hoping the man was hard of hearing. 'Harry Hassemer.'

He scratched his head. 'Must be two of yez. I

know a Harry Hassemer. Opal miner. Used to be a fencer.' He peered at Kelly. 'A relation of yours?'

'Not that I know of.' Kelly, his stomach churning, tried to flash his most disarming smile. 'What a hell of a coincidence.'

They had reached the blockade. Boris hadn't closed his door and slipped from the wagon. 'Hey fellers, you'll never believe this. Guess what this bloke's name is.'

A bald man with a grey beard peered at Kelly. 'If he had a beard like mine, I'd say Santa Claus.'

'Shut up, Charlie. No, his name's Harry Hassemer. Same as Harry's.'

Charlie moved closer. 'Poor bastard. I thought one of them was bad enough.' He scratched his stomach.

Another man, balancing a rifle casually in both elbows, moved to the front of the Toyota. 'It's Harry's vehicle, but.'

'What is, Frank?' Boris limped to join him.

'This is.'

Boris swayed back, to get the number plate in focus. 'Could be.'

'No fucking could be. It is. I should know the bastard. Me and Harry went up to Vanderlin Island on a fishing trip in it two years ago. It's Harry's all right.'

Boris moved towards Kelly's door but Kelly held up his hand. 'Don't come any closer. This thing's full of dynamite. Six cases of it. Move one foot closer and I'll blow it up. You too.'

Charlie stepped back. 'What are you talking about?'

'I'm talking about blowing all of us sky high. Now get that truck out of the way and let me through.'

Without moving his feet, Boris leaned forward. 'Are you Huddlebutt?'

Kelly nodded vigorously. 'Harry Huddlebutt.' He

tilted his head back and laughed, unable to control himself.

'Jesus, why are you laughing like that?'

'Because I'm crazy. Mad Harry Huddlebutt. Now move the truck. Quick. Or else I'll blow everything up. You and me and the bridge. And your Falcon. I'll move it for you all right — about six miles.' He shrieked with laughter.

'The bloke's nuts,' Charlie said but looked alarmed.

Frank said, 'I don't think that's the name of the bloke we're looking for, Boris.'

'Doesn't matter,' Kelly yelled. He fumbled for one of Hassemer's matchboxes and struck a match. He held it up. 'Quick. I feel the urge coming on.'

Frank raced for the truck. Charlie had retreated and stood scratching his stomach and gazing nervously at the bridge. Maybe he'd helped build it, Kelly thought. He leaned out of the window. 'Hurry, I have to be with God by lunchtime.'

'The bloke's a raving loony,' Charlie said.

Boris stood his ground. 'What did you do that's got the coppers looking for you?'

'I blew up Captain Cook's cottage.'

Boris half turned to Charlie. 'I never knew he was still alive.'

'Well, now he's got nowhere to live,' Kelly shouted. 'Just a big hole in the ground where his cottage used to be.'

'I thought it was something to do with diamonds.'

'I eat diamonds.'

'Jesus Christ,' Charlie rumbled from the distance, 'let the bastard get going. He's probably been bitten by a mad dog.'

'I ate a blue heeler for breakfast.' The truck jolted forward and Kelly headed for the gap. He threw the box of matches on to the road. 'Don't go near it,' he yelled. 'It's full of the world's most deadly reverse explosive. If it goes off, all of you'll be sucked into the matchbox.'

Kelly drove across the bridge.

'What did he say?' Frank said when he rejoined the others.

Boris hadn't moved. 'Something about the fucking matchbox, I think.'

'The man's a raving lunatic.' Charlie scratched his navel. 'I don't know that we should say too much about this. People would reckon we were on the bloody piss.'

'But he was in Harry Hassemer's Landcruiser,' Frank said.

Kelly laughed for a full minute and had to stop to wipe his eyes. He reached in the back and grabbed an open packet of biscuits and ate two at once. He was famished. There were cans of tinned meat, beans and fish in the back. No time to stop though. He checked his watch. If he could find all the tracks he needed, he should be at the Cooper by late afternoon.

He drank some water and ate some more biscuits. He scanned the sky, searching for a helicopter, but the sky was empty and as bleached as a plain cotton sheet. He drove off, his course set for south of Tobermory homestead.

'Harry Huddlebutt,' he shouted and began to laugh again.

Kolvenbach was certain. The woman had seen Hunnicutt. He leaned towards Laura. 'Does your husband know a woman artist?'

'Not that I'm aware of.'

'But you wouldn't necessarily know. You haven't been living with him for a long time. He could have many friends you know nothing about.'

She nodded slowly. 'I suppose so.'

'Do you think she could be an accomplice?' He stood at the window. Hands clasped behind his neck, he bent right, then left, stretching one set of muscles, then another. 'He might have needed help for a job like this.' A grunt as he bent low. 'You know, someone who'd arranged to meet him somewhere, someone who could help him hide out for a few months.'

'A woman?' Instinctively, she resented the idea. 'You forget, he kidnapped me. He forced me to go with him. He wouldn't do that if he were meeting another woman.'

He dismissed the theory in five words. 'He got rid of you.'

She clasped her hands. Kelly with another woman? And one who didn't even comb her hair?

'You don't like the idea?'

He had turned. She could see he was amused. Flashes of jealousy were for other, less steely-minded people. 'I hadn't thought about it,' she said.

'But it is possible.'

She tried to appear casual, unconcerned, but her fingers continued to grapple. 'Possible, I suppose, but most unlikely. Kelly is a loner.'

'Ah.' He stared down at her, his eyes wide and even brighter than normal. He shook both arms, loosening the muscles. 'But that woman has seen Hunnicutt. I'd swear to that. Maybe a casual acquaintance. Someone he met by chance. And it led to a romantic night camped beside some outback river, eh?'

She laughed. 'You don't know Kelly.'

He raised a finger. 'Maybe *you* don't. Did you ever think he would steal diamonds, kill someone, plan an elaborate escape like this?' The finger wagged. 'No. So, you see, anything is possible with a person you don't truly know.'

Kelly with another woman? She felt a curious

202

burning somewhere behind the eyes. The bastard. He'd pay. 'If you're right, he'll come here,' she said.

'Or come to where she is. She's not staying here.'

'So what do we do?'

'Find out where this woman artist is camped. We can do that by air. Then make a quick flight over the country to the east. That's where he's been. We might see him. If not, we wait. He'll come to us. Either to the Cooper, as you've been telling me, or to the woman.' He smiled, still sniffing the faint aroma of jealousy. 'And we'll be waiting for him.'

20

The man who owned the motel at Innamincka was
curious about the couple in Room Three. They were
an odd pair. The big man had a strange voice; the
woman didn't speak at all. And they didn't behave
like a married couple. Not that whether they were
married or not worried him. He was sure a few
of the 'married couples' who stayed at his motel
did so because it was about as far away from their
respective spouses as they could get. The thing that
puzzled him was that this pair didn't even behave
like a friendly couple. They stood apart and the
man always did the talking. When he'd come to
the office to make his phone calls to Canberra and
Melbourne earlier that morning, the woman had
waited outside. In view, but out of hearing.

The owner's wife had been observing them too
and she, bedevilled by her feminine intuition, worried for the woman. She reckoned the woman was
frightened of the man. Even she felt intimidated
by him, if just a little attracted. The man was huge
and always seemed to be flexing his arm or shoulder
muscles. Her husband reckoned he must have a
bad back but that was just her husband's way of
trying to make so impressive a man seem flawed,
liked ordinary males such as he.

If the woman wasn't frightened — they argued
about this too — she was certainly cowed or, at

the very least, respectful in a way that wasn't normal.

The woman didn't look the subservient type. She stood straight and had the sort of fire in the eye you saw in good horses. She smiled occasionally, but the wife thought it was more a plea for something, rather than a cordial greeting. She thought of getting the woman to one side and talking to her but her husband forbade it.

The motel owner's wife was a perceptive woman and another fact intrigued her: the couple didn't dress in the same style. The woman was well, if uncertainly dressed; like a city type venturing into the bush for the first time. She wore discreet but costly jewellery and a watch that the wife yearned to see close up. By contrast, the man was dressed in real country gear — high quality, hard-wearing stuff with boots that would have cost at least 300 dollars — which he wore naturally, as though he'd spent his life in the bush. But whose bush? Not Australia's.

They were discussing the couple when two South Australian policemen arrived, racing into town with their four-wheel drive's two tall aerials whipping the wind. They had driven up the Strzelecki Track. They'd been ordered to Innamincka in case the notorious Diamond Killer, Kelso Hunnicutt, crossed into South Australia. Hunnicutt, they explained, was the focus of a manhunt that had moved from northwestern New South Wales to far western Queensland. He was thought to be heading east but if he drove into South Australia, Innamincka was his most likely entry point.

The policemen, stretching and brushing their clothes after the long drive, described Hunnicutt and his vehicle to the motel couple.

'Sounds a bit like the man our friend in Room Three's waiting for,' the wife said and laughed nervously, scarcely believing what she was suggesting.

The senior policeman seemed to grow a little taller. He stretched his back, squared his shoulders, and demanded more. He listened with great interest. The other policeman made notes and kept glancing at his companion, becoming more agitated as the conversation progressed.

'Can you describe the man who was making the enquiries? Where is he now?'

The woman looked to her husband.

'Out in his plane,' the husband said. 'He spends a lot of time flying around, searching for his friend.'

They talked for another five minutes. 'Anyone else come into town in the last day or so?' the senior man asked.

'A woman drove in this morning. Just for fuel. She's an artist.'

The policemen exchanged glances. 'Where did she come from?'

'Western Queensland. Not sure where.'

'And where's she staying now?'

'She's camping up at Nappa Merrie.' The man's eyes darted from one policeman to the other, watching their reactions. Nappa Merrie was over the border in Queensland, beyond their jurisdiction.

While the motel owner refuelled their vehicle, the two men had the wife show them Room Three.

Whereas most of the world's rivers start small and grow in volume, Australia's outback rivers do it the other way. They start impressively, cruelly stirring the dreams of those who chance upon them, but lose their water to a hostile sun and thirsty plains and finish their journeys as dry channels or potholes in the desert.

Cooper's Creek was a classic example. It was formed by the junction of two Queensland rivers, the Thompson and the Barcoo. Each had its origins on the western slopes of the Great Dividing Range and each ran generally to the southwest. The Thompson flowed through Longreach, the Barcoo through Blackall; and they met at the town of Windorah. From that point, the two rivers became the Cooper and were downgraded, at least on maps, to the status of a single creek. The Cooper retaliated by splitting into a confusion of channels which spread across a vast area. Eventually they merged, to head south. On its new course, the Cooper passed Durham Downs and Karoma cattle stations, then hooked to the west, splitting once more into many channels. It gathered itself into a single stream to pass Nappa Merrie station, to cross the Queensland–South Australian border and to touch Innamincka. West of that tiny settlement, it broke up into a bewildering series of channels and water holes as it snaked through some of Australia's most menacing desert country.

Further west, the river regathered to cross the Birdsville Track, before ending its long journey on the shores of Lake Eyre. It was a journey infrequently accomplished. True to its kind, the Cooper rarely flowed. In normal times, it was no more than a series of water holes, big and small, awaiting replenishment from downpours in distant places.

It was among the maze of water holes that lay between Innamincka and the Birdsville Track, and in a region that formed the southern border of the appalling Stony Desert, that Kelso Hunnicutt proposed to hide.

Kolvenbach was returning to Innamincka, flying west above the road from Karoma homestead. He'd seen no sign of the white Landcruiser. No sign of any vehicle, in fact, until he had circled Karoma, where the Cooper's sandy bed still ran north to south, and there seen a Land Rover stopped at a gate. The stockman opening the gate, a man with the dark face and flashing teeth of an Aborigine, had waved.

Innamincka was to the southwest but Kolvenbach continued on his course. He was trying to anticipate which way Hunnicutt might be travelling. By now he was developing a respect for his quarry's bushcraft. Whatever he might be, whatever he might have done, Hunnicutt was good in the bush. And tricky.

If he were heading towards the Cooper, he would choose the most unlikely route. That was his *modus operandi*. Since leaving Melbourne, Hunnicutt had been travelling generally in a northerly direction, which meant he should reach the Cooper from the south. Therefore, he was likely to come in from the north. That could explain why he had been travelling where the woman artist had seen or met him. He'd been driving wide of Innamincka so that he could complete a big loop and swing back down to the Cooper from the north.

He turned to Laura. 'I think this man of yours could be playing a very cunning game.' He saw her eyes flash; she didn't like him referring to Hunnicutt as 'her man'. No matter. He was tired and in a bad temper from all the hours of unsuccessful searching. 'I think he may have driven in a large circle. First north, then east, then north again, then west, and now south.'

Her eyes became dull. She'd become lost on one of the turns.

'In other words, I think he may have driven around us.' He pointed ahead. A track scarred the landscape. Far beyond it, rising from the emptiness of the Stony Desert, was a puff of dust. Kolvenbach narrowed his eyes, fascinated by the telltale signal. 'If I'm correct, he'd be coming down from the north. To meet up with his woman.'

She folded her arms and closed her eyes. She

was exhausted, and tired of Kolvenbach needling her. Kelly had no accomplice because he'd done nothing more serious than get involved in a silly bet. And he wouldn't have a girlfriend who drove a truck and dressed in baggy clothes and wore no make-up. Or would he? She'd often accused him of having bush whores. Never seriously, though; merely to forestall or counter his accusations. However, he'd spent so much of his time wandering through the outback that it was possible he'd met that woman somewhere. It was feasible that he'd arranged to meet her; to spend the rest of his anticipated week in the bush with his outback lover.

At least she was white. She smiled.

Kolvenbach noticed the expression. 'Ah, so you've seen it, too. A car. Could be a Landcruiser. Still a long way away.'

The dust trail was slight. The vehicle was travelling slowly, not following any track but making its own path to the south. The squared shape became more distinct.

'Landcruiser,' he announced.

'Wrong colour.'

'Or just dusty.' He was irritated by the note of satisfaction in her voice. She was scoring a point because he had said Hunnicutt was on his way to see his woman. How like a female.

'Not dusty. It's brown.' Now she was bored.

'And the wrong model.' He clicked his tongue in disappointment. 'That one's too old.'

In silence he flew over the Landcruiser. He tried to see who was inside but saw only a hat and a raised hand. He flew on until he picked up the track from Cordillo Downs and turned towards Innamincka.

'So Kelly's not coming from the north,' she said.

'Maybe not at the moment. Give him time. He may prefer to travel in the dark, but he will come to the river, I am certain.' He reached over and briefly squeezed her wrist, pressing hard enough to hurt. 'Give credit where it's due, my dear Laura. This man of yours is as cunning as a rat. All we have to do is set the trap and wait by it.'

She rubbed her wrist.

'I had some interesting conversations on the phone earlier today.'

'I'm pleased.'

'Of course you know Hunnicutt's partner, Gerry Montague?'

She caught her breath. What had he learned? She shrugged. 'Yes.'

'And what does that gesture, that graceful toss of the shoulders, mean? Yes, I know him but not very well?'

'I've met him, of course. I haven't had a lot to do with him. As I told you before, I didn't get involved in Kelly's business affairs. Certainly not in recent years.'

'Ah.' He checked his instruments and gave the glass on the fuel gauges a nervous tap. It was an old habit, born in the days when he had flown a rickety biplane whose few gauges suffered from sticking needles. 'And how about a Mr McCarthy?'

She was silent for a moment, careful not to rush into one of his traps. But McCarthy? She shook her head. 'I don't know a Mr McCarthy. Who's he?'

'I was hoping you could tell me. He's not involved with the film company?'

'No.'

'But he is involved with Montague.'

'McCarthy?' A firm shake of the head. She looked at him doubtfully. 'I've never heard of the man.'

'Strange. He seems to be spending a great deal of time with Montague.'

She tried to look disinterested because Kolvenbach kept glancing at her, probing for a sign that she recognised the name. McCarthy. Gerry hadn't mentioned him. What was Gerry up to? Cooking up some little deal of his own with this McCarthy? She wriggled in the seat.

Kolvenbach was still watching. 'What sort of man is this Montague?' Now he sounded jovial, which made her even more wary.

She answered slowly, choosing her words with care. 'He's the businessman in the organisation. Kelly is the creative man. At least, that's what he likes to call himself.'

'Wasn't Montague the boss and Hunnicutt a junior partner?'

'Are you kidding?' She laughed, pleased to find his thinking so wide of the truth. 'Kelly started the company. Gerry — that is, Montague — joined later, when things got moving and Kelly couldn't handle the book-keeping and the marketing side of things.' She paused, sensing a need to be less definite. 'At least, that's what I think happened.'

Kolvenbach checked his chart, then said, 'So what sort of man is Montague? Be frank. I value your judgment.'

She took a deep breath to steady herself. 'I really don't know. Good at selling, I believe. You know, going out and getting new contracts.'

'And he handled the books?'

'I just said so. Yes, he looked after that side of things. Kelly couldn't tell a ledger from a comic book. Gerry Montague made the money, Kelly made the pictures. He was always away.' She glanced right, across the spiked shadows of the desert. 'He hates being in the one place. He should have been born a Tuareg.' She turned. 'You know, crossing the Sahara on a camel with a salt caravan or something. He's a nomad.'

'So.' He was wrestling with some private problem. 'Why? Why are you so curious about Kelly's partner?'

211

'Just something I heard today.'

'Who were you speaking to?'

He looked at her and his eyes were alive with challenges. 'Someone in Canberra.'

'And he knows Gerry Montague?'

'He mentioned the name. And the other man, McCarthy.'

'And?'

Suddenly Kolvenbach banked the aircraft in a sharp turn. Laura grabbed for support.

'What's wrong?'

'I'm a fool,' he said, levelling the twin as he settled on the new course. His eyes searched for the dust trail of the brown Landcruiser. 'Why would someone be driving across the land, not on a road?'

She squirmed into the seat and used her fingers to comb her hair into place. 'Because the man probably works out here and he's looking for cattle or something. And I wish you'd warn me before you do something like that.'

Kolvenbach was not listening. 'Hunnicutt could have changed vehicles. He *should* have changed vehicles. Everyone is looking for a white Landcruiser.'

'He'd never get rid of his beloved truck.' She said the word disparagingly. 'I used to say to him when he was talking about buying that thing that at least he should get something with a bit of style, like a Range Rover. But no, Kelly wanted another one of those ugly things. Something good in the bush, he would say. He imagines himself as some sort of outback adventurer.'

Kolvenbach frowned. The answer disturbed him. He filed it away, to think about later.

Kelly saw the plane returning. Immediately he turned to the left, away from Innamincka, meandering among low spines of sand that rose from the

Stony Desert. The plane swung in the same direction, flew well ahead of him and then banked. Now it came towards him.

It wasn't the police because he'd seen a woman in the cabin when it had first flown over him. It was an unusual aircraft: high winged, with long-range tanks drooping from each wingtip and a round, almost tubby fuselage. The two engines emitted a turbocharged scream, so it was powerful and fast. Expensive. Not the average bush runabout. He'd seen one like it before. Where?

The answer came as the plane dived low, heading for him as though on a strafing run. *Along the dingo fence*. Before he met the man who had posed as a boundary rider. The man who was after the diamonds.

The aircraft swept by on his left, no more than ten metres above the ground. The pilot stared down at him. Kelly sunk low in the seat, to look like a smaller man and waved, using the hand to obscure his face. A violent wash of tortured air, alive with the screams of the whirring propellers and turbocharged motors, rocked the Landcruiser.

In the aircraft, Laura said, 'Could you see?'

'Not clearly. Just one man, though. Hold on.' Kolvenbach applied more power, climbed and banked. 'I'll make a slower run. Your side. Tell me what you see. And cover your face. If it is Hunnicutt, we don't want him recognising you.'

He lowered the flaps and the undercarriage, throttled back and fishtailing the aircraft to lose even more speed, prepared for another fly-past.

'My God, don't land on top of him,' she screamed, alarmed by their low altitude and the constant bleeping of the stall-warning device.

'Just look at the man. Leave the flying to me. Now.'

At that moment, the old Landcruiser swung sharply to the left, into the path of the aircraft.

213

Inside the vehicle, Kelly yelled, 'You're the one that'll come crashing down, not me, you crazy bastard'.

In the aircraft, Kolvenbach shouted and yanked the wheel to lift the nose. He poured on more power and climbed. Laura hadn't spoken. Her hand clutched her throat.

'Well?' he said, when they were a hundred metres up.

'Well what?'

'Was it him?'

'I didn't see anyone.' Her voice was shrill. 'I just saw the roof. He almost rammed us.'

'Cheeky bugger.' He grinned. 'Or else the man's deaf and needs glasses.' As he completed his turn, he studied the terrain. 'Could have been dodging a rock, I suppose. Ready?'

Her hand still held her throat. She was having trouble breathing. 'Ready for what?'

'Another run. This time, have a good look at him.'

'Are you crazy?'

'I'll be further away from him. He won't be able to do that again. Don't forget, cover your face.'

She was shaking.

'Come on,' he said, throttling back and losing altitude once more as he settled on course. He reached across to touch her arm. 'I'd pass him on my side and have a look myself, but I'm busy trying to keep us in the air. Besides, you know him better. Here we go.'

They were, it seemed to her, even lower than before. She felt a bump as one wheel touched the ground. The plane yawed and growled; Kolvenbach fondled the controls. 'Now,' he called and she looked to her right, hands raised like blinkers. Through the window of the Landcruiser and across on the far seat she could see one man. Hat on. Head tilted towards her so that the face was shielded. Sitting low.

214

Then they were past. The plane wobbled its wings and rose steeply. There was a small tree ahead.

She hadn't been breathing and took in great gulps of air as Kolvenbach climbed. Up came the wheels, up came the flaps. They settled into steady flight and she tried to assemble her impressions.

'He's wearing a hat. The face was partly obscured. He seems small.'

'You mean you don't know.'

'I'm not sure.'

He nodded, understanding. 'But it could be.'

'Yes. It could have been Kelly. Whoever the driver was, he was hiding his face.'

He was still nodding. 'Let's say the chances are fifty-fifty that it was Hunnicutt. A normal man would have looked at us. Smiled, waved, shaken a fist, done something, but not hide his face.' He tapped the wheel. 'Okay.'

She took a deep breath. 'What does that mean?'

'It means I've decided. We're going on to the Cooper. I had thought of landing and having a little chat with whoever's in the wagon. The ground's too rough, though. Too many rocks and sandy ridges. No matter.' He gave her his steely, confident smile. 'He's going to the river. To be near his friend. We'll wait for him there.'

She glanced back. 'He's still heading east. That's the wrong direction.'

'Which makes me think it is Hunnicutt. Always laying false trails. And he's changed vehicles.' He glanced at Laura. 'Do you think that's why he met that woman of his? Because she had another vehicle waiting for him?'

She shook her head. 'I don't know.' His eyes danced across hers, searching for a reaction. She turned away.

215

Kelly was still in shock. The face staring at him from the cabin of that plane, the eyes open wide in terror, the hands held high in an appeal for help, belonged to Laura. Somehow, that man had caught her.

Kolvenbach checked his watch. They'd be at Innamincka in thirty minutes. Time to think about a few things. First, to consider the problem of Laura's remarks about the white Toyota. She'd wanted Hunnicutt to buy a Range Rover and they had argued about it. Yet the white wagon was new; less than a year old. And she had claimed she'd left Hunnicutt years ago and saw little of him. So she was lying. Why? Just a womanly whim, or something more serious?

Then he thought about the morning's telephone calls. Montague said Hunnicutt had rung him the previous night from somewhere near Cunnamulla. That tied in with his theory about the woman artist. Hunnicutt was definitely coming to meet her. Montague also said the police were now looking for two men. They had no name for the other man. No, they didn't suggest Magnus Kolvenbach was the second person. Why should they? Montague was puzzled and Kolvenbach was pleased to leave him that way.

And then the conversation with Lister. He said he'd lost two men trying to find out more about Montague. Lost? Kolvenbach had been intrigued by the word.

'Just that,' Lister had replied. 'They're lost. We don't know where they are.'

Montague, it seemed, had some tough men working for him. Was that the role of the mysterious McCarthy: a minder for Montague? Why? Innocent men didn't need bodyguards. Montague was up to something, but was it connected to Harald's death?

216

The sooner he returned to Melbourne, the better. In the meantime, he had to find Hunnicutt and get back the papers and the diamonds. In that order. Maybe tonight.

21

He had to join the track to pass through a fence. This was part of the huge Innamincka cattle station. If there were people waiting for him, they could be in this area. His senses sharpened, Kelly drove on, eyes constantly checking the sprawl of land on either side of the track. There were patches of tufty grass down here, and trees, robust trees that dotted the countryside for as far as he could see. The site was at least eighty kilometres from the river but this was flood plain, land over which turgid waters spilled when there'd been heavy rains in western Queensland and the Cooper was running.

Behind the trees the sun was setting, splitting the air with shafts of sunbeam and shadow.

Kelly saw the small building and braked. It was an outstation for the Innamincka property. It was not always manned, he remembered, but he couldn't recall whether there was a landing strip nearby. Probably. An outpost that had once been several days' hard ride by horse from the homestead would be no more than twenty minutes by aircraft. He parked behind a tree, got out his binoculars and used them to study the building and an even smaller shed, and to search beyond the yards and through the trees.

The plane might have landed. The big man who had seized his wife could be waiting for him, one shadow among hundreds.

Kelly moved among the grey trunks, bending with each twist of dappled bark, pausing regularly to check for any sign of the plane or the man. He saw no movement, not even cattle. There was no aircraft. He returned to his vehicle.

Ever since seeing Laura's face, Kelly had been sick with worry. How had that man caught her and what had he done to her? He'd thought of the worst questions and the most terrible answers. Now, leaning against a tree and waiting for night to come, he determined what to do.

He had to get to the plane while it was on the ground. It would almost certainly land at Innamincka. A twin of that type probably had the range to fly to Adelaide but if the man was searching for him, as he undoubtedly was, then he would wait at the Cooper. What would he do with Laura? That puzzled him. How could the man land and refuel with Laura on board and not have her seen by other people? Where would they sleep? He thought about Laura being roped hand and foot and grew angry. Bastard. He'd kill him if he hurt her.

He forced himself to forget what might have happened to his wife and to think clearly about what he had to do.

The brown Toyota was a liability, so he would get rid of it. The men on the bridge had seen him. Now the man in the plane had seen the wagon and even if he wasn't sure who was driving, he'd be watching and waiting for it to reach the river.

Kelly crept closer to the outstation. There might be some stockmen preparing to bed down for the night. There could be a ute or a four-wheel drive parked on the other side of the building. If so, he'd wait until late and do a repeat of his car-pinching trick. If not, he'd get to Innamincka before dawn and steal something else.

It was all very airy-fairy, he realised, but he

couldn't think of anything else. He had to change vehicles. Only in something different could he get close to the plane, and only by reaching the plane could he rescue Laura. After that, it didn't matter what happened to him. All that mattered was that, somehow, he had to set her free.

Bent low and moving with great stealth, he crept towards the building.

Monica Tate saw the vehicle flickering through the spangled shadows of dusk and cursed. She didn't want other people camped on her water hole. To ensure her seclusion, she'd moved down the river, well away from the Burke and Wills Dig Tree where all the tourists went, and almost ten kilometres from the Nappa Merrie homestead. It was a large water hole, rimmed by gnarled gums of enormous width and home base to a squadron of pelicans. Tourists would frighten the birds away.

She closed her sketchbook. People looking over her shoulder and making clucking noises of admiration drove her nuts. She stood up, brushed dust from her shorts and waited.

They were not ordinary tourists. The vehicle had two big aerials and writing on the side. As if to oblige, the driver turned side-on to negotiate a dip in the track, and she read the word *Police*.

It stopped near her and two policemen got out. One stayed beside the vehicle; the other approached her, nervously pushing and pulling the holster on his hip as he walked. She imagined a cricketer adjusting his protector before facing a fast bowler. When everything was in place he stopped. Perspiration stains spread from his armpits.

'Hot day.'

She agreed.

'You wouldn't be Monica Tate?'

She concealed her surprise by scratching the

back of one leg with the toe of her boot. 'I would be.'

They had been searching for her for two hours and the policeman nodded with satisfaction. 'You were on the Bulloo River a few days ago. You saw the fugitive, Kelso Hunnicutt.'

'Yes.' She wet her lips. 'How did you know I was here? And why have you come? Is anything wrong?'

He raised a hand. 'No, no. No problems. Just wanted to make contact and make sure you were all right. I presume you are?' The other man had been staring intently at the water hole and checking its shoreline, tree by tree. Now this man did the same.

'Certainly. I was just doing some sketching.'

'Yes. You're an artist.' He was not looking at her. She found it disconcerting, talking to a thick, sweaty neck.

'That's right.' She'd been bitten by an ant and rubbed her ankle. 'How come you know so much about me?'

'We've had several bulletins about you.' He faced her, inspected her as though seeing her for the first time, then explained their assignment to watch for Hunnicutt.

'You think he'll come this way?'

The policeman was staring at the trees and shuffling his feet to get a better view. They were such large trees; wide enough to hide several men, not just one. 'Who knows?' he said. 'Possibly not. He was last seen heading east, towards Cunnamulla, but you never know. Not with this fellow. In any case, the police have been anxious to talk to you since the other day. It seems you drove off in a hurry.'

'I just wanted to get away. The whole affair frightened me.'

'Understandable.' His hand was on the holster with his fingers rapping a nervous beat on the

221

leather. 'Did Hunnicutt say anything to you about where he might be heading?'

She shook her head. 'He said he was investigating sites for some film he was making. He said he needed a quiet place. He didn't mind birds but he didn't want people.'

'I'll bet he didn't.' The policeman turned to scan the country beyond the river. 'But he didn't say where he might be heading?'

'No.'

'You're certain. Not even a hint?'

'Nothing.'

His chin compressed in doubt. 'Did you see any signs of weapons or explosives?'

She shook her head vigorously. 'He had nothing.'

'How can you be so sure?'

'I looked.' And when he seemed surprised, 'I found him sleeping near where I was camped. I wanted to take photographs and I needed him to move his car. Before I woke him, I looked in the Landcruiser. There was no rifle.'

'You got in the Landcruiser?'

'I looked through the windows.'

'Were they opened or closed?'

She was sounding foolish. She could see it on the man's face. 'Closed. The vehicle was locked.'

'And it was dark?'

'Well, the sun wasn't quite up.'

'Very hard to tell, miss, under such circumstances.' He nodded several times. 'We have information that he has weapons, including a machine gun, and a substantial quantity of explosives on board his vehicle.'

'I don't believe it.'

'Our informant was a passenger in the vehicle.'

'Oh.' She was silent.

'You were lucky.'

'Yes. Possibly.'

Once more he scanned the area. The shadows troubled him. 'You don't expect Hunnicutt to come this way?'

'Of course not.' She shrugged. 'How would I know? Look, I only met him for a brief time. He seemed pleasant. A very normal man, in fact. He didn't say he was going anywhere. I was surprised to find him gone when I came back with the men from the homestead.'

The policeman's head bobbed up and down as she spoke. She imagined him dismissing the words as those of a naive young woman.

'I believe you saw the man with the aeroplane today.'

She was intrigued. 'I haven't seen anyone with an aeroplane.'

'A big man. Speaks with an accent. He talked to you while you were refuelling your truck this morning.'

'Oh. I didn't know he had a plane.' She frowned. 'I didn't like him.'

'Have you seen him before?'

She shook her head.

'Did Hunnicutt say anything about meeting a friend?'

'No.'

'Did you know that we're searching for two men?'

'I haven't been listening to the news and I haven't seen a newspaper in months.'

'Well we are. There are two of them, apparently. The second man attacked a police sergeant who had apprehended Hunnicutt down at Tibooburra. They may well be travelling independently.'

'And you think the second man is that man who spoke to me this morning?'

'Who knows, miss. But he's apparently waiting for someone and the description he gave the people at the motel matches that of Hunnicutt. May I ask what you and that man talked about this morning?'

'He was asking me whether I'd seen a friend of his.'

'That's all?'

'Yes. He said his friend was supposed to have passed through Tibooburra on his way up here. He said he was worried about him.'

'A normal conversation, eh?'

'More or less.'

'You said you didn't like him. Why?'

She was still holding her sketchbook and passed it from one hand to the other. 'I just didn't. Instinct, I suppose.' She thrust the book under her arm. 'So you think Hunnicutt's coming to the Cooper?'

'Possibly. The man's a bit of a will-o'-the-wisp.' He began fiddling with the holster again. 'You'd never met Hunnicutt before, had you?'

'Never seen him in my life.'

'Or heard of him? You're in similar pursuits. He's a film-maker, you're an artist.'

She smiled, remembering the conversation at the Bulloo camp. 'I had no idea who he was.'

'Who did he say he was? He must have given you a name.'

'David something-or-other. I don't remember the surname. I'm terrible with names.'

'But not Kelso or Hunnicutt?'

She shook her head.

He walked to the edge of the water hole. 'Beautiful spot, this, but very lonely. It'll be dark soon. Don't you think it would be a good idea if you moved into Innamincka?'

'No.'

'You could be in danger if he came along and saw you again. After all, you were the lady who put the police back on his track.'

Resolutely she shook her head. 'Why would he come here? Surely he'd be more likely to go to Innamincka?'

224

He frowned. 'I'd be happier knowing you were with other people.'

'That's thoughtful of you, I'm sure, but I'm happiest when I'm on my own.'

The man nodded several times and walked back to his vehicle. 'You'll let me know if you see anything?'

'You mean other than pelicans?'

He stopped and gazed out across the water. 'You're not underestimating this man, are you?'

'I haven't even been thinking about him.' She thought that was not only a stupid thing to say but a lie. She'd thought about David — Hunnicutt — constantly since leaving the Bulloo. She couldn't imagine him doing all the things people said he had done. And what was it now — carrying a machine gun and a load of explosives?

The policeman had been speaking. He repeated himself. 'I was saying, would you promise to do one thing for me? I'd like you to drive on in to Innamincka every morning, just for a few minutes, for the next day or so.'

'Is that like asking me not to leave town but to report to the police station every day?'

He laughed. 'No. It's just so we can be sure you're all right.'

'I'd rather get on with my work and not lose valuable time driving up and down this river.'

'I'd appreciate it if you could.'

She sighed. 'Okay, I will. I promise you.'

He waved and got in the vehicle. When they had gone, she walked to the water's edge and sat down. In the distance, she heard the sound of an aircraft.

There were no stockmen at the outstation. Using his torch, Kelly searched inside the building. A long table, chairs, some bunks, pots, pans, a few plates. He rattled a drawer full of worn knives and bent forks. He went outside again and looked around. The shed's door was locked but a hinge was loose. He yanked it clear and squeezed through the gap. In a corner of the shed and partly covered by a tarpaulin was a motorcycle.

He pulled the cover away and examined the bike. It was reasonably new and had a rack over the back wheel and knobbly tyres with plenty of air in them. He swung the bike from side to side, listening to the sloshing of fuel in the tank. Nearly empty. No matter, he had plenty of fuel in the wagon.

He laughed, moved by the absurdity of his situation. He was reduced to riding a motorbike. Never mind. He'd put the Toyota behind the shed, out of sight of any passer-by, and ride down to Innamincka. Whatever the man who held Laura would be looking for, it wouldn't be a man on a bike.

22

Gerry Montague was up in the ceiling when the telephone rang. Hastily, he slipped the plastic bag with the extra 100,000 dollars back in its hiding place and scurried for the ladder. He had had a busy half hour: confirming that the money was safe, checking the compartment in the deep freeze, and burning more of his handwritten notes. He was out of breath when he reached the phone.

McCarthy seemed amused. 'What have you been doing? Riding that exercise bike of yours?'

'Got to keep fit.' He tried not to pant and succeeded only in sounding even more breathless.

McCarthy needed money. Expenses were soaring. Earlier today, he had dispatched men all over Australia. One man had flown to Perth, one via Darwin to Kununurra in the Kimberleys, and another to Canberra. 'Amex are going to want some money soon and I'd like to be able to pay them on time. My expenses have been exceptionally heavy.'

Which meant, Montague knew, that his costs were rising sharply. He was still panting. 'Why, George? Canberra I can understand. But why Western Australia, for God's sake?'

'I'll explain.' So many of McCarthy's conversations were back-to-front, Montague thought. George would begin with peripheral matters and then work

227

his way towards the core of the subject. Not that bills for first-class air fares to Canberra, Perth and Kununurra were going to appear too peripheral.

'I think I was right about this Rob character. The blackmail that your partner got involved in almost certainly was to do with Kolvenbach.'

He waited for a response but Montague was striking a match to burn a surviving fragment of his notes. The rest were ash. 'Go on,' Montague said when the paper was well alight.

'Have you heard of a man called Robin Lister?'

Montague pushed the ashtray away from the phone. 'No.'

'You should take an interest in Federal affairs. He's the minister I mentioned yesterday. The one to do with Aboriginal affairs.'

'He's Rob?'

'No doubt. When we started linking your mysterious Rob with Kolvenbach, it became much clearer. You say the South African was developing a diamond mine in the Kimberleys?'

'Correct.'

'An area prone to Aboriginal claims, wouldn't you say?'

'I wouldn't have a clue.'

'Don't be so modest, Gerry. I think you've got a clue.' He coughed, to shed the sarcasm that had curled his words. 'Anyhow, trying to start a mine wherever there are people talking about sacred sites and land rights is a difficult business. Fraught with complications. Makes it very hard to get started. So it's worth spending a bit of money to ease the way, grease a few appropriate palms. Good, old-fashioned bribery. Follow me?'

'Who bribed who?'

'A man who wanted to make tens of millions on his diamond mine probably reckoned it was worth spending a million or two to smooth the way.'

'Kolvenbach paid Robin Lister?'

'He was probably asked to.' McCarthy slipped into his police voice. 'The information I have so far suggests a great deal of cash or kind may have changed hands.'

'Kind?'

'Cars, fishing boats, a house or two, refrigerators, video recorders. That sort of thing.'

Montague snorted his disbelief. 'You're telling me a government minister demanded a fishing boat... a house... a video recorder?'

'Not so fast, my old mate. More people than merely the honourable gentleman from Canberra are involved.'

He thought for a few moments. 'Which, I presume, is why you've sent men to Western Australia?'

'Precisely. Perth is where the State government sits, and there would have to be considerations paid there, too. We don't know too much about that at the moment but we will soon. I've sent a good man there.'

'And Kununurra?'

'That's the nearest airport to the proposed mine. Some of the locals who were claiming that the mine site was near and dear to them would appear to have been given favours — the cars and houses and the other trinkets I was talking about. The modern equivalent of beads and axes. All in return for having a good think and deciding that a sacred site wasn't so sacred after all, if you get my meaning.'

'I do, George, I do.'

'Thank heavens for that. The man I've sent to the Kimberleys will find out who the people are.'

Montague was silent for a few moments, then dared ask the critical question. 'So why was Kelly blackmailing Robin Lister?'

'He must have found out. Was Kelly close to Harald Kolvenbach?'

'He'd been working with him on a film we were going to make.' He hesitated, then decided to expand on the theme. 'They'd gone together to Western Australia, to the site of the mine. He and Kolvenbach were going to fly back up there.' Wrong, he knew instantly, and searched for more words. 'At least that's what Kolvenbach wanted. Not Kelly, of course.'

McCarthy made a low, growling sound. He was laughing. 'Your partner found there was more money in shooting clients than in shooting films.'

Montague leaned back, cradling the phone in his shoulder. 'So you've had a busy day, George.'

'Indeed. But expensive. I'll need that money soon.'

'Thank you, George.'

'Oh,' McCarthy said, 'a word of caution. This Robin Lister has a rather bad reputation.'

'Meaning?'

'The word I hear is that he's ruthless.' He laughed but this time the noise was a burst of sound. 'What politician isn't?'

'What are you getting at, George?'

'I'm passing on a warning. People who know him in politics say he'll stop at nothing to get his way. Nasty type. Climbed to the top up a ladder of knives planted in other people's backs. Know the type?' His voice rose into a register of doubt. 'You realise he's the one employing these visitors who've been calling on you?'

'Lister?'

'Of course. He was being blackmailed by your partner. He must think you're involved too. That first man we caught in your apartment was looking for the evidence — whatever it was Hunnicutt was using to blackmail Lister. Probably Kolvenbach too. My theory is that Hunnicutt was blackmailing both men. Kolvenbach refused to pay up and Hunnicutt shot him.'

230

Montague liked the theory. 'And Lister?'

'He's terrified that with Harald Kolvenbach dead, news of his little deal will slip out. And he knows what that would mean. No more plush office with hot and cold running secretaries, no more cheap meals in the parliamentary dining room, no more VIP flights or gold passes on the railways; public disgrace, gaol. He'd do anything to avoid that happening. So I'm just letting you know that we're not dealing with an ordinary criminal. This man has great influence and he's facing disgrace... as well as the loss of a million dollars or so, or whatever it was that Kolvenbach paid him. Just be extra careful, Gerry. Don't do anything without checking with me. Okay?'

'Fine, George.'

Montague hung up. He got the notes from Harald Kolvenbach's file and read them again. Those strange names: Woolaru, Kalalpaninny, Mumpi. Now they made sense. He grinned. Who'd got the new house and who'd got the video player?

He thought about Kelly. Elusive bugger. He probably would have won the bet. He wondered how long it would be before Kolvenbach caught up with him.

McCarthy didn't know about the dead man's brother. Jesus, what would happen when the big man came back to town? And where was Laura? He'd tried all the places where she might be but there was no sign of her. He had an uneasy feeling; she might have become a free agent and would try to squeeze him out of the deal. The trouble was she was so clever.

Things were becoming too complex. He poured himself a drink.

Kolvenbach took the motel owner's car. The man hadn't wanted to hire it out, hadn't wanted the big man to leave before the police returned, but Kolvenbach had placed a wad of notes on the counter and joked that he'd left his aircraft as a deposit. He and his wife merely wanted to drive down the river to a beautiful spot they'd seen from the air.

They'd miss dinner.

No matter. They'd be back in time for supper. He'd gone, the quiet wife in tow, before the owner could point out that they didn't serve supper. Confused by the exchange, he went to the kitchen to tell his wife to cut some sandwiches and leave them in Room Three.

An hour later, Kelly rode through the Cooper crossing. With the engine stuttering at idle and the motorbike's lights switched off, he moved slowly towards the airfield. The high-winged twin was the only plane there. He parked the bike on the edge of the strip and fossicked in his bag. He had brought only a few things: a dark jumper with a pullover hood, his big torch, a tomahawk, and his well-used Swiss Army knife. He also had a flask of water, a packet of nuts and some dried fruit, in case Laura hadn't been fed. He put on the jumper, pulled the hood over his head, slipped the tomahawk through his belt and the knife into his pocket, gripped the torch and crept towards the aircraft.

It was big and sleek; a real corporate, tax-deductible conveyance. He flashed the light through the windows. He was prepared to see Laura bound and gagged and lying on the floor, but the plane was empty. He tried the doors but they were locked. He could force them with the axe but that would make noise; no point if Laura wasn't inside.

With the knife, he started to hack through the sidewall of the front tyre. It was a slow, onerous job. All the time, he kept his eyes on a brightly lit building in the distance. It was probably the motel. An occasional sound — a voice, a door slamming

— drifted across the airstrip. Then the blade was through and a rush of air cooled his hand. Gradually the tyre flattened on its rim and the plane nosed down, poised like a great bird preparing to feed.

He set to work on one of the other, bigger tyres. The sidewall seemed tougher but when the tyre eventually deflated, the air made such a shrill whistle that Kelly grimaced, fearing someone would hear. But the only response was the distant jangle of a telephone.

Folding the serrated blade into its housing, he stood clear and examined the results of his butchery. The plane was tilted and crippled — totally unflyable. He felt a surge of satisfaction.

'Now,' he muttered, addressing the unknown man who had seized his wife, 'try and follow us.' Us, because he planned grabbing Laura, sitting her on the back of the bike and riding up the track to the outstation. There, they'd get in the old Toyota. He'd make straight for the water hole where he intended hiding out. And then they'd be safe. Just the two of them.

He hadn't worked out how he would rescue Laura. It depended where she was. And what the big man was doing.

First, he had to find them.

He returned to the motorbike and pushed it towards the motel. The brightest light shone from the office window. It was the candle attracting tourist moths in from the desert. Or Kelso Hunnicutt into a trap? He stopped. No. No trap. Things were normal. It was just a beacon to guide weary travellers. A vehicle was parked near the office. A twinkle of reflected blue puzzled him and he moved closer. After fifty metres, he stopped again. The vehicle was a police car. He thought of turning back but there were no sinister silhouettes within the cabin, no shadowy figures propped against the sides. The policemen could be inside the motel, having dinner. He thought of food and his stomach twitched from hunger. Other people ate three times a day; he'd spent recent meal hours either driving lonely tracks or creeping through the dark.

He pushed the bike closer.

The parked vehicle was another Landcruiser, a well-equipped vehicle, sitting high on big tyres and with two thick radio aerials, big enough for the crew to talk to Adelaide. Its sides were covered in bright, reflective signwriting and there was a blue light on the roof. A set of powerful driving lights, identical to the ones he had on his hidden white wagon, projected from the front bull bar.

For a moment he thought of stealing it.

He muffled a laugh, enjoying a brief vision of the police jumping up from the dining table and giving chase on foot. Ridiculous. Stealing the Toyota with all its flashing lights and bright signs would be as sensible as pinching a merry-go-round. Still, he had to admit he'd enjoyed stealing Harry Hassemer's old Landcruiser. He stopped, realising that he was aglow with excitement. Okay, Laura was in danger but the sheer excitement of the last few days was invigorating, infectious. He wanted more, the opportunity to do daring things. He'd never had such an exciting time.

He parked the motorcycle around the side of the building and walked to the front, where a throng of insects buzzed around the window. He thought he might stroll into the office, enquire about a room and find out who else was staying there. And make a casual inquiry about the police car out front.

Near the office he heard voices and stopped. A man's voice said 'sergeant'. Immediately, Kelly sought somewhere to hide. Next to the window was a coin-operated Coca-Cola machine, an old unit rendered pink by a plastering of dust. The machine cast a triangle of shadow and Kelly pressed himself against the wall, twisting his body to fit within the shadow.

The motel owner was describing his Fairlane. He laughed impatiently. Kelly heard him say, 'It's the only one up here. You can't miss it.'

The other voice, deeper, was less distinct. 'And you say... down the river somewhere... and the woman... back for supper.' The voice rose. 'Supper?'

'The wife's made sandwiches.'

The office door opened and a wedge of light, crowded with shadows, spilled across the plain. A third voice, projecting into the night, said, 'You've no idea how far they might have gone?'

Kelly sank into a crouch, pressing his cheek against the dusty flank of the Coke machine.

'He said he and his wife were going to a water hole they'd spotted from the air. I guess they were getting sick of just flying around and wanted to see something from the ground.'

'He does match the description of the second man, Mr Wilkinson. We were anxious to ask him a few questions.'

'Anyhow,' the deep voice interrupted, in the tone of someone anxious to get moving, 'what's done's done. We'll be on our way. You said they went east, up river?'

'Yes, sergeant.' One shadow remained. The others became two policemen in khaki uniforms.

'If we do miss him and he comes back, don't let him take your car out again, eh?'

The taller policeman waved, more of a dismissal than a farewell. The office door closed, wiping away the last elongated shadow. The darkness around Kelly deepened but he was still vulnerable. If the Toyota turned to the left, its lights would sweep across him.

The bigger man, the sergeant, opened the

Toyota's cabin door, reached in and withdrew a microphone on a curly cord. He put on a set of earphones, called his base and went through the rigmarole of identification. He had his back to the office.

'When's the plane coming in?' he asked and began to doodle on a notepad resting on the seat. '0900 hours? Good. We think we have a positive identification on the second suspect... That's right, in an aircraft. He's travelling with a woman. They've registered here as man and wife... Yes, LH. No name, just the initials. Gold-embossed... Have you got any information on that address we found?' The sergeant began writing, then whistled. He lowered the microphone and spoke to his companion. 'That address on the woman's bag. It's where Hunnicutt lives.' He picked up the microphone. 'Is someone checking on LH?... It could be. Let me know, eh?... No, they're not here at the moment... We just missed them... They borrowed a car and went up river... Yes, borrowed.' He laughed, enjoying what the voice in his earphones had said. 'Only for a couple of hours, apparently... No, no, we're about to follow them... Because that woman artist is camped there. You know, the one Hunnicutt ran into in Queensland... Yes, Tate. She's here... Near Nappa Merrie... I sent the details down by phone earlier... That's what I reckon too... Right. I will. You'll still be there?... Good, talk to you later.'

He clipped the microphone into its bracket. 'There'll be another six men here at nine in the morning,' he said and swung himself up on to the seat. 'They're going to find out if LH could be L. Hunnicutt and ring back tonight. LH. What say she's our man's wife? And she's travelling with our man's partner and they're all planning to meet here and get away in that aircraft? Interesting, eh?' Gently, he slapped the other policeman on the shoulder.

'What do you reckon this Monica Tate's involved too?'

The other policeman started the engine and his words were lost. Kelly, face level with the hinges of the Coke machine, saw the sergeant twist in his seat and reach for something in the rear. 'Back the way we came,' he said in a tired voice.

The lights were switched on, even the big auxiliary ones, and Kelly, blinking in the sudden glare, rocked back on his haunches and pressed himself against the wall. No matter how he twisted, his right shoulder, elbow and knee were brightly illuminated. He held his breath.

With a crunch of gravel, the vehicle's front tyres were dragged to the right. The Toyota turned in a slow semicircle and headed for the track to Nappa Merrie.

Wearily, Kelly got to his feet. Dazed by what he had heard, he watched as the police vehicle drew away from him. The tail lights narrowed to a single blur of red, then turned towards some trees.

Kelly ran for the motorbike. He had to follow.

23

The patch of brilliant white weaved and bobbed through the riverine trees. Following was easy. All Kelly had to do on the unlit bike was get reasonably close and ride where the lights had gone, noting the dazzling trunks, dodging the stark shadows.

The police avoided the main track. They went along the Cooper, stopping frequently to sweep a spotlight across a water hole or illuminate a stretch of sandy and secluded channel. Each time the vehicle stopped, Kelly sheltered behind a tree, in case the light was flashed in his direction.

Progress was slow but after an hour, they came to the place where Monica Tate was camped. She had a small campfire going. Kelly smelled the sweet burning of eucalypt wood before he saw the tent and the familiar truck. He saw Monica rise, wiping her hands on her hips and peering anxiously into the battery of approaching lights.

One hundred metres from the campfire, Kelly cut the motor and glided to a halt. He pushed the bike clear of the wheel tracks and lay it on its side behind a fallen tree. Crouched low, he hurried to a wide bush that was close to the campsite, and knelt behind it.

The police vehicle had stopped. The spotlight stabbed the night, its narrow beam dancing across the surface of the water hole and scattering reflections among distant trees. On the far side, the mass of pelicans ruffled their wings, creating the shimmer of black and white curtains touched by a breeze. Then the Toyota turned sharply and drove in a circle around the camp site, with the sergeant sweeping the bush with his light.

'What was all that for?' Kelly heard Monica say when the Toyota stopped. The vehicle's lights were on her and she shaded her eyes.

The sergeant got out. 'Sorry, miss. We're looking for that man you were talking to this morning. The big fellow. He's travelling with a woman. Have you seen them?'

She shook her head. 'Why? What's happened?'

Kelly crawled under the bush. As he watched, the sergeant turned and signalled his companion to extinguish the Toyota's lights. Abruptly the area changed. The bright, full figures were transformed into black outlines. Only Monica's fire gave light, glowing a dull yellow and flickering small flames. The trees around the site faded to ghostly shapes and wisps of smoke became grey phantoms curling among the branches.

Kelly relaxed. He was now in total darkness and hidden under the bush. But he could see the others.

'That's better.' The sergeant sighed like a man adjusting his belt. 'We just want to ask him some questions, miss, that's all. Sure you haven't seen him? Not even car lights in the distance? He's driving a white Fairlane.'

'Sergeant, I haven't seen a thing.'

They walked to the other side of the fire until Kelly could no longer hear them. The other police-man got out of the vehicle but stayed beside it. As Kelly's eyes grew accustomed to the darkness, he could see that the second man was holding some sort of gun — a rifle or shotgun. The man held the gun in both hands, ready for use.

Kelly heard a noise. The sound was faint, a stick being dislodged or the rustle of dry grass, but it was close and to his right. He strained to hear any further sound but Monica and the sergeant had raised their voices. The sergeant was insisting that she return to Innamincka. She was refusing.

'I am perfectly all right,' she said.

Kelly saw a movement. Someone was creeping through the bush. A different shadow, a man, bent low and carrying something. He was close, so close that Kelly felt a shiver of fear, thinking he had been seen. He pressed his fist against his lips to stifle any sound.

The man moved one step, stopped, moved another, and stopped again. Now he was no more than two metres away. He was facing the faint light, intent on the figures around the fire.

He stayed motionless for a full minute, long enough for Kelly to make out every detail. It was the man from Tibooburra, the man who had Laura. He was holding a rifle and looking around, as though seeking somewhere to hide. For a few moments, he seemed to be examining Kelly's bush but then he went the other way, sinking into the blackness behind a tall tuft of dry grass.

Where was Laura? Kelly wanted to twist around, to see what was behind him, but he dared not; the slightest movement, the faintest sound might betray his presence. Already his frightened body seemed to be generating an alarming amount of noise: his ears boomed to the beat of his racing heart and every breath rasped through his throat like a saw through wood. He pressed his face to the ground until he had calmed and the sounds diminished.

'How certain are you?' Monica was saying.

'Reasonably.' The sergeant acknowledged a gesture from his partner. 'We should be moving. We want to have a word with this gentleman.'

240

'And we're sitting ducks here.' The other police-man glanced anxiously around him and climbed into the vehicle.

'One last time...' the sergeant began.

'No,' she said.

He shook his head ruefully and walked back to the Toyota. 'But you will come into town in the morning, as you promised?'

'Of course.'

Muttering to himself, the sergeant climbed aboard.

Kelly waited, wondering if the big man would make a move, wondering why he was armed, won-dering why he was stalking the police — or was it Monica? — and wondering where Laura was. If she were still with him. If she were still alive.

The police Toyota roared into life, the driver so anxious to move that he was punishing the motor. Once more the spotlight stabbed the bush. Kelly kept his head on the ground while the light swept across the bush, across the tuft of grass, and through the trees. Then, with a crunch of gears, the Toyota moved forward. The light quivered as the vehicle bounced through rough ground. It detoured around Monica's camp and continued its course along the river.

The man rose. He slung the rifle casually across one shoulder, and walked towards the campfire. Monica, watching the lights of the departing vehicle, had her back to him.

'Good evening,' the man said and lowered the gun.

Monica turned and sank to the ground.

'Got any coffee?' He walked to the edge of the fire and lifted the lid of a pot that was sitting in the embers. 'Good. Mind if I have some?'

She watched while he filled a mug.

'Have I taken your cup?'

She shook her head.

'They were looking for me, I gather. Did they tell you why?'

She took a deep breath. 'They said they wanted to ask you questions.' Quickly she added, 'I don't know what about'.

'Ah.' He tried the coffee and grimaced. 'And, of course, you wouldn't ask them. You'd be too polite.'

She said nothing.

'Do they think I'm involved in some way with this man Hunnicutt?'

She shrugged; the shock was beginning to wear off. 'Why don't you run after them and ask them yourself?'

'I'm not Hunnicutt's friend, you know. Just the opposite.' He squatted beside the fire, mug in one hand, rifle laid casually across his lap.

Kelly wriggled backwards out of the bush.

'I get the feeling they think you *are* his friend,' Monica said, bolder now. She threw a large branch on the fire.

On all fours, Kelly slithered back to the log where he had hidden the motorbike. The man was saying, 'Ah, so they said more than just "We'd like to ask him a few questions," did they? Amazing, isn't it? The police are so pompous. They talk the same all over the world.'

'I wouldn't know.' Her voice was faint now.

'What else . . .' The words blended with the sigh of a breeze stirring the highest branches of the river gums.

Kelly reached the log and lay beside the bike. He stayed there for at least a minute, content to be shielded from the faint firelight and to have the comforting touch of the bike against his hands. Now if anything happened, he had the means of getting away. It was quiet here. Vague sounds drifted to him but no longer was he able to distinguish any

words. Good. If he couldn't hear them, they wouldn't
hear him. He pushed himself into a sitting position
and began to search for the Fairlane and for Laura.
Left, straight ahead, right. Once more. Nothing. It
was too dark. He thought of moving off, to search
on foot, but there was a flaw in that scheme: if
he found Laura, he'd need the bike immediately,
to take her away. He had no use for the Fairlane.
It was too big, too low and too obvious.

He lifted the bike on to its wheels and, moving
with great care, started to push it away from the
fire. He tried to follow the line he had taken in
reaching the water hole. He went slowly, feeling the
way with the bike's front wheel, stopping, reversing
and trying another direction whenever the tyre
touched a bush or rolled against some other
obstacle.

After a while, he stopped, sensing that something or someone was near. He could see only the
tops of the trees, vague forms against an indistinct
sky, but he sensed he was close to some object that
was foreign to this bush. He took a deep breath.
His nostrils picked up the faint but distinctive
aroma of burnt oil. Not from the bike. This was
different, the noxious smell made by an engine that
had leaked oil on to a hot exhaust pipe.

The bike's wheel hit something, and wood
snapped. He cursed silently and leaned forward,
hand outstretched. He touched the branch of a
fallen tree and traced it to the trunk. With great
care, he leaned the bike against the tree and groped
his way to the exposed roots. The oily smell was
stronger, more pungent. He crept forward a few
paces. Now he could define a lighter shadow: a white
object, wide and low and square at the edges.

The car. There was no sign of another person.
No whispered plea for help. No squealing from a
bound and gagged woman.

Kelly had the torch in his shoulder bag but dared not use it. He moved forward until his fingers touched the car. He rapped the window.

'Laura?'

From behind him a light flashed. He spun around and the beam shone in his eyes. 'Magnus! He's here.' It was a woman, shrieking. 'Quick!'

Laura.

'For God's sake,' Kelly said, his voice hushed but urgent. He stumbled towards the light. 'It's me. Turn off that damned thing and let's get out of here.'

The light retreated. 'Magnus!' She was moving backwards and fell.

Kelly could hear the sound of boots crashing through the bush. He reached Laura. The torch had spilled from her hand and shone on her face. She was terrified. What had that man done to her?

He bent down. 'You're all right, you're safe, it's me, darling, me — Kelly — I've come to take you away.' The words gushed out, each thought tripping on the last.

With flailing fists, she hammered his chest.

'Stop.' The man had a torch. The beam, weak at this distance, hit the car, swung left, then right and settled on Kelly's bent back. 'I have a gun, Hunnicutt. Stand up. Raise your hands.'

Kelly fell on Laura and grabbed her shoulders. She was screaming. My God, he thought, she's doped. The bastard's drugged her. He rolled with her. He heard the crack of a rifle and the whine of a bullet. Even as he rolled and clutched her and felt her fingers clawing his face, he knew that it was a deliberate miss; a warning shot. They rolled through a bush. She was screaming and sobbing, and punching and scratching him.

Another shot, another command to stand up, but now the man couldn't see him; the torch was slashing the bush above their heads. They rolled down an incline, then over the ridged roots of a broad tree. Shielded by the tree, Kelly dragged Laura to her feet. She was making strange, angry, growling sounds. He slapped her.

'Calm down. Do what I say.' He grabbed her hands. 'We can get away. You'll be safe. Just follow me. Ready? Run.'

'No!' she screamed. 'Magnus!'

He lifted her, kicking and punching, on to his shoulder and set off in a loping, awkward run for the bike. He crashed through a bush that tore at his legs and brought him down on one knee. He got up and ran several steps but stumbled on a root and fell. Another bullet whistled through the night.

For a moment, Kelly stayed on his knees, desperately sucking in air. He held Laura by the wrist. 'For God's sake, it's me,' he gasped. 'Laura, what's he done to you?' She wrenched herself free. He had to let her go; he couldn't carry her any further, could never put her on the bike like this.

She blundered towards the torch. 'Here.' She was waving her hands like a drowning person. 'He's over here.'

The torch flashed through the bush, too high to pick out Kelly but bright enough to show him the way. He slithered behind a tree, under a bush, and around the clumps of grass, dodging the dancing beam, scrambling towards the fallen tree that supported the bike.

He saw a flash of chrome and ran straight towards it. The torch beam was above him, beside him, on him.

'Stop!'

He threw himself forward. The rifle barked twice. The man began shouting orders, not to him but to Laura. The beam looped through the tallest branches of the trees, then descended and searched for him. The man had handed the torch to Laura. She was helping him. The bastard. What had he *done* to her?

The log was in front of him, with the motorbike's shiny handlebars and headlamp winking back at the probing light. Kelly dived over the tree, somersaulted on the ground and, rising quickly, grabbed the handlebars. He spun the bike away from the tree, jabbed at the starter and jumped on.

The torch beam was too high. The man was shouting, 'Lower, lower'.

The only discernible path led to the fire. Monica was standing beside her truck, partly shielded by its open door, peering towards the place where the torch flashed and the gun had been spitting fire. Body bent forward, head low like a racer, Kelly rode towards her, weaving between the clear silhouettes of the trees.

Again the rifle sounded. With a scream of tearing metal, the front wheel wobbled violently and he almost fell. The bullet had torn through the mudguard. He swerved to the left, almost toppling over as the bike plunged down a steep slope. Feet down to steady the machine, he accelerated up the other side, monowheeling through a clump of bushes until he brought the front tyre down to earth. He almost fell, regained his balance and began a series of zigzag turns.

He didn't hear the next shot but felt it. The bullet hit the engine somewhere, and the bike shuddered and clanged as though it had struck a rock. It still ran. He turned sharply in the other direction.

The man was a great shot. He was aiming at the bike, not the rider. But how was he seeing him so clearly? Then he realised — the campfire. Kelly was riding between the shooter and the fire, weaving backwards and forwards, presenting a target as clearly defined as a mechanical duck in a shooting gallery. Immediately, Kelly turned at ninety degrees, switched on the headlight, and selected a path away from Monica's camp. He gunned the bike through the bush. Off with the light. He'd memorised the track. A little to the right and he heard the crunch of bushes under the wheels. Big trunks flashed past. Slightly to the left. More bushes. A leap over a mound. Then he was in clearer country and turned left, away from the rifle. He slowed; no point in hitting a stump and breaking a leg.

There was no more shooting. He looked back. The lights of the car were turned on. The man was going to chase him.

Ahead of him, a bright light bobbed on the horizon. The police were coming back. The lights were a brilliant pinpoint: dazzling white with a sporadic blue flash. They must have heard the shooting. Kelly braked and twisted in the saddle. Behind him, the Fairlane was flying, its lights slicing the air as the driver pounded the big car over rough ground in an effort to catch Kelly before the police got to him.

Kelly turned left, back to the Cooper, back into the trees. He'd cross the river, where neither vehicle could follow.

Among the trees, he could see nothing and slowed to a walking pace, trailing one foot to steady himself. He rammed a log and fell. He picked up the bike and manhandled it to clear ground. Glancing back, he could see that the Fairlane was close, maybe two hundred metres behind; but the police vehicle was still a kilometre or more away. He could hear the plaintive wail of a siren.

Suddenly, he was descending. The front wheel slithered in sand. This was the river bank, he realised; but he braked too violently, and the bike skidded sideways and fell on him. He crawled clear, lifted the bike back on its wheels and peered into

247

the gloom. There were no reflections. No water. He had chanced upon a dry part of the river. Slowly, he let the bike trickle forward, using his feet to paddle alongside, and to help maintain his balance at such a slow pace.

He was in reeds. A lignum swamp. The reeds were tall, twice his height, and they snatched at his knees and slapped his cheeks. He opened the throttle to get more power and raised one hand to protect his face. The front wheel turned violently and he was thrown forward. Scrambling to his feet, he picked up the bike and rode on, keeping both hands on the handlebars and suffering the slaps and slashes as the bike carved a path through the swamp.

The motor began to slow. And stink. It smelled of cooked oil and hot metal. With a final squeak of protest, it stopped. Kelly got off and let it fall. The bullet had put a hole in some vital part and the oil had drained out. The motor had seized.

Grabbing his bag, he blundered on, becoming entangled in dense clusters of lignum, occasionally sinking ankle deep in mud. A light flashed over his head. He stopped, frightened that he would give away his position by stirring the reeds.

The siren was strong now. He heard a male voice curse; heard the sharp click of a rifle bolt and the slam of a bootlid, then the drone of a dying siren.

The squeal of brakes. The clunk of a door. 'All right, get away from that car,' a strong voice demanded.

'And keep your hands in the air,' a second voice added.

'Thank heavens you're here.' It was Laura.

'Where's the man you've been travelling with, lady?'

'I don't know.' She sounded, Kelly thought, exactly like a woman close to hysteria. Maybe the effects of the drug were wearing off. He wanted to be with her, to calm and reassure her.

'He just came out of the bush and tried to shoot me,' she said. 'I was with the car and Magnus tried to help me and he kept shooting at Magnus...'

'No,' Kelly said to himself, prompting her to get the story right.

The first policeman said, 'Just a minute, lady. Try and calm down. Who came out of the bush? Who tried to shoot you?'

'My husband.'

'And who is that?' The voice was slow, anticipating one answer.

'The man you're looking for. Kelso Hunnicutt.'

'Oh Jesus, Laura,' Kelly whispered and thumped his forehead.

The second policeman said, 'And what happened to your friend, lady? What did you say his name was?'

'Magnus. He got hit on the head. Such a terrible blow.' She sucked in her breath in distress. 'He's back there somewhere, unconscious. Oh, thank God you came along. I thought Kelly was going to kill me. He had this gun and he forced me to get in the car and he kept on saying all these wild things. He brought me here and when...'

She didn't have to finish. Kelly heard two thuds, two grunting sounds, and two heavy noises, like sacks falling.

After a few seconds' silence, Laura said, 'My God, that was quick'.

The man grunted. 'You were good.'

'So what about Kelly?'

There was a metallic click. 'I'd say he's gone, for the time being. Don't worry. He won't get far on that thing. Quick, help me do this.'

Kelly crawled towards the far bank.

24

The fire had not died; it had been deliberately extinguished, doused with water to blacken the last glowing embers. Monica Tate did not want to attract any more visitors. Kelly stayed crouched against the tree for several minutes until he could distinguish the features of her camp. He saw pots and pans near the mound which had been the campfire; a folding kitchen-table laden with jars, cans and bottles; an easel where she had been drawing. There was no sign of Monica. The tailgate of the truck was open. She was sleeping inside.

He did one cautious lap of the site, moving from tree to tree, listening for sounds that might indicate a trap. Once he thought he heard a light cough from the truck, but that was all.

All night the clouds had been thick. Now, only a few hours before dawn, they thinned and became dappled, then parted to reveal a fine slice of moon. Around Kelly, the land, the trees, even Monica's truck, were bathed in a ghostly blue. For a full ten minutes he watched the campsite from behind the trunk of a gnarled old giant which lifted arthritic limbs towards the moon. When satisfied that he was the only one observing the camp, Kelly moved to some shrubs near the truck, waited one more minute and crept to the tailgate.

She was asleep in the back, legs drawn up into

her body and covered untidily by a couple of blankets. He flashed his torch on her face. Gently, he shook her foot. She sat up, eyes wide in fright.

'Would you mind moving your truck?' he said, briefly shining the torch on his face. 'I want to take some pictures and you've parked right on my spot.'

She seemed shocked, then half smiled. Throwing aside the blankets, she shuffled forward until her legs dangled over the back of the truck. She leaned out and looked around. 'Are you on your own?' she whispered.

'Yes.'

'What are you doing here?'

He switched off the torch and stood back, in a place where he was well lit by the moon. 'I guess I'm looking for somewhere to hide. Even someone to talk to. I've had a difficult few days since I saw you.'

'You're not David whatever-his-name-is.'

'Correct. I'm Kelso Hunnicutt.'

She slid to the ground. 'The police are looking for you.'

He made a short sardonic grunt.

'Did you do what they said you did?'

'No.'

She pursed her lips. 'Have you got a machine gun and explosives in your Landcruiser?'

'I haven't even got a Landcruiser any more.' He tried to smile cheerfully. 'I had a motorbike for a while but that got shot from under me. Now there's just me.'

'Why do they think you killed someone?'

'I don't know. They've been chasing me all over the place.'

She avoided his eyes. Rubbing her hands to counter the cold, she walked to the remains of the dead fire. 'Do you want coffee or tea?'

'I drank water from the last water hole. But I'm starving.'

251

'There's a man looking for you too.'

'I know.'

'Who is he?'

'I don't know.'

'He has a woman with him.'

'She's my wife.'

She looked up quickly, then bent to retrieve a blackened billy can. 'I can make coffee on a gas stove. It will only take a few minutes. You should have a hot drink. I've got fruit cake. Coffee and cake. Will that do?'

'Wonderful.' He folded his arms to keep out the cold and turned in a slow circle, checking the trees for movement.

'Why is your wife with that man?'

He shook his head. 'I don't know.'

'There's not much you do know, is there?'

'No. She was with me until Tibooburra. She was going to catch a plane home. He must have grabbed her there.' Kelly shivered. He hadn't felt cold until now. 'I think he must have drugged her or done something to her. She's behaving so strangely.' Monica looked at him and Kelly thought he saw disbelief. Maybe pity. 'He's after the diamonds. Which I don't have. He certainly thinks I've got them, and he thinks I killed that man in Melbourne.'

'Everyone seems to think that.' She put the little stove in the back of her truck to shield the light. She struck a match and a crater of blue hissed into life. 'They were here a couple of hours ago.'

'I know. I saw them, remember? That was me on the bike.'

'No, no. Since then.' They had returned with a story about the man being struck down from behind. According to them, he had only just recovered consciousness. The woman, Monica added, said Kelso Hunnicutt had done it. He had tried to kill her. She seemed confused.

252

'I think she's drugged.' He fingered the scratches on his cheek. 'How long ago was this?'

She lifted a shoulder. 'Three, maybe four hours. They were in the big white car. The police have been here again, too.'

Instinctively he moved into the shadow cast by the truck's tailgate. Since abandoning the bike, he had seen only the Fairlane pass, but he had walked most of the way below the level of the Cooper's banks. He said, 'You're sure it was the police? The same ones?'

Her head tilted in curiosity. 'Of course.'

'When was that?'

'Possibly an hour and a half after the others.'

'What did they say?'

'Almost nothing. They just whizzed into the camp, shone their light on the truck and wanted to know if I was all right. Then they blasted off. They seemed in a hurry to get into town.'

'How did they look?'

She was puzzled. 'All I saw was the light shining in my eyes. Why?'

'Because I think that man attacked them and flattened them both. You know, knocked them out.' He told her what he had heard. 'I didn't see anything. I was hiding in the reeds but there were noises like two men falling, and then that man and Laura were talking.'

She was silent for some time, frowning, pursing her lips, stroking her nose. She said, 'What did you do?'

'Got out of there before he tracked me across the river. He's a pretty good shot with that rifle of his.'

'That man told me you did all the shooting.' She spoke slowly, not accusing but giving him time to change his story. 'According to him, you were firing at them, you hit him on the head, you threatened

253

to kill the woman... I mean, your wife. They said you did all those things.'

'Sure. You can see my gun.' He raised his empty hands, then touched the scratches on his face. 'She did this to me over there.' He nodded towards the distant bushes where he had found the car. 'That was when I was trying to *rescue* her.' He grunted and stared into the ground. 'He's done something terrible to Laura to make her behave like that. God knows what.'

She shook her head. 'I don't know what to believe.'

'Me either.' Kelly squatted on the ground. 'I don't know who this man is. By the voice, I'd say he's a South African. Possibly a mercenary. Probably knows diamonds and wants Kolvenbach's lot for himself. What I *do* know is that he's ruthless. I'm dead if he catches me. And probably dead if anyone else catches me, too, because I think the police are in the mood to shoot first and ask questions afterwards.'

'That man kept holding his head as though he'd been hit. Like this.' She put a hand to the back of her head and grimaced in mock pain.

Kelly nodded. 'It's all part of the act. He's going to say he was unconscious when those two policemen were attacked, but he was there. He must have done it. Laura said, "My God, that was quick", or something like that to him.'

Monica joined him in staring at the ground. 'You know who's going to get the blame for that. Everyone'll hold you responsible for whatever happened to those two policemen.'

'Sure. I've been blamed for everything else.'

She stood, stretched her arms and gazed up at the moon and the scudding clouds. 'So what are you going to do?'

'Get away, if I can. Hide somewhere. I've left a

254

Landcruiser — not mine, but another one — up north at an outstation.' He saw the question on her face. 'Mine's hidden in Queensland. I stole this one.'

'I see.' The water was beginning to boil and she turned down the gas. 'What will you do after you get away from here?'

'Try and sort this mess out.' He laughed bitterly. 'Would you believe this started as a drunken wager?' He told her about the bet. Listening intently and shaking her head every now and then, she rattled through a box until she found a second enamelled mug, a coffee jar, spoons, powdered milk, and sugar. He was still talking as she measured out the coffee and cut several large slices of fruit cake.

'It sounds to me as though you were set up.'

He shook his head. 'I am totally confused. I want to get to a phone and ring Gerry. I tried to phone him once but I got interrupted. He might be able to sort things out for me in Melbourne. I need someone there to ask a few questions.'

'This Gerry... he's a good friend?'

'We've been partners for years.' Not waiting for the coffee, he bit into the fruit cake.

She turned off the gas. 'I want to get out of this place. I'm tired of armed men calling in at all hours. They frighten me and they'll frighten away the birds.' She took a deep breath. 'Like a lift?'

He straightened his back. 'Where to?'

'Where are you heading?'

He nodded down river. 'Back to the old Landcruiser. Then further along the Cooper. I know some pretty remote places.'

She waved a hand, like a teacher hurriedly erasing a chalked slate. 'The police have got a plane coming up in the morning. The sergeant told me. More men in cars too. Now these are South Australian policemen, which means they'll search South

Australian territory, which means the Cooper. They'll find you within a day or two.' She filled his cup, then hers. 'Do you know what you should do?'

He waited, mouth full of cake. He was exhausted and his head was sore from Laura's scratches.

'Get as far away from here as you can. And quickly. Go somewhere where there are masses of people. They've been looking for you in isolated places. They won't expect you to hide among crowds. And you need to be near a telephone so you can ring your friend, the one who's going to straighten things out for you.'

As she expounded her theory, his head bobbed up and down, agreeing with the logic. 'If you could just take me up as far as the old Landcruiser...'

'Do you need anything from it?'

'It's full of my gear.'

'The explosives and the machine gun?' There was a hint of a smile.

'You can have a look for yourself.' He took a long draught of coffee and sighed with satisfaction. 'But if you could take me there — it's about a hundred kilometres — that would be terrific.'

She was shaking her head. 'You're not going to drive that thing another inch. You can get what you need out of it but you're staying with me. With me you've got a chance to get away from here. On your own, you're a dead rooster.'

He ate more cake. 'Where are we going?'

'Well, I've got to get back to Melbourne. So have you, if you want to clear yourself.'

He caught a crumb that had escaped his mouth. 'We can't go south or east. The roads would be crawling with police. They've even got helicopters looking for me.'

'So where do we go?'

'North. I know a way.' He looked up. 'You'd really do this for me?'

She avoided his eyes. 'I don't think you killed anyone.'

'I didn't. They say I did; they say they found all sorts of evidence that says I did — my footprints, a rifle of mine, things like that — but I didn't.'

She glanced doubtfully at him, seemingly more convinced by her intuition than his words. 'I don't like that big man,' she said. 'He frightens me.'

'He scares me too.' He grinned.

'I was thinking we should just drive on down to Adelaide. I could hide you in the back.'

'And meet all these police rushing up to give their mates a hand? No, we'll do the grand-circle route. Up north towards Mount Isa and then either east to the Queensland coast or west towards Tennant Creek. Probably the latter.'

'Into the Northern Territory.' She got up and began gathering her things. 'Then where?'

'Wherever seems best. It depends where the police are searching. Maybe we'd head south through Alice Springs.'

'That's a hell of a roundabout way to go home.'

'But it could be safer.'

She was clearing the table and stopped. 'Who'd pay for the petrol?'

'I would. The fuel's on me. The food too. You provide the vehicle. I look after everything else.'

She wrinkled her mouth in doubt. 'How long would it take?'

'Depends on how fast we drive.'

'That big man who's got your wife and who's after the diamonds... he's going to keep on looking for you. He's got an aeroplane.'

Kelly took a slow, satisfying drink of coffee. 'I reckon he won't be flying anywhere for a day or so.'

'Oh?' She scratched her hair. 'What did you do to his plane?'

'Let a couple of tyres down.'

She seemed disappointed. 'He'll pump them up again.'

'Not these tyres.'

Her head bobbed forward, like a bird pecking at seed. 'So you've been stealing cars and sabotaging planes since I last saw you.'

'I also pinched the bike.'

More pecking. She took a deep breath, checked that the moon was still there, and said, 'Tell me, what should I call you? Mr Hunnicutt? Kelso?'

'Kelly.'

'Good.' She nodded approval. 'Well, Kelly, if you got up off your bum and helped me pack, we'd be out of here twice as fast.'

Kolvenbach hadn't slept and he was still angry. His plane was crippled and even if he could get new tyres sent up quickly on a charter flight, he'd be stuck in Innamincka for at least a day. He paced the room, muttering to himself.

From the smaller bed, Laura said, 'Look, they believed you'.

'It's not that. It's that damned husband of yours. Now they'll catch him before I do.'

'Maybe not.'

He grunted. The police were already off, searching for Hunnicutt.

'Magnus, you're lucky you're not behind bars.'

'Those police are fools.'

'Well that's your good luck. Just thank God they weren't a pack of Albert Einsteins.'

He sat on his bed. The damned cut stung. He touched it again and checked his hand for blood. He took a deep breath. She was right. The police had swallowed their story, never doubting it was Hunnicutt who had attacked them, destroyed their radio and manacled the sergeant to the bumper bar of the Toyota. Believing that, they had readily accepted his story. After all, he was a fellow victim. When they burst into the room, Laura had been bathing the cut behind his ear. Had they looked closely, they might have seen that it was made by a sharp knife run lightly across the skin; but they hadn't bothered. The blood on the shirt, the pained and still dazed expression on the face were sufficient.

They were stunned to find he was the dead man's brother. They expressed sympathy, but warned him off the hunt.

'Your comrades in New South Wales and Queensland haven't been doing too well,' Kolvenbach had said, taking care to blame other forces for past failures, and narrowing his eyes in pain.

'We'll get him. You just keep out of it.' They had told him not to leave the motel and then driven off.

Kolvenbach got up and walked a few paces to the wall with the faded picture of Mount Kosciusko. He turned to face Laura. 'He won't get far on that bike. I'm sure I hit it.'

'Kelly hasn't ridden a bike for years.' She kept her eyes closed. 'He'll probably fall off.'

'He seemed pretty damned good on it to me.'

'If you've hit the bike like you reckon, it'll run out of petrol or something and you'll soon find him.'

'Maybe not before the police.'

'If you hit the bike, he won't get far which means he'll have to hide somewhere along the river. Probably near here. The police don't know that. They'll think he's ridden off, trying to get as far away as possible. Let them go haring off into the distance. You can look for him around here.'

He swung back to face Mount Kosciusko.

'I wish you'd go to bed,' she said. 'All of this standing and walking backwards and forwards is driving me crazy. At least take your boots off.'

He walked to her bed and bent to grab her wrist.

'You were very cool tonight.' She tried to shake free of his grip. He held on. 'Very impressive,' he continued. 'Very inventive. You think quickly in an emergency. What you said back at the river was clever.'

She turned her head like someone anxious to sleep. She didn't like the way he was looking at her. This praise was the prelude to one massive 'however...'

'And the way you behaved when they came here... You're a very good actress. Totally convincing.'

'Thank you.' It was the whisper of a person who is almost asleep.

'Damn you, look at me.' He shook her wrist.

Slowly, she turned round to face him. He sat beside her on the bed. 'You were so clever, in fact, such an accomplished actress, that I've been thinking.'

'You're always thinking. You should try sleeping.'

'Tell me, Laura,' he said softly, reaching for her other arm and pulling her so that she had to face him, 'are you in league with that husband of yours?'

She closed her eyes and moaned. 'Not that again, please.'

'Did the two of you plan all this? Or did you plan it and did he merely execute your plan?'

She tried to shake free but quickly gave up. 'You've got the strength of a gorilla and the brains of one. You were out there tonight when he attacked me. You heard me calling to you. You heard me shouting out where he was.'

He let her go but sat with an arm on either side of her, pinning her to the bed.

'He got away, didn't he? What were you whispering in his ear while you two were rolling in the grass? What sweet words did he say to you?'

260

'Nothing, you stupid bastard.'

'Why was it that when I gave you the torch, you kept shining it in the trees, not on him?'

'Because I'm not good at aiming torches. Because you kept shouting at me and pushing me on the shoulder. Because Kelly had been hitting me and rolling on me and I was winded. Because I couldn't see him. Because I'd had a fright and my hands were shaking. Enough reasons?' She thumped his chest with both fists. 'For Christ's sake, Magnus, who do you think I am? Wonder Woman?'

'Watching you, I was thinking,' he said, as though she had not spoken, 'that here is a woman with the brains and the cool head necessary to plan something like the murder of my brother and the theft of a few million dollars' worth of diamonds. I was thinking that maybe you were cleverer than your husband. I was thinking that he was no more than the means of carrying out your scheme.'

She folded her arms. 'You were thinking all that?'

'Yes.'

'You're nuts. I'm going home.' She tried to sit up.

He pressed her against the bed. He needed only one hand. 'I was also thinking that you were wasted with a man like that. With any other man, in fact.'

She went limp. 'Any other man except you. Is that what you're saying?'

'The other day, I was thinking how good you'd be in Africa.'

'Good at what?'

'At running safaris. At handling clients, organising and controlling the staff, making things work properly. I have no one like that.'

She smiled. 'And who'd shoot the lions?'

'Don't mock me.' He held her shoulders. 'Tell me, did your husband plan this thing on his own?'

She tried to prise one hand loose. No hope.

'Was it his idea and did he ask you to help him?'

She tried to bite his hand. He seized her jaw. 'Tell me. If you didn't plan it in the first place, if you weren't the mastermind, did he come to you and seek your expert assistance? He'd know the way you think. He'd value your skills.' He shook her. 'Did he promise to give you a percentage? Was that it?'

Again she tried to bite him.

He moved her face from side to side. 'And he has no partner? This other woman, for instance?'

He took his hand away and she glared up at him, still defiant. 'I don't know. Kelly hasn't told me a thing. I thought you believed me.'

He sat back and folded his arms. 'Tonight your performance under pressure, your ability to improvise and come up with such fanciful, yet logical stories impressed me. And so I thought: if she can invent such plausible lies for the police, why couldn't she have been lying to me? If she can make up, on the spur of the moment, a tale that satisfies an angry policeman, why couldn't she make up a tale that would fool a simple bush fellow like myself?'

She laughed. 'You're about as simple as a Swiss watch.'

Once more he grabbed a wrist. 'You're hurting me,' she said, but he ignored her.

'You're either a magnificent woman, the sort I need, the sort of partner I've been looking for, or you're a devious, scheming witch.'

She looked away. 'Take your pick.'

With a finger he turned her face until their eyes met. 'Which one?'

She shrugged. 'All this talk bores me.'

He put his hand behind her and lifted her towards him. 'Does this bore you?'

He kissed her. It was a gentler sensation than she might have anticipated. His lips were rough and

262

his skin was covered by a bristly stubble but the act itself was tender. He continued to hold her close.

'No,' she said, breathing into his chest. 'It doesn't bore me.'

'Good.'

'But it does surprise me.'

'Why? Because the monster shows he is human?'

'No.' She let her nose rub the open flap of his shirt. 'I thought you did only one thing at a time. I thought now was the time to hunt a man, not do something like this.'

He spoke into her hair. 'We have no means of moving from here. There will be no hunting for a while.'

Gently, he laid her head on the pillow. He went to the wall and turned off the light. She lay there, not moving, while he stood above her and slowly removed the belt from his trousers.

25

Before dawn, they reached the old Landcruiser. Kelly, who had been struggling to stay awake, got out and, stumbling with fatigue, began transferring his gear into Monica's truck. At first she was hesitant and stood back as though expecting to see him emerge with a case of TNT, but the most aggressive things she saw were a few digging tools and a box of fish hooks.

'No machine gun?'

He was carrying the final item, a drum of petrol, and shook his head. 'That was silly. I said that to a man I gave a lift to. The police believed it.'

'My father always said never joke with a policeman.'

'Wise man.'

'My father was a drunkard who liked telling jokes. He was arrested a lot.'

Not knowing how to respond, Kelly said, 'Ready to go?' He avoided her eyes by looking at the eastern sky. The morning star was fading.

'As soon as I have a wee.' She went behind the shed. 'What will you do about the motorbike?' she called out.

'Let them know where it is, I suppose. And then pay whatever I owe them.' He gave the Landcruiser a friendly pat. 'The same as I'll do with the bloke who owns this.'

'That's if you're in a position to pay.' She hurried back, still adjusting her pants. 'Come on. I'll drive. You sleep. First, tell me where to go.'

Kolvenbach rang early and Gerry Montague, still in his pyjamas, was in his study and thinking about what the man had said. The plane was sabotaged. Kelly was still loose. And on a motorcycle. He wouldn't last long. There was a good chance the police would get to him first.

The phone rang again.

McCarthy. 'That was an interesting call, wasn't it? Kolvenbach's brother. Now, you haven't been telling me about him. More secrets, old chum?'

'You bastard, George.'

McCarthy laughed. 'We've been through that, Gerry. I'll be around at ten. Got a proposition for you. Don't go away.'

Ten. Montague dressed quickly. He had to ring the diamond broker and he couldn't do it from the apartment, now that he was certain George McCarthy was tapping his line.

He went out the back, through the garage. He took the Porsche and drove quickly along a maze of lanes and small streets. The engine ran roughly, but he knew what caused that; he'd have it fixed when this business was over. He stopped after a few kilometres to check his mirror, then, seeing no following car, drove off at a more modest pace.

He went north and followed the Yarra to Hawthorn. He saw a telephone box in a side street, checked his mirror, and parked.

The broker was anxious. He'd heard from no one. Not even Laura? No one. The man sounded genuine. Montague arranged to meet him that night, with the diamonds.

Montague rang Mary Calibrano and told her he'd be late at the office. Then he rang Harry Turner, the accountant, to see if he'd had any luck tracking down the money Kelly had allegedly stolen. He used the word allegedly because, after all, he was still Kelly's most loyal friend. All Turner was sure of was that the money had gone. It surely has, and it will come in handy, Montague thought, and hung up.

He drove back to the apartment, parked in the garage and went upstairs to wait for George McCarthy.

McCarthy had a notebook. Just like a private detective hired to follow a straying wife, he began to read. 'At 8.33, subject entered garage and started up car. A Porsche Turbo.' He looked up. 'Want the registration number?'

Montague's face faded to white.

'Subject drove in an irregular pattern until he reached... no, we can skip all this.' He flipped over a page. 'Turned left off Church Street and stopped at phone booth. Called three numbers. Spoke to his secretary and said he'd be late. Spoke to Harry...' McCarthy looked up. 'That's your accountant, isn't it? Yes, of course. Harry Turner.' He put down the book. 'Anyhow, you asked old Harry if he'd found any trace of the money your esteemed partner absconded with. Negative. Which means you're still in deep shit.' He smiled. 'Or are you?'

Montague leaned back, eyes closed, face tilted towards the ceiling.

'Praying, old boy?' McCarthy's stomach rose and fell like a passing wave. 'It's the other phone call that interests me, Gerry. To someone called Lucas. He wanted to know where you'd been, did he? And you were concerned about Laura. Laura?' He waited until Montague opened his eyes and let them slide towards him. 'Isn't that Mrs Hunnicutt, the wife of your esteemed but missing partner? And did we hear you mention the word diamonds?'

A long silence, during which neither man took his eyes off the other, ended when another wave passed over McCarthy's belly. A rumbling sound emerged. He patted his mouth.

'What an interesting morning, Gerry. First, we discover Kolvenbach has a brother and you've got some sort of deal going with him. Then I check with a friend of mine at police headquarters and it transpires that this second Kolvenbach...' He reopened his book and checked. '... by the name of Magnus Rickard Kolvenbach, has taken the company plane and is presently at some place called Innamincka, where the police have been talking to him and where someone, presumably your close friend Kelso Hunnicutt, has put holes in the tyres of his expensive flying machine. And now I find that you're talking to a man called Lucas who's interested in diamonds and is wondering why he hasn't seen you; and that you're concerned about Hunnicutt's wife.' He smiled. 'And you've made an appointment to see this Lucas tonight. You did say, "I'll bring the diamonds", didn't you?'

Montague had difficulty swallowing. 'What do you want, George?'

'Before I tell you, let me put a few things to you, just to show you what a clever bloke I am. If I'm wrong, correct me, eh?' He went on without waiting. 'You've got the diamonds. I don't know what this Hunnicutt character is doing racing around the country, dodging police and putting holes in the tyres of people's planes, but you've got the diamonds. Right?'

Montague blinked.

'One blink for yes, two for no? Okay, let's go on. Who's got the papers that our friend in Canberra is so interested in? You? Or is it Hunnicutt, and is that why this second Kolvenbach is up there trying to catch him? To hell with the diamonds, he wants those papers. Is that it?'

Montague got up. 'I need a drink.'

'Get me a beer, will you, Gerry?'

'What's all this leading up to, George?'

'Simple. You've got the diamonds. Maybe you were involved in the killing.' He waited but Montague had his back to him and said nothing. 'Look, it doesn't matter to me whether your mate shot Kolvenbach or Blind Freddie did it, but speaking off the top of my head, the most likely scenario is that Hunnicutt pulled the trigger and then either dropped the bag of diamonds or tossed them to you. I'm not interested in who shot who. I'm interested in the diamonds. And I'm very interested in the meeting you've got with this Lucas character tonight. I might go in your place.'

Montague turned. 'The diamonds aren't yours, George. Hands off.'

McCarthy opened his mouth as though whistling. 'Oh, but you're wrong. Everything's mine now. Do you know what I'm going to do?'

Montague handed him the beer.

'I'm going to sit down and you're going to sit down and we're going to start from the beginning and you're going to tell me the truth. Now, won't that be a change? We're going to forget all that nonsense you've been feeding me. This time, there'll be nothing but the truth. A nice game of truth or consequences, played to my rules.' He examined the beer can, as though suspecting poison. He sniffed the opened top. 'You're a real character, Gerry. A gem. Every time you swear to God that what you're about to tell me is the truth and nothing but the truth, you come up with another heap of bullshit. You're wasted in the film business. You should have been writing fairy stories.'

Montague slumped in a chair.

'Now, before we start the game,' McCarthy said, still eyeing the can, 'you and I are going to run through the facts. At least, today's version of the facts.' He lifted the book and waved it at Montague. 'I know a few more things I haven't mentioned, so be warned. If I hear some fanciful tale that has the smell of make-believe about it, I'll stop being polite and go straight into truth or consequences.'

Montague, a little more settled now, sighed. 'What are you talking about, George?'

'Spiro's outside. He's the footballer with a taste for ears. Remember?' He waved an apologetic hand. 'Of course you remember. He's the man who saved your neck just the other day. Very strong fellow. Well, if I'm not happy with the trend in our conversation, I'm going to call Spiro in. Then I'm going to start again. Every time you don't answer, or don't give me a satisfactory answer, I'm going to turn Spiro loose. First, he'll bite off one ear, then the other.'

Montague laughed.

Up shot McCarthy's eyebrows. 'I'm pleased you've still got your sense of humour. You'll need it.'

Montague managed to retain the smile. 'Bite off my ears?'

'You will have a choice.' McCarthy leaned forward. 'You can nominate which one you'd like to lose first.'

Nervously, Montague scratched the back of one hand. 'George, this is a very sick joke.'

'No joke, my old mate. You see, after Spiro bites off your ears, he'll break your fingers, one at a time. If you're still in the mood for lying to me, he'll take off your shoes and socks and start down there. Ready?'

Montague stood. 'You wouldn't.'

'But Spiro would. He likes doing that sort of thing. I've seen him do it. He's good. This trick of his with the ears is a bit messy but the way he breaks fingers is remarkable. Clean. Quick. Just like snapping a pencil in half.' He closed his eyes in admiration. 'He's never bitten anyone's balls off but I think he'd like to try that sometime, too.' McCarthy paused to sip his beer. 'Remember that visitor you had the other night? He's not hearing too well at the moment and he won't be signing any cheques for a while.' He wiped froth from his lips. 'Now, let's start with a simple question. Where are the diamonds?'

An hour later, McCarthy had twelve pages of notes and Montague still had his ears. There were a few lies, either through omission or inventive fabrication but to Montague's relief, McCarthy seemed to have accepted it all. The main lie was that Hunnicutt had shot Kolvenbach and then given the diamonds to his wife, who was in league with him. But she had been shocked by the killing — she hadn't expected that — panicked and handed the diamonds to the only man she trusted — Montague. She had since disappeared and he had no idea where she was.

'We'll get rid of her,' McCarthy announced. 'Let's hope that either this brother of Kolvenbach's or the police catch up with Hunnicutt and dispose of him quick smart. In the meantime, I'll get someone on the job of tracking down Mrs Hunnicutt. We'll make it look like suicide.'

Montague took a deep breath. He needed time to think, but having Laura out of the way could be advantageous. There'd be no question of sharing anything with her and he didn't want her coming back and confronting McCarthy and thereby causing him to end up with no ears. 'You're a callous bastard, George,' he said.

'Indeed, but I do the things that are necessary.

And this has to be done. We don't want a hysterical woman running around telling people she handed you a bag of diamonds, do we?' He reached over to pat Montague's knee. 'Don't worry. I'll put a good man on to the job. He'll find her and dispose of her. There'll be no questions.'

The police sergeant was grey-faced from weariness. He rested his bandaged head in his hands. They'd searched for Hunnicutt but found no trace of him or the motorcycle.

'There's one thing I should have asked you earlier, Mrs Hunnicutt.' He drank some of the tea that Laura had made for him. 'I didn't think of it, frankly. I still felt as though a ton of bricks had landed on my head and the constable and I were in a hurry to get back on your husband's trail, so I overlooked it.'

'What was the question?' Laura sat demurely in a corner of the motel dining room, hands folded on her lap.

'What are you doing out here with Mr Kolvenbach?'

Her face flushed. 'I thought you'd ask. It's a little embarrassing, really.'

'I have to ask.'

'I understand.' Her hands changed position. 'As you may know, Kelly and I have not been living together. In effect, the marriage failed a long time ago. And I found someone else.'

There was a long silence. The constable rattled his tea cup and glanced at the sergeant.

'It happens,' the sergeant said with the wistful expression of a man who had not found someone else but wanted to.

'The someone I found was Harald Kolvenbach.'

The sergeant looked up. 'The dead man?'

Her teeth gnawed at her lower lip. 'He was a

271

fine person. So gentle. Kelly knew, of course. I think it was one of the reasons why he did what he did. Kelly just went crazy.' The last words were whispered. She coughed, restoring volume. 'It must have been straight after the shooting. Kelly came around to the house where I was staying and kidnapped me. He beat me and theatened me with a knife, then he tied me up and carried me out to his car.'

'On the night of the shooting? Hunnicutt did that?' The sergeant was stony-faced, like a man who has discovered treasure but is intent on keeping his secret. 'Were there any witnesses?'

'I think half the street would have heard. A few of them must have seen me being carried out on Kelly's shoulder.'

'He had you over his shoulder?'

'Tied hand and foot. I was in such pain.'

'What happened then?'

She spread her hands. 'He forced me to stay with him all the way to Tibooburra.'

The second policeman moved closer to the sergeant. 'This explains...' he began but was waved into silence.

The sergeant glanced at Kolvenbach, who was sitting at another table and nursing his head; he seemed to be suffering from a mild concussion. 'Where did you meet up with Mr Kolvenbach and how come you're travelling with him in his plane?'

'I got away from Kelly at Tibooburra while he was putting fuel in the car. By chance, I ran into Magnus. I didn't know he'd flown up there but I knew him of course, and he knew me. He also knew that his brother and I planned to marry when the divorce was through.'

The constable said, 'So he put you in the aircraft?'

'He felt it was the safest place for me. I was in a pretty bad way. I was badly shocked. I was bruised. And thirsty... Kelly hadn't given me any water.'

'Nice bloke,' the constable said.

'You were lucky,' the sergeant said.

'Very.'

'Were you aware that Mr Kolvenbach was intent on trying to track down your husband?'

'He told me.' She glanced at Kolvenbach, who was staring into his coffee. 'Magnus was angry that the police seemed to be doing so badly. He's so impatient. Not like Harald.'

'Well, we don't want any private hunting parties out there trying to do our job for us. This man's dangerous.'

'Magnus is well and truly aware of that now,' she said, and smiled gently at Kolvenbach.

The police left, heading for the airstrip to await the arrival of reinforcements. Kolvenbach went to the window. When the last of the Toyota's dust had settled, he turned slowly. 'You were in love with my brother?'

Her eyes drooped into a bereaved pose. 'We planned to marry. In the spring.'

He walked up to her, put his hands on his hips, swung back his head and laughed. 'You're incredible. You almost had me believing you.'

'Good.'

'Did you ever meet Harald?'

'Never. What was he like?'

He raised a hand above his head. 'Twice as big. Twice as rough. Had no time for the ladies.' He pulled her to her feet and put both arms around her. 'What you said made me jealous but it made their eyes sparkle. Now they are certain they know why Hunnicutt killed my brother.' Gently, he pushed her away until she was at arm's length. 'Why did you feel you needed to say something like that?'

She avoided his eyes. 'I was trying to think of a reason for being with you. One they'd understand. One that would turn their attention away from you and back towards Kelly.'

'You certainly did that.' He grunted, wrestling with an unresolved problem. 'But why would Hunnicutt kill Harald? He didn't have to. Have you thought about that?'

She shook her head and pulled him close to her.

'It doesn't make sense,' he continued, his voice soft and worried. 'He could have taken the diamonds without shooting Harald. It's got him absolutely nowhere. He did such a clumsy job of the robbery that everyone knows who did it.' He stopped. An aircraft was flying overhead.

'The tyres for your plane?' she asked.

'The police.' He twisted his wrist to read his watch. 'Our charter isn't due for another three hours.'

Laura led the way back to their suite. 'So what will we do?' she said, letting her hips sway as she walked in the bright sunlight. 'I know you hate wasting time. So do I, and we'll be stuck here for hours. Any ideas?'

She went straight to the bathroom mirror, where she brushed her hair and checked her make-up. With delicate dabs, she perfumed the skin behind her ears.

He had followed her into the room. 'Why do women do that?'

Their eyes met in the mirror. 'Do what?'

'Put scent on themselves.'

'To smell nice.'

'But you already smell nice. And behind the ears... why such a strange place?'

She laughed softly. 'I don't know. All women do it. And here, too.' She dabbed her throat, stretching her neck in a tantalizing way. 'It makes me feel good.'

He moved closer and lowered his head until his nose tickled her ear. 'I was burning deep inside when you were talking about Harald. You were so convincing that I was feeling jealous. Very jealous.'

274

'That was foolish — but nice.' His hands were on her hips. She put the bottle down and pulled his arms around her.

'I imagined you with him and then I thought about us last night.' He let his tongue explore her ear. 'I nearly went crazy thinking of you doing all those things with my brother. It was a terrible feeling.'

She turned in his arms and touched his lips to silence him.

He nibbled her fingertip, then breathed deeply. 'The perfume smells good. It makes you very desirable.' He squeezed, a little too hard, and she whimpered. 'But it's not my favourite. Do you know the smell I prefer?'

She had to gasp to get her breath back. 'What?'

'You, when you're freshly washed. Just out of the shower. You have a clean, feminine smell. Delicate. Pure.'

She touched the perfumed area behind her ear. 'And I've spoiled it for you?'

Effortlessly, he picked her up and carried her into the shower.

'What are you doing?' She was kicking her legs, but laughing.

'I am going to wash away that artificial aroma and get back to the real you, to the freshly bathed, essential female.'

'You wouldn't dare put me under the shower like this.'

'I would. Right now I'd dare anything.' He kissed her savagely. 'I was watching you in that room. Watching those men too. They couldn't take their eyes off you.'

She kicked harder. 'Don't get me wet. I didn't bring many clothes.'

He turned the shower tap and a few drops of water splashed on the floor. He held her to one side.

'Magnus, please.' She grabbed his shirt and undid a button. 'You'll get wet too.' She undid another button, her fingers working frantically. 'Take it off, please.'

He lowered her into a corner of the recess. She stood still and he knelt to remove her shoes.

'Mustn't get these wet.' He threw them on the floor and began to unhook her skirt. She wriggled to help him pull it over her hips, and let it slide to her ankles. She lifted one foot, then the other, and moaned softly as he pressed his face against her belly.

'Please put the skirt where it won't get wet,' she whispered, and he threw it into the other room. 'Oh Magnus, be careful, that cost a fortune.' Because he was bending and moving so much, she was having trouble with the final shirt button.

'You worry about the wrong things,' he said and, still on his knees, opened her blouse. Working with speed and dexterity, he slid the blouse from her shoulders and tossed it after the skirt.

Without looking up, he undid her bra. With his teeth, he drew her minuscule panties down over one hip, then the other.

She ripped his shirt from him.

Very gently, he slid the panties down her legs and flicked them into the other room. He kicked off his boots and the last of his clothes and rose slowly, pulled her under the dripping shower and letting his tongue track a sensuous, wandering course up her belly, into the navel, between her breasts, around the nipples, along the perfumed throat, up to her lips.

As they kissed, Laura's fingers ran down the hairs of his back and dug into his buttocks. He reached to turn the shower on full force. She stood with her face raised, compliant and trembling, awaiting his next move.

The water beat down. He lifted her until her lips were level with his and he kissed her again. Mouths open, tongues touching, each probed and explored deep within the other. She locked her legs around him.

He pulled back, shaking water from his hair. 'You could have met Harald, you might have been lovers,' he said and gripped her thighs.

'No.'

He spun her slowly under the shower. She leaned back and he kissed each breast, fondling and stroking and squeezing as he kissed.

'True? You were not lovers?'

'No.' She sighed in ecstasy. 'Oh, keep doing that.'

'He was a very impressive man.'

'No man could be more impressive than you.'

He sucked on one nipple, drawing out the breast. He let go and pressed his face against her. 'You have a fantastic body.'

'And you're so strong. I love strength.' She reached down for his erect penis and groaning, lowered herself on to him. 'You feel huge,' she said, and bit his shoulder.

He licked each ear, then her throat. 'You taste better. More like a woman.'

She lifted her face, letting water cascade from her overflowing mouth. Slowly, evenly, she rocked on him. 'Oh God, this is wonderful.'

Abruptly, he stepped from the shower, carrying her into the other room. He lowered her, dripping and protesting, on to the bed.

'Why did you stop?'

'Too quick.'

She lifted a corner of the sodden bedspread. 'But I'm so wet.'

'You feel good wet.'

She let an arm fall limply across her face. 'But Magnus, that was so very, very good.'

'This will be better. And slower.' He sat on the edge of the bed and with ease, lifted her on to him. 'Let me show you a way I learned in Africa...'

Kelly had set a course that took them deep into the northeastern corner of South Australia. It meant crossing the worst of the Stony Desert but it was the one area, he reasoned, where no one would be looking for them. The Queensland police would not cross the State border — even if they were in the region — and the South Australian police, according to the information Monica had been given, were either back at Innamincka or still travelling up the Strzelecki Track. None of them was north of the Cooper. Therefore, he had Monica drive straight up the track to Cordillo Downs and Birdsville. He slept. It was a rag-doll sleep, with his head bobbing on every bump, but he was exhausted and slept until Monica shook him awake a few hours later.

'There's another road,' she said.

He sniffed, rubbed his face and sat up. The upholstery was hot and his cheek streamed with perspiration. He looked around. They were on a sea of stones, with waves of sand rippling its surface. A track came in from their right. It was no more than two sandy ruts with a central ridge of rounded stones, all the colour of burnished bronze. He checked his watch and bent to check the odometer.

'You've come a long way,' he said and stretched his back. To his left was a flat stone, raised on its edge and signwritten in crude white letters: *Bus Stop*. He laughed. 'I know the man who put that there.'

'Where are we?' Her face sagged from weariness.

He jerked his thumb to the right. 'That's the wet-weather road from Betoota. Ever been there?'

She shook her head.

'I thought all you artists would know of Betoota. Russell Drysdale used to go there every year or so, when he felt like painting some really depressing scenery.'

She managed to laugh. 'Any birds?'

'Hawks. Thousands of them. Have we got any water?'

She passed him a flask. 'So where do we go?'

'Left, towards Birdsville.' Anxiously, he peered first left, then right. The view was the same: an unrelenting landscape of polished stones and wind-rippled sand. In the distance, a flock of long-necked birds flew low, stitching an erratic hem on a sky of bleached blue.

Monica followed his gaze. 'Black swans.'

He'd been trying to count. 'Maybe a hundred.' Still watching the birds, he drank more water, then splashed a little on his face. He pulled out a map and showed it to her. 'We're just about in Queensland so we'll have to be careful. I know a way to bypass Birdsville. There's a police station there, so we should go around. Let's swap places. You sleep. I'll drive.'

She seemed reluctant to surrender the wheel.

'I'm a reasonable driver.'

'It's not that. What'll happen if we run into a police roadblock somewhere?'

'We won't.'

'But if we do? I don't want any shooting.'

'Neither do I. I won't do anything to endanger you.'

She ran her tongue across her teeth, made a clucking sound and nodded, her mind made up. 'Okay, but wake me if you think there's going to be any trouble. And won't we need petrol?'

'We've still got a lot in drums. We'll need that later. I reckon we should refuel at Boulia.'

She nodded, meaning she knew the town.

He tapped the map twice. 'Birdsville and Bedourie are too small. People there notice every vehicle that comes into their town. Boulia's a bit bigger. They won't be so intrigued by a girl and a bloke in a Ford truck.'

She was already out of the door. 'Whatever you say. Just try and keep it quiet so I can sleep.' When she climbed on to the passenger's seat, she said, 'Hungry?'

He made a face. 'Not desperately.'

She reached in the back and found an opened packet of dry biscuits. 'Munch on these while I have a snooze. When I wake up, I'll make you something decent.'

The Diamantina River hadn't run for more than a year and the ford that Kelly remembered was dry. The crossing was rough but simple to negotiate. The only spectators were a few egrets which, disturbed by the truck, soared beyond the coolibahs and settled in a water hole downstream. Monica stirred, mumbled a few incomprehensible words, then lapsed into a deep sleep.

Once over the Diamantina, Kelly stopped. Far to the left, he saw sunlight flash on a windmill's rotating blades. Birdsville. He hadn't meant to come so close to the town. On the northern side of the river was a track that wound through tall rushes. He turned right, away from the town, and followed the track for almost a kilometre. Then, at a place where the rushes thinned, he swung to the left and drove on to a stony plain. He stopped, got out and relieved himself, then looked around. The windmill wasn't visible from there and even the river was hidden behind a fuzz of grey that was a mixture of coolibah leaves and heat haze. He heard a bird squawk but nothing else; only the steady rumble of the truck's idling motor. Satisfied, he got back behind the wheel and set a course to the north across the stones.

He intended running parallel to, but many kilometres to the east of, the graded road running up from Birdsville. After the gibber plain, he would cross the huge Bipa Morea claypan and skirt the swampy fringes of Lake Machattie. Then, by using a succession of minor roads, he would bypass the tiny township of Bedourie, follow tracks past Coorabulka and Springvale stations and finally join the Kennedy Highway between Hamilton River and Boulia. Thus, they would drive into Boulia from the east.

Surely, he reasoned, a man and a woman crossing Boulia's Robert O'Hara Burke bridge in a dusty F100 and presumably having travelled all the way from Winton or Longreach, would not be linked with the motorcycle-mounted desperado Kelso Hunnicutt, whom police were hunting down south at Cooper Creek. Or so he hoped.

While Kelly was playing with these thoughts, the police aircraft from Adelaide was landing at Birdsville. The two men on board, having dropped six colleagues at Innamincka, had flown up to Cordillo Downs and then crossed to the Birdsville Track, in case Hunnicutt had decided to make a dash for Queensland. They had seen no sign of him. The passenger, a detective-inspector, sought out Birdsville's policeman and gave him the latest information about the manhunt. He also had a request: that the local man watch the Diamantina crossing south of the town in case Hunnicutt somehow managed to ride this far.

He had one additional bit of information. The woman artist Monica Tate, who had first reported sighting Hunnicutt in western Queensland, had disappeared. She had been camping near Innamincka. She was an eccentric person, not inclined to cooperate with the police, and it was likely that she had decided to go home, which meant driving south to Melbourne. However, there was a possibility that Hunnicutt had commandeered her truck and either disposed of the woman or forced her to take him somewhere. The detective-inspector passed on the relevant details about Monica Tate and her truck. Just in case.

After the plane had taken off, to fly over the Birdsville Track all the way south to the Cooper crossing, the Birdsville policeman stood at the edge of the airstrip and thought. He'd heard a lot about Hunnicutt. He didn't sound like the sort of man who would now be following defined tracks and passing through towns. So the policeman drove down the road to the hospital where the Flying Doctor radio was based and began calling all the homesteads within a range of two hundred and fifty kilometres.

It was five hours later that the man from Monkira homestead radioed in. He'd been travelling back from Bedourie and he'd had a puncture. He'd stopped under a tree to change the wheel. About ten minutes later and a long way up the road, maybe four or five hundred yards from where he was parked in the shade, he'd seen a light blue truck, possibly a Ford F100, drive straight across the road. What struck him as being strange was that there was no track there. The truck headed north across the gibbers. He wasn't sure but he thought a man was driving. No, he couldn't say what he looked like but there was no one else. Just one man.

26

There was a time — a brief but vivid moment — when Montague thought of giving McCarthy only a portion, at most half, of the diamonds. He'd hide the rest. After all, no one knew just how many gems had been in Kolvenbach's safe or what they were worth. There'd been press speculation of four or five million dollars but that could be dismissed as normal newspaper nonsense. McCarthy would accept a couple of million as a realistic figure. Initially, he might be disappointed because he'd been dreaming of villas in Spain and yachts in the Caribbean, but his innate greed would prevail; after all, two million was about two thousand times more money than he'd ever seen in his bank account.

McCarthy was using the telephone in the study. He'd been making calls all day but this conversation seemed particularly animated. He was talking to someone called Trevor, and he was busily writing notes and making contented, clucking noises. It seemed a good time for Montague to make his move: to stroll casually to the refrigerator, get the diamonds, bury half of them — the best half — in the bucket of Neapolitan ice cream, and then present the rest to George. Ahead of the deadline he'd been given. He'd smile modestly, exuding goodwill and honest intentions. George would be transfixed by the sight of all those sparkling gems.

Just as long as he didn't feel like eating Neapolitan ice cream. George was keen on ice cream.

The dream ended at the door of the deep freeze when Montague found McCarthy right behind him. The man had a remarkable ability to distinguish the strategic manoeuvre from the trivial ramble. With a snap of his fingers, McCarthy summoned Spiro to his side.

Within an instant, one arm was being bent behind Montague's back and McCarthy, standing clear, was saying that if there was a gun hidden in the deep freeze, Spiro would change his priorities and break an arm first. Even as Spiro's pressure forced him up on his toes, Montague was wondering what he had done wrong. Maybe it was going to the left door and not the right where the beer was kept. Anyhow, it was too late. Spiro was twisting his wrist and growling and McCarthy, who hadn't let him out of his sight all day, was smiling.

'What's in there, Gerry?'

Still on his toes. 'Ice cream.'

'You were going to put ice cream in my beer?' McCarthy thrust Montague to one side. Legs bent, body leaning forward, puffing loudly, the fat man examined the interior of the deep freeze. He prodded a few frozen packages, then straightened and, rocking on his heels, regarded Montague with an angled look that was suspiciously close to respect.

'Some people refer to diamonds as "ice",' he mused. 'You haven't been playing jokes on everyone, have you, Gerry? You wouldn't do something as irreverent as freeze a few million dollars? You haven't been chilling all those lovely sparklers?' He signalled to Spiro, who released the hold.

Shelf by shelf and with savage sweeps of his arms, McCarthy cleared the deep freeze, creating frosty cascades of chops and steak and chicken, and scattering misted packets of peas and carrots and bright plastic tubs of ice cream across the floor. He picked up the tricoloured bucket of Neapolitan ice cream and went to the sink. With a carving knife, he cut out chunks of strawberry, vanilla and chocolate ice cream and let them thud on to the corrugated metal surface. With the tip of the blade, he pushed some of the larger chunks into the sink bowl and sliced them into mush. Nothing but ice cream. He did the same with a tub of plain vanilla. No diamonds. Then, cutting himself a corner of ice cream, he stared at Montague, his mouth crinkled by cold and doubt.

'Let me show you,' Montague said, trying to sound as though McCarthy's performance had been a vaudeville act which he had truly appreciated. His own performance was strained because he didn't fancy the thought of McCarthy with a carving knife in front of him and Spiro with his eager jaws behind him. With forced joviality, he said, 'May I?' and extended his hand for the knife. A reluctant but curious McCarthy handed it to him. Montague used the knife to chip away a layer of ice at the back of one shortened shelf. With the blade, he prised open the cover and handed McCarthy the bags of diamonds.

McCarthy held one frozen chamois by its drawstring and prodded the sides. 'Is this what I think it is?'

'Probably.'

McCarthy opened the bag and peered inside. 'And this, of course, is what you were going to give me?'

'Of course.'

'Why did you let me go through all this business?' McCarthy waved the bag across the scattered meat and chopped ice cream.

'Because I found it amusing.'

'Ah.' He moved to the sink and put more ice cream in his mouth. Cheeks bulging, he regarded Montague with eyes that were brittle with cold. 'You liked seeing me make a fool of myself.'

Montague shook his head and made sure not a hint of a smile showed.

'What do you think, Spiro?' Holding up the diamonds, McCarthy looked beyond Montague. 'Do you reckon our friend here has outlived his usefulness?'

Montague's feet did a nervous jig. 'Just a minute, George. We were sharing, remember? And you need me. There are still things to do. Lucas, remember? He'll take fright if someone else goes to see him.'

McCarthy smiled. 'Just joking, Gerry, just joking.' He hurried back to the telephone, which was lying on the table. 'Still there, Trevor? Sorry about that. Just a little emergency. Nothing serious.' He nodded vigorously several times. 'Thanks for the news. That's a favour I owe you.' He laughed. 'All right, two favours. Be seeing you.'

He replaced the phone and beckoned to Montague. He upended the second chamois bag and spilled the diamonds across the table. Casually, he began sorting them into piles: big, medium, small. 'We now know where the missing Mrs Hunnicutt is.' He caught Montague's startled expression. 'She's with Kolvenbach's brother, up at this place Innamincka. Travelling with him in his aircraft. Strange that, isn't it?'

'Kolvenbach.' The voice was flat but Montague's mind was juggling possibilities. The first, the strongest, was that Laura and Kolvenbach had been making some private deal.

'Kolvenbach's still stuck at this town, waiting for new tyres. Trevor was reading the latest police telex from Adelaide and it said there were two people on the plane.' He held one large diamond up to the light and turned it slowly, gawking at the flashes of brilliance. 'That'll buy the Rolls.' His smile promised Montague a ride. 'Now, back to the problem of Mrs Hunnicutt. There's no point in sending anyone up to Innamincka. Too far, too expensive, too slow. She and Kolvenbach will be gone by the morning.' He put the diamond on the table but apart from the others. He wagged a finger. 'But the pilot will have to file a flight plan. Yes?'

Montague had been fascinated by the diamond and depressed by the fact that McCarthy had obviously claimed it as his own. He shrugged. He didn't know what pilots were required to do.

'So we'll just keep tabs on him. We'll know where he's going and when he's due. When he lands somewhere closer to civilization, my man will fly there to meet them. And zap.' Like a boy playing marbles, he used one of the small diamonds to pot another. 'We'll get her. Good news, eh, Gerry?'

McCarthy put the big diamond in his pocket. Roughly, he scooped up the others and started to pour them back into the bag. 'Tell me, old mate, have you got any idea what this woman would be doing with Kolvenbach's brother? Any theory?'

Dazed, Montague shook his head. 'No. It's a mystery.' As he spoke, Montague realised that this was the first honest answer he'd given all day.

Laura Hunnicutt was on her own. It was the first time Kolvenbach had left her and, instead of trying to run off, to take the first steps in getting back to Melbourne, she had fallen asleep. She was still tired from the activities of the previous twenty-four hours. The hunting, the shooting, the bashing, the phoney stories, the wild lovemaking.

Kolvenbach was out at the airstrip, helping fit the new tyres, and Laura was in the motel room. She'd been dreaming of her father. It was a good dream, not as confused as some of the others, and he'd been with her, not with that sleazy woman he'd run off with all those years ago.

She sat up and thought of the things she should do and the things she would like to do, then became worried because they were so different. Her emotions were getting in the way of reason and that hadn't happened for years. Reason said she should be in Melbourne. She, not Gerry, should be handling the disposal of the diamonds. He'd stuff it up. Lucas preferred to deal with her and he might renege if Gerry showed up. So she should be there to sell the diamonds, get the maximum from Lucas, and keep clear of any police trap.

Another thing — Gerry might be panicking about the shooting and carrying on in such a way that people would become suspicious. Left on his own for too long, he would start worrying and making his own decisions and then he'd foul up everything. He was good when you told him what to do but he didn't have the head for handling the unexpected.

Her thoughts drifted to Kolvenbach. That was the silly thing: he bullied her and she enjoyed it. She, who was irritated beyond endurance by people who tried to dominate her, just as she despised those who lacked the will to be dominant (people like Kelly, who were satisfied with being second best), found herself filled with a strange, almost euphoric feeling of contentment in his presence.

She closed her eyes. Her father had left when she was eleven and the memories were mixed. Some had become intense and exaggerated whilst others were blurred. He'd been strong. Brutal to some people, or so others had told her; but never to her. She'd loved him and he adored her. He used to stroke her hair. She remembered that. Her mother would be screaming and spitting profanities at him, and he would ignore her and put Laura on his knee,

288

stroking her hair and saying soothing words as though the woman weren't in the same room. He was a big man too. Maybe not as big as Kolvenbach but it was difficult to be sure. Her memories were little-girl memories and they made everything seem bigger: the house she'd lived in, the tree she climbed to get away from other people, the family car her father took when he left with the other woman.

'I know what I want, Laurie,' her father used to say. He called her Laurie; no one else had. He would wink, sharing a secret. 'I know what I want and I'm going to get it.' Just like Kolvenbach. Magnus was a clear, analytical thinker with a will that was as unyielding as cast iron. His outlook on life matched her father's philosophy exactly. Know what you want, go for it, and let the rest be damned.

Magnus was rich. Her father was always going to be rich. Maybe he was; she'd never heard from him after he'd gone away.

Already, Magnus was immensely wealthy. Now that his brother was dead, he would be the sole owner of the diamond mine up in the Kimberleys and that would be worth tens of millions of dollars. And then there was the safari business in Africa and other enterprises Magnus had only hinted at. If she aligned herself with him in some way, there'd be enough money to do all the things she'd dreamed of, and never been able to; not with Kelly constantly dithering about, making his little films.

She needed to clear her head. She went to the refrigerator and opened a bottle of soda water.

She drank half the bottle, burped a few times and sat on the bed. What to do? The first thing was to find out what was happening with Gerry back in Melbourne. She would have to be cautious. Ring him collect.

She went outside. There was no sign of Magnus or the man who'd flown up with the tyres and all the equipment. They must still be at the airstrip. She went to the office. The owner's wife was there, her face frozen in surprise, as though she'd been caught with her hand in the till.

'Why Mrs...' she began and let her voice trail away because the couple had registered in one name and now she knew that the man had that long, strange Dutch-sounding name and this woman was not his wife. She cleared her throat. 'How nice to see you.' She meant without the man.

Laura asked her to book a reverse-charge call, gave her the number and asked her not to mention this to Magnus — it would soon be his birthday and she was arranging a present for him. The woman didn't believe her but said, 'That's so sweet of you'.

The woman made a great and laboured show of leaving the office; she tidied some papers on the desk, moved to a cabinet nearer the door and put a file in a drawer, rearranged a withered flower on top of the cabinet, and flicked a dead fly from the window sill. When Laura said, 'There's no need to close the door entirely; just part of the way will do,' the woman was propelled from the room as effectively as if she had been shoved.

A strange voice answered. Laura asked for Montague. 'Who is this?' the man asked, but he already knew; the operator had been through all this, giving the caller's name so that the number would accept the reverse charges.

She felt uneasy. 'Mr Montague, please,' she repeated and said no more until the man put down the phone. She heard him shout, 'It's for you'. It was not a friendly voice. She thought of hanging up but Gerry was already there.

'Laura? Where the hell are you?'

Laura saw the owner's wife flit past the window, on her way from one unnecessary job to another.

'It's about that birthday present we were discussing,' she said in a loud voice, and watched the window, waiting for the return journey.

'What?' The line became quieter, as though Gerry were covering the mouthpiece. Talking to that other man? The crackle returned. 'Right,' he said. 'I know what you mean.'

'I'm at Innamincka. It's a long story. Can't explain now. I'm trying to get back.'

Again the silence, then the crackle as the hand was removed. 'How will you come back? When?'

'I don't know at the moment. As soon as I can. Gerry, who's that with you?'

He ignored the question. 'I have to know when you'll be back. It's very important.'

'I'll let you know as soon as I know. Gerry, is it safe to talk?'

'Yep. Fine, fine.'

So glib. Now she was really worried. 'Are the police there with you? Is that who answered?'

He hesitated for so long that she thought they had been disconnected. 'Yes. No problems, though.'

'You're sure?'

'What are you doing up there?'

The woman passed the window again and, apparently dropping something, bent near the door.

'That sounds great. A bit more than I wanted to spend, but great.'

'What? Laura, what was that?'

She left the phone and went to the doorway. The woman had gone into one of the rooms. Back to the desk. 'Is anyone else listening in?'

'No.'

'Have you seen L yet?'

'Who? Oh.' He coughed. 'Soon. Very soon.'

'Not tonight, please.'

Montague didn't answer. So it could be tonight.

Lucas preferred to have his meetings at night. 'Wait for me, eh?' she said.

'Pardon?'

'Let me see him, Gerry. It's better. Believe me.'

'Well, that depends.'

'On what?'

'When you're in town.'

'I'll be there. Don't move until I get back.'

'Okay,' Gerry said in a voice slowed by doubt. 'What was that about spending too much? I didn't follow all that.'

'Nothing. I have a passing audience, that's all.'

Again the hand across the mouthpiece. Then, 'Laura, be sure to let me know exactly when you're leaving and how. Give me your precise schedule.' He paused, as though getting instructions. 'Will you be flying out?'

'Like I said, I'll let you know. Is everything going well?'

'Fine.'

The silence generated mutual suspicion.

'Got to go,' she said.

'Will you be leaving tomorrow?'

'Bye, Gerry.' She hung up and, deeply troubled, returned to the room.

The truck had been misfiring. What began as an occasional stammer became a regular stutter. Near Boulia, the engine backfired several times. Monica woke and Kelly stopped. The road was clear so he got out and for the first time checked the engine.

The bonnet rose, a monstrous mouth revealing rotting teeth. Kelly put the prop in place and stood back, dismayed by what he saw and smelled. The engine bay stank. His nose, twitching in disgust, detected the sharp aroma of leaking petrol, the sour smell of battery acid and the acrid tang of scorched oil. He got a cloth and began wiping things. The dominant, circular air-filter canister, once blue, was blackened by a thick scum of grit and oil mist. Each spark plug was hidden beneath a greasy black paste. The radiator was stained orange and the battery terminals had grown corrosive stalagmites of white.

Monica might be a great artist but she was no mechanic, he thought, and removed the spark plugs. He kneeled at the side of the road to clean and reset each one.

Monica got out, went behind some bushes, then watched him replace the plugs.

Kelly began removing the air filter.

'Shouldn't we keep moving?' she said, nervously glancing up and down the road.

'We should, but we can't.' They were parked on the side of the Kennedy Highway, no more than ten kilometres from Boulia. He held up the filter. It was filthy.

'I don't know the first thing about cars,' she said breezily. She walked around the Ford, ignoring it and the upraised filter, and gazed at the flat landscape. 'All I know is that you turn a key and it goes.'

'You know how to change a tyre.'

'That's different. I can change a wheel, add petrol, clean the windscreen. All the things that need doing on the outside. The engine's a mystery. I pay a mechanic a fortune to keep this thing going. The engine's his responsibility. I make it a point never to open the bonnet.' She caught his accusing glance and added quickly, 'Except occasionally to have a look at the oil. And water.'

Kelly was pounding the air filter against his leg. He coughed, overreacting to the rising cloud of dust.

'You were the one who wanted to drive across the desert,' she said.

'Most of this dirt's been here for months.'

'I told you, my mechanic looks after those things.

And he's in Melbourne.' She made it sound as though it were the man's fault for not being there.

'How old's the truck?'

'I forget.'

'When was the last time this mechanic of yours looked at the motor?'

She shrugged. 'The last time I was in Melbourne, I suppose. Or maybe the time before.' She scratched an elbow. 'Will you be long?'

He lifted the filter to the sun and squinted into its latticed filthiness. 'This thing's old enough to be on the pension.'

'But it's better than nothing.' There was a hint of criticism in her voice — here they were in a hurry and all Kelly could do was nitpick about a bit of dust. And then, a concession: 'Do we need a new one?'

He put it back in place and began sealing the canister. 'A new truck mightn't be a bad idea.'

She turned her back to him. 'Maybe you should have stuck to your stolen motorbike.'

He made a show of wiping oil from the top of the motor.

'Someone's coming.'

He turned. A car was approaching from the east. It slowed. He could see a man and a woman in the front. The man was wearing a wide-brimmed hat. A local. Which meant he could have come from anywhere within a thousand kilometres.

The car stopped behind them and the driver got out. He was big, the sort of man who raised raw-boned cattle, and he had a belly that overhung his moleskin trousers like a wave about to spill over a weir.

'Having trouble?'

Kelly was still shielded by the raised bonnet and Monica stepped in front of him. 'My husband's just fixing something. We'll be right, thanks.'

294

The man rubbed his shoulder. He seemed, Monica noted with dismay, pleased to be out of the car. 'Nice day.'

'Hot.'

He glanced at the numberplate. 'You Victorians wouldn't be used to it.'

'No.'

The woman got out of the car, her face preset in a smile that was part good humour and part perpetual squint.

Under the bonnet, Kelly thought: now they're dividing us, attacking from two flanks. They'll want to talk. I'll bet they know someone who lives in Victoria.

'And where are you from?' the woman was saying. 'Melbourne?'

'Near there,' Monica said. The man had walked past her. Kelly had to face him.

'G'day,' Kelly said, sparing the man only the briefest of looks.

'Having a spot of trouble?'

Kelly nodded and tried to give the impression that tightening the wing nut took a great deal of effort.

'We have a daughter who lives near Warrnambool,' the woman said. Kelly had to smile.

'Nearly fixed?' the man said.

'Right as rain.'

'They raise sheep,' the woman was saying.

The man was examining the engine bay. 'Done a lot of miles, by the look of it.'

'Close to two hundred thousand.'

'I drive a Ford too.'

Kelly was compelled to look. 'A bit newer than ours.'

The man agreed. 'The last one did over a quarter of a million miles. Ended up hitting a bullock at night. Didn't do either of them much good.'

'No.' Kelly wiped his hands, unmistakably signifying his eagerness to be under way.

The man massaged his shoulder. His brow wrinkled in pain. 'What was the problem?'

'Engine's been misfiring.'

'There's a good man in town. Knows Fords.'

'I think we'll be right.'

The man's wrinkles fractured in doubt. 'The plugs don't look too good.'

'We're getting a proper service in Darwin.'

The man whistled. 'Long way.'

'She'll make it.'

The woman was saying, 'We're going to see our son'. She laughed, a nervous, apologetic sound. 'He's the black sheep of the family. All the others are on the land but he's a policeman.' Another nervous ripple. 'He's twenty-five. Married. Has a lovely wife. They seem to like it here.'

Monica said, 'Oh?'

'Yes. They've just had a little boy. We're going to see the baby for the first time.'

'Oh that's nice.'

'They're calling him Hastings. As a first name.'

'That's a strong name.'

'It's not a family name.'

Kelly called out, 'Come on, love. We're right now and we mustn't keep these good folk any longer.'

The man was still worried. 'Do you reckon you'll get to Darwin?'

'We call the truck Old Man River. It just keeps rolling along.'

The man stood back and had a good look at the truck and at Kelly. He frowned. 'You're not from up this way?'

Kelly concentrated on wiping his hands. 'No.'

'I feel as though I know you from somewhere.'

'Don't think so.' Kelly turned to Monica. 'Come on, love, we've got a long way to go.'

'Strange,' the man said.

'I hope you like little Hastings,' Monica said.

'It's such a curious name for a baby,' the woman said, her face worried but still set in a smile.

'And where is your son?'

'Boulia. He's at the station there.'

'Of course. Well, have a good time.'

Monica climbed in beside Kelly. The other couple waved.

The starter whirred for a long time before the engine fired. It coughed once, then ran evenly. The couple waved again. Kelly drove off, waved once and turned to Monica. 'That was a stroke of good luck, wasn't it?' he said bitterly.

'You're the one who wanted to stop.'

'We had to. We'd have gone through town with this thing backfiring and farting and making as much noise as a bloody machine gun.' He slapped the steering wheel. 'That's if we'd have got that far.'

'You can always get out and start hitchhiking.' She bent to look in the outside mirror. The couple were getting in the car. 'I'm sure you could get a lift with the local cop's parents as far as Boulia.'

He looked at her, ready to snarl. She laughed.

'What's so funny?'

'You. Your eyes look as though they've been stuck on your face and the glue's slipped. In other words, you look dreadful.' She scratched her scalp. 'God I'm tired. You must be worn out.'

He turned towards the open window and took a deep breath. His fingers drummed the rim of the wheel. 'Sorry. You've been wonderful. Amazing. I'm really very grateful. It's just that I'm tired and cranky, that's all. And worried.' Another drum roll. 'About Laura.'

'Your wife?'

He nodded. 'That man's done something terrible to make her like that. Drugs, I'm sure.'

She was quiet for a while. 'It must have been a great shock. I mean, the way she behaved when you were trying to rescue her.'

'It was awful.' He leaned towards the wheel, to emphasise what he was saying. 'It was as though she was someone else. A totally different woman. She seemed frightened of me. She wanted him to shoot me. Would you believe that?'

Quietly, Monica said, 'I hope she's all right'.

A sigh of despair. 'I can't do a bloody thing.'

'No. Not at the moment. You've got enough problems of your own.' She squirmed in the seat to make herself more comfortable, played with her seat belt which was twisted, and spent some time straightening it. 'Sorry about the motor.'

'Sorry about the outburst.'

'That just about makes us square.' She checked the mirror again. Far behind them, the car was moving. 'Their son couldn't have been the postmaster or the storekeeper or the town undertaker. He had to be the policeman.' She pulled his sleeve. 'I think that man half recognised you.'

'So do I. As soon as he gets to the police station, he'll see my picture above the mantelpiece and that'll be that.'

'So what do we do? Give Boulia a miss?'

He shook his head. 'Can't. We need fuel. And we're heading west from Boulia. There's no fuel out where we're going.'

'And where's that?'

'Across the top of the Simpson Desert. Then into Alice Springs.'

She frowned, trying to picture their route, then bent forward, listening to the engine.

'You seem to have fixed it.'

'I haven't fixed it. It's just better than it was.'

With a sudden rush of noise, the other car overtook them. The driver pressed his horn. It played the first bars of 'Colonel Bogey'. Kelly waved. The other car sprouted hands and drew rapidly away, the driver anxious to demonstrate its superior performance.

Near the bridge leading into Boulia, Kelly stopped. He crawled into the back. It would be better if only Monica were seen in town, he said, and started to cover himself with a blanket.

'Just be quick. Straight in for petrol and straight out.' He held up a corner of the blanket so he could see her.

She pulled the blanket over him. 'Keep down. And stop talking. And while you're down there, why don't you have a sleep?'

'Fill it up.' His voice was muffled. 'Get every drop into the tank that you can.'

'Yes, master.' She pulled a box of supplies on top of him.

'What are you doing?'

'Making you look less obvious. Now shut up.'

'It hurts.'

She moved the box. 'Should I use your credit card or your cash?'

'Very funny.' He wriggled into a new position. 'Do you know where the money is?'

She straightened the blanket. 'I do.'

'Don't forget. Fill the tank to the brim. We've got a long way to go and it'll be hard going.'

'If I didn't need a new truck before this, I'm going to need one when we get back.'

'I'll get you one.'

'What are you going to do — steal it? Now shut up. We're coming into town.' She drove across the bridge spanning the Burke River and entered Boulia.

27

The motel owner felt sorry for the big man who was checking out of Room Three. The police sergeant had told him Kolvenbach was the brother of the man who'd been murdered back in Melbourne; and so when he heard the news, he felt compelled to pass it on. The man might have caused the police a little trouble earlier, but he had a right to know.

Hunnicutt had been sighted up north, near Monkira.

Hunnicutt? On the motorbike?

The motel owner became confused. Not on the bike. In a truck; the one belonging to that woman artist who had camped along the river. Someone had seen the truck heading north, not on a road but across rough country, and the police theory was that Hunnicutt had stolen or commandeered it. Or murdered the woman and taken the truck.

'He murdered the woman?'

The man blushed, caught expounding his own theory. 'It's possible. You never know with a man like Hunnicutt. They saw a man in the truck but no woman.'

'When was this?'

'Just a while ago. At least, that's when they got the report.' He checked the office clock. 'No more than half an hour ago. They were on the phone. Right here.'

'And Hunnicutt's on board? They're certain? It's not just someone's guess?'

The man's shoulders quivered like jelly prodded by a spoon. 'I don't know, Mr...' He checked the register but that held the wrong name, the alias Kolvenbach had used when he checked in. 'I'm only telling you what they said. It's their theory.' He smiled, relieved to shift the blame. 'They're pretty sure, though. They've alerted the Queensland police. You see, Monkira's up north in Queensland.'

A map of the State was pinned to the wall and he searched for the name. His finger wandered through the far west of Queensland until he tapped one spot in triumph. 'Here. It's only a cattle station.' He stood back and examined the map. 'Funny place to be. I wonder where the devil he's heading for.'

Kolvenbach stood beside him. 'Yes, I wonder.'

Kolvenbach sat beside his packed bag and studied the road map. Laura faced him. 'I think it's time we went our own ways.' She spoke quietly but resolutely. 'You don't need me any more. I'd only get in the way and I should be going back to Melbourne. There are things I must do. People will be worried about me.'

He looked up briefly. 'Who?'

'My sister.'

'You haven't mentioned a sister.'

'Well, I have one.' He was studying his map again. 'And she'd be worried. She's a great worrier.'

'Ring her.'

'It's not the same.'

He put down the map and looked at the wall, ignoring her. 'Monkira... going north. Where would he be heading?'

'I have no idea.' She sat beside him. 'Why don't you go up there and see if you can find him? I'll go home.'

'Has he ever mentioned Monkira?'

'I've never heard of the place.' She touched his wrist. 'Please, Magnus. I'd love to stay with you but I must go home. You go on. I'll go back to Melbourne.'

'Boulia, Dajarra, Duchess, Mount Isa,' he prompted.

'Look, I've never heard of any of those places.' She thought again. 'Mount Isa. That's a big mining town. They'd have an air service.' She gripped his wrist more tightly. 'Take me there. Please.'

Kolvenbach prised her fingers from his arm and spread the map. 'Okay. Tell me, Laura, has Hunnicutt spent much time up in this part of Queensland?'

'Oh for God's sake, Magnus, he's spent a lot of time everywhere. I don't know where he goes. The more obscure the place, the more he likes it.'

'Why is he going north?'

'How would I know?' She calmed herself. No point boiling over while Kolvenbach remained icy cool. 'Probably because there was nowhere else to go.'

His eyes were bright with discovery. 'So this is not planned. He is running. Running blind, perhaps?'

'Perhaps.' She clasped her hands. 'Magnus, will you take me to Mount Isa?'

'I said yes.' With his fingers, he formed a slim steeple and used it as a chin rest. 'Do you think he's going to Mount Isa?'

She blinked. 'You said yes?'

'You should listen. I said okay. I meant it. Now, about Mount Isa. Why would he be going there?'

She was about to say 'How the hell would I know?' but Mount Isa was where she wanted to go so she took a deep breath and said, 'May I see the map?'

He pointed out Monkira, Boulia, Mount Isa. Then his finger swung towards Winton and Longreach. 'Or would he go this way — east — and then across to the coast?'

East would mean missing Mount Isa. Frowning with concentration, she let a finger trace circles across the white spaces to the west of Boulia. 'What's out here?'

'Desert.' He narrowed his eyes and drew away from the map, like a person needing glasses. 'Bad desert, by the look of it. It's all sand ridges.'

'He wouldn't go there.'

'But he likes desert. We must not underestimate this man of yours.'

He hadn't said that for a while and she held her tongue. 'But he's not in his four-wheel drive. He's in this truck.' She almost said 'this woman's truck'.

He hadn't thought of that; she could see it in his eyes.

She added quickly, 'And he definitely won't go to the east, towards the coast'.

'Why not?' He was ignoring the map and concentrating on her. The steeple had moved forward and now touched his nose.

'Too many towns, too many police. He wouldn't head back towards civilisation. You see,' she said, convincing herself as she talked, 'Kelly has this silly pride about his knowledge of the outback. If he's in a desperate situation, as we believe he is...' She looked at Kolvenbach for support but his eyes, while bright, were blank. She coughed, unsettled by the look. 'Believe me, Magnus, the last thing Kelly would do is head to the east, towards heavily settled country. He'll stay in the bush. As deep in the outback as possible.'

'That's what you think?'

'Yes. He'll go north.' On the map, her hand hovered around Mount Isa. 'And then either up here...' She indicated the tangle of rivers cutting the emptiness south of the Gulf of Carpentaria. 'He talks about this area a lot. Or else he'll go west.' She pointed to the Northern Territory. 'This is his favourite part of Australia.'

303

Kolvenbach folded the road map and an aerial chart of the region and put them in his briefcase.

'You'll take me to Mount Isa?' she asked.

'We'll be there tonight.'

'Thank God. Do you think I could ring from here and make a booking on a flight?'

'Why not?' He regarded her with amusement. 'Are you sure this interesting little exposition wasn't for the purpose of getting you to the nearest airport?'

'It's what I think Kelly will do.'

He seemed to be judging her. Finally, he said, 'I agree,' and scratched his chin. 'But with Hunnicutt, who knows?'

McCarthy handed Montague a handkerchief. He took it and dabbed his face. His mouth and cheek hurt and one eye was closed. With his good eye, he looked down and saw the blood spattered across the front of his shirt. A new shirt, too.

'Bit of a mess, my old mate, isn't it?' McCarthy was not so angry now. He had been furious when he'd returned. 'Don't worry. Things are going to get worse before they get better.' He laughed. It was an unpleasant sound and Montague, holding the handkerchief to his eye, wondered how much worse it could get. Spiro had amused himself for half an hour. Just practising, as he put it.

'So you still say there's no one else?'

Montague sniffed up some blood that was trickling out of his nose, and nodded.

'And you can't tell me why this Lucas seemed to be expecting someone else?'

Slowly, mouthing the words with difficulty, Montague said, 'He was expecting me, George'.

McCarthy lifted his face to the ceiling. 'No, no, no. I can tell, old friend. He was expecting someone else. Not me. Not you. Someone else.'

304

'What did he say?' It was about as defiant a question as Montague dared ask.

'It was what he didn't say. I get a feeling about people, Gerry. It comes with practice and this bloke was expecting a third party. And all I'm asking is this: who? Just tell me and I'll let Spiro have a rest and you can go and clean yourself up.'

If he mentioned Laura he was dead. Montague looked up, eye swollen, mouth bleeding, bright blood still leaking from his ear. All on the one side. Spiro was right-handed. He said, 'You just made him nervous, George. Believe me'.

'Sure, Gerry, sure.' Suddenly McCarthy laughed. 'You look awful. All right. Have a break. You too, Spiro.' He nodded to his man, a teacher letting a student off early.

Montague used the handkerchief to cover his eyes. Yes, you have a break, Spiro. That's kind of you, George. Poor Spiro must be tired. And at that moment, Montague swore to kill George McCarthy. Or have him killed. Yes, that was better; get someone else to do it.

He sucked air through his mouth, wiped his ear and studied the bloodstains on the handkerchief. He knew who could do the job. And he'd get the diamonds back. It was perfect.

McCarthy had become cheerful. 'I'll send them to someone else. Stuff Lucas. In fact,' he said, winking towards Spiro, 'we might do more than stuff Lucas. We might do him a severe mischief. What do you reckon?'

Spiro raised an eyebrow.

The telephone rang. It was McCarthy's friend from police headquarters. The conversation was short; just grunts from McCarthy, who wrote throughout. He said a curt 'thank you', hung up and immediately rang an interstate number.

'They're on their way to Mount Isa,' he said. He

gave the aircraft's registration number, listened and frowned. 'That seems a roundabout way to get there... Okay. You ring me when you land there and I'll confirm that they're still at Mount Isa. When are you leaving?... Good. You know what to do.'

He leaned back, both hands behind his head, and stared wistfully at Montague. 'We're doing all right, Gerry old son, we're doing all right.' He inclined his head towards the bathroom. 'Go and clean your-self up. Change your shirt. Have a lie down.'

When Montague had gone, McCarthy beckoned to Spiro. 'I think it's about time we thought of getting rid of our friend. Work something out, will you? Something neat. Make it look natural.'

Spiro frowned. Not because he didn't like McCar-thy's proposal but because he had planned a rather messier ending for Gerry Montague.

Kolvenbach had landed at Monkira and told the startled grazier that he was from Interpol. Laura stayed in the aircraft, wearing a baseball cap and sitting in the left-hand seat; she was the Interpol inspector's charter pilot. The grazier was impressed and told his story once more.

Now airborne and back in his rightful seat, Kol-venbach was racing the sunset to Mount Isa. 'I don't like it,' he said, his finger tapping the map spread across his knees. 'That man saw a blue truck, that was all. It was possibly a Ford F100 and he saw it from a distance. He thought he saw a man behind the wheel.' He gazed left, then right. Beneath them, lengthening shadows spread deep stains across a pink land. 'It was not a good sighting. Far too indefinite.'

Laura said nothing. They were heading for Mount Isa and that was enough. Kolvenbach might have doubts about the grazier's story but he was still searching for the truck. It was the only lead they had.

From Monkira, Kolvenbach flew west to pass over the Birdsville–Mount Isa road. Then he turned north, but well away from the road. If Laura was right, Hunnicutt might swing into the Northern Territory. Kolvenbach had been trying to imagine himself in Hunnicutt's position. He would do the unexpected. Even without four-wheel drive, he could be tempted into the big desert east of Alice Springs. Or at least, to its fringes, where a truck might be able to pass. Kolvenbach checked the map. There were tracks to the north of the desert. Those tracks could be Hunnicutt's goal.

He throttled back. Laura, numbed by the monotony of the landscape scrolling past her window, was jolted into wakefulness. It was too soon for Mount Isa. Were they turning, or landing?

He pointed to the left. 'Down there. A vehicle.'

It was still far away. Something, travelling along a faint track and distinct only because of the spiralling dust trail. The track followed a row of trees that snaked into the distance. A river — dry, of course — but a big river. Kolvenbach checked his map. The Georgina.

'Quick. The glasses.'

She handed him the binoculars.

'Take the wheel.'

'I can't fly.'

'Just hold it straight.'

'How?' Her voice rose.

'Don't let the wheel move. Now be quiet.' He held the glasses, twiddled the focusing ring and let out a series of little grunts. He put down the glasses and took the wheel again. 'Very good.'

She sat in silence, counted to ten and said, 'Well?'

'It's the truck.'

'Can you see who's inside?'

He was gazing down at the land, searching for other tracks. There were none; just the one that followed the river. 'Of course not. But it's a blue Ford. I'd say it was the one that woman artist had.' Another sharp grunt of satisfaction. 'Hunnicutt's friend.'

She ignored the jibe. 'So?'

His eyes were alive with good humour. 'So we fly on, passing Mr Hunnicutt as though we had absolutely no interest in him, because we don't want to alarm him. If he sees us, he will think we're merely a disinterested aircraft flying north.'

'You're sure it's Kelly?'

'That woman would not be driving out here.' His hand swept from horizon to horizon. 'No one but Hunnicutt would be driving out here.'

'But we will go to Mount Isa?'

He discarded the road map and began checking one of his aerial charts.

'Magnus?'

He lifted a hand. She could see his lips moving. He was making calculations. Eventually he said, 'How would you like to go to Alice Springs instead?'

Alice Springs! She slumped in the seat. Then she thought: there would have to be more planes through Alice Springs than through Mount Isa. And it would be quicker. Down to Adelaide, across to Melbourne. 'How long will it take?'

He had taken out his calculator. 'An hour and a half in this aircraft. Maybe longer. We will loop to the north, to make sure they don't see us.' He squinted at the instruments. 'We have the fuel. And we can land in the dark.' He seemed pleased. 'I'll have you there for dinner. What would you like to eat?'

She blinked. 'I hadn't thought about it.'

'Something special. It will be our last supper.' He slapped the map. 'He's heading towards Alice Springs. Mr Hunnicutt is trying to make fools of us by driving in a great big circle.'

'You're certain?'

'No.' He laughed. 'How could anyone be certain with such a slippery character as Hunnicutt? But I have a feeling. The closest roads I can see that run around the edge of the desert..,' he checked the map, '... the Simpson Desert, seem to end up near Alice Springs. Surely after such a journey he will have to buy fuel? Maybe food. Where else would he go but to Alice Springs? Therefore, we will go there, we will have dinner, you will buy a plane ticket and I will hire myself a four-wheel drive. You will fly to Melbourne and I will go out to meet the elusive Mr Hunnicutt.'

Kolvenbach unhooked the radio's microphone and called Mount Isa to advise of his changed flight plan.

It was night and they had stopped on the edge of the Simpson Desert. All around them were eroded hills, stark trees and great masses of red rocks flashing tiny reflections from the fire. The rocks were in mounds, like bricks that marked the site of a demolished building; there were thousands of them, glossy and sharp-edged, and so clean-cut they could have been shaped by hammer and chisel. Low sand drifts, the probing fingers of the moving desert, stretched from one rocky pile to the next.

It was not a pleasant place to camp but there was an abundance of dead wood and the rugged hostility of the terrain made it seem safer. It was not a place where humans would willingly gather.

Since leaving Boulia, they had seen only one other vehicle, a big stock truck that was heading for Glenormiston, the last cattle station before the Northern Territory border. Unaware of their presence, the driver let his truck rumble ahead of them, swirling dust into a tunnel of brown which hid them all the way to the station turnoff.

After that, nothing. Only a spreading wilderness of worn land and shattered rock.

Kelly had made the fire. It was small; an Aborigine's fire, big enough to cook a meal but not so bright that it might attract some curious stockman camped over the horizon. Monica was frying sausages and onions. Two billycans simmered in the coals; one contained boiled potatoes, the other held the water for their tea.

They had crossed the Georgina two hours earlier but Kelly was still talking about it. The inland rivers fascinated him. Monica listened, occasionally prodding a sausage or turning it over and sending the dripping into a paroxysm of fatty explosions.

One day, Kelly said, staring with unfocused eyes into the flames, he was going to drive along the entire course of the Georgina.

'Any good birds?' Monica asked in a way that meant she was humouring him.

'Loads,' he said, although he'd never noticed; but surely there'd be enough birds along a river that skirted desert country to keep her pen busy for weeks. 'It's got so many different names,' he said while she turned all the sausages. The Georgina started up on the Barkly Tableland, near a homestead called Gallipoli. Then it was joined by three other rivers, the Buckley, the James and the Ranken. And that was before it left the Northern Territory.

'You know your rivers,' she said, with a lilt to her voice that made Kelly move his eyes from the flames. She'd make a great teacher of little children, he thought as he caught the patronising smile; but the flames were mesmeric and he continued. Once across the Queensland border, it attracted the Templeton River, then a couple of creeks; then south of Boulia it was joined by the Burke and the Hamilton Rivers.

'That's where we were today?' She knew, but was trying to sound interested.

'Yes. You crossed the Burke with me under the blanket and the Hamilton's not far from where we met that couple with the Boulia cop for a son.'

She laughed. It was funny now that they were well clear of Boulia.

'So how many's that?' He went through the list. 'Six rivers so far. Seven if you include the Georgina itself. And who's ever heard of it? The Georgina — our great unknown river.'

'Fascinating. Dinner's almost ready.'

He was starving, he said, but kept his eye on the fire. He'd really do this journey some time. Across three states and half of Australia.

Did she remember where they'd crossed that big claypan north of Birdsville? No, she'd been asleep. Well, west of there, the Georgina changed its name and became the Eyre Creek.

She lowered the frying pan. 'Why?'

His eyes left the fire. He stared up at the night sky for inspiration but he was still dazzled by the fire's glow and saw nothing. He laughed. 'I don't know. Probably two different explorers gave it two different names.'

'An erudite explanation. Would you get the plates?'

Between passing the plates and taking the first bite, he recounted how the Eyre Creek was joined by the Mulligan River and how it was then joined by the Diamantina and how all of them became the Warburton Creek.

'And then what?' She knew the story was close to its end and asked the question brightly.

'The Warburton runs into Lake Eyre. Right up near the top. There's a big groove across the salt, like a muddy stain, where the river flows in. When it flows.'

'And you're going to drive along its entire length?'

He was tackling a hot sausage and nodded, teeth bared to spare his lips from burning.

311

'Which river? It sounds like you've got a dozen to choose from.'

'I'll start with the Georgina, near Gallipoli station and ignore all the tributaries, until it becomes the Eyre Creek. Then I'll follow that and the Warburton down to Lake Eyre.'

She joined him in staring into the fire. 'That would be a mammoth trip. But great.'

'Full of beautiful birds,' he said. 'But not much water.'

They talked during the meal, while they drank tea and while they stretched out their bed rolls. Before lying down, he put out the fire, using a shovel to cover the coals with dirt.

A deep blackness, an intense quietness, closed around them.

'What sort of films do you make?' she asked.

'Little films. Trade films. Not important, except to the people who pay for them.'

She seemed worried. 'Aren't they any good?'

He lay on his back, one arm tucked behind his head and with his eyes searching the skies for familiar constellations. 'Yes, of their type, they're very good. We make good money.' The last part was defensive, he realised, and regretted having said it. It was the sort of thing he used to say to Laura. He was talking to an artist who couldn't afford to buy a decent truck but was dedicated to her work. She would probably be famous one day and be remembered long after she died. No one was going to remember his epics about floor tiles and new motors.

'That's important,' she said with a laugh.

He propped himself on one elbow. 'Being remembered?' His voice kinked in surprise.

She matched his pose. Their eyes were growing used to the night and they could just see each other. 'No. Money. You said you made good money.'

'Oh. Yes, I do. Or I did.'

'Which is why you can afford to pay for all this petrol we're using.'

He laughed and lay on his back again.

She was still looking at him. 'Do you want to make any other sort of films? You know, documentaries for TV or movies for the cinema?'

He sighed. 'I don't know.'

'You don't know whether you want to or not?'

'I don't know whether I'm good enough.'

She was quiet for a long time. 'You're honest. That's rare.'

He had a good feeling about Monica. She was not thinking critically of him; she understood him and was even impressed — unlike Laura and so many of her friends with their pretentious ambition.

She said, 'There's one way to find out'.

'By trying?' He shifted in his sleeping bag. 'Feature films cost millions. There aren't too many people around these days willing to risk that sort of money on some unknown film director.'

She sat up, pulling her bag around her shoulders. 'Back to the first question. Would you like to make feature films?'

The Milky Way was particularly brilliant. He loved the outback skies. They were so clear, so far removed from earthly worries. He sighed and spoke slowly, as though the words hurt. 'To be frank, I don't think so. Making a big film would be a huge headache. You deal with hundreds of people. You fight with the producer, the writer, the actors, everyone.' He found the Southern Cross and its pointers, and fixed celestial south. She was waiting, not satisfied with the answer. 'I'd rather make small films. Good, small, high-quality films.'

'Like you're doing?'

'Maybe ... I think what I'd like to do,' he said, folding his arms across his chest with great

313

deliberation, 'is make good documentaries. One-hour features. Something for television. The industry used to be able to make short features for the cinema but those days are gone, unhappily. So it's TV or nothing.'

'What sort of documentaries?'

'Who knows?'

'You should.'

A couple of grunts suggested a laugh. 'You don't give a man any rest, do you?'

'No, come on. I'm interested.'

'Documentaries about some interesting subject.'

'Like your trip down the Georgina?'

He hadn't thought of that. 'I'd have to get someone to act as presenter. Someone to write it.' He was spinning a web of problems.

'You could star. You could write it.'

'I've never been in front of the camera in my life.'

'Well, it's about time you were. Come on, Kelly, you'd be good. You're not bad looking.' She paused, as though reconsidering and he heard a snicker. 'And you certainly know the subject.'

He was silent.

'Well, that's one subject,' she continued. 'And let's face it, Kelso Hunnicutt, notorious diamond-killer, the most talked-about man in Australia, when all this is over and you've straightened everything out, there'll be people clamouring for your story. You could probably get a million for appearing in a documentary like that.'

He gave a short, derisive grunt. 'The way Australian television is at the moment, they'd be scratching to pay me a hundred dollars.'

'All right. Say half a million. Think big, Kelly, think big.' She wriggled deeper into her sleeping back. Her voice was lower, closer to sleep. 'Now, what's going to be the second documentary? Another one about the outback, I presume?'

'I'll have to make you my manager.'

'You need someone.' She made an oohing sound, having dredged up an unexpected thought. 'How about a film on birds?'

'I don't know anything about birds.'

'They fly. Some of them nest in trees. Many of them have pretty feathers. Anything else you need to know, I'll tell you. I'll be your expert adviser.'

'I could always make a film about you.'

She made a smug little sound. 'I thought you'd never think of it. You could call it "A Bird in the Bush".'

'A Bird...' He laughed. 'You're right. It'd be good. Lone girl wandering the outback, sleeping on river banks, waking strangers before dawn to get them to move their cars.'

'You see? You've got the story outline already. Can I ask you a question?'

'You haven't been doing too badly so far without seeking my permission. What's on your mind?'

'When should we get under way again?'

He reached for the torch and shone the light on his watch. 'About midnight. That's in three hours and ten minutes' time.'

'See you then.' She rolled on to her side. Within minutes, her breathing had become heavy and slow. She snored. Only lightly, and rather pleasantly, Kelly thought, like a woman enjoying her sleep.

He rolled on his side but couldn't sleep. His mind was afire with thoughts.

The message came through late that night. McCarthy had just gone to bed. He grumbled all the way to the phone but his bad temper ended when his contact, who was on night shift, gave him the news. Kolvenbach had changed his flight plan. He was now heading for Alice Springs. Correction; he would have landed in Alice Springs. According

315

to the amended flight plan, he was due there about seven. Four hours ago.

So Kolvenbach would be there all night, McCarthy mused. How extraordinary. Alice Springs was where Harry was flying to. Adelaide to Alice Springs, Harry had said; then he would charter an aircraft to fly him to Mount Isa. No need, no need. Again McCarthy shook his head, scarcely believing his good fortune. He searched for the number of the Adelaide motel. Harry would be surprised.

Harry, who was going to kill Laura Hunnicutt, had had his victim delivered to him.

28

Just after dawn, Kelly and Monica came upon a Land Rover parked at the side of the road. A rear wheel was off, tools were scattered around the vehicle, and a man was sleeping on a camp stretcher strategically placed across the wheel tracks.

As they approached, the man sat up, rubbing his face with a filthy hand.

'We've got to stop,' Kelly mumbled, the reluctant humanitarian triumphing over the hunted fugitive.

'Agreed,' Monica said in a worried whisper.

They stayed in the truck. The man approached, hitching up his pants and touching the brim of an imaginary hat when he saw Monica.

'Got troubles?' Kelly said.

'You could say that. Not carrying a spare diff for a Land Rover by any chance?' His face was smeared with grease and when he grinned, it cracked into the patterns of a rumpled old road map.

'Sorry.'

The man stopped opposite Kelly and peered inside the truck, checking for himself. He had keen eyes. He was the sort of man, Kelly feared, who would miss nothing and remember everything.

'Been here long?' Kelly asked, scratching his face so that his hand covered his mouth and chin.

'Day before yesterday.' He glanced in the back of the truck. 'Got room for a passenger?'

Kelly hesitated. His eyes must have registered dismay because the other man stepped back. Kelly forced himself to smile brightly. 'Where are you heading for?'

'Jervois. The copper mine. Only a couple of hours down the road.'

'Sure,' Monica said quickly and slid closer to Kelly. She began talking the moment the man climbed on board and didn't stop until they reached the copper mine. She and Kelly were photographers on an assignment for *National Geographic*. The man asked their names — Des and Jen Bartlett. Normally they did movies but they'd switched to still photography in recent years.

The man snapped his fingers. He had seen one of their films. About a goose? In the US or Canada or somewhere up there. For Disney?

Yes. That was one of their favourites.

He loved the shot of the goose flying beside the station wagon.

That had taken days to get.

It must have. He was a photographer himself. Only an amateur, of course. He liked taking pictures of birds.

Really? She showed him her camera and brought out the biggest lens. He clucked in appreciation.

He introduced himself apologetically; after all, he was travelling with famous people. He was the manager of the Jervois mine. He'd been to see friends at Manners Creek. The radio wasn't working. He knew that when he set off. Stupid, in country like this.

At the mine, he said, 'I don't suppose you've got time for coffee or a drink?' and they concurred; they had to film magpie geese at a lagoon up in the north and a friend was waiting for them.

When they were under way, Kelly laughed. 'Gee, you can talk.'

'I didn't want him staring at you any more or asking awkward questions.'

'Why Des and Jen Bartlett? Do you know them?'

'I know of them, of course. They do those lovely wildlife documentaries. I just thought of their names. Better to pretend to be someone famous rather than just a pair of nobodies. Now if someone asks him if he's seen a desperado running from the police, he'll say "No, but I met this famous pair of photographers, the Bartletts," and start telling them about the goose film.'

'You hope.'

She nodded agreement. 'I hope.' She reached in the back for the pack of food. 'Hungry?'

The first thing the mine manager did was to get a beer. The second thing was to go to the radio. His hands had begun to shake by the time he had raised the man he wanted. 'That you, Mick? Listen. I've spent the last day or so broken down about eighty kilometres east of here and I just got picked up by a couple in an old blue Ford ute.'

He sipped the drink and wiped his mouth with the back of his wrist. 'Yes, yes, I'm okay. Listen. There were two of them, a man and a woman. I don't know who the woman is but the man's Kelso Hunnicutt... that's him... absolutely no doubt.' He laughed and his hand shook violently. 'Scared shit- less. I thought he might want to take a look inside the Land Rover and that would have been the end of me because I had Saturday's paper on the seat and his picture was all over the front page... No, I didn't see any explosives or things like that but the back of the truck is full of drums and boxes and he could have had anything in there.' He drank more beer and felt better. 'They're heading west... Yeah.' He gave a detailed description of the couple and the truck. 'They gave me some cock-and-bull

319

story about being a pair of wildlife photographers. She's got cameras... No, they're cameras, I'm sure of that. Expensive stuff... They said they were going north.' He laughed and beer frothed from his lips. 'They said they were going to shoot something.' Another laugh. 'No, geese.'

Kelly saw the old man and thought of driving around him but it would have meant running the man down because he was dancing across the road, waving his arms and shouting for them to stop. Anxiously, Kelly looked around. There were faint wheel tracks on the left. Almost out of sight, an old, old utility truck was parked beside a boulder. He could see no one else.

Monica had been dozing. 'Who is it?'

'Don't know. He seems harmless.'

The old man held up his hands, to show that he had nothing in them. Tentatively he approached Kelly's door. 'No need to get alarmed, young fella.' He leaned against the door and acknowledged them both with a sly smile. He wore a hat that looked as though it had spent most of its life under a mattress. 'They're waiting for you down the road so you'd better turn off here.' He indicated the track. 'Just follow me.'

Kelly looked around them. The country here was dry but colourful. It had flourishing trees with broad, white trunks, clumps of large boulders and in the distance, a strip of mountains that stained the horizon a pale blue. But apart from the old man, it seemed devoid of life.

'Who's waiting?'

'The cops. They're setting up a roadblock or whatever they call it, down at Harts Range. Come on.' He began hurrying towards his utility.

Kelly got out and ran after him. 'Just a moment. What are you talking about?'

The man's forehead set in rows of knotted cords. 'You're this Hunnicutt bloke, aren't you?' When Kelly's mouth opened but no words came out, he added, 'I was just listening on the radio and I heard Perry calling up Mick Nelson and telling him he'd just been given a lift by you and a sheila'.

'Who's Perry? Who's Mick Nelson?'

'Perry Gilquist. He's the manager of the mine back there. The bloke you gave a lift to. Mick Nelson's the cop at Harts Range. He's just down the road. Come on.'

'Who are you?'

The man's glance swept from Kelly's boots to his hat. 'I'm the bloke who's trying to bloody well save your skin. We're wasting time. Come on.'

Gerry Montague expected to be caught so he had his excuse prepared. It was simple, even naive, but he couldn't think of anything better. He desperately needed fresh air. That was the only reason he'd slipped out of the apartment. He was feeling nauseous. If they doubted him, he would vomit over their feet. He could do it; he still felt bad. But no one was following him. George had been shouting at Spiro about something and the third man, who'd been watching him all night, had been asleep in the other bedroom. No one had seen him go out the back.

A taxi came around the corner. He blessed the driver, signalled the cab, and scrambled across the rear seat. The city, he ordered. The top end of Collins Street.

Montague made the journey sitting sideways in the corner, so he could look through the rear window. He saw no sign of pursuit but he hadn't seen anyone the last time and that episode had ended disastrously. He was wearing sunglasses and a hat but the taxi driver still asked him what had happened to his face.

321

'The woman's husband has a bad temper,' Montague said, and the driver smiled sympathetically.

'Some men just can't handle that sort of thing,' he said and Montague agreed. 'Think he's following you?'

'You never know.'

The driver peered into his outside mirror. 'What's he drive?'

'A semitrailer.'

The driver laughed. 'You're clear.' He turned to make eye contact. 'Next time, pick a woman whose man rides a pushbike.'

When they were in Collins Street, Montague said, 'Stop here. Wait. I won't be long.' He went into a leather-goods shop and used one of his sheaf of credit cards to buy a briefcase. He stayed in the shop for another minute, to see if anyone approached the taxi. No one did so he hurried back and had the driver do a slow lap of the block, then drive into the Regent.

Montague paid the driver handsomely and hurried inside. After browsing through a few shops to make sure he wasn't being followed, he went upstairs to the hotel reception area. The telephone booths were nearby. First he went to the men's room and reached into the fold in his underpants for the slip of paper with Rob Lister's number. Then he went to a booth and rang Canberra.

'Yes, it's about Kolvenbach,' he said when he had Lister on the line. 'And never mind who's calling. I believe you want some papers?'

There was silence.

'Look, this isn't blackmail. I'm just ringing to tell you who's got the papers. You can get them back and then you can do what you like with the bloke. Okay?'

After a pause, Lister said, 'I don't know what you're talking about'.

'Of course not. But if you've got a pen handy, I'll give you his name and tell you where you can find him. And the papers.' He gave him McCarthy's name, his office address and the address of his own flat. 'You'll know that last one,' he said with grim humour. 'That's where McCarthy is at the moment. He's going to blackmail you until you haven't got a cent left. But be careful, he's got two good men in there with him. You've already seen what they can do to your hired hands.'

There was a scratching noise. Lister was still writing. 'Who is this I'm talking to?'

'Someone who knows everything. By the way, there is something you can do for me, Mr Lister.'

'You said you weren't after money.'

'The deal is you get the papers, I get the diamonds. McCarthy has some diamonds.'

Montague heard a clicking sound.

'I'll ring you tonight, Mr Lister. Can I get you on this number?'

'I really don't know what all this is about.'

'I said, can I get you on this number?'

'I'll be here.'

'Good. Let me know what happens.' Montague hung up and with his new briefcase under one arm, walked to the reception desk. He booked a suite for the night, giving a Sydney address. He would pay cash.

The clerk looked at his face but said nothing.

'I had an accident at the airport,' Montague volunteered, touching the side of his face. 'Hit by a taxi.'

'Do you need a doctor, sir?'

'I've seen a doctor, thank you.'

'Some of these drivers...'

'Indeed.'

Once in the room, Montague rang his office. Mary Calibrano was frantic. She had been trying to ring

Montague but those detectives who were minding his flat in case Kelly made contact kept answering and they refused to put him on the line.

'I've had enough of them,' he said. 'So I've moved out for a while. Forced out of my own place. Lovely, isn't it?' She thought it was disgraceful. He gave her his room number but said he wanted no one else to know where he was. There was one exception. He might get a phone call from Laura Hunnicutt.

'Where is Mrs Hunnicutt?' Mary said, her voice fragile with worry.

'It seems she's been with Kelly.' Montague heard the surprised intake of breath. 'I don't know the story but I do want to talk to her. Will you please give her this number. No one else.'

'Can I call? If it's urgent?'

'Sure. But only if it's important.' He hung up, checked that the front door to the suite was locked, and went to the desk. He took out some sheets of hotel writing paper and began making a list of things to do.

The track led into a jumble of scalloped hills. The old man lived in a hut made from rough wooden planks and rusting sheets of iron. The hut projected from the side of a low hill that was so encrusted with broken rock it resembled the crumbling ramparts of an ancient fortress. The back door of the hut opened into a tunnel. It used to be the entrance to a gold mine, the old man said, and began boiling water for tea.

'You're the first visitors I ever had. 'Cept for Wally.'

'Who's Wally?' Kelly stayed near the open door. He had to bend to look out.

'An old blackfella. He comes every few days. Brings me a few things. Don't go into town m'self, not if I can help it.'

324

Monica said, 'You live here on your own?'

'Just me.' He'd lived there for more than eighteen years, he said, but didn't say why. Kelly wondered about the gold mine. The man had the ruined hands and secretive face of an old-time prospector.

'Now,' Kelly said as the man poured tea into chipped cups, 'why are you helping us? What's all this about?'

'It's not about nothin'. I just don't like seein' a bloke on the run and bein' hounded by every bastard around.' He looked up. 'Only got powdered milk. That do?'

'That's fine.'

'Don't particularly have a likin' for the law,' he said with a mischievous grin. 'Or the taxman. Or wives.'

'You're keeping clear of all three?' Monica suggested, and he burst into a cackling laugh.

He turned sharply towards Kelly. 'This your wife?' His voice had the low whine that men reserve for a fellow sufferer.

'No.'

'Well, that's somethin'. Wives are a curse.' He looked at Monica as though she needed convincing. 'I know it for a fact.'

'Really?' she said and seemed prepared for an argument.

'What's your name?' Kelly asked.

'Percy.'

'Just Percy?'

'That'll do.'

'Well, I'm Kelly.' He held out his hand.

Percy took it. His palm felt like bark. 'I thought your name was Kelso?'

'It is but everyone calls me Kelly.'

He frowned, lost in a half-forgotten memory. 'People used to call me Spider.'

'Do you prefer Percy?' Monica said.

He seemed to have forgotten she was there. He nodded, acknowledging her presence. 'I don't talk to no one 'cept Wally these days so it don't matter.'

'And what does Wally call you?'

'Nothin'.'

Kelly, back at the doorway, bent to look outside. He felt uncomfortable inside a building. 'Are the police looking for you, Percy?' he asked.

Percy cackled and wiped tea from his chin. 'Not any more.' He grinned at Monica, eager to share the joke.

'But they were?'

'Maybe.' He winked at Monica.

Kelly took a few steps outside the building and gazed up at the rocky slope. 'Do you know why the police are after me?'

'Nope. I just heard them talkin' on the radio.' He jerked a thumb towards a radio set that stood against the far wall. 'Have you got dynamite or gelignite or somethin' like that on board that thing of yours?'

Kelly ambled back inside. 'No. Why?'

'They reckoned you were carryin' explosives.' He frowned into his mug of tea. 'Pity. I could of used some.'

'I'm wanted for murder, Percy.'

'Oh.' The old man looked into his tea and then slowly let his eyes wander across to Kelly. There was awe on his face. 'Jesus. I never killed anyone.' He made it sound like an omission.

'Well neither did I.'

With great precision, Percy removed a tea leaf from the rim of his cup. 'No?'

'No.'

'But they're after you, just the same?'

'Yes.'

'Bloody coppers — won't leave a man alone.'

Monica put more sugar in her tea. 'What were they saying on the radio?'

'Perry Gilquist said you'd picked him up on the road. He'd been broken down somewhere east of Jervois?'

'He'd done a diff,' Kelly said.

'He's a city bloke, not a bushman. Always on the radio. Sends a lot of telegrams. The man'll end up perishin'. Third time he's broken down.' He bent his head in thought. 'Could be four. Always breakin' something. Should go back to Brisbane. Anyhow, he said you reckoned you was gonna take pictures of geese or somethin', but he recognised you.' He pointed a bent finger at Kelly. 'He had Saturday's paper in his car and it had your picture on the front.' He grinned. 'A bloke can be stiff, can't he?'

'Apparently my picture's been in all the papers.'

'Fair dinkum?' He was impressed. 'Who do they reckon you killed? Someone important?' He leant forward eagerly. 'Not a politician?'

Monica laughed. 'No.'

'Pity.' He was genuinely disappointed. 'Who then?'

'A man in Melbourne. I knew him. He was a good man. He was starting a diamond mine up in the Kimberleys.'

Percy's head tilted to one side, as curious as a puzzled puppy. 'A miner. What was his name?'

'Harald Kolvenbach.'

He scratched the stubble on his chin. 'Was he up in north Queensland once? On the Palmer?'

'I don't think so. He was South African.'

Percy moved his head, trying to shake the name into place.

Monica said, 'What else did they say on the radio?'

Percy put down his cup and clasped his hands in concentration. 'Mick Nelson, he's the cop, asked if you was carrying dynamite. You said you wasn't?'

'No.'

'Why would he say that if you didn't have any?'

'Because they think I have. They also think I've got a machine gun on board.'

'Jesus. I'd like to see that.'

'I don't have it. Never did.'

He shook his head profoundly. 'Bloody cops. That's typical. If you haven't done nothin', they'll soon think of somethin' to hound you for.'

'You said they were setting up a roadblock,' Monica prompted.

'Well, Mick Nelson is. I met him once. Be a nice enough bloke if he wasn't a cop. Only young. His wife had a baby that died.'

Kelly waited a respectful time. 'So there's just this one policeman waiting down the road?'

'Suppose so. He's got one of those new four-wheel drive Japanese things.'

'And he's waiting at Harts Range?'

'Yeah.' Percy got up and walked to the door. 'Where are you heading for?'

'Melbourne eventually. I want to get back and try and clean this business up.'

His eyes darted from Kelly to Monica, to make sure he wasn't being teased. 'Isn't this a bloody funny way to be goin' to Melbourne?'

'I haven't got much choice. Do you know Melbourne?'

'Never been there. It's not over that way, is it?' He angled his head towards the west.

'It's to the south. We thought we might go through Alice Springs.'

'Ah.' He was happier with familiar names. 'They'll be looking for you in the Alice. Young Nelson would of radioed through. They'll have police up The Bitumen waiting for you.' He laughed and slapped his thigh.

'What's so funny?'

His face became wreathed in wrinkles of cunning. 'You want to get to the Alice?'

'If we can?'

'I'll get you there. You can go Wally's way.'

The police four-wheel drive was parked sideways across the road. When Kolvenbach saw it, he checked that the rifles were covered and then continued, changing down through the gears until it was time to brake. Slowly, like someone disturbed from rest, a policeman got out of the driver's seat and raised one hand. Broad-brimmed khaki hat, light brown shirt, light brown pants, boots; good hunting gear, Kolvenbach thought and noted the revolver on the man's hip. Another policeman, an Aborigine, was sitting under a tree, using his knees to prop up a rifle.

The policeman kept his hand in the air until Kolvenbach had stopped and turned off the engine. Like so many whites up here, he had red hair and freckled skin. Warily, he approached the rented Pajero and looked inside before speaking.

'Morning, driver. Where are you heading?'

'I was just sightseeing. Lovely country.' Kolvenbach made a show of studying his map. 'I thought I'd go as far as the Jervois Range.' Earnestly, he added, 'What's the road like?'

The policeman noticed the rent-a-car sticker and chewed at his lower lip. 'I'm afraid you can't go any farther. We have an emergency situation.'

So someone else had seen Hunnicutt. Play the tourist. Find out what you can, then get out of here. 'It's my first time in the Centre. I wanted to get out of town and have a look around. You know, see some of the real country.'

'Sorry.' The policeman had pale, nomadic eyes. They avoided Kolvenbach's face but roamed across his hands, the Pajero's windscreen, the roof with its empty rack, the knobbly front tyre. 'I can't let you go up there, sir. Not to Jervois.' He squinted towards the end of the road, up at the sky, across to the distant mountains which were turning a smoky grey as the day grew hotter. Finally, he returned to Kolvenbach's face. 'I'm afraid you'll have to turn around and go back.'

Kolvenbach seemed crestfallen. 'Why?'

The policeman's boot played with the front tyre. 'Like I said, we have an emergency situation. We can't allow anyone up that road.'

'Can I do anything to help?'

'Thank you, sir. No.' He looked around, measuring a turning circle for Kolvenbach's vehicle. 'I wouldn't linger. We don't want people on this road.'

Kolvenbach was about to move when the policeman stopped. 'May I see your licence, sir?'

Blast. 'Of course.' Kolvenbach handed the man his international driving licence.

'From overseas?'

'Africa.'

'Kolvenbach?' The man stumbled over the word, then frowned, troubled by a slovenly memory.

Kolvenbach laughed. 'A very common name where I come from. It's like Smith.'

The man was still worried. 'Just visiting?'

'Yes.'

'When did you arrive in Alice Springs?'

'Yesterday. By air.'

The man's lower lip ballooned, inflated by growing doubt. With reluctance, he handed back Kolvenbach's licence. 'Where are you staying, sir?'

No point lying. 'The Oasis.' Time to give the policeman another problem. 'Where would you suggest I go? Somewhere where there are mountains...'

The constable took a deep breath and put both hands on his hips. 'Most people like to see the MacDonnell Ranges.'

'Good.' Kolvenbach selected first gear. 'I'll go

there.' He waved, turned in a half circle, shouted his thanks and drove off.

The policeman stayed in the middle of the road. Kolvenbach could see him in the mirror, his hands on his hips, a figure set in the classical pose of doubt. It was the name. Sooner or later he would connect Kolvenbach with Hunnicutt and then he'd radio Alice Springs and the police would check his story. Which meant he had to go back to the Oasis motel.

He glanced in the mirror again. The police vehicle's windscreen was flashing in the sun. He shook his head. Even without the reflected light, Hunnicutt would see the vehicle a mile away. Which meant that somehow he would drive around the roadblock.

But which way? Kolvenbach slowed and checked his map. Hunnicutt would have to be heading for Alice Springs. If there was a roadblock out here at Harts Range, there'd be roadblocks on the Stuart Highway, the main south-north road out of Alice Springs. That meant Hunnicutt would avoid the highway. As he drove back along the road, Kolvenbach's eyes followed the ranges rimming the horizon. It looked like rough country. Perfect terrain for Hunnicutt.

Henry Delacombe was in the middle of the crowd that poured from the Ansett 737. He followed the leading group across the tarmac and into the Alice Springs air terminal, sweating a little because he was dressed for the cooler south. He was an ordinary-looking man, of ordinary size and wearing ordinary clothes, like a dozen of his fellow passengers. He had on a white shirt and tie, fawn pants, tan shoes, hat and sunglasses, and he carried his coat over his arm. He was a man you wouldn't look at twice, which was precisely what Henry Delacombe wanted. He had

331

dressed with great care, even cut his hair and shaved off his moustache so that he would not be noticed.

To the few people aware of his vocation, Henry Delacombe was known as Harry the Hatchet. Not that he ever used a hatchet. Usually it was a gun, although he had been known to poison, to drown or to strangle. He preferred the latter. It was more satisfying and there was no doubt when the job was over that the assignment had been brought to a successful conclusion.

When he entered the terminal, he was still wondering how he was going to find Laura Hunnicutt. Presumably by doing something as simple as going to a telephone and ringing hotels and motels and asking for her. That's if she were using her real name. McCarthy had said she might be registered as Kolvenbach.

He collected a handful of hotel brochures and went to the public phones. They were all busy. He stood behind a Sikh who was talking rapidly and waving his free hand. The man was dressed in a lightweight suit of gunmetal grey and a cerise turban. Stunning. It would make a great disguise some day. He could even hide something in the turban. He would wear his thick-rimmed glasses and all people would recall would be the turban and the glasses. The man's watch was gold; worth at least 3,000 dollars, Harry guessed, unless it was a copy he'd picked up in Bangkok. He looked again at the clothes. No, the watch would be real. You didn't spoil a two-thousand-dollar suit by wearing a twenty-dollar watch. The Sikh turned and offered a liquid smile of apology, but kept talking.

At the next phone, a woman was trying to get through to someone and apparently having no luck, because she was becoming increasingly agitated. She put her coins in again and rang another number. Avoiding the woman's face — Harry the Hatchet didn't want anyone staring back at him — he watched her fingers. Good rings. Real diamonds. She dialled 03 — Melbourne. She asked for a room number. Only then did he study the woman with any interest. Head down, his favoured pose, he started from the bottom. Good shoes. None of those horrible, striped sneakers that people wore these days. Italian shoes, tan with beige panels. A nice rounded toe, low heels but not too low; a woman's ankle needed elevation to make it enticing. No stockings, but who could wear stockings up here? Good legs, tailored skirt with pleats that slimmed already slim hips. Off-white cotton blouse with three-quarter length sleeves, appliqued in a fine but subtle pattern. Elegant. Very expensive. French? No, Italian; designed in Milan. He'd bet money on it.

He should have been a tailor; he loved good clothes. Never mind, he made more money than any tailor he knew.

She wore an expensive watch; ultraslim case, a jewelled bezel, gold band. Swiss or French, he guessed; not Japanese, although it was becoming difficult to tell. Two plain gold bangles on the right wrist. A fine gold chain around the neck. Hair upswept. Good face. Straight nose, high cheekbones. He looked again, transferred his coat to his other arm and moved away from the phones. He lit a cigarette and, face shielded by his hands, looked again.

No doubt. It was the Hunnicutt woman.

29

It was several hours before a furious George McCarthy thought of ringing Montague's office. His men had searched the building, combed the streets and checked the car, but there was no sign of Montague. Would he have done something as stupid as go to his office?

Mary Calibrano answered. She was feeling happier because, only ten minutes earlier, Laura Hunnicutt had telephoned from Alice Springs and as requested, Mary had passed on Montague's number at the Regent. And then Gerry himself had rung back. Good news — Laura was returning to Melbourne and when she got home later that day, they might be able to prove Kelly's innocence. It was all very mysterious but Gerry sounded happy. He also sounded a little drunk.

McCarthy introduced himself as Superintendent Wilson of Russell Street. He had been trying to contact Mr Montague at his apartment but Mr Montague had left without leaving a forwarding address.

'He's not here,' Mary said dutifully.

The caller emitted the sad sign of a disappointed but sincere man. 'This is so important. We have information that casts a whole new light on this wretched business of Kelso Hunnicutt.'

She tingled with interest. 'New light?'

'Completely. In fact, we have information that points to a new suspect. But Miss . . .'

'Calibrano. I am — I was — Mr Hunnicutt's secretary. You said a new suspect?'

'Yes, but Miss Calibrano, we must talk to Mr Montague. He is the vital link in this investigation. We need him to prove the innocence of Mr Hunnicutt. And we can't find the man. He seems to have disappeared.'

'Oh.'

'Every hour the hunt for Mr Hunnicutt continues, he's in great peril. I'm sure you're aware of that.'

'Indeed. I've been so worried, Superintendent.'

'I'm sure you have, Miss Calibrano. But if I'm to call off this manhunt and possibly save Mr Hunnicutt's life, I have to talk to Mr Montague.'

She was twisting the piece of notepaper with Montague's room number on it.

'You say he's not in the office?'

'No. There's no one else. I'm on my own.'

'And he hasn't been there all day?'

'No.'

'Miss Calibrano, why do I get the feeling you're withholding something from me?'

She mumbled a few incomplete phrases.

'Please, Miss Calibrano. Mr Hunnicutt's life may depend on our finding Mr Montague quickly. Do you know where he is?'

Fidgeting with uncertainty, she said, 'He's in a city hotel, I think'.

'You think?'

She straightened her back and lifted her head. 'He's staying at the Regent Hotel.' She gave him the room number.

'Thank you, Miss Calibrano. We'll call him straight away.'

'You'll let me know what happens? I mean, about clearing Mr Hunnicutt.'

'Immediately. Thank you for your help.'

McCarthy hung up, pushed himself out of his seat and, waving his hands like a triumphant boxer, yelled for Spiro.

'He's at the Regent.' He gave him the room number. 'And Spiro,' he added, slapping his man on each of his broad shoulders, 'make it neat, won't you?'

He called to his other man. 'Let's tidy up this place. Leave nothing to show we've been here. It's time for us to get out.'

Percy the hermit wasn't sure if it was Tuesday or Wednesday and neither Kelly nor Monica could help; they'd lost track of the days. 'Don't matter,' Percy said, eyes fixed on a distant gap in the hills. 'I got a feeling Wally'll be here today.'

'Do we need Wally?'

'If you wanna get into the Alice without no one seein' you, you do.'

'Don't you know the way?'

Percy gave Kelly a look that was part tolerant good humour, part pity. 'You need Wally, son. The old bloke's better at this sort of thing than me. He goes into town a lot and he moves through these hills like a bloody shadow.'

'What if he doesn't come today?'

'Then he'll come tomorrow. Or the day after. What's up? In a hurry to get to the pub?'

Kelly tried to match Percy's good humour but he was restless. The hut seemed a perfect hideout and the truck was out of sight, parked within the entrance to another hillside tunnel; but he was frantic with worry about Laura and anxious to get back to Melbourne. He could do nothing up here.

Monica was lying on a mattress in one corner. She was trying to sleep but tossed continuously.

Percy took Kelly by the elbow and led him outside. 'She been any trouble to you?'

'No.'

He seemed to doubt the answer; Kelly might have been trying to convince him day was night. 'Where'd you find her?'

Find her? Kelly stumbled for an answer. 'In Queensland.'

Percy frowned. That answer worried him too, as though he'd had bad times in Queensland. 'Whereabouts?'

It all seemed so long ago. 'On the Bulloo River. She was camped there. She's been terrific.'

Percy dismissed the last bit of information. 'What was she doing there?'

'Painting birds.'

The answer astonished Percy. 'What the hell for?'

'She does it for a living.'

The old man turned for another look at the woman in the corner. 'Never heard of that in my life. I thought they was colourful enough as it was.'

Kelly took Percy by the shoulder and pointed up to a tree. 'She sees a bird up in a tree and she gets her brush and paints and some canvas, and she paints a picture. She's an artist.'

Percy slapped his knee. 'I thought you meant...' He stopped abruptly. The big radio in the corner of the hut had crackled into life. He put a finger to his lips and led Kelly back inside. 'The police band,' he said softly, sitting on a stool near the set. 'Usually spouts a lot of bullshit but it gives a man an occasional laugh. Tells him when to keep outa sight too.' He waved a hand when he recognised the voice. 'That's Mick Nelson at Harts Range.'

Nelson was calling Alice Springs. He had stopped a man on the Plenty road and sent him back to town. The man's name was Kolvenbach. He spelt it and Kelly, astonished, sank to the earthen floor.

Nelson was asking, 'Isn't that the same name as the bloke who was killed by Hunnicutt?'

337

Affirmative. 'I thought it rang a bell. He's staying at the Oasis. Better check him out, eh?' Nelson then gave a detailed description of the man. He was driving a hired Mitsubishi Pajero. He read out the registration number and the name of the rental company.

'He's thorough, isn't he?' Percy said, his scowl spoiled by the taint of admiration. 'If you had a pimple on your nose, he'd report it.' He noticed how pale Kelly had become. 'What's up?'

Monica pushed herself into a sitting position. 'Isn't that the same man who was chasing you?'

Numbed, Kelly nodded. 'Kolvenbach.'

'The man who was killed?'

'Jesus,' Percy said and put a hand to his chest, as though about to bless himself.

'Kolvenbach.' Kelly stood up. 'I've been such a bloody fool.'

Bewildered, Percy looked from Kelly to Monica. 'Didn't he kill this bloke after all?'

'Harald had a brother,' Kelly said. 'He mentioned him. He said he was coming out to Australia sometime soon.'

'That big man is the dead man's brother?' she said.

Kelly spread his hands. 'He thinks I killed Harald. He thinks I've got the diamonds. That's why he's after me. And he's got Laura.' He faced the splintered timbers framing the door to the tunnel. 'That's why he's got her. It's a swap. Laura for the diamonds.'

Monica seemed doubtful. 'You've seen him a few times. Why didn't he try to make the exchange before?' She got up, brushing dust from her clothes. 'When I last saw him, he seemed pretty intent on putting a bullet through you.'

Percy said, 'Who's Laura?'

'My wife.'

Percy's eyes narrowed to defensive slits. They darted from Kelly to Monica and back again. 'And this bloke's got your wife?'

'He's drugged her.'

Percy's lined face became a sea of worried ripples. 'Like doping a horse? You mean, he gave her a needle?'

'Something like that.'

The frown deepened. He turned to Monica. 'And you're helpin' him get this Laura back? That what this is all about?'

Monica raised her hands in a helpless gesture.

Percy carried on, ignoring Kelly. 'This woman, Laura ... is she the reason why Kelly shot this bloke?'

'Kelly did not shoot Kolvenbach.'

'No.' He frowned at the door. 'That's right. I forgot. Is this Laura worth all the trouble?'

'I've never met her.'

Percy leaned against the door, next to Kelly. He whispered so Monica wouldn't hear. 'I don't follow much of this, son.'

'Neither do I, Percy.'

'At least you know something.'

'What's that?' Kelly sighed, not greatly interested. He walked to the open doorway. Percy followed, reaching out to tug at his shirt.

'You know where to find this bloke who's got your missus.'

Kelly stopped, arms braced against the doorway.

'He's at the Oasis. That's a big motel in town.' He grinned. 'Why don't you get Wally to take you there? Could be interesting.' Cackling, he went to a cupboard, unlocked a padlock, and produced a shotgun. 'Want this?'

Harry the Hatchet had used one of his fake driver's licences to hire a car. He had produced a credit card in the same name, been told where to find

339

the vehicle, taken the keys and then gone to the bookstand where Laura Hunnicutt was shuffling through paperbacks while waiting for her flight to be called.

She'd been surprisingly calm. Shocked at first; then inclined to shake when she understood what he was saying; then angry by the time they reached the car. But she had never seemed really scared. He'd told her he had a gun under the coat and she was in no doubt he meant to shoot her; but she hadn't panicked, screamed, or done any of the things he was prepared for. Fantastic. The calm ones were always easier than the ones who were shitting themselves.

At the motel, he pulled on one glove, picked the lock to her room and pushed her inside.

'My luggage will be on that plane,' she said.

'Believe me, sweetheart, that's not your major worry at this point in time.' He looked around. A worn leather and canvas bag was beside the bed. 'Who's that belong to?'

She shrugged. 'Probably whoever's taken this room since I left.'

Harry hadn't been carrying a gun under his coat, but now he produced one. It was small, lethal only up to about ten metres, but handy in situations like this. He went into the bathroom: shaving gear, toothbrush, a man's deodorant.

'This guy was here last night, sweetheart.'

'Maybe we're in the wrong room.'

'You're cool. I like that. I'll remember this visit with affection.' He waved the gun airily. 'Would you like to smoke? Go ahead if you want to. One of yours, of course.' He could do with one of his own cigarettes but that would be sloppy. When the police came, they'd examine everything. Especially things like drinking glasses and ashtrays. Even with suicides, they were thorough.

340

From his folded suit carrybag, he took a leather toilet case and extracted a small bottle. He put it on the table between the beds.

'Who are you?'

'A very important person in your life.' He found that amusing.

'Who sent you?'

'Santa Claus wrote and said you'd been a bad girl.'

She looked at the bottle. 'What's that for?'

'Headaches. Those tablets end headaches people like you cause other people.'

She was sitting on the bed and, nervously, she shuffled closer to the wall. 'You won't get away with this.'

He gave her his Jack Nicholson impersonation. Open eyes, open mouth, all bizarre innocence. 'Sweetheart, if I had a dollar for every time I've heard that line, I'd be a millionaire, believe me.' Nicholson became the Joker. 'I exaggerate, which is one of my failings. In truth, I'd only have enough to pay for a few good meals at a top restaurant. With the best wines, of course.' He pulled on a second glove. 'But you get my meaning, I'm sure.'

She was against the wall. 'I'd like to know who sent you.' It was a reasoned request, not the remark of a woman who had a few minutes to live.

He raised an eyebrow. 'Not *why*? That's the usual question.'

'Sure. But tell me *who* first.'

'I like you, sweetheart. You got big balls.' His expression suggested he was waiting for applause. For some reaction.

What happened was not what Harry the Hatchet was expecting.

The door burst open and Kolvenbach charged in, chest puffed up, eyes blazing like a wild bull. Harry was a pro and he was quick. He swung towards the door and he had time to lift the gun, but he didn't have time to press the trigger. Kolvenbach, bent forward, hit him with a shoulder charge and, grabbing him around the hips, lifted him and rammed him into the wall.

Harry gasped and slumped to his knees. He dropped the gun. Kolvenbach seized him by the shoulders, lifted him off the ground and folded his arms around the man's chest. With a sharp grunt of exertion, he squeezed.

Laura heard the snap of ribs.

Kolvenbach threw him against the wall. The back of Harry's head struck the bricks. He slid to the floor and didn't move.

Kolvenbach took a deep breath, wiped his hands and turned to Laura who was sitting, goggle-eyed, on the bed. 'Are you all right?'

She couldn't speak.

He touched her shoulder and shook her gently. 'I said are you okay?'

She nodded, clearing the way for words. 'Where did you come from?'

'I had to come back to the motel.' He moved forward and prodded Harry's inert form with the toe of one boot. 'I went to the office to get the room key. The manager said he thought you'd come back. He said he'd seen you with a man ... he was embarrassed, poor chap.'

'Oh Magnus, thank God you came back when you did.'

'I listened outside the window for a few moments.'

'He was going to kill me.'

'I heard. Nasty sense of humour.' He carried the unconscious man to the bathroom and dumped him in the shower recess. He rifled through his bag. 'Any idea who he is?'

She had to hold her hands to stop them jiggling on her lap. 'No.'

342

'Or who sent him? I assume someone sent him.'

'I suppose they did.' She shook her head. 'I've never seen him before. He just came up to me at the airport.'

He held up a folder. 'Three driver's licences. All with his picture. All in different states. William Young, from Glenelg, South Australia. Does the name mean anything?'

'No.'

'Allan Wilkinson from Figtree Pocket, Queensland?'

'Magnus, I've never heard of those men.'

He examined the third licence. 'Cedric Bayliss, from St Leonards, New South Wales.'

'Whoever he is, he was going to kill me.'

He put the folder in his pocket. 'I'll get you a drink.' He went to the refrigerator. The phone rang.

'Mr Kolvenbach? Some police were just here in the office asking about you. They're coming to your room to have a word with you. I hope you don't mind.'

'Police,' Kolvenbach said, and rapidly checked the room. The man's pistol was near the wall. He kicked it under a bed and closed the bathroom door.

'I need to do my face,' she protested.

'No time.' He studied her. 'You're a little pale. But still beautiful.'

She was stunned. He'd never said anything like that, even when he was making love.

There was a knock. Two plainclothes policemen were at the door. Yes, he was Kolvenbach. He invited them in.

'This is Laura. We're travelling together.'

They mumbled polite greetings then turned back to Kolvenbach. They'd had a report that he was seen at a police roadblock at Harts Range earlier that morning. What was he doing there?

'I told the policeman. I'm a tourist.'

'You're also Harald Kolvenbach's brother.'

'That's right.'

They waited. He waited.

'Sir, what are you doing in Alice Springs?'

'I'm on the way to the Kimberleys. My brother and I have — had — extensive mining leases up there. Because of the recent...' he blinked and compressed his lips, '... the recent tragedy, I have to go up there. There is a matter, an urgent business matter, that needs the attention of one of the principals. And I'm the only one left.'

The detectives nodded in unison. The older man said, 'Mr Kolvenbach, why were you driving to the Jervois Range?'

'Our company is in the mining business.'

'And?'

'We've been contemplating an investment in that area.'

'Copper?'

He shrugged noncommittally.

'You told the officer at Harts Range that you were a tourist.'

Kolvenbach raised his hands. 'Would you tell someone that you were thinking of making a ten million dollar bid for a company?'

The men looked at each other and tried to imagine themselves as mining entrepreneurs. 'Possibly not,' the younger one said. He was disenchanted with life in the police force and fancied himself as a businessman.

The other detective looked around him. 'The manager mentioned that there might be another man in the room.'

'There was. He left.'

'Who was he, Mr Kolvenbach?'

'The driver who brought Laura from the airport.'

'He was kind enough to give me a lift,' Laura said, and both men looked at her, the older with

344

the eyes of one who was compiling a detailed report, the other with the blatant stare of a virile man admiring a good-looking young woman.

The senior detective stroked his chin. 'We had a report that you were at Innamincka in South Australia, only yesterday.'

'Yes. That's right. I was.'

'Why?'

'I landed there on my way to the Kimberleys.'

'The report suggested you were looking for Kelso Hunnicutt.'

Kolvenbach waved a large hand. 'I was disappointed with the progress the police down there were making. I heard Hunnicutt was in the area. I wanted to have a look.' He turned to the younger man; he seemed the more malleable. 'You can understand that.' Involuntarily, the man nodded. 'What is this all about? Is it something to do with Hunnicutt?'

'Do you know where Hunnicutt is?'

'Somewhere near Innamincka, I suppose. Is that what the roadblock was for? Is he up here?' Neither answered. 'Surely not. He wouldn't come up here?'

'Who can say?' The older man extended his hand. 'Thank you, Mr Kolvenbach. Good luck in the Kimberleys.'

The other man said, 'You're flying your own plane?'

'Yes.'

'Have a nice flight.' He nodded to Laura and his look lingered. She recognised the expression: strong, highly sexual interest, tempered by the realisation that he couldn't compete with a man like Kolvenbach.

'Goodbye,' she said sweetly. They left.

'What do we do now?' Laura said when their footsteps had faded.

'Get rid of our friend in the shower. Get you back to the airport and on the next plane out.'

345

'No.' She shook her head. 'Remember, they sent that man to meet me at the airport. They expect me to fly out.'

'Is there a train?'

'I'm not going on any public transport.'

He took her hand. 'Then you'd better stay with me.'

She gripped his hand. Whoever was trying to kill her might try again. Who was it? And why? It couldn't have anything to do with Harald Kolvenbach's death or Magnus would be the one who wanted her dead. 'Yes, please, Magnus,' she whispered. 'I'm so frightened.'

'I'll look after you,' he said. 'Don't worry.'

She pulled his hand to her chest. 'And what are you going to do?'

'First, get rid of that man. I'll drive his car and take him in the boot. You follow in the wagon. We'll take a little journey into the ranges.'

'Are you going to kill him?'

She asked the question so casually that he hesitated before answering. Did she really expect him to kill the man? He looked at her wide open eyes. No, she couldn't; she was still in a state of shock.

He licked his lips, still troubled. 'I'll just dump him where he'll be found and rushed to hospital. We'll remove all his money and his watch to make it look like a robbery. And I'll leave him one of his licences.' He produced the folder. 'How about we make him Cedric Bayliss?'

He retrieved the assassin's pistol and put it in her bag. 'A souvenir,' he said. 'Come. We must hurry.'

Spiro rang with bad news. Montague had checked out of his hotel suite. McCarthy said, 'How do you know?' and the question confused Spiro. 'What do you mean?'

McCarthy had not hired Spiro for his intellectual

abilities and so he was patient. 'Have you gone to the reception desk and asked if he's checked out?'

'No. I don't know what name he's using. Probably not Montague. I didn't want to make them curious.'

Good point, McCarthy conceded. 'Spiro, how do you know he's checked out if you haven't been to the desk or even rung the desk, to make sure he's checked out?'

'Because I've been inside the room. It's empty. No bags, nothing.'

'Spiro, he didn't take any bags.'

Spiro was silent while he tried to process this information. 'So what should I do?'

'Use the phone you're on to ring the reception desk.'

'Boss, I can see the desk.'

'Ring them. Believe me, it's safer. Got that?'

'Yes.'

'Then ring me and let me know.'

'In the office?'

'On this number, yes. And Spiro, if he hasn't checked out, I'd like...'

For the next few seconds, Spiro became very confused. McCarthy seemed to have put the phone down but he was still speaking. 'Get here, Spiro,' he was saying, not talking any louder than before but a long way from the mouthpiece.

Spiro heard the sound of something breaking — a glass door? McCarthy was swearing. Then, in a low, barely audible voice, he said, 'Spiro, emergency. Get here. Take care.'

There was a loud noise and the phone went dead.

Wally arrived that afternoon. Kelly was sitting outside the hut, near a stunted tree that had limbs like battered and blackened exhaust pipes. It was an ugly tree but the shade was good and the flies left him alone. He'd been there for hours, watching

347

for the Aborigine, willing him to come and peering at the distant gap that had intrigued Percy. As always, he looked for a smudge of dust or a flash of sunlight on metal or glass.

The rattle of small stones came from behind him, down the hill. Kelly stood up and got his first look at Percy the hermit's only regular visitor.

He had been wondering what Wally might drive. In his mind, he'd conjured images of a battered Jeep with grossly worn tyres, no windscreen and no seats — just a wooden box wired to the floor. Or maybe something more ancient to rival Percy's venerable Chrysler utility.

Wally came by camel.

The animal padded down the hill, delicately placing each foot to avoid the worst rocks and making a sound only when its great, pliant pads sent loose pebbles slithering down the hillside. Wally was fat and rode the camel with the easy grace of a stuffed toy; he might have had no bones, for he swayed and bounced with a comfortable softness.

The camel stopped near Kelly. It seesawed to the ground in a torrent of obscene gurgling. Wally got off.

He wore a football jumper that had as many holes as stripes, his pants were held up by a length of rope tied around his waist, and he wore no shoes. He was old. Certainly sixty, maybe seventy, but Kelly was not good at guessing Aborigines' ages. Without doubt, he'd had a hard life. Wally's face had more folds and creases than a worn leather bag.

He had only one eye, which he fixed on the stranger near the tree. Kelly raised a hand in greeting.

Percy emerged from the hut and shouted a greeting. Wally smiled, revealing teeth that resembled a row of weathered tombstones.

Kelly felt a surge of dismay. This was their guide, the man who moved through the mountains like a shadow?

Once inside, Percy explained who the others were and what they wanted to do. 'Reckon you can get them into town without being seen by any of the coppers?'

Wally nodded. Percy was right, Kelly thought, Wally never called him by name. In fact, he rarely spoke. He grunted a lot. He'd known many Aborigines and this one didn't impress him; not as a guide into a town ringed by police roadblocks.

Percy might have read his thoughts. 'Not too sure, eh?' He was on the verge of one of his cackling laughs. 'Don't worry. He's good.'

Kelly nodded and smiled at Wally, whose forehead had settled so low that he could have been blind in both eyes.

Monica posed another question that had been troubling Kelly. 'Are we going by camel?'

Kelly was glad he hadn't asked because Percy erupted into laughter and Wally displayed his tombstone teeth. 'We'll leave Sarah here. We'll take the two utes.'

'You're going too?' Kelly was surprised. There'd been no suggestion of Percy accompanying them.

'Thought I might. Could be interesting. I'll take this.' He brandished the shotgun. 'Anyhow, it's a year or two since I been into town. Might as well go tonight.' He laughed, and Wally, happy to see him pleased, smiled.

Being a cautious man, Spiro parked the van around the corner and hurried into the narrow street that ran behind McCarthy's office. He arrived in time to see the private investigator being escorted down the fire escape. McCarthy, puffing badly, was in front. Three men followed. Spiro did a rapid

349

sidestep into an alley. The four men reached the bottom of the stairs and turned right, away from Spiro. One man had McCarthy by the arm; the other two stayed close, constantly glancing around them.

A Jaguar was parked at the end of the street. Stolen, Spiro presumed. The four boarded the car, which departed with rubbery squeals. Spiro was able to make out the first letters of the numberplate before it was obscured by the rising cloud of tyre smoke.

He ran around the corner to his parked van and felt a twinge of satisfaction. At least the driver was an amateur; either nervous or a show-off. That left two. If they'd grabbed George and somehow disposed of Freddie Porter, those two were good. He drove past the fire escape and wondered what they'd done to Porter. He'd check later. Right now, he had to get within sight of the Jaguar.

30

The old Chrysler had once been a sedan but a previous owner had hacked off the back half and converted it into a utility truck. Percy had owned it for thirty-seven years. The wooden sides to the tray were almost nonexistent; only a few jagged scraps of timber clung to the metal uprights. The metal floor had rusted away in the mid-1960s and Percy had replaced it with a decking of old railway sleepers.

Kelly drove the Chrysler because Percy reckoned it would be safer; the police wouldn't be looking for him in something as decrepit as the old ute. Kelly had told him the full story of the robbery, or as much as he understood of it. Percy had said, 'A man who's got four million dollars in diamonds ain't gonna drive around in a heap of shit,' and then, his eyes twinkling, apologised to Monica for the language. Despite his distaste for people and towns, he seemed to be looking forward to the trip.

Percy went with Monica in her Ford.

Kelly took Wally. They led, with the old Aborigine pointing the way whenever there was doubt or a choice. Wally sat with one foot resting on the inside of the screen. It was a large foot, as black and veined as a burnt leaf on top but as rough and pale as sandpaper on the sole. Wally didn't speak. Occasionally he grunted when he meant yes. When the answer was no, he said nothing but wiggled the toes of his broad and upraised foot. Just wait on, the toes were signalling, and we'll let you know when the answer's yes.

They followed a rough track that took them near the ruins of the Arltunga goldfields. Sometimes Kelly could see the faint marks of previous traffic. On other occasions, Wally merely pointed to a distant tree and they would drive there, dodging large rocks and sprawling bushes, and crossing soft and sandy creek beds. Kelly tried to memorise the way. When he had a moment, he would write it all down in his special book.

Percy had a good time in Monica's truck. He tried the radio and cooed with surprise when he located the Alice Springs ABC station. He'd never been in a vehicle that had a radio. Monica showed him how to play one of her tapes. He chewed a finger, not daring to appear too delighted or too foolish in front of this woman.

He looked in the back and saw the easel, sketch-books and bundles of pens and paint brushes. 'Do you really paint birds?' he asked and she wondered why he laughed so much.

'Whatta the two of you gonna do when you get to the Alice?'

'Fill the tank and the drums. We need fuel.'

'I coulda got that for you.'

'Kelly has to make a phone call.'

'Ah.' The answer made more sense although he seemed doubtful. 'Not to this wife a his?'

'No. Percy, we have to pass through Alice Springs to go south. We have to get back to Melbourne. To clear Kelly's name.' That was essential, she said, and he nodded sagely.

'How'd you get involved?'

She laughed. 'I don't know.'

The answer didn't puzzle him. Women did things

for no reason. He said, 'He hasn't got no diamonds with 'im; is that fair dinkum?'

'Absolutely.'

'And no dynamite or nothin'?'

'No.'

He growled his disappointment.

'Be handy in that gold mine of yours?' She was busy steering between a rock and the branch of an overhanging tree so he couldn't see her eyes, but her lips were curling in a smile.

'What gold mine?'

'Oh, come off it, Percy. I know what you're doing out there.'

He made a low, gurgling noise, like Sarah the camel. 'Just mention gold in town and a bloke'll have every no-hoper in the place camped on the doorstep.' He scratched his neck.

'I wouldn't do that, Percy.'

'There's none anyhow.'

'No. I was joking.'

He grunted. 'Mind you, youse two could stay out there if youse wanted to. Plenty a room in them hills.'

'That's very kind of you.'

'Might be safer than Melbourne.' Another grunt. 'The coppers never give up.'

'We could be neighbours.'

He gave her his sly smile. She was joking. She knew he couldn't stand neighbours, not people who could see each other. Over on the other side of the hills, a few miles away, might be all right.

They drove on for a while, following Kelly's path. Percy rolled his jaws, chewing at a problem. Finally, he said, 'You won't get ten mile out of the Alice. You know that?' The inference, she felt, was that Kelly might know but she wouldn't.

'Why not?'

'There are more police up here than maggots in a dunny and they're all looking for this truck a yours.'

Of yours. She frowned. 'I'm aware of that.'

'Gonna do anythin' about it?'

'We'll avoid the police.'

'How?'

She wasn't sure. 'That's Kelly's territory. He's terribly good at finding his way around police roadblocks.'

Percy sniffed derisively. 'He'll wanna be bloody good.' He didn't apologise for bloodies. 'They'll have every creek bed covered. It's the truck that'll give yez away.'

She was thinking.

'So waddaya gonna do, eh?' Somehow, he was making this all her fault and, therefore, her problem.

'I have an idea,' she said.

'Wazzat?'

Her eyes challenged him. 'You get us into Alice Springs and you'll find out.'

His eyebrows rolled a few times. Once, he shot a quizzical glance at her.

'You don't like women, do you, Percy?'

He began rolling a cigarette. 'Not particularly.' He met her frank stare. One eyebrow up, the other eye almost hidden beneath compressed lids, he said, 'You can only judge people by what they does to you. True or false?'

'Depends. Are you hiding from a woman?'

He seemed to find the remark so amusing he couldn't find the breath to make a noise. His mouth opened wide, his eyes rolled with mirth. When he was able to breathe, he said, 'It wasn't a sheila that did it'.

'Did what?' She followed the tracks of the old Chrysler through a shallow patch of sand.

Both his eyes narrowed into slits surrounded by folds of mirth. 'What you're askin' is why in the name of hell would a good-lookin' bloke like me be livin' out where I'm livin'?'

'And avoiding the police. Yes, I suppose so.' The truck became stuck and she had to reverse out and try again. 'Were you married?'

'You ask a lotta questions.'

'Sorry.'

He was silent for a while, then lifted a hand in a Papal gesture. 'It's all right. Got nothing to hide. 'Cept meself.' He gave one of his thin, cackling laughs. 'You know what maintenance is?'

'I think so.'

'A bloke leaves a woman because he can't stand a bar of her and she goes runnin' to the court and the court reckons he's gotta pay her money, even if it's more than he's got, and when he don't pay up they come lookin' for him. Y'can go to gaol for that.'

'How long ago was this?'

He was grinning, pleased she'd begun to unravel the mystery, anxious to share a triumph. 'Thirty-eight years.'

'You've been running from the police for thirty-eight years?'

He searched her face for a sign of admiration but she was aghast. Concern for him? Or for that rotten woman? Women stuck together.

He puckered his lips and made a whistling sound. 'There was other things.'

'Like what?'

'You know Croydon?'

She thought. She knew three towns called Croydon. It wouldn't be the one in Melbourne and it probably wouldn't be the one in Sydney. 'Up near the Gulf?'

'Yairs.' He was surprised.

'I've painted birds near there. Along the Gilbert.'

'Well, I worked for a bloke who ran a station out of Croydon and he didn't pay me what he owed me. Mean old cunt. 'Scuse me.' He touched his lips

355

in admonition. 'So I took the money. It was my money. He owed me.'

She said, 'And he went to the police?'

'What's more, the bastards believed him.' He didn't apologise for bastards. 'They gotta warrant out for me. Theft. Seventy-five lousy quid. The mean old bugger owed me more. Owed others too, but nunnavem had the guts to take what was theirs.'

'So now you're living in a hill?'

He settled more comfortably into the seat. 'It's not a bad hole, is it?'

'No. Not if you're happy there.'

He nodded contentedly. 'It'll do me.' He sniffed and looked around. 'We're getting close. Wally'll have him stop soon.'

Never before had Gerry Montague walked out of a hotel without paying but he'd had a niggling apprehension of danger, and so he'd taken his bag, caught the lift and walked down Collins Street to the Hyatt. He'd booked in there, given the same Sydney address, and taken a room two floors from the top.

His window looked out across the Jolimont railway yards. It was like watching a model-train system with dozens of miniature lines all feeding into each other; little, silent trains rolling into the city or fanning out on the suburban lines. He stood at the window, watching and thinking. After twenty minutes, he sat down beside the bed and rang Mary Calibrano.

He'd changed hotels. He'd ordered a club sandwich at the Regent and been given toasted cheese so he walked out. Mary would believe that. She knew he had a short temper when it came to poor service.

He gave her his new room number. 'I want you to do something for me. A little mission, and then I want you to ring me back and tell me what happened.'

She was intrigued. Willing to do whatever he wanted, of course.

'Go to my flat. Take a parcel of correspondence. Any innocuous business papers that look legitimate. Knock on the door and ask for me.'

There was a stunned silence. 'Whatever for?'

'I want to find out if those detectives are still camped there. I've got a feeling they might have left.'

'There's not a Superintendent Wilson among them, is there?' she asked nervously.

'Wilson? No.'

'He rang the office. He said he had information that might prove Kelly is innocent.'

Montague tried to swallow but his throat seized. He coughed. 'When was this?'

'A little while ago. He said they had some new suspect. Gerry, isn't that wonderful news?'

Jesus. Montague stared out the window. A helicopter was passing and he looked away. A new suspect? Gerry Montague?

'I didn't know what to do,' she was saying, 'but he said it was absolutely essential that he talk to you so I gave him your number at the Regent.'

So the police were on to him. How? 'Well, I'm not there now,' he managed to say.

'Did he speak to you?'

'No.'

'Gerry, please get in touch with him. Ring him as soon as you can. He said Kelly's life was in danger. His name is Superintendent Wilson and he's at Russell Street. Do you want me to look up the number?'

'I'll do it, Mary.'

'Superintendent Wilson.'

'Got that. Okay. I'll call him straight away.'

Hope made her voice ring. 'Won't it be wonderful if they can clear Kelly?'

'It certainly will.' Deep breath. Back to the other

business. It was more urgent than ever now. He needed to know if McCarthy and his apes had left the apartment. They probably had. With him on the loose, they would clear out. Which meant the hundred thousand was still in the ceiling, waiting to be collected.

'Now Mary, I want you to go to my place and find out if the police are still there.'

'Why don't you ring them?'

'Because then I'll be caught up again with all their questions and their haranguing. Honestly, Mary, they've asked me the same questions about Kelly a hundred times. I can't even get a proper sleep. They're driving me nuts.'

He knew what she was thinking: Gerry is being neurotic again. But she'd do it for him.

'And if they are there?'

'Give them the parcel. Say it's for me.'

'And if no one's there?'

'Make sure. Knock a few times. Wait. Then ring me.'

He hung up and went back to the window. So the police knew it wasn't Kelly. They had a new suspect. And they wanted to talk to him. Urgently. Jesus Christ, this was awful. He checked his watch. Laura was due back that night. He'd go out to the airport and meet her. He needed her; he didn't know what to do next.

He began scheduling his time. Mary should ring in about half an hour. Then, if the flat was empty, he'd collect the money and a few of his things. That would take another hour. Then he'd drive out to meet Laura. He stopped, his thinking disrupted by a terrible possibility. Supposing it was Laura who had told the police? Supposing she and Kolvenbach were working together and had done this to get him out of the way?

He'd run. Take the money, get in his car and

go. He'd go to the airport all right, but instead of meeting Laura, he'd catch an international flight to somewhere. Maybe Bangkok or Hong Kong. Some place where it was easy to disappear.

The diamonds. He'd forgotten about them. And Lister. Had he done something about McCarthy? Once more he looked at his watch. He'd told Lister he would ring again that night. All right, he'd call him from the airport. He could leave the country and still get the diamonds. He'd work out some way.

He went to the mini bar and poured himself a Scotch. The world was full of scheming, devious bastards, he thought and, drink in hand, lay on the bed to wait for Mary's call.

The Jaguar stopped at an address in St Kilda. It was a double-storeyed brick building, possibly a block of flats. There were a dozen others like it in the street. Spiro used his mobile phone to call Govorko. They used him sometimes. He was big and inclined to move awkwardly, as though his joints and limbs didn't match, but he lived nearby and he was reliable.

He'd be there in ten minutes. He'd be driving a white Commodore.

Only one man got out of the Jaguar. The others stayed, one guarding George in the back, the driver remaining behind the wheel. Spiro thought of doing something immediately, before Govorko arrived. He could probably get one of the guards but he wasn't sure about the second.

It was too risky. He waited.

The first man returned, bent to talk to the man in the rear of the car and then hurried back into the building. He was back again within thirty seconds. He checked to make sure the footpath was clear and then hauled McCarthy from the car. The man in the back seat got out too, and the three of them went into the house. Not good, Spiro thought. One man was still in the car and George was in the building. He looked in his mirror. A white Commodore had just turned the corner.

Govorko parked two cars behind him and casually walked up. He stopped near the van to light a cigarette.

'It's the green Jaguar up ahead,' Spiro said. 'One man on board. Two inside that building on the left. They've got George.'

'How's George look?' Govorko seemed to be having trouble lighting his cigarette. He tried a second match.

'Bit staggery. Can't see any sign of injury. These fellows are good. They must have taken care of Freddie Porter.'

'That so?' Govorko wasn't concerned. He sounded impressed, challenged. 'So what do we do? Go in after him?'

'We'd have to take care of the driver first.'

'That's okay.' The cigarette was burning now and he inhaled deeply.

Spiro was worried. He had no idea where in the building McCarthy had been taken, nor did he know how many men were inside. Almost certainly, there were more men than the two guards he'd seen. The first man had been talking to someone, getting instructions.

'I'll drive up,' Govorko suggested, looking back along the street. 'I've got a street directory. I'll go through the lost motorist routine.'

'Okay.' Spiro didn't like it but he couldn't think of a better scheme.

'And you'll come from the other side?'

'I'll walk up. Take your time from me.'

'Got you.'

Spiro was still worried. If the driver was waiting in the car, then the others planned to come out again. But when?

No sooner had he thought of it than it happened. A shaken and stooped George McCarthy reappeared on the steps of the building. There were two men with him. One was new. Spiro recognised him. He was known around town as the Turk. Nasty reputation. George wouldn't like this; he'd once put the Turk in Pentridge for five years.

Govorko saw, nodded slightly and ambled back towards his car. When he was in the Commodore, he phoned Spiro. 'You want us to follow them?'

The Jaguar was pulling out from the kerb. 'You go first,' Spiro said. 'They might have seen the van before. I'll follow you. I'll be a long way back. You talk me around the corners.'

Within ten minutes, Spiro knew where they were going. They were taking George to Montague's apartment.

'Keep talking,' he said. 'I know where they're heading. I'll go a different way. When they get near there, we might have a little accident.'

'How little?' Govorko sounded cheerful.

'Just a bump. Not enough to hurt George but enough to start an argument.'

'Good. I like arguments. Are you having the accident or me?'

'I'll handle that,' Spiro said. Govorko had done stunts in films. He was the sort of man who considered a triple roll-over a minor bump.

'I'll take the man in the back and get George out of there. Can you handle the two in front?'

'Sure.' Govorko began to hum a tune.

'They're good,' Spiro warned.

'That's okay.' He continued to hum.

A block from Montague's apartment, Spiro turned into a narrow street and waited. He'd been driving hard and his heart rate was up. This was like the start of a game, those last nervous seconds before

361

the referee blew his whistle. He put on the grey dust coat and the cap with Hot Pizza written across the front, and examined the street. Cars were parked on both sides. Perfect.

The Jaguar came into view, cruising towards him.

'I see them,' Spiro said on the mobile phone, and accelerated. There was room for two vehicles but, as the other car drew close, he let the van veer towards the middle. The Jaguar swerved. He went with it, then, when a crash was inevitable, jerked the wheel hard to the left. He braked. The back wheels locked and he slid into the side of the car, blocking the driver's door.

Spiro leaned out of the window. Broken Italian would be good. 'What the hell you doin'? You think you own the road, eh?' He pounded the roof of the Jaguar. 'You seen what you done a my van?'

The driver rolled down the window. 'And look what you've done to my fucking car, you stupid cunt.'

'Who you calling stupid, eh?'

'You, shovel face.'

Govorko's Commodore was in the street and getting close.

The man in the back of the Jaguar leaned forward and tapped the driver's shoulder. 'Let's just get out of here.'

'I can't move an inch. This stupid prick's wedged us in.'

The Commodore stopped. Govorko blew his horn.

'I said who you calling stupid?' Spiro bellowed a string of profanities and got out through the passenger's door.

Govorko blew the horn again. 'Come on,' he yelled. 'Get out of the way.'

The Jaguar driver thrust two fingers in the air. By now, Spiro was storming around the van. He

362

went to the Jaguar's back door. The man guarding McCarthy partly lowered the window.

'You hear what your man calling me?' He bent to look inside. The man had a gun on his lap. The Turk, in the front, had his hand in his coat.

Spiro extended an arm in complaint. 'He ruin da van. You see dat?' He gestured towards the van and then, with extraordinary speed, swung his arm through the narrow opening. He grabbed the man behind the neck and pulled his head hard into the window. The man's face spread grotesquely across the glass.

Govorko appeared on the other side of the car. One boot smashed the Turk's window. He had a gun at the man's head.

Spiro leaned towards the driver. 'You want to try something? I'd like it.' He smiled and the driver raised his hands.

The man in the back was bleeding from the nose and making snuffling noises. Spiro opened the door and dragged him out. 'Hi,' he said and gave the man a head butt. The man collapsed on the road.

Spiro reached in and helped McCarthy out of the car. 'Reckon you can get in the van?' he asked and McCarthy nodded.

On the other side of the Jaguar, Govorko had reached in to grab the Turk in a headlock. Now he was pulling him, arms thrashing and legs kicking, out of the car.

'Don't kill him, mate,' Spiro said and Govorko rammed the Turk's head against the roof. He slid him back into the car. The driver's arms shot higher in the air.

'Reckon you can back out of here?' Spiro asked. The driver nodded.

Spiro picked up the man on the road and laid him across the back seat. He slammed the door. 'Well, go. And drive safely.'

With a rip of metal, the Jaguar reversed out, turned and sped down the road.

Nearby, a white-haired man was standing at his front gate. 'Some people should never have been given a licence, isn't that so?' Spiro called out.

The man was open-mouthed.

'Did you hear the language they used?'

The man nodded.

'Have a nice day,' Spiro called, and got in the van. 'Thank you for your help, friend,' he shouted to Govorko, and drove off.

McCarthy reached across and, with a feeble grip, grasped Spiro's arm. 'Good man,' he said softly.

'How are you feeling?'

'Not as bad as someone's going to feel.' He reached for a handkerchief and wiped his mouth. 'Oh boy. Just like the old days, except this time, it was me on the receiving end.'

'Where do you want to go, boss?'

McCarthy took a deep breath and held his ribs. 'Seeing we're close, make it Montague's place. I've got a feeling we must have missed something.'

The phone buzzed. It was Govorko. 'What do you want me to do?'

'Follow.'

Spiro reached into his trouser pocket. 'By the way, I found this in Montague's room.' He produced a pad of hotel notepaper. 'He'd been making some sort of list. He must have pressed real hard. I think we can read what he wrote down.'

Laura held up her blouse, checking it for rips. It had cost her the earth at that shop in Toorak Road and Kolvenbach had taken it off with all the finesse of a bulldozer.

'What are you doing?' he asked.

'Seeing if it's in one piece.' He'd been an animal — brutal, eager and inconsiderate.

Kolvenbach looked across at her. How like a woman to be thinking of what to wear. Only a few minutes ago, she had been a primeval creature, lustily celebrating the fact that she was still alive.

So was that man still alive, he thought, but only just. The potential assassin was lying in a creek bed at the side of the road, about twenty kilometres out of town. He'd be discovered soon. Maybe he already had. He wouldn't talk and he certainly wasn't in any shape to come after Laura again. Kolvenbach lay back on the pillow, worrying about who might have sent him.

There were no rips. Laura brushed a dirt spot. 'I've got nothing else to wear. All my clothes are on that plane.'

'Buy some more.'

Normally she liked buying clothes but that suggestion worried her. She was frightened to go out. 'You'll come with me?'

'No. I have things to do.'

'More important than looking after me?'

He kept his eyes on the ceiling. 'There's still the matter of that husband of yours.' He wouldn't have said 'husband of yours' twenty minutes ago, she thought. 'That's why I came here and I'm running out of time. And patience.'

'What are you going to do?'

'Look around. Check a few roads. Ask a few questions.'

'Let's face it, Magnus. You don't know where he is.'

'I hope he's coming to Alice Springs.'

'You hope.'

His eyes swung towards her. He should get rid of her; she was in the way. Damn that man. He got up and went to the bathroom. 'Get dressed. I'll take you into town. Buy what you need.' He reappeared at the bathroom doorway. 'Have you got money?'

'I have credit cards.'

'Good. Go shopping. Take your mind off things. It will do you good.'

Sure. Forget that some man I've never seen before picked me up at the airport and tried to kill me. Calm down. Deep breaths. Think clearly. She needed to ring Gerry again. She'd have to do that from town.

'You'll drive me down to the shopping centre?'

'Sure.'

'I don't want to walk.'

'Laura, I'll drive you to town and you can get a cab back. Get dressed.'

31

Kelly sat near the truck, slowly breaking a long stick into small pieces. Wally had ambled over to the narrow water hole that lay between the walls of the gorge, and was sitting in the shade cast by a grove of gums. Motionless, he was a speckled darkness, almost impossible to see.

Kelly heard the splutter of the Chrysler's engine before it came into view. Percy waved when he saw him and Kelly wondered whether Percy and Monica had done well or whether the old man was merely pleased to be out of Alice Springs.

Monica got out, clutching several brightly labelled plastic shopping bags. She handed Kelly his bank keycard.

'Doesn't work,' she said. 'I put it in the machine and it spat it out. The police must have closed your account.'

He frowned. He hadn't anticipated that and he was running short of cash. He pointed to the plastic bags. 'So what did you do?'

'Used mine. The machine loved it.'

'You've got enough?'

'Not all artists starve. Here.' She threw him a soft cotton hat. 'That's what the well-dressed tourist is wearing this year. You too can be mistaken for a Japanese. And this.' It was a T-shirt, orange and blue and with the words *A TOWN LIKE ALICE* written across the belly. 'You've had a wash?'

'From head to toe. The water was cold but clean.'

She studied him. 'You look better.'

Percy, who was stiff from driving and had taken a long time to get out of the Chrysler, joined them. 'The town's crawlin' with coppers,' he said.

'It's true.' Monica reached into another bag and produced a pair of stonewashed jeans. 'You'll be a ball of style in these and they're a different colour to the one's the police are advertising.'

Kelly nodded his thanks. 'How many police are there?'

'A couple on every corner.'

'Lots of tourists?'

'The town's full of them. Go and get dressed.'

'Yes ma'am.' He saluted.

'And bury the old clothes.'

'But they're still good.'

'They look as though a pack of dogs slept on them. And the police are searching for a man dressed by R M Williams, not Just Jeans. Put the new gear on. It may not be as good but it's different. And clean.'

With a mischievous chuckle, Percy produced a set of numberplates.

'Oh yes,' Monica said, 'look what our light-fingered old friend found. Genuine Northern Territory plates.'

'You stole them?' Kelly said.

Percy seemed delighted. 'Got the pair of 'em off in five minutes flat. Bet the bloke never wakes up that they're gone.'

'It was an old car parked beside an old hut at the end of an old road.' Monica emitted the tired sigh of someone who disapproves of a necessary action. The numberplates were for the Ford. The police would ignore a vehicle with Alice Springs plates. At least, that was Percy's theory.

'True,' he said and signalled to Wally, who ambled, bow-legged, towards them. 'They're lookin' for an interstate truck. Youse'll be right with these.' He followed Kelly, who was walking to the far side of the truck to get changed. 'What now?'

'Fuel. A phone call and a visit to...'

'Hey,' Monica called out. 'I've got another present for you.'

He was unbuckling his trouser belt. 'I don't need any more clothes.'

'It's not clothes. It's a holiday.'

He peered around the front of the Ford.

'You're going to Ayers Rock. I've bought you a ticket on a coach. You leave tomorrow morning, so don't get your new clothes dirty.'

'What are you talking about?'

'You want to get out of town? Well, I've got a plan. The first part is that you disguise yourself as a normal person and you travel to Ayers Rock. No one's going to look for you on a tourist coach that's full of rich and smiling Japanese tourists.'

'Japanese? Tourist coach?'

'I think you're the only Australian on board.' She laughed, testing his humour.

'No.' He shook his head.

'Yes. It's best. Believe me.'

'What about you?'

'I've got things to do.'

'Like what?'

'Never you mind. You just get on your bus and have a good time. I've booked you in for a sunset tour of the Rock and a night's accommodation at Yulara.'

'But I don't want to go to Ayers Rock.'

'It's the only way you're going to get out of Alice Springs. There are more police on the roads around town than...' She hesitated.

'Maggots in a dunny,' Percy prompted.

369

'Quite. They're here in force. We even saw two helicopters. Two.' She paused and he lowered his head, burdened by grim thoughts. 'Kelly, we'd never make it. Not together.'

'What name did you use for the coach ticket?'

'You're my son. Dennis Tate.'

He leaned against the bonnet. 'How old am I supposed to be?'

'Old enough to need an adult ticket.' She noted his doubtful expression. 'None of your Japanese fellow adventurers are going to know you're supposed to be a boy.'

'But splitting up.' He waved a hand helplessly. 'I don't like it.'

'You'll just have to do without me for a day or so. I'll meet you at Ayers Rock. You spend your day there having a good time and working out where we have to go from there.'

He considered. 'I think I know a way.'

'I'll bet you do.' Pleased, she began to walk away.

'Monica,' he called after her, his voice sharp with worry, 'when am I going to see Laura? She's probably in town with Kolvenbach. I've got to reach her somehow. I've got to try and get her away from him.'

'I only bought one ticket.'

'I can't just leave her with him.'

She let her head droop and lowered her voice. 'Kelly, do you reckon she's worth the risk?'

Shirt off, pants loose at the waist, he walked to her. 'What do you mean worth the risk? She's my wife.'

She turned her back. 'That doesn't make her the perfect woman.'

'He's drugged her or done something to her, to make her act the way she's been behaving.'

'She didn't seem too drugged when I saw her the other night.'

'What are you saying?'

'That if I were you, I'd think long and hard about sticking my neck out to try and help her when there's a fair chance she doesn't want to be helped. I think she's feeling nice and cosy with that big man.'

'How can you say that?'

'Easily. And don't say it's just female intuition, although I've got plenty of that. I've also got eyes and ears and I know what I saw and heard.'

He was silent; wounded and offended.

'Oh for Christ's sake, Kelly, she's had plenty of chances to get away, surely. And if she were doped, she'd be walking around like a zombie, not jumping up and down and screaming out for that big man to help her; and not coming into my camp in the middle of the night and giving me a long and lucid account of an attack that you were supposed to have made on the pair of them. Face up to it, Kelly. She's your enemy.'

He took a deep breath. 'Thanks for the clothes,' he said and walked away.

Gerry Montague had the taxi drop him one block from his apartment. He walked past the front entrance and went around the corner, then down to the alley that ran behind his place. A quick look because the alley made him nervous. A few cars. No people. He walked back. There was a man sitting in a car parked near the opposite corner, a tall man in a white Commodore, but he was looking the other way and almost immediately started up the car and drove off. Just to be safe, Montague waited a few minutes, walked in the other direction and then turned and strolled past the front of his apartment once more. He went around the corner and entered the alley from the other side. It was still deserted so he quickly unlocked the garage, patted the Porsche, and went inside.

The place was empty, just as Mary had said. It was also remarkably clean. McCarthy and his men had washed all the glasses and put them away. The bottles were in the cabinet. The beds were made. The plates and coffee percolator were washed and drying in the rack.

He gathered some clothes and put them in his best suitcase. He went to the bathroom, studied his bruised face in the mirror, and packed a few creams and vitamin pills. He took off his coat, got a torch and the stepladder and went into the spare room. With difficulty, he climbed through the inspection hatch in the ceiling. He crawled to the corner of the roof where he had hidden the plastic bag behind the loose piece of insulation. He checked that the money was still there. Back to the ladder.

Getting down was more difficult. His extended leg searched for the topmost rung. A hand touched his ankle and guided his foot to the ladder.

'Welcome home, Gerry,' McCarthy said.

McCarthy stood in front of him, brandishing the Hyatt notepad. 'Very interesting stuff, this, you treacherous lying little turd. See what we've done.' He held up a pencil and rubbed its point sideways across the paper. 'Remarkable. You and Laura, eh?' He looked at the notebook with exaggerated interest. 'Due tonight, was she?' He shook his head. 'She won't make it, old boy. Gone. Snuffed it. Having a big sleep. Departed this earth.' He put down the pad. 'Now it's your turn.'

He snapped his fingers and Spiro moved forward.

'Let's hurry before those goons figure out where we are,' McCarthy said, and, bag of money in one hand, led the way out of the flat. Behind him, he heard Montague yelp.

Without turning, he said, 'Not yet, Spiro, not yet'.

Kolvenbach was in his usual postsex phase of feeling unclean and guilty but, this time, he didn't feel guilty about what he had done to the woman; it was the wasted time. While he was amusing himself, Hunnicutt could have slipped into town. Or been caught. There were dozens of police ringing Alice Springs and they were stopping every vehicle. It would be a disaster if they found him. He had to hope that Hunnicutt had somehow eluded them. He was clever enough.

If Hunnicutt had reached Alice Springs, he would head for a service station or some place where he could get fuel. Large quantities of it. No matter where he was going — north, south, east or west — he would need petrol.

Laura was down the street. Damn her. She was nothing but a nuisance now. He would make a booking on the next plane south and force her to take it.

He thought again about the man who had come to kill her and was puzzled. Why would anyone send a hired killer to dispose of Laura Hunnicutt? What had she done? What did she know that made her dangerous? The man had intercepted her at the airport. It had to be someone who knew she was flying home.

Who knew?

Still pondering, Kolvenbach drove to the northern outskirts of town, where he had seen large service stations and fuel depots. Hunnicutt must be carrying drums in the back of that truck. He would probably need a couple of hundred litres of fuel. That should make his task easier; people would remember someone who bought vast quantities of petrol. He tried all the stations on the highway leading out of town. No one had filled a Ford F100 carrying drums. He parked near the northernmost station.

Half an hour passed. The highway carried only light traffic. A couple of road trains rumbled past, laden with motor spirit, huge shipping containers and caterpillar chains of motor vehicles destined for the north. One express coach arrived from Darwin. Six cars called into the service station.

Kolvenbach, his desire returning, began to have other thoughts about Laura. He couldn't send her back to Melbourne. She wouldn't be safe there. He fossicked in his bag for the airline schedule they'd used to select her original flight. There were direct services to Darwin, Adelaide, Sydney, Cairns and Perth. Perhaps she could go to Sydney and stay with a friend. He would discuss it tonight.

And ask who knew she was returning to Melbourne.

He frowned. She was an intriguing, desirable woman, but dangerous. That was the critical word — dangerous. Obviously, someone else thought the same about her. Who?

Monica had been right about the hat. A few people, visitors affecting a Territorial swagger, wore new Akubras but most people had on a floppy cotton hat like the one she'd bought him. He was one of hundreds. Kelly looked in a few shop windows and smiled at his own reflection, enjoying the anonymity of his tourist uniform of T-shirt and jeans, and relishing the opportunity to move among people.

He found a phone booth, waited until it was empty, and tried to ring Gerry Montague. He was not home. He rang the office. Mary Calibrano answered.

For a few moments, she was too shocked to speak. Then she started to laugh and the words poured out. Thank God he was safe. It might be over soon. The police had another suspect. A superintendent from police headquarters had told her. They wanted to speak to Gerry. They needed his help.

'I can't reach Gerry.'

'He must be at Russell Street now, talking to them. Where are you?'

'Alice Springs. In a phone box. Surrounded by people. It's a weird feeling.' Yes, he was all right. No, he was not going to give himself up.

'But they have someone else.'

'You think.' And there's someone else hunting me and trying to shoot me and he's got Laura, he thought, but said nothing. Mary would have hysterics and collapse. 'What did the man say?'

She paused, trying to recall the superintendent's words. 'I forget exactly what he said but it sounded so promising. He said they had new information which pointed towards a fresh suspect. I think that was it. He said once they'd spoken to Gerry, to clear up a few things I suppose, they'd be able to call off the hunt and arrest the other man.'

'They said that?'

'That's what I understood. The man's name is Wilson. Superintendent Wilson.'

Confused, not daring to believe everything she was saying, Kelly looked through the glass panels surrounding him. A man had stopped at the nearest shop window and was staring at him.

He hunched over the phone. 'Got to go, Mary.'

'Take care. Are you eating?'

He laughed. 'I am. Not as much as I'd like but enough.'

'Will you ring again?'

'Tomorrow. From Ayers Rock.'

'You're going to Ayers Rock? Do they have a phone there?'

'They have big hotels there, Mary. I'll call. Take care.' He hung up. He held the door open for the other man, who mumbled thanks in German and showed no interest in his face.

Kolvenbach got the information he wanted at a small service station south of the main town. Yes, a blue Ford truck had pulled in with drums in the back. About forty-five minutes ago. They'd taken nearly two hundred litres of super.

They?

That's where it became confusing. The two in the Ford were a woman and an old man. What was she like? Nothing special. Rather scruffily dressed. Shorts, shirt, hat — all brown, like military gear. Loud voice. She did all the talking. And the man? Old and stooped.

Not a stooped *young* man?

Definitely not. The service-station operator held up his hands. He'd noticed the old man's hands. They were thin and bent, as though he had arthritis.

The truck. Did it have Victorian plates?

The man shook his head. No, it was a local. Alice Springs registration.

Kolvenbach parked down the road and closed his eyes in thought. It was the vehicle Hunnicutt had been travelling in. No doubt. He'd switched numberplates. No problem there. The woman must be the artist Hunnicutt had met in Queensland, then met again on the Cooper. And the old man? A third person in the plot, one who'd been waiting to take them to their ultimate hiding place, who would feed them and shelter them until the hunt had died down.

He ran through that again. It made sense. Hunnicutt had been heading for the Centre all the time. He would hide out somewhere in the Alice Springs district. And now there were three people, any of whom could have the papers. Hunnicutt would have the diamonds but, not realising the value of the papers, he could have given them to one of the others. Or hidden them or tossed them out somewhere along his tortuous trail across Australia.

God forbid. He'd be searching the country forever.

Typical of Hunnicutt to approach from the north, then come in from the south, through Heavitree Gap. Knowing the way the man operated, he should have started on the wrong side of town, not up north. But where was Hunnicutt? Hiding out in the ranges, waiting for the others to return? Or would he be in Alice Springs? All he knew for certain was that he was now hunting three people and they were driving a Ford with local number-plates.

He turned and drove into town, to look for an old blue F100 with Northern Territory number-plates.

Laura changed in the shop and put her Melbourne clothes in the carry bag. She looked in the mirror once more. The turquoise blouse was great. She adjusted the collar, lifting it at the back. Turquoise was such a good colour for her; it blended with her eyes and highlighted her hair. Navy slacks, wide navy belt, navy shoes. Discreet and elegant. Slimming too. A small straw hat. Good for the sun and cheeky. She adjusted the angle. A jungle print scarf. Slightly outrageous but it added a splash of colour. She unclipped the gold chain and put it in her handbag, loosened the scarf until the knot was exactly where she wanted it, and pulled back the curtain of the changing booth.

Feeling a little less obvious, a little less of a target, she went to the counter, signed the credit-card slip for 575 dollars and walked to the shop entrance. There she hesitated. People were milling on the footpath. Supposing one of them was waiting for her? She looked left, then right, took a deep breath and stepped out. A woman turned as she passed. No danger there; merely admiration or envy and she was used to that.

She entered another shop and bought casual gear: shorts, T-shirts, sandals. Another shop for underwear. Then she went to a chemist and replaced all the cosmetics, combs, brushes and toiletries that were locked in her suitcase at some air terminal down south.

She was looking at shoes in a small shop window when someone tapped her shoulder. It was a man; she could see the shadowy reflection in the mirror. She dropped the bags. Her hands wouldn't work and her knees trembled.

The man bent and offered her the fallen bags. It was Kelly. He took her by the elbow and led her into an arcade.

'Kelly?' She spread one hand across her chest.

'I saw you ten minutes ago.' His face was trying to restrain a smile, his eyes were darting in all directions. 'I've been following you.' He leaned forward until his face almost touched hers. He whispered, 'Are you all right?'

She was looking beyond him. Where were the police? She tried to free her arm. 'Kelly, what are you doing here?' Her voice was high, frightened.

'Have you got away from him?'

'Who?'

'Kolvenbach.'

She noticed a man watching them. He was staring. He hadn't moved and he had one hand in his pocket. She gripped Kelly's wrist. 'A man's looking at me.' She lowered her head until her face was hidden by Kelly's shoulder.

'Not at you, my love. More likely me.' He let his head touch hers. 'Don't look. Just move.' He led her through the arcade and turned the corner. 'Keep going.' They came to a travel agency's display window. 'Stop here.' They faced a large model of a Boeing 747 and a panel of posters advertising trips to the USA. Kelly glanced to the right, past an Ayers Rock display. 'Is he still there? Look now.'

'No.'

He whistled softly, making the noise of a deflating tyre. 'Oh Laura, thank God you're all right. You are, really?'

She nodded vigorously.

'How did you get away from him?'

The shock was over. Her mind was racing. She said, 'From Magnus Kolvenbach?'

'I've been so worried. I was thinking of going down to the Oasis motel and busting you out of the room.'

Her mouth sagged in surprise. 'How did you know we were there?'

He wobbled his eyebrows. 'I know everything.'

'You were going to *bust me out*?'

'I couldn't leave you here. Laura, you look wonderful. Did he give you a hard time? I mean, with drugs and... you know.'

She hesitated, then shook her head.

'Has it been awful?'

A slight nod. Too awful to talk about. He put his arm around her, and squeezed her.

'You're safe now. I'll look after you.'

He felt her head moving against his chest.

'Where is he now?'

This needed a special answer. What was better: to get Kelly back to the motel and wait till Kolvenbach returned, or get rid of him now? She didn't know. Damn it, she couldn't decide.

'I don't know.'

He took her in his arms. 'I can't believe that you're safe and we just met like this. Out in the street.'

She gave a little relieved laugh. She still needed time. 'Where did you get those clothes?'

He wasn't going to say another woman bought them for him. 'In town. Like them?'

'I hate stonewashed jeans. You're too old for them.'

That's the normal Laura, he thought, and felt cheered. Whatever Kolvenbach had given her had worn off; she was over it. 'We'd better keep moving.' Putting one arm around her shoulder and carrying her bags in the other, he led her down the street. 'Got to keep moving when you're in the fugitive business,' he said breezily.

She must show concern. 'You've been all right?'

'Sure.'

'I've been so worried.'

'I'm okay. Where would you like to go?'

She shook her head. 'I've got a motel room.'

'Where?'

'At the Oasis.'

He stopped. 'But Kolvenbach's there.'

She was committed. 'He's gone. He left today.'

'He just left you? Let you go?'

'I got away from him.' She lifted a hand to adjust the new hat. 'I had no clothes. That's why I was buying all this.'

'I was wondering.'

'I've got nothing. Just my bag and the clothes I was wearing. I ran away. I couldn't take anything.'

'Where's he gone?'

'Looking for you.' That was safe.

'Do you know where?'

'I've got no idea.'

'He thinks I shot his brother?'

She nodded sadly. 'Like everyone else.'

He wheeled her into a coffee lounge. No one else was there. He ordered two cappuccinos. He hadn't had one since Melbourne. This was so normal; and to be with Laura felt wonderful. When the waitress had gone, he said, 'What happened the other night? Out on the Cooper.'

The stop had given her thinking time. Kelly had mentioned drugs. She touched her forehead. 'It's all so hazy.'

'You can't remember?'

'Not much.'

'I was on a motorbike.'

Her face was a mask of surprise. 'You, on a motorbike?'

'You don't recall?'

'You're joking, Kelly: you can't ride a motorbike.'

'I used to.'

She grasped her forehead. 'Truly? You were riding a motorcycle?' He nodded and she let her head sag in bewilderment. 'I don't remember a thing. Are you still on it?'

He lifted a hand. 'Right now, I'm on foot.'

'I mean, how did you get here?'

'Long story. But I'm a bit short of transport.' He took her hand and kissed her fingertips. 'I knew that bastard had given you something.' His hand moved up her arm. 'Has he been giving you needles?'

'I don't remember.' She folded her arms protectively. 'I'm so glad to be away from him. Kelly, can we go to the motel?'

'Why?'

'My things are there.'

'You've got new things.'

The waitress delivered the coffee. Laura sipped the milky froth. 'I want to be with you, Kelly.' She put down the cup and regarded him with wide, innocent eyes. 'You've no idea how much I've missed you. I just need to be with you. On our own. To touch you. To lie with you. To feel safe again.'

He looked out on the street. 'I was supposed to meet someone.'

'Who?' That woman? She'd love to have a good look at her.

'Just someone who's been helping me.' People were passing and he turned away from the window. 'You're sure Kolvenbach's gone?'

'Oh, he's gone. He was in a foul mood. You've

381

been too smart for him and that's made him mad. I think he's driven out of town, way up the highway. He thinks you're up north somewhere.'

He nodded, his mind on many things. 'I have to come back though. I'm meeting him at five.'

'Him?'

'An interesting character. Black as the ace of spades. Moves through the hills like a shadow.' He smiled. 'I'll tell you about him later.'

Him. And black. She hadn't expected that although she should have; Kelly had a twisted admiration for Aborigines. She said, 'You're not going to leave me? I couldn't stand that.'

'No. Never again.'

She held his hand. 'I can't believe it's you. I can't believe that I'm safe at last.'

They went out, walking hand in hand until Kelly hailed a taxi. 'By the way,' he said, as the cab slowed, 'I love the outfit.' He touched the collar of the turquoise blouse. Already, he was planning how he would remove all her clothes, item by item. He'd leave the crazy scarf until last.

32

It won't last, Percy was saying. Red is a bad colour out here. It fades. That didn't matter, Monica replied, the paint only had to last a few weeks. Did she reckon she could do it? He'd known blokes in the old days who made a fortune doing that for a living and they'd reckoned it was a terrible job. All the different coats and all the rubbing down. She was a painter, she reminded him; but he said, with all the clucking of a hen, that she only painted birds. Birds, trucks: who cared? This would be a simple job, turning a blue Ford into a red Ford, and she'd get it done more rapidly if he stopped complaining and did what he said he would do.

Muttering about the way all women were the same, Percy went to fetch the old Chevrolet grille that he'd found at the wreckers and reckoned he could wire in place.

Wally didn't know the woman in the hat and bright scarf but he stayed within range, watching. When Kelly and the woman were in the arcade, he was outside at the plaza end, sitting on the brick wall of one of the ornamental gardens. He put himself near a group of Aborigines who were resting in the palm tree's shade. The men wore red headbands and had the lean, loose build of desert men. They stared at him with some curiosity. He ignored them.

Percy had said people were looking for Kelly, so Wally looked for people who looked as though they were looking for Kelly. He saw a few who glanced suspiciously at Kelly, but they always walked away. When Kelly and the woman were in the coffee lounge, Wally watched from beyond the road, squatting against the trunk of a tree growing on the sandy banks of the Todd River. When Kelly and the woman were getting in the taxi, he was crossing the road behind two tourists. He heard Kelly say 'Oasis'.

Walking slowly, Wally headed across the river to the street where he had left the old Chrysler.

McCarthy was worried. He hadn't heard from Harry the Hatchet and Harry had promised to ring him as soon as he'd made contact. Harry's plane had landed in Alice Springs many hours earlier and yet McCarthy had heard nothing. He had a bad feeling about that project. He also had a bad feeling about his own situation. He was vulnerable. Freddie Porter was conscious again but he wasn't mobile; he had a violent headache and couldn't see properly and had to lie down every ten minutes. Only Govorko, who wasn't one of his regulars, was guarding him.

McCarthy got on with packing the essential papers. He had to quit the office quickly before the goons came back.

Spiro walked in frowning.

'What went wrong?' McCarthy's voice rose like the growl of an aroused guard dog.

Spiro shook his head. 'Nothing. It's done. It's just such a waste of a good car. It must have been worth a quarter of a million dollars.'

McCarthy relaxed. 'You can buy your own Porsche one day.'

Spiro seemed dazed. 'It's wrecked. That's a big drop.'

384

'Nothing suspicious?'

'A classic accident. Man has too much to drink. Runs off road. Plunges to his death. Another name, another number is added to the tragic road toll.'

McCarthy grunted. 'Don't get poetic on me, Spiro. Give Freddie a hand. We've got to get out of here.'

Kolvenbach's clothes were still in the room. A jacket hung in the wardrobe. A pair of boots was on the floor, near an open suitcase. A crumpled shirt and pair of pants lay across one bed. There were two beds, Kelly noted.

Nervously, he looked around him. 'I thought you said he'd booked out.'

'He's gone.' Laura began gathering Kolvenbach's things and cramming them into his case. 'The man's irrational. It's just like him to go storming off and leave everything behind like this.'

She was folding a shirt. Folding? Why the hell was she being so tidy? He said, 'He must be coming back.'

'No,' she said firmly. 'Not today. Probably not tomorrow. He's gone out in the bush, way up north, looking for you.'

'Looking for you, too.'

'Yes.' She hadn't thought of that. She put the shirt in the case and moved forward to grip Kelly's arm. He had been edging towards the door. 'Darling, don't leave me now.'

'I won't.' He kept his eye on the window. 'Not ever. But I don't like this. What if he changes his mind? Jesus, Laura, let's go somewhere else.'

She put both arms around him and squeezed. 'You can't go anywhere. You'd be recognised if you tried to book in at any other motel. And darling, I wouldn't have come back to his room if I thought he was returning. For heaven's sake, Kelly, I've just managed to get away from that monster. I wouldn't come back to him.'

385

Kelly looked around. There was no other bag, none of her gear. 'Where's your stuff?'

'We didn't sleep together,' she said, as though offended.

'You had another room?'

'Yes,' she said, but knew it was a mistake.

'Always?'

She said nothing.

'Laura, how could he keep you prisoner if you were in another room?'

'He had a key.' She shrugged helplessly. Better to follow Kelly's drug scenario. 'Or something. I don't know.' She touched her forehead. 'I don't remember. I do recall him coming into the room in the mornings and getting me.' She lifted an arm, the symbol of a returning memory. 'Rope. He had me tied.'

'To the bed?'

She nodded.

'I thought that. I thought he must have had you tied up.'

'Kelly, it's been awful.'

He thought of what Monica had said. There was so much that didn't make sense. He looked around Kolvenbach's room again. 'How come you've got his key?'

She was ready for that. 'He brought me into the room this morning. I was feeling better, clearer. Able to think. He was in the bathroom. I ran. I took the key with me.'

He shook his head. 'I don't like it in here, Laura. It's as though Kolvenbach is watching me.'

She sat beside him. 'He's not. Darling, relax. Please, hold my hand.' And when he did, 'Kelly, it's been so long.'

'Only a few days.'

'It seems like a lifetime.'

'What happened at Tibooburra? How did he get hold of you?'

She put her fingers over his lips. 'We can talk about it later.' She began untying the loose knot in her scarf.

He stopped her. 'I want to leave that to last.'

Kolvenbach returned at four-thirty. They were still in bed. Kelly, weary from his days of running and exhausted by the frantic lovemaking, was almost asleep. At the moment when the conscious fraction of his mind was worrying that he might miss the rendezvous with Wally, the door opened quietly and there stood the big man. Hat in hand, leather satchel over one shoulder, legs apart, he almost filled the doorway.

Kolvenbach hesitated for a few seconds. He made a hissing sound, a snake judging the striking distance to its prey, then lunged forward. Kelly tried to sit up but he was too sluggish and the other man was too fast. Kolvenbach grabbed Kelly by the shoulders and shoved him against the wall. His head bounced off the bricks.

Laura pulled the sheet up to her chin. 'It was the only way I could make him stay until you got back.'

'Where did you find him?'

'What is this?' the dazed Kelly demanded, seizing Laura's arm.

She pulled free and stood up, dragging the sheet with her. Kelly was left naked on the bed. Kolvenbach snapped his fingers at Laura. 'I said, where did you find him?'

'I didn't find him. He found me. He was in the main street.' She began gathering her clothes.

Kolvenbach reached into his satchel and withdrew a large pistol. Casually, he waved it at Laura. 'Get dressed. You're leaving.' He pointed the gun at Kelly. 'Have you still got everything with you?'

Kelly spread his hands across his groin. 'Are you kidding?'

'The diamonds, the cash, the papers. Where are they?'

'Let me get dressed.'

He aimed the pistol.

'You won't shoot. You're not that stupid.' Kelly heard himself saying the words and was surprised. He sounded brave and confident, yet he was terrified and humiliated. He'd been outwitting this man in the bush and now he'd been trapped in bed. Caught with his wife, who was apologising to this man for being with her own husband. Like a lover found with another man. He felt destroyed, so he laughed.

Kolvenbach lowered the pistol. 'You're right. I won't.' He smiled. Terrible eyes, like his brother; Kelly could never look into Harald Kolvenbach's eyes. 'But you will tell me what I want to know. I can make you talk. Believe me.'

'I didn't shoot your brother. I didn't steal anything.'

'We've been through this conversation before.'

'Look, I rang Melbourne today. I called my secretary. She told me the police now know who killed Harald. They know it wasn't me. It's someone else.' He tried to recall the name Mary had said. Wilson. 'You can ring the Victorian police and ask for a Superintendent Wilson. He'll tell you.'

Kolvenbach glanced at Laura, who was edging into the bathroom clutching a handful of new clothes. She shrugged. 'I know nothing about it.'

Kelly sat up again and Kolvenbach, with contemptuous ease, pushed him back down. 'You're as slick with words as your wife, Hunnicutt.'

Kelly shook his head. 'I didn't kill your brother.'

'The last time we met, you said the things I want were hidden in the winch of your car. Where are they now?'

Kelly was trying to think clearly but all he could

think of was what Laura had said: 'It was the only way I could keep him here...' And Monica's warning: 'She's your enemy'.

'Well?'

His head ached. Of course. He'd hit the wall. He touched the back of his skull. The man would never believe him. Better to stall; he'd stay alive longer. He said, 'They're still there. All of them.'

'In the winch?'

'Hidden within the good old Toyota's winch.'

'And where's that?'

'Buried.'

Kolvenbach repeated the word.

'In Queensland.'

'The winch?'

'The whole car.'

Kelly thought the big man was going to strike him. He covered his face but Kolvenbach lowered his arm, closed his eyes and, after a huge intake of breath, turned away. He rapped on the bathroom door. 'You've got ten minutes. I'm putting you on a plane.'

Laura opened the door a fraction. 'I'm not going on any plane.' She saw the determined look on his face. 'Magnus, please. Remember what happened.'

'I've bought the ticket. You're flying to Sydney. Once you get there, you can go where you like. I just want you out of here.' He lifted his watch so she could see its face. 'Nine and a half minutes. I'm taking you whether you're dressed or not.'

Kelly lifted himself on to his elbows. 'What's been going on between you two?'

Kolvenbach threw Kelly's clothes at him. 'Get dressed.'

'I asked you a question.'

'And I said get dressed.'

'I want to know.'

Kolvenbach struck him across the face with the

back of his hand. 'You're lucky I've let you live this long, murderer. Now, do what I say. Do not talk. Do not ask stupid questions.' He prodded Kelly on the chest. 'You might be good in the bush, Hunnicutt, but obviously you're not much good in bed.'

'You bastard.'

He raised the pistol. 'I have no time to waste. Get dressed.'

Glaring at Kolvenbach and with blood trickling from his mouth, Kelly put on his T-shirt and jeans. While he was dressing, Kolvenbach went to the bathroom, barged past Laura, and returned immediately with an elasticised clothesline. He ordered Kelly to lie on his face. He tied his hands behind his back, then stretched the line to the ankles and bound them together. He used Kelly's belt to secure his neck to the bed post. With his own belt, Kolvenbach strapped Kelly's bound ankles to the other end of the bed.

'I'm taking your wife to the airport,' he said, stuffing one handkerchief in Kelly's mouth and completing the gag with another. He knotted the second one so tightly Kelly grunted with pain. 'When I come back, we'll go for a little drive and you'll give me a few answers.'

At the airport, Kolvenbach checked with Telecom and was given the number for police headquarters in Melbourne. He rang and asked for Superintendent Wilson. There was no one by that name, but there was a Superintendent Williams. He spoke to him. No, there was no other suspect in the Kolvenbach case. The police were still hunting for Kelso Hunnicutt. Was the caller ringing from Alice Springs? Did he have information to pass on?

Kolvenbach hung up and went to Laura, who was sitting against the wall, far from the phones. 'There's no such man. Your husband is a liar.'

She had her hands locked together. 'I know that.'

'I will get what I want.'

'I'm sure you will.' She looked up. 'Those papers must be important.'

'They are.' He looked around. He could see no one who seemed to be displaying particular interest in her. 'Do you need money?'

'No.' The flight was being called. 'Magnus, I only did that with Kelly to delay him, to make sure you caught him.'

He took her by the elbow and led her out of the terminal. 'Are you going to stay in Sydney?'

'No. I'll go home.' She twisted, trying to face him. 'I want you to believe me.'

'It's not important.' Near the gate he stopped and gripped both her arms. 'And you're sure you didn't tell anyone you were returning home on that other flight?'

'No one.' A flutter of uncertainty left her lips. 'Except...'

'Yes?'

'Gerry. I rang him. He was going to pick me up at the airport.'

'Gerry Montague?'

'Yes.'

'Would he tell anyone?'

'No.' She frowned. 'I don't think so.'

'Well, there you are,' he said, pushing her towards the gate. 'The man who wants you killed is either Montague or someone he's been talking to. Have a nice trip.'

He turned and hurried away.

It was dark when Kolvenbach reached the motel. He let himself in the room and released the gag. Kelly coughed and gasped for air while Kolvenbach undid the straps holding him by the throat and ankles.

391

He rolled Kelly on to his back and went to the bathroom, returning with a roll of adhesive plaster. Kelly was sitting up. He tried to talk but could only make guttural noises.

'Had enough air?' Kelly opened his mouth and Kolvenbach stuck a wide strip of plaster across it. 'It's only for a few minutes. You and I are going on a little trip.'

He slung Kelly over his shoulder and carried him to the door. He looked out and, sure no one was watching, carried him to the back of the rented Pajero. He slid him into the back and covered him with a canvas sheet.

He hurried back into the room, got his jacket and satchel and checked that his hunting knife was inside. He took the motel laundry bag and filled it with drinks from the refrigerator, then returned to the car.

Out on the road, he searched for the big tree that marked the turn-off to the MacDonnells. 'I know a nice, quiet place where we can talk without being interrupted. And then you can tell me exactly where you've buried that vehicle of yours. That's if you have buried it. Are you telling me the truth, Hunnicutt?'

Kolvenbach reached back, found the canvas and groped for Hunnicutt's head. He intended giving it a hurtful squeeze but the canvas collapsed. He stopped and felt again. The bulging canvas covered nothing but the floor. Hunnicutt had gone.

Laura stayed in the ladies room until the crowd had dispersed. The Ansett man saw her emerge and beckoned to her. 'A lot of people are frightened of flying,' he confided. 'My wife's the same. She always has to take Valium before she'll get on a plane.'

'Thank you. I'll get some.'

He checked a list. 'Do you want me to put your name down for tomorrow's flight?'

'I'll think about it.'

He smiled. 'You might end up staying here permanently.'

'There are worse places than Alice Springs.'

'Indeed. And I've probably worked in most of them.' He moved from behind the counter.

'You've been very kind,' she said. 'I'm sorry to have caused so much trouble and held up the plane like that.'

'No trouble. Would you like a taxi to take you back into town?'

She nodded.

'Come on,' he said, picking up the plastic bags she had deposited on the floor. 'I'll come out with you.'

33

The birds had stopped their screeching chorus of complaints and were now fluffing their feathers and twittering. Wally, kneeling in the sand and bird droppings at the back of one of the larger cages, was intrigued by the elasticised rope.

'Keep it,' Kelly said, rubbing his wrists to restore circulation. 'Call it a gift from the big man.'

The Aborigine reached out and touched the corner of Kelly's mouth. 'Blood.' It was the first word he'd said all night.

Kelly wiped his chin. 'He roughed me up. Very tough guy.' He began to rise and a parrot squawked. Wally put a hand on Kelly's shoulder and pressed down. He shook his head. 'Wait.'

Two words. This was a good night. 'Wait for what?'

Wally raised a finger to his lips and sunk low to the ground. Kelly did the same, lying behind a log that supported one of the nesting boxes. Wally had been in the cage earlier and had laid in a supply of small uprooted bushes. Now he spread them across Kelly's back.

Bright lights flooded the alleyway formed by the rows of motel units. The Pajero raced past the aviary and headed towards Kolvenbach's room at the far end of the complex.

Kelly felt Wally's hand gently pressing on the

394

back of his head, keeping him down. He could hear Kolvenbach slamming doors and cursing. The man was running, his boots crunching on gravel. A torch beam flickered across the gardens and the vines growing on the tall cages, then brightened the doorways and staircases along the two-storeyed blocks. The boots crunched back to the Pajero. More door slamming.

The vehicle raced past them again, slowed briefly as Kolvenbach glanced into the office and restaurant, and turned on to the main road.

'He's gone,' Kelly whispered.

Wally's rough hand touched his cheek and stayed there, keeping Kelly on the ground for another five minutes. 'Okay,' he said eventually, and began removing the layer of bushes.

'Where are we going?'

Wally rose to his feet like smoke curling from a dying fire. He beckoned and Kelly followed. They went to the rear of the motel and climbed a fence. They padded across the sands of the Todd, keeping well clear of a small fire in the middle of the dry riverbed where a group of men and women sat drinking and chattering.

'It's been quite a day,' Kelly whispered, feeling the need to break the silence. 'Found a wife, lost a wife, captured by a giant, rescued by a shadow.'

Wally turned and flashed his graveyard smile.

Laura took a room in a small motel not far from the Oasis. She stood in front of the mirror and gazed in disgust at what she saw. Laura Hunnicutt, Woman of Steel, was scared to go home. No, that was an understatement; she was terrified. Someone in Melbourne wanted her dead and she didn't know who.

Only Gerry had been aware that she was flying back, but he wouldn't send someone to kill her. That would be idiotic. He needed her in Melbourne. Whatever fascination he had for her body, he was even more dazzled by the prospect of the millions she was going to make for him — and she had to be in Melbourne to conclude the deal with Lucas. No, Gerry was too greedy to kill her. At least, not kill her until she'd sold the diamonds and he'd got his money.

Unless Gerry had done a deal with someone else. Who?

Back at Innamincka, Kolvenbach had asked her about another man. He'd telephoned someone in Canberra and been given a name. Some man who was supposed to be involved in a business deal with Gerry Montague. She concentrated.

McCartney? No, McCarthy.

Kolvenbach had asked her if she knew a McCarthy.

She would have to contact Kolvenbach, think of the right words to make him take her back again (because she would only be safe with him to protect her), and then get him to tell her what he knew about McCarthy.

First, she had to call Gerry Montague. She could always tell when Gerry was lying.

She tried to ring him at his flat. He didn't answer. She rang the office and got the recording machine, with Mary Calibrano's voice asking her to leave a message or telephone after nine o'clock in the morning.

She had Mary's home number.

'Welcome back to Melbourne.'

'I'm still at Alice Springs. The flight was cancelled.'

'Oh.' And then, in a voice that rose with excitement, 'Have you seen Kelly?'

She couldn't know. What did she know?

Mary laughed delightedly. 'Laura, Kelly's up there. He telephoned me this afternoon.'

'Oh my God.' She pumped excitement into her voice. 'In Alice Springs?'

'Yes.'

'Is he all right?'

'He said he was fine. A little hungry, I think, but all right. He said he was going to Ayers Rock. He'll be there tomorrow.'

A long pause.

'Are you there, Laura?'

'Sorry. I was surprised. How long ago did he call you?'

'A few hours.'

Ah. Before Kolvenbach caught him. He certainly wouldn't be going to Ayers Rock now. She hadn't been thinking about Kelly. Poor Kelly. He had no diamonds, no papers. She wondered what Kolvenbach would do to him.

'You haven't seen him?' Mary said.

'No.' She hesitated, trying to put a rush of thoughts in order. 'Ayers Rock? I might be able to catch a plane there in the morning.' That sounded proper. The worried wife trying to be near her husband.

'Do you want me to tell him you'll be at the Rock? He's ringing me from there.'

You'll wait a long time for that phone call, she thought, and said, 'Yes'. Then, 'No. I mightn't get on the plane. I wouldn't want to disappoint him, or have him put himself in danger, trying to find me.' She liked that.

'You ring me tomorrow. I'll find out from Kelly where he is and tell you.'

'Wonderful. Mary, I'm so thrilled.' She started the preliminaries to a farewell and then asked, as though the thought had just occurred, if she knew where Gerry Montague was.

Possibly back in his flat. He had left it for a while because there were detectives camped there. She thought they had gone.

'Detectives?'

'They've been there for days. It's been awful for him.'

A feeling of cold dread spread through her. Detectives, camped in Gerry's flat. Doing what? Searching for the diamonds? She and Gerry had prepared good hiding places but would they withstand a really thorough search — one that lasted a few days? She'd heard of police literally dismantling a house or a car in their search for drugs. Would they do the same for diamonds? Yes, when there was murder involved. Was Gerry the suspect the police superintendent had mentioned to Mary? And if he was, how long before they linked Gerry with her?

Trying to sound slightly amused, as though the whole thing was nonsensical, she asked, 'Why on earth have they been staying in Gerry's place?'

'Gerry said it was in case Kelly tried to get in touch with him. They could trace the call, I suppose. He said they kept on asking him questions about Kelly, over and over again. That's why he moved to the hotel.'

'The Regent?' Of course. She'd forgotten.

'No. The Hyatt. He was only at the Regent for a few hours. He must have moved just after you called him. The Regent served him the wrong sandwich.' She laughed.

'I beg your pardon?'

'Crazy, isn't it? But you know how touchy Gerry gets about food.'

'He's at the Hyatt?'

'I think he might be back in his apartment.'

Mary gave her Montague's number at the Hyatt — just in case.

Laura said, 'Do you know a Mr McCarthy? I believe he's a friend of Gerry's.'

Mary repeated the name, making it sound like bits that didn't belong together.

'Someone was telling me he's a business acquaintance. A partner or something.'

Mary was silent for a while and Laura could imagine her ruffling through her mental filing system. M for McCarthy.

'No. I've never heard of a Mr McCarthy. Why, is it important?'

'No, I was just curious.' She said goodbye, then rang the Hyatt and asked for Montague's room. There was no answer and she left no message.

She sat on the bed and tried to fit the pieces of the puzzle in place. The police were not camped at Gerry's flat — to use Mary's expression — just to intercept a phone call. They could do that, more effectively and more economically, by other means. They must suspect Gerry. They'd probably been searching the flat. Had they found what they wanted and left?

And if Gerry had moved to the Regent and then gone immediately to the Hyatt, he was running from them. Had he taken the diamonds?

She had to return to Melbourne, to find out what the devil was happening. But only with Kolvenbach. He had the strength, the ability to protect her. He also had his own plane.

She went to the bathroom to do her hair and stared in the mirror. After all her work — the meticulous planning, the duping of Kelly into accepting the bet, the flawless way the robbery had been executed — everything was dissolving into a mess of nightmarish uncertainty. The police were suspicious of Gerry, who had somehow taken a secret partner called McCarthy; Kolvenbach had thrown her out, and someone was trying to kill her.

She threw the brush at the mirror.

It bounced without breaking the glass. She leaned on the hand basin. There was only one good thing. Magnus had Kelly.

Kolvenbach returned to his room in a foul temper. He had driven south through Heavitree Gap and followed the road past the airport for more than twenty kilometres, gambling that Hunnicutt had either gone or been taken that way. He had seen no sign of a white man on foot and no one remembered seeing a blue Ford truck. He had raced back into town, been up and down every street, checked every park, driven north along the highway and driven west along the ranges.

He still hadn't worked out how Hunnicutt could have escaped. He must have had help. The woman artist and the old man with the arthritic hands? Impossible. He had been in the room for less than a minute and he'd heard nothing.

He was chasing a ghost.

He drank a brandy, then another and calmed himself by cleaning his favourite rifle. He handled it lovingly, fantasising that Hunnicutt was visible in the sights.

He put down the rifle and rang Canberra. Rob Lister was not available. Parliament was sitting and the Minister was required in the House. Kolvenbach gave his name as Mr Kay and left a message. He'd finally caught up with the gentleman he'd been trying to see for a few days. Unhappily, the gentleman had had to rush off. He hoped they'd meet again soon. The secretary, obviously puzzled, promised to leave the message for the Minister but she warned that the House would sit until late. Was there a number the Minister could ring? No. Kolvenbach said he'd call tomorrow.

He put the rifle away and refilled his glass. He'd almost finished his third brandy when the telephone rang.

'Laura?' He was astonished but not displeased. The brandy had mellowed him. When he heard her story, he laughed.

She hadn't expected that.

'One Hunnicutt runs away and another comes back.'

What was he saying? That he'd disposed of Kelly? With her voice shaking because the prospect of Kelly being dead was as shocking as it was desirable, she said, 'Magnus, don't talk in riddles. What's happened?'

'Your husband has got away.'

'Kelly?'

'You have more than one husband?'

He sounded tipsy. 'Magnus, what happened?'

Now he was belligerent. 'Maybe you know. Did you come back here and spirit him away?'

'Don't be infuriating. Tell me what happened.'

He emptied the last drops from the glass. 'That man of yours has disappeared. I had him tied up hand and foot with a big piece of sticking plaster across his mouth. I had him under canvas in the back of my wagon and he disappeared. I'm interested in theories. You know the man; what's your theory? Is he Harry Houdini or the Invisible Man? Tell me.'

'When did this happen?'

'Soon after I got back from the airport.' He reached for the brandy bottle. 'I asked whether you had any theories.'

'No theories,' she said, suddenly realising she had the means of forcing Kolvenbach to take her back. 'But I do know one thing.'

'What?'

'I know where he's going.'

'Where?' He drank half the glass in one gulp. 'How do you know? Have you seen him?'

'Of course not. Kelly rang Melbourne earlier today. He told his doting secretary. I rang her. She told me.'

'And where is he going?'

'No. Before I tell you, you have to make me a promise.'

He grunted.

'I presume that means okay. The deal is you come and get me and you keep me with you until we get back to Melbourne. Promise me that, and I'll tell you where Kelly has gone.'

'You're a devil.' He sounded amiable.

'Maybe.'

More grunts, which became a low laugh. 'Funny, just before you called I was thinking of you. I was angry with you, and puzzled by you: yet I was missing you. I was wanting you.'

'All those things?'

'I've had a very bad day.'

'Well, I'm just down the road.'

'And you'll make my day better?'

'Who knows?'

'I've been drinking. I get rough when I drink too much.'

'So do I, and I could do with a drink.'

He gave a little rumble of amusement, then sighed. 'I'm disappointed in you, Laura. The sight of you and that man...'

'I told you why that happened.'

More brandy. 'No man likes to see such a thing.'

She was silent.

'I'm better than he is.' The voice was a low growl, meant for himself rather than her.

'I know.'

'I might be very rough.'

'So?'

He took a deep breath and put the glass down. 'You really know where Hunnicutt is?'

'I know where he'll be tomorrow.'

He coughed, trying to clear his mind. 'Are you close by?'

'Just down the road.'

'Well, come here. I'm in the same room.'

'You come and get me. I'm not leaving this place.'

'Giving orders?'

'No. I'm too frightened to leave on my own. Surely you can understand why?' She waited but he said nothing. 'Magnus, I feel safe with you.'

He was having trouble linking his thoughts. It was the drink. A wave of cynicism washed over him. Safe with him? Bullshit. She meant she wanted to use him for something, one of her little schemes. He rolled the glass in his fingers. Well, two could play that game. She had one good card; he held the rest. 'All right,' he said. 'I'll come and get you. Where are you?'

She told him. He put down the phone and stretched out on the bed. Let her wait a while. His head swirled with confusing thoughts. He was pleased she was back but he didn't trust her. She was a devious woman, working her own schemes, trying to use him and thinking he was enough of a fool not to realise it. He relished the thought of penetrating her, of expunging the memory of seeing her lying naked with another man. It would be a wild and savage night.

He thought about that and got up to wash his face.

Whenever she was around and Hunnicutt was within range, the man got away. He wrestled with the problem of whether she was working with Hunnicutt or whether she truly wanted him caught and out of the way. And if she did want him killed — she had an appallingly ruthless streak — why? Was it just the spiteful wish of a wronged wife? Wronged wife! She'd been in bed with the man, fucking like a rattlesnake.

Savagely, he towelled his face.

She was much more deeply involved in this affair than she'd admitted. So deep that someone wanted her killed and had sent an expensive professional to do the job.

He'd drunk too much, and was too befuddled to think properly. But as he left the room, something from deep within the functioning part of his brain told him that Laura Hunnicutt was the key to getting the papers back.

34

Kelly was wearing his *G'DAY MATE* hat, dark sunglasses and the T-shirt with the map of the Northern Territory on it. He was surrounded by a milling crowd of Japanese, most of whom seemed to be dressed in variations on the same theme. The man behind the desk handed him a large envelope, looked at him curiously, and said, 'This was left for you, Mr Tate'. By my mother, thought Kelly, and quickly left the counter.

Out on the footpath, he opened the envelope. Inside were two fifty-dollar notes, a travel voucher, a map of Ayers Rock, a Japanese phrase book and a handwritten note.

> *The money is for your play lunch. The book is so you won't be short of conversation. Your travelling companions are staying at the Sheraton and so are you. Why not splurge? Everything has been prepaid except drinks. Aren't credit cards wonderful, as long as your name's not Hunnicutt... I'll meet you tomorrow morning on top of the Rock. Say nine o'clock? Wait for me. I'll be there. M.*

Two policemen were approaching, marching in step and regarding everyone with keen eyes set in expressionless faces. Kelly squeezed into the queue entering the coach and, knees bent to disguise his

405

height, shuffled down the corridor to a window seat at the back of the vehicle. He wriggled low in the seat and pulled the hat over his forehead. He opened the map and held it in front of his face.

A Japanese man, middle-aged and hunched, either from the worries of the world or from the weight of two Nikons slung around his neck, edged into the adjoining seat. His white baseball cap was emblazoned with a green and pink palm tree and the word *CAIRNS*. The front of his T-shirt featured a smiling crocodile with a pair of feet projecting from its jaws. The Japanese had a tired face that was more than lean; it seemed to have been devoured from within. He nodded politely to Kelly and tried to bring his swinging cameras under control.

The two policemen stopped outside. One climbed up the steps, acknowledged the driver and, spreading his legs until they blocked the corridor, surveyed the interior of the coach.

Kelly had been to Japan to shoot scenes for one of his double-overhead-camshaft movies and said to the man beside him, '*Ohayō gozaimasu*'.

The man, who was almost seated, rose, displayed a set of misaligned teeth and returned the greeting. He nodded several times and the cameras banged the back of the seat in front of him.

He should be seen to be involved in conversation, Kelly thought, and said, 'You've been to Cairns?' He nodded several times as though the other man were replying and the Japanese, who was finally settled in place, raised both eyebrows in ridges of perplexity.

The policeman had advanced by two rows and was facing a sea of uplifted and alarmed faces. He moved a finger, as though counting bodies.

'Cairns,' Kelly repeated and pointed to the man's cap.

The man bowed slightly and smiled. 'Very nice place.'

The coach's air brakes hissed. The policeman, looking embarrassed, smiled and retreated. The bus door closed.

Kelly relaxed but stayed low, his head level with those of the other passengers. 'I've been to Japan. Nagoya.'

The man's expression suggested that Kelly might have been to the moon. 'Nagoya?'

Kelly bowed. It was contagious.

'Me.' He tapped the crocodile.

'You come from Nagoya?'

He nodded vigorously and smiled so broadly Kelly thought the teeth might tumble out. They shook hands.

At the front of the coach, a young Japanese woman had risen and, using a microphone, said 'good morning' in English and Japanese. The interior rippled with soft replies.

The police had gone. The coach pulled out from the kerb and into the early morning traffic. Kelly looked forward to the trip. He had never travelled on a tourist bus.

The morning edition of the Melbourne *Herald-Sun* carried the news of Montague's death. It was not a big story. Just five paragraphs at the bottom of an inside page, under the headline: FILM MAN DIES IN CAR CRASH. *The Age* had an even smaller story and a shorter headline: CLIFF DEATH. The accident had been discovered late and Montague was not well known. The morning television news bulletins all ran the story, principally because of the car. They had videotape of the floodlit and mangled Porsche being hauled up the cliff face soon after midnight.

McCarthy was pleased. According to his friend

at police headquarters — who'd rung on another matter — there was no hint of suspicious circumstances. The corpse's blood-alcohol reading had set a new record for the month. McCarthy was interested, he said, because he'd been thinking of buying a Porsche and now there was one going cheap. Both laughed.

The friend was ringing because Kolvenbach was off again. He had lodged a flight plan early that morning to travel from Alice Springs to Ayers Rock. 'We're losing interest in him, George. The man's become a tourist, apparently.'

'Still travelling with a woman?' McCarthy asked casually.

'So it would seem. The flight plan says one passenger.'

McCarthy put down the phone. He was in Spiro's house in Fitzroy, where he had set up a temporary office. He went to the kitchen and made himself a coffee. Where was Harry the Hatchet?

He had no doubts that it was Lister's men who had grabbed and beaten him. Maybe they were tapping his phone again and had intercepted Harry. Or got to Harry and offered him more money to forget about Laura Hunnicutt and dispose of George McCarthy instead. He shivered at the prospect.

He thought about the Kolvenbach papers. Hunnicutt had them. Obviously, Lister didn't know that but he wanted them back so desperately they must be worth a lot of money. A desperate man could be put under pressure. Time to take the fight to Canberra.

He rang Lister's office.

Parliament had sat until the early hours of the morning and the Minister was not yet in his office. McCarthy left a message. The matter was urgent and related to the Kolvenbach papers. He would ring in one hour. He hung up while the secretary was asking for his name.

Then, on a whim, he rang Montague's office. Mary Calibrano was in tears.

'This is Superintendent Wilson. Miss Calibrano, I've just read the newspaper and I have to ask: is that the same Gerald Montague we've been trying to contact?'

It was, she sobbed.

He expressed his deepest sympathy and waited several seconds, sharing a profound silence with the grieving woman. 'Unhappily, Miss Calibrano, I was never able to get in touch with Mr Montague.'

She was trying to bring her voice under control. 'I thought he rang you.'

'No. Why I'm ringing is because we now have more evidence and it shows, quite conclusively, that Mr Hunnicutt did not murder Harald Kolvenbach.' He waited.

'Well, thank God for that.' She blew her nose. 'Does that mean Kelly's in the clear?'

'Absolutely.'

She sounded as though she might cry again.

'The trouble is, Miss Calibrano, that Mr Hunnicutt doesn't know and there's no way we can tell him. The man keeps well and truly out of sight.' He laughed; a modest, defeated sound, suitable for a day of such mixed news.

'Well,' she began and then didn't know what else to say.

'The simple fact is we don't know where or how to find him so that we can pass on the good news and tell the poor man to stop running. He's in the clear.'

'That's wonderful.' Her voice was a whisper.

'Yes.'

She sniffed. 'He's calling me later today.'

'Is he now? Where will he be, Miss Calibrano?'

'At Ayers Rock. He's going to call me from Ayers Rock. Do you have police there?'

'Yes, indeed we do, Miss Calibrano.' Another modest laugh. 'Well, not Victorian police, of course, but Northern Territory police. There's quite a large squad up there.'

'Can you let them know? Maybe they could put up signs or broadcast messages on loudspeakers or something.'

'Maybe they could. When do you expect him to ring?'

'Sometime today. He didn't say when.'

'Miss Calibrano, would you know if Mrs Hunnicutt is up there with him?'

'Laura? She's in Alice Springs. She may go to Ayers Rock today. She's trying to get on a plane.'

He was silent for a few moments. 'How do you know that?'

'She told me. She rang last night.'

'Laura Hunnicutt rang you last night?'

'Yes. This was some hours after Kelly had rung me in the office.'

'Did she ring *late* last night?'

'Late enough. I was at home having dinner.'

'And Mr Hunnicutt. He rang you from Ayers Rock?'

'No. Alice Springs.'

'And she rang from Alice Springs?'

'Yes, but she didn't know he was there. She was going to try and get a flight to the Rock so she could be with him.'

'And she told you this last night?'

'Yes.'

He breathed heavily. 'Thank you, Miss Calibrano. Again, my condolences on the sad loss you've suffered.'

She mumbled thanks.

McCarthy sat back. Harry the Hatchet was either dead, incapacitated, or he'd been bought by Lister. At least Harry didn't know of Spiro's house. They were reasonably safe here.

McCarthy tipped the remains of the coffee down

the sink and went to the refrigerator for a beer. He needed to think.

Even Kolvenbach, with his mind full of conflicting plans and persistent worries, had to admire the scene drifting towards the aircraft. It was a stunning sight: some of nature's most glorious gems displayed on a cloth of wrinkled red sand.

The great rock was brightly coloured and vividly striped, long and humped like the carapace of a beached turtle. It was orange where the early sunlight touched its broad flanks; pinkish grey where the rolling striations gave its back the look of a ridged shell; purple, flaming red and even a deep blue-black in the valleys and folds that caught the brightest rays and hid the deepest shadows.

To the west were the Olgas, a jumble of domes that glowed pale violet in the early light. They lay across the horizon like a bunch of translucent melons.

The air was pure and the morning clear and the sky was a watery blue. Later in the day, when the sun was high and the air thin and warm, the blue would bleach to a calico grey and the Rock would simmer down to sandy hues.

'Ayers Rock,' Kolvenbach said, and Laura, who had been dozing, awoke as he banked the plane in its first turn prior to landing at the Yulara strip. He pointed to the west. 'Mount Olga.' He pointed to the southeast, where the shadowy silhouette of a table-top mountain erupted from a supremely flat horizon. 'Mount Conner.' He had been reading his chart.

He's a real poet, she thought, rubbing her eyes. Better than Kelly, though. He would have been gushing about the three mountains and pouring out all of his geographical and historical knowledge. How high, how far around, which explorer discovered them, who were the first white men to climb them.

'Lovely,' she said and hung on.

At the airport, Kolvenbach took delivery of a rent-a-car and, after checking the car park, followed the bitumen road into the landscaped desert gardens of Yulara village. He had a map and went first to the camping area and caravan park. He found one F100 but it had Queensland plates and was beside a caravan which was overflowing with small children. He then followed the looping road that led to the Red Desert motel. He entered the motel, passing the *Private, Guests Only* sign and let his car trickle past the units, but few vehicles were parked there. He examined the crowd of back-packers sunning themselves on the grass beside the pool. Most were blonde. Swedes or Germans, he guessed, and drove back to the road. Next, he went to the Four Seasons hotel, checked the car park and walked inside, wandering through the bar and the lounge and out, into the swimming pool area. When he was satisfied he had checked the whole village, he stopped at the Sheraton, where he had made a reservation.

They walked to the reception desk. 'No sign of him,' he said softly to Laura. It was meant critically, the preliminary to a protest at having been led on a wild goose chase.

Laura said, just as softly, 'Amazing. I expected to find him sitting on the steps, waiting for us'.

Neither was in a good mood.

They booked in as man and wife. A porter bulging with the load of plastic shopping bags led them to the room. As soon as he had gone, Laura went to the bathroom. Kolvenbach rang Rob Lister.

The Minister had just entered his office. He was highly animated. Did Kolvenbach know that Gerry Montague was dead? His car had gone over a cliff. It was in the Melbourne papers. Very slowly, Kolvenbach said 'No', and wondered. Over breakfast, he and Laura had been discussing Montague and his mysterious colleague, McCarthy. She didn't know McCarthy. Neither did he. It was a discussion that soured the morning because neither believed the other. The one thing that seemed clear to Kolvenbach was that either Montague or someone he confided in, maybe McCarthy, was responsible for sending that man to Alice Springs.

Now Montague was dead.

Lister read out the details. It appeared to be an accident but that was too convenient. More likely to be the work of professionals.

'What do you know of McCarthy?' Kolvenbach was watching the bathroom door. He'd heard the toilet flush.

'He's a private investigator in Melbourne,' Lister said. 'Ex-detective with the Victorian police. Has a reputation for being a hard man. I had an anonymous phone call about him. Very interesting. Just a moment.' Someone had entered the Minister's office and Kolvenbach heard Lister say 'Not now Peter', and ask him to leave. 'Sorry. My anonymous telephone caller wanted to tip the bucket on McCarthy. He said that McCarthy was at Gerry Montague's apartment and that McCarthy had the diamonds — and the papers.'

Kolvenbach whistled. 'The papers?'

'He was specific. He said I could have the papers but he wanted the diamonds. Any idea who it might have been?'

The bathroom door was still closed. Kolvenbach didn't want her listening to this. He said, 'None. How about you?'

'I didn't recognise the voice although it sounded like a Pom. Montague was English.'

'Montague?'

'That's my guess.'

'Which could explain why he went over a cliff.'

'Precisely. I sent some men to talk to McCarthy.'

Lister sounded amused.

'What happened?'

'They got him. Roughed him up a little. They were taking him to Montague's apartment when they were waylaid in the street and very efficiently put out of action.'

'Dead?'

'No, no, no. Two were KO'd, the third shit himself. Quite an operation.'

'McCarthy did this?'

'His men.'

'So he got away?'

'Yes. If I understand your cryptic message of last night, a similar thing happened to Hunnicutt. That so?'

'I had him. He got away.' Kolvenbach gave a concise summary. He finished as Laura emerged from the bathroom. He signalled for her to sit down.

'So what should we do next?' Lister asked. 'Who's got these bloody papers, Hunnicutt or McCarthy?'

'I don't know. I've got a few thoughts that might help us resolve things. Let me polish them up and come back to you. Can I reach you on this number today?'

'You can reach me or leave a message. I'm wanted back in the House at four.'

They hung up.

'Who was that?' Laura said.

'An acquaintance. Ordinary business must go on.' He said nothing about Montague or McCarthy.

He sat looking at her and she fidgeted, not liking it when he stared at her. 'Why are you looking at me like that?'

'I beg your pardon,' he said with exaggerated courtesy and walked to the window. He could see the tip of Ayers Rock in the distance. 'I'm sorry. I do that sometimes when I'm thinking about something serious.'

He was thinking that he could use Laura as bait

414

to attract whoever had the papers — Hunnicutt or McCarthy.

Spiro had been outside, talking to Govorko. When he came back into the house, McCarthy stood up and stretched. 'Feel like a nice long plane ride?' he said, and Spiro waited to learn of his latest assignment. 'You and me are off to Ayers Rock, Spiro.'

The two of them? That was unusual. Spiro knew better than to ask why. When McCarthy was in a bad mood, the answer usually was 'Because I said so' — and McCarthy was in a bad mood.

'Kelso Hunnicutt's wife is at Ayers Rock. So is the elusive Mr Hunnicutt. Do you think we could find them?'

Spiro shrugged.

'I think it's worth a try. One of them has these stolen papers that seem to be sending our friend in Canberra into such a frenzy.' McCarthy was pensive for a moment. He had rung Lister again. Lister wanted proof and he was demanding a fax of the letter. Just the top part, showing the date and the first line. To fax even that much, McCarthy had to have the letter. Blackmail by fax; he hadn't heard of that. He might be a pioneer. Smiling at such an appealing thought, he turned back to Spiro. 'Be nice to get our hands on the Hunnicutts, wouldn't it? We could get Lister off our backs and indulge in a spot of high-class blackmailing at the same time.'

'I never been to Ayers Rock.'

'Neither have I, my little friend. I've made the booking. We leave this afternoon.' He tossed a glossy photograph on to the table. 'Mrs Hunnicutt used to be a model. This is what she looked like five years ago. Do you think you could find her?'

Spiro grinned. 'I'd like to do more than just find her.'

'You may get the chance. Now get packed. We

415

should leave here in an hour.'

Spiro frowned. 'How will we know where they are?'

McCarthy tapped his forehead. 'My good friend Superintendent Wilson will find out later today. We will be told exactly where to go.'

The coach swung into the driveway of the Sheraton. It passed rows of palms, masses of shyly blooming grevillea bushes, spiky outbursts of native grasses, and swelling mounds covered by chopped spinifex mulch, then stopped at the entrance to Yulara's only four-star hotel. Kelly was among the last to get off. He waited for the man from Nagoya, who was having trouble with cameras that persisted in hooking over seat armrests.

The guide raised her arms and began an address in Japanese. Two porters brought out trolleys for the group's luggage. Kelly, head bent forward to appear less conspicuous among so many short people, looked beyond the coach and saw a police Landcruiser stop in the car park. A policeman got out, hitched up his pants, and began to walk towards the hotel entrance. Kelly turned the other way.

Kolvenbach and Laura were at the top of the steps.

Kelly swung back towards the coach. The policeman was approaching. Kelly held up the map of Ayers Rock. '*Ohayō gozaimasu,*' he called out and the tour leader stopped. The other Japanese turned to face him. '*Konnichi wa,*' he continued in a loud and authoritative voice. He smiled with great vigour and tapped the map. 'Ayers Rock.' He pointed to the gardens. The Japanese turned and searched for the Rock. *'Ichi, hai, dōmo arigatō.'* He'd run out of Japanese words and began inventing some. Waving the map, he said, *'Wah nomo domo michi dichi. Hai chai, wulu walu, nagoyen doyen walu'.*

The policeman glanced at him, nodded to one of the Japanese men who had stepped out his way, and walked into the hotel.

'Ayers Rock. Mount Olga. *Dōmo arigatō*,' Kelly said and bowed.

The man from Nagoya spoke to the others and they laughed. Some clapped.

'I said you were learning Japanese,' he confided.

'Thank you.'

Kolvenbach and Laura were still on the steps, facing each other, their heads bent in conversation. Kelly took off his hat. 'Here — a gift from Australia to Japan.' He presented the man with his hat — the hat Laura had seen in Alice Springs.

The Japanese blinked, bowed, and gave Kelly his Cairns cap. Kelly put it on and pulled the peak down until it touched the top of his sunglasses. The men smiled at each other and, together, walked up the steps. Kolvenbach and Laura walked down. They passed, with Laura speaking earnestly to Kolvenbach and with Kelly flourishing one hand and speaking gibberish to the man from Nagoya.

Inside the hotel, the Japanese said, 'So sorry. I did not understand.'

'Ah.' Kelly clapped his hands. 'I must have been speaking Chinese.'

'You speak Chinese?'

'Not well. I get confused.' Kelly smiled modestly. 'Japanese and Chinese. They are difficult for us.'

'Very admirable.'

'Thank you.' They shook hands. Kelly joined the crowd at the reception desk and presented his travel voucher. He was taken to his room and stayed there. The Japanese tourists were going on a Champagne Sunset Tour of the Rock. He had the voucher, prepaid by Monica, but he had no desire to leave the room.

Kolvenbach was here. With Laura. Monica was right. Laura was in love with the South African.

He felt sick, and too frightened to go out.

How did Kolvenbach know he was at Yulara? He lay on the bed but then almost immediately got up. He had promised to ring Mary.

She was not in the office. He checked his watch. Mary was always there at this time. There was only her recorded voice, asking that the caller leave a message. He waited for the pips and gave Mary his phone and room number.

She telephoned much later. She had left the office for several hours — she was most apologetic — because she had been too distressed by the news about Gerry Montague. She told Kelly. He was appalled. 'It was an accident,' Mary was saying. 'Gerry's car went over a cliff. I don't know what he was doing down there, especially at night. He never drove that far from the city. You know that.'

'When did this happen?'

'He was found around midnight. The police were here this morning.' She hesitated, reluctant to pass on the next news. 'They say he was drunk. They asked me if he drank a lot. I didn't know what to say. After they left, I went home. I'm sorry.' He heard her cry.

She sniffed several times and then tried to brighten her voice. There was some good news. Very good. Superintendent Wilson had rung twice. The first time was to say Kelly was definitely, positively in the clear. The superintendent confirmed that another person was now known to have killed Harald Kolvenbach.

Kelly sagged on to the bed. 'You're sure?'

'Yes. They know it's someone else.'

'When did he ring?'

'He telephoned me this morning. That was the first time. He'd read about Gerry and he said he was sorry and then he told me you were no longer a suspect.'

'Did he say who murdered Harald?'

'No.' She coughed, embarrassed about something. 'The second time he rang was a few minutes ago. I'd only just come back to the office and heard your message. I hope you don't mind but I gave him your number.'

'Up here?'

'Yes.' Her voice was finely balanced, ready to share his pleasure or tumble into guilt. 'Should I have done that? He sounds nice. Kelly, he's so much on your side.'

'Have you met him?'

'No.'

Kelly tapped the bedside table. He spoke slowly. 'Here's what I'd like you to do, Mary. Ring this Superintendent Wilson at police headquarters. Confirm that the search is off. Ask who the new suspect is. Tell them I'll give myself up if they'll tell you who it was that shot Harald. Then call me back. Okay?'

She rang ten minutes later. Her voice was shaking. There was no Superintendent Wilson at police headquarters. The search for Kelso Hunnicutt was more intensive than ever and had been extended to cover all of the Northern Territory and South Australia.

Kelly grabbed his small bag and left the room immediately. He went out the back way, through the hotel gardens and around to the front of the building. Who was this Wilson? Not a policeman, so he must be someone working with Kolvenbach — who was at Yulara, staying in the same hotel, and who now knew Kelly's room number.

The foyer was empty. Outside, a group of Japanese tourists were being loaded onto a transit coach. Kelly recognised his friend. He joined him and went on the Champagne Sunset Tour of Ayers Rock.

35

It was several years since Kelly had been to Ayers Rock and he had never stayed at Yulara. In fact, the tourist village had been no more than a grand plan when he was last there. He had always camped near the eastern end of the great monolith. It had been a wonderful site, a mile from the Rock but seemingly close, so that when he crawled from his tent at dawn, the glow of light on the bulbous walls radiated a warm greeting. Yulara made it all so different, so remote. He was surprised how far the coach had to travel before the passengers could glimpse anything other than the top of the Rock and how much further they had to go before they could see it all.

That moment came when the coach glided over a sandy rise and, with a groan of brakes, rolled to a halt at the first photographic stop.

The coach filled with sighs, then titters of excitement. Even Kelly made a little mumbling noise, his own nostalgic greeting to an old friend. This was a wonderful angle and even to someone who had seen it as many times as he, the spectacle was as grand as ever. The full northern face of Ayers Rock, almost trapezoidal in shape, was like a great fossilised tent, solidified at the moment when its folds were billowing in the wind. The colours were soft: vertical bands of pale apricot and watery red, with mottled patches of grey-green where the rays of the setting sun touched the lichens growing on the cliff faces.

Kelly glanced to the west. Beyond the Olgas a few thin clouds stretched across the horizon like fluffy strands of cotton wool. It would be a brilliant sunset. In an hour, the colours would be spectacular. The Rock's great walls would ripen and change into fiery reds and intense purples.

The man from Nagoya was most impressed and smiled at Kelly as though offering personal congratulations. Cameras swinging, he joined the stream pouring from the coach to take pictures.

Kelly stayed in his seat. Several cars and a smaller bus passed, bearing people anxious to film the sunset from one of the obligatory viewing points. One car slowed, either to view the Rock or examine the coach, and he slid lower in the seat.

The next stop was at the ranger station. It had public phones. While his fellow passengers were collecting pamphlets, studying colourful wall charts and buying books, he rang the Sheraton. Were there any messages for Mr Tate? The operator checked. No messages but a gentleman had been enquiring if Mr Tate were in. The gentleman had telephoned? No, he came to the desk. He was a short, rather stout man. Kelly's teeth played with his lower lip. Not Kolvenbach. Not even Laura.

'Did he ask for me by name?'

She checked. 'No, Mr Tate. He asked if the gentleman in Room One Eleven was in.'

He hung up and rang the hotel again. Affecting what he hoped would be taken for a Japanese accent, he asked for Mr Kolvenbach.

'The room is not answering. Would you like me to page Mrs Kolvenbach? I think I saw her going into one of the lobby shops a little while ago.'

421

'No thank you. I'll ring later.' No, there was no message.

Mrs Kolvenbach. So she was playing the part of the South African's wife. Even shopping. Spending his money, no doubt. Great. She was living with the man who was trying to kill him. And he'd even driven her to Tibooburra and delivered her to Kolvenbach. He walked outside and sat on a bench.

He took out his handkerchief and wiped his eyes. A hand touched his shoulder. It was the man from Nagoya.

'Are you well, my friend?'

Kelly nodded. He touched an eye. 'Dust.'

'Ah.' The man's ravaged face mellowed into hollows of concern. 'Very bad?'

Kelly shook his head. He had a wild urge to hold the man's hand.

Gently, the Japanese said, 'We are about to drive around the Rock. You must come.'

They got off at Maggie Spring. Kelly took his bag; it was small enough to carry over his shoulder. He walked with the others into the narrowing gorge that led to the pool, gazed up at the flaring colours on the three-hundred-metre-high cliffs and used one of the Nikons to photograph his friend at the water hole.

On the way back, he dropped to the rear of the group. 'I will not go back in the coach,' he told the man.

The Japanese seemed greatly concerned.

'I have someone coming to pick me up,' Kelly lied. 'A very old friend who will take me back to the hotel. We are having dinner together.'

The man nodded understanding. 'Have a good night. Enjoy yourself.'

'You too.' Kelly stopped near a tumble of fallen rocks. The group walked on, studiously following their leader. Once, the man from Nagoya, who was trailing behind, turned to wave. Kelly returned the farewell, then walked up the rocks. He climbed beyond the first level. He'd used this area in a film he'd made years ago. There were caves up here, low but with sandy bottoms. Warm enough to sleep in. He had no intention of returning to the hotel.

He had a block of chocolate in his bag. Half for dinner, half for breakfast. In the morning, he would climb the Rock and wait for Monica.

McCarthy had been sitting at one end of the lounge, Spiro at the other. Each read a paper and lingered over his drink. Folding his newspaper and leaving it on the table, McCarthy went to the nearest telephone and rang the hotel's number. He asked for reception. Across at the desk, he saw the girl — a Filipino, he guessed but possibly Malaysian; very exotic, whatever she was — pick up the phone.

No, she didn't think the gentleman in Room One Eleven had returned although his key was not in the rack. She tried the room. There was no answer. Possibly he was on one of the tours. They normally returned about an hour after sunset. Was this the gentleman who'd rung before?

It was.

'Mr Tate rang and enquired whether you'd called.'

McCarthy was stunned. 'He did?' His voice was flat.

'About half an hour ago.'

'From his room?'

She had to think. 'No, it was an outside call. Would you care to leave a message?'

He assured her he wouldn't bother and went back to the lounge. Ignoring Spiro, he picked up the paper and ordered another drink. Hunnicutt was using the name Tate. And he'd rung to see if anyone had called. Cunning fellow. Now he was aware that someone knew where he was staying. He wouldn't come back to the Sheraton.

He finished his drink, folded the paper under his arm and left the hotel. A minute later, Spiro followed.

They met in the car park, beside the hired car. 'Go back inside and ring each of the hotels,' McCarthy said, passing his man the three brochures. 'Ask for Mrs Kolvenbach. If Hunnicutt's wife is travelling with Kolvenbach, it'll be pounds to peanuts that she's using his name.'

'What if she answers?'

'Say you're from Room Service and ask if she just phoned down to order French champagne and oysters. She'll say no and you'll say is that Room Two Fifty Two, and she, like a good little girl, will give you her room number and tell you you've made a mistake.'

'What if she's not there?'

McCarthy gazed imploringly into the fronds of a palm tree. 'In that case, don't speak to her. Just come back and tell me what hotel she's staying in.'

It was after midnight and Kolvenbach was thinking he was wasting his time. Since sunset, he had stationed himself near the entrance to the camping area, figuring that Hunnicutt, the woman and the old man wouldn't stop at one of the hotels. Such a scruffy trio would attract too much attention, even among the backpackers at the Desert Sands. They'd camp. The woman had all the equipment. They'd come in at night, and this was the only place where camping was allowed.

He was puzzled by Hunnicutt's decision to travel to Ayers Rock and had spent the last couple of hours trying to work out why. This was such a bizarre, unlikely place for a man on the run to come to. But when he thought about it, that was precisely

424

the sort of thing Hunnicutt would do. He always took the unlikely road, went to the unexpected place.

He had developed a certain affection for Hunnicutt. It was a grudging respect, the sort of feeling that sometimes grew when he was hunting dangerous game in Africa and his quarry either eluded him or led him on a long and exhausting chase. He'd get Hunnicutt, but the man was good.

All his thinking led to one conclusion. Hunnicutt must be here to dispose of the diamonds. Ayers Rock was where he was meeting the buyer. Kolvenbach doubted Lister's story of the diamonds and papers still being in Melbourne, and he didn't believe Hunnicutt's tale about everything being buried with the vehicle in Queensland. Hunnicutt would have the diamonds with him. Having killed for them, he would never abandon them; not four million dollars worth. He'd chosen Ayers Rock because it was the most unlikely place for such a big and illicit transaction. It also had a regular jet service. The buyer could fly in and be out of the country within twelve hours.

All this was speculation. One thing Kolvenbach didn't doubt: Hunnicutt had murdered his brother. For that reason alone, he'd hunt him down.

At ten to one, a small tourist bus went by. Kolvenbach saw it enter the camping area and back into a space. He began to wonder. It was a strange hour for a tourist vehicle to reach Yulara, and there was only a driver on board. He watched and saw the driver walk in front of the lights. It was a woman. He left his car and walked closer, waiting in the shadows as she went into the women's toilet block. The woman emerged and he recognised her. It was the artist, the one he'd met at Innamincka.

She climbed back into the minibus. *MURRAY'S TOURS — King's Canyon, Mount Conner, Ayers*

Rock, Mount Olga was written on the side. Kolvenbach stayed hidden for another hour until he was certain she was asleep. He saw no sign of any man.

Quietly, he returned to his car.

There was a cold wind that night and Kelly got little sleep. Long before dawn, his legs stiff and his hips and shoulders aching, he climbed down from the rocks and followed the sandy track to Maggie Spring. He drank some water and splashed his face, which was still sore from Kolvenbach's beating. He touched his cut lip and rinsed his mouth, then sat on the sand at the edge of the pool while the first hint of light brought flushes of colour to the rock faces that soared above him.

He ate a little chocolate, drank more water and set off to walk around the Rock to the climbing place. The sky was a pale violet with the surviving stars spluttering and fading like burnt-down candles, but the southwestern side of the Rock remained in deep shadow and Kelly had trouble finding the path. The walk took him more than an hour. When he reached the climb, with its array of signs and car parks, dawn was near and the Rock was a towering mass of sloping shadows. But the horizon was afire and while Kelly gazed up, the topmost folds flamed into slices of bright light.

Already, a couple of cars were parked there. People who had come to pit themselves against the Rock were drinking coffee or holding cameras to their eyes and complaining that there wasn't enough light.

He began to climb.

Kelly had made the ascent several times. Eleven hundred and ninety-two feet. He knew the height above the plain in feet, had never learned it in metres. The summit was almost three times higher than the Sydney Harbour Bridge. That fact always

426

impressed him and sustained him when, muscle-weary and breathless, he had felt like surrendering and turning back. He never had.

The climb was further than you thought, harder than most people imagined. He knew the worst was the early part, where the slope was steep and the aftershock of that early effort made the knees and thighs of city people scream for rest, and the rocky ridges towering above seemed even higher and more intimidating than they had from the ground.

When he reached the chain which marked the route along a thin and sharply angled ridge, he stopped and looked back. To the west, the magical domes of the Olgas were a transparent pink, as elegant and ethereal as stained glass. The way north towards Yulara was marked by the sparkle of head-lights. Cars and coaches were pouring out for the compulsory dawn visit and to unleash squads of eager and innocent climbers.

The first sliver of sun broke the horizon. He climbed on, enjoying the sudden warmth. With one hand on the chain, the other steadying the bag over his shoulder, he climbed for another five minutes, then stopped and sat with one arm locked around a metal post. Other climbers were following. They were spread down the slope like ants on the trail of honey. Two youths, wearing only caps, shorts and Reeboks, strode past him. Heads down, legs pumping, they were too intent on the climb and their own personal race to offer greetings. Each was after the honour of being the first to the top for that day. Young men had been doing that every day for the last twenty years, Kelly reflected, and concentrated on getting back his breath. He scanned the groups of people fanned out across the land below him. He was searching for a man of exceptional size. That was the good thing about Kolvenbach — he stood out in a crowd.

Would he bring Laura for the climb, just like other newlyweds? The thought of them together made him sick and then he felt ashamed for having thought it. Taking a deep breath, he rose and resumed climbing.

Two young men and a girl passed him while he was traversing the deep undulations that added agony to the final phase of the climb. They ran past him on the way down one dip and scrambled, laughing, up the other side.

When he reached the highest point, they were sitting beside the stone marker with their arms spread back for support, their chests heaving, their faces flushed with the mixed reds of exhaustion and triumph. Their laughs were fractured by breathlessness.

The first two youths were signing the climbers' book. Kelly put down his bag, nodded greetings, and looked around him. A stream of climbers was approaching. No sign of Monica. She'd said nine o'clock.

He picked up his bag and casually walked beyond the marker towards the rising sun, crossing the ripples and gullies that formed the corrugated roof of the Rock. In the distance, some shrubs and a few wind-bent trees had taken root in a fertile hollow. He would wait there. Out of sight and with the sun behind him, he could see who approached.

A disgruntled Laura was sitting beside Kolvenbach. He had offered to let her stay in the room but she had refused. Not because she wanted to see Ayers Rock — she had already seen it from the plane — but because she thought Kolvenbach would be out all day and she didn't want to be left on her own. They had been parked here since four in the morning. She was cold and hungry and she would kill for a cup of coffee, but he just sat behind the wheel, never taking his eyes off the minibus.

'If you'd told me we were going to be sitting out here like this, I could have had the hotel people prepare us a food pack and a thermos of coffee.' He hushed her into silence.

'Who are Murray's Tours?' Another shush.

'You can be extremely irritating.'

'So can you.'

'My God, the man can speak.'

He spared her a glance. 'The woman who is your husband's accomplice, the artist who was camped at the Cooper, is in the bus.'

'Why?'

His fingers drummed the rim of the steering wheel. 'That is what we are going to find out.'

At 7.15, they saw Monica emerge. She went to the toilet block, returned about ten minutes later, and drove out of the camping area. Kolvenbach slid low in his seat and had Laura do the same. When the bus had passed, he started up the engine and followed.

A hundred metres down the road, they passed a stationary car. A man was standing near it, photographing a flowering tree. For some time, he had been walking near the base of a sandhill, constantly taking pictures. He was a stout man and had Kolvenbach not been so intent on following the minibus, he might have been surprised at the man's dress. He had on a white business shirt, dark grey pants and leather shoes. Only the tie and coat were needed to complete a business suit.

The man let Kolvenbach pass and then, pausing to take another photograph, got back in his car.

Spiro raised his seat. 'Do we follow them?'

McCarthy tossed the camera on to the back seat. 'Of course. Just make sure they don't get interested in us.' Immediately, he regretted the remark. Spiro was the best tracker in the business.

429

'I thought the big bloke must have been screwing the legs off her,' Spiro said cheerfully.

'Why leave a comfortable bed in a luxury hotel to do it in a car?' McCarthy rubbed his hands to warm them. 'And on a morning like this.'

'Who's in the bus?'

'No idea. She must interest Kolvenbach, though.' He reached in the back for the flask of hot coffee. 'In any case it's Laura Hunnicutt we're interested in. Wherever she goes, we go.'

The parking area was almost full but Monica found a space in the zone reserved for coaches. That was another benefit; now she could park in loading zones and special areas normally forbidden to cars. She was preparing her arguments for Kelly; he'd have cutting things to say about her getting rid of the Ford and buying a bus, especially one that had done 323,000 kilometres. At least it was a Toyota and it had four-wheel drive; he was as biased as hell towards four-wheel-drive Toyotas, so he might shut up. She could never have got here in the old truck — even painted red and with the phoney grille. In the minibus, she'd been waved through three roadblocks between Alice Springs and the Rock. Other vehicles were being searched and anyone in a small truck was being given a hard time.

She got her bag, made sure it contained the water and fruit and the parcel that Sue had sent her, put a double knot in her bootlaces, tightened the chinstrap on her hat, and walked to the place where the mottled slab of sloping rock merged with the ground. She saw some plaques and began to read them but soon stopped. They were in memory of people who had fallen to their deaths. Ignore such things, she told herself, and began the climb, but almost immediately stopped. The surface was as speckled as sunburnt skin and broken into small plates. The Rock was peeling, breaking away in scales. She hadn't expected that. In awe, she gazed up at the great folds towering above her. Uluru. She preferred the Aboriginal name. Ayers Rock sounded so... colonial. Named after some government official who'd never seen it. But Ul-u-ru. A word that should be breathed, not spoken, a word that flowed like a wind sighing through the caves and canyons that gave the walls shape and shadow. Uluru — the name given by the nomadic tribes who revered it as some mystic object. She bowed slightly, as though entering an ancient cathedral, and resumed the climb.

She was excited. She had never been to the Rock. That was one reason for suggesting she meet Kelly on top. That and the fact that no one would expect to find him up there.

The climbing path was easy to distinguish. It was a pale strip that followed the sharp edge of the ridge and was as distinct as the honed blade of a knife, having been polished by the slips and slides of several hundred thousand pairs of boots, shoes, runners and sandals. Above Monica, at least a hundred people were stretched along this strip. Some were going up, a few were returning, but most had stopped. The chain that began at the steepest part of the climb had drawn clusters of people to it. Some were sitting down, determined to go no higher and grimly grasping the links, not caring about the spectacular view but summoning the courage to go back down.

She would not stop. She was used to walking through rough bush and her legs were strong. Ignoring the increasing drop on either side of the ridge, Monica climbed all the way to the end of the chain. Only then did she stop and turn around. The view was stunning: a vast spread of desert, crinkled with

431

sandhills, dotted with bushes and trees, and ending in the floating uncertainties of remote heat hazes. Yulara was a grove of trees and roofs. The Olgas were domes of fire, not vivid red but the light, searing colours at the heart of the flame. She must go there one day to paint.

She forced herself to look straight back, down the chain and the worn pathway to the rows of coaches and the people milling around the flat area at the bottom of the climb. There was not one policeman in sight.

She took several deep breaths, turned and tackled the next stage of the climb.

Laura did not want to climb. She was wearing light slacks and a simple pair of white shoes with rubber soles — some of the things she'd bought in Alice Springs and, coincidentally, good for climbing — but she had no desire to pit herself against the mountain. It looked too steep and too big, and she had no desire to fail in front of so many people.

Kolvenbach had his glasses on Monica. 'She's left the chain. She must be going all the way to the top.'

'Can you see Kelly?'

'No, but it's too far to be sure.' He put the binoculars down. 'I'm going. You can stay here.'

Laura looked around her. There were dozens of coaches, scores of cars, hundreds of people. Even a caravan selling ice creams and cold drinks.

'I'm not staying,' she said. 'Not on my own.'

'Well, don't forget to lock the door.' Checking that his pistol was in the bag, Kolvenbach got out.

'I've got no idea what's going on.' McCarthy scratched his ear. 'Woman from bus goes up mountain. Couple sit in car. Woman gets near top of mountain. Couple go up mountain.' He turned to

432

Spiro, who was leaning across the steering wheel to get a better view. 'You tell me what's happening.'

'Got no idea. What do you want me to do?'

McCarthy blew air against the windscreen, rounding his lips as though forming smoke rings. 'As far as I know, there's only one way up and one way down. But if something's going to happen up there, I guess we should know about it.'

'You want me to follow her?'

'Be a good idea, Spiro.'

'You coming too?'

McCarthy laughed. 'Not unless you want to carry me up.'

Spiro was still following the progress of the big man and Laura Hunnicutt. 'What do I do when I get up there? Do you want me to take that big guy?'

'Reckon you could?' McCarthy knew Spiro couldn't resist a challenge.

'I reckon. A man that size should bounce a few times before he hit the bottom.'

McCarthy tapped his fingers on the dashboard. 'Nothing desperate, Spiro. Just see what happens. If you have a chance to get the Hunnicutt woman on her own, grab her.'

'How do I bring her down if she doesn't want to come down?'

'Persuade her. If you have to, put her to sleep and carry her down. Bandage her ankle. Say she sprained it and fainted from the pain.'

Spiro liked that. 'Do you mind if I mess the big fellow up?'

'Just be discreet. We don't want attention. All we want is the woman.'

433

36

Kelly checked his watch. Eight forty-seven. Monica
had reached the summit ahead of schedule. Even
from this distance, he recognised her immediately.
Khaki shirt, brief shorts, stout boots. She had the
floppy hat pulled well down and she wore her big
sunglasses. He looked beyond her to the trickle of
climbers that rose and fell through the undulations,
as even as a slick of debris awash on an ocean
swell. Not one person in police uniform and no
Kolvenbach.

Monica was carrying a bag over one shoulder.
He saw her stand beside the monument, as though
celebrating her achievement in reaching the top:
then join a short queue to sign the visitors' book.
He laughed. She'd make a great spy. Book signed,
she looked around. When she turned in his direction, with her eyes shielded against the sun, he
stepped out and waved. She saw him and he took
cover behind the bush again.

She followed a roundabout route to the trees.
First she went south and pretended to admire the
view. Then she ambled to the east, passing well
beyond the place where he was hiding. There, she
sat down and ate some fruit. Kelly watched. He
was hungry. She took her time, then rose and
headed back towards the monument. When she
reached a gully that ran towards the trees, she

stopped and, bending low so as not to be seen by those at the summit, hurried towards him.

She was breathless. 'You got here all right,' she said, her face alive with excitement. 'Isn't it wonderful up here? So big. It must cover hundreds of acres.'

'Did I see you eating something?'

She delved into her bag. 'Orange, banana, apple. What would you like?'

He started with the banana.

'I've got water too.'

He drank some. 'Did anyone follow you?'

'I kept checking. No.'

She took out a large brown package that was covered in air-freight stickers and had her name printed in bold letters across the front. 'I've a little surprise for you. Two in fact. This is the first.'

He was eating and nodded, ready for anything.

'Did you know I used to work in the film industry?'

'No.' He drank some more water. 'Is this why you kept on spouting famous names at me when we first met? Beresford, Weir, Schepisi. All of those?'

'I worked with a few of them. I did make-up. To earn a few dollars, not as a career. I painted faces during the week and birds at weekends. It was fun and I made a few friends, one of whom sent me all this stuff.' She held up the parcel. 'I got it air-freighted from Sydney yesterday.' She pulled out a beard. 'I'm going to transform you. Change you so that even your own mother wouldn't recognise you. Or more to the point, your own wife.'

Kelly had no intention of telling her what had happened with Laura in Alice Springs. Monica, eyes shining like a mother on Christmas morning, was pulling out brushes and bottles and arranging them on the rock.

'Here?'

'Why not?' She held the beard against his chin. 'Perfect. When you go down, no one will recognise you. I've also got a moustache and bushy eyebrows. I could even make you bald.'

'No thank you. Not bald.'

'Who said women were the vain ones?'

'I think a beard and moustache would be enough. Will it take long?'

'Not if you keep your mouth closed.'

Kolvenbach had stayed within one of the hollows, supposedly resting but in fact able to observe Monica without showing more than his face. Using the glasses, he saw her reach the monument, walk south, then east, then disappear. He stood up. In the distance, not far from where he had last seen her, was a grove of stunted trees and scrub. She must have gone there.

'What now?' an exhausted Laura asked. She was sitting, arms wrapped around her knees, in a depression near the bottom of the hollow. 'And when do you think we might be able to get something to drink? I am dying of thirst. And starving. Or don't you suffer from such human foibles?'

'I think I know where she is.'

He could have been talking to himself. Probably was, Laura thought and, with great difficulty, got to her feet. She limped. One heel was blistering. 'I can tell you where she is without looking. She's on top of this damned rock.'

'You stay here.'

'I will not.'

'I thought you were tired?'

'I'm dying. But there's no way I'm going to be left sitting here on my own.'

He helped her up the slope. Some other climbers scrambled past them, panting noisily. When they had gone, he pointed to the trees. 'See over there?

436

That's where she is. I'm going to approach those trees and I have to do it without being seen.'

'Why? Do you want to surprise her with her pants down? Women have to do it too, you know.'

He ignored her. 'I presume she's meeting Hunnicutt.'

She laughed. 'Up here? That's crazy.'

'Which is precisely why your husband would meet her here. He has survived by doing crazy things.' His voice became soft. He was speaking to himself again. 'There could be someone else there, too. Someone he'd arranged to meet.'

She lifted her face to the heavens, seeking divine protection from men who went mad and climbed mountains in pursuit of mythical beings. And who didn't eat or drink.

'I can't sneak up on them if you're tagging along. So you will stay here.'

'I will not.'

He turned to her and smiled. 'You will help me overpower them?'

She returned his smile. 'There's going to be a fight?'

'Who knows?' Impatiently, he glanced around him. 'Look, we're wasting time. Come with me for part of the way. I will tell you where to hide.'

'You Tarzan, me Jane.'

'I'm not playing games, Laura. If you do something to scare them away, even innocently, I'll throw you over the edge.'

'Sure.' She brushed dirt from the seat of her pants, then looked at him. He meant it.

'Walk behind me. Exactly behind me. Step for step.'

'Don't take such big steps.'

'Don't talk. Save your breath.'

Spiro saw them move. He waited for the next group of climbers to pass, then followed. Instead of going

437

to the summit, the big man and the Hunnicutt woman turned left along one of the shallower gullies. Both could be seen, but an observer would have no idea of their height. Then they disappeared.

Spiro increased his pace. He liked to think he was as fit as in his football days and he drove himself hard, turning off in one deep hollow and jogging along the thin stain of sediment marking its bottom. The surface was smooth, polished over the ages by rushes of rainwater, and it sloped towards the precipitous northern wall. Quite suddenly the slope became steeper and broke into a series of deep gutters. Far enough. Spiro stopped and crawled up the side. He sprawled across the top and waited. After a minute, he saw the big man appear from one of the undulations about a hundred metres ahead of him. Very slowly, the man raised his head and looked to either side. Up came his shoulders and his body, then his legs, kicking himself forward. He slithered belly-down across the rock. The woman followed. They crossed a shelf, then the man disappeared, snakelike. The woman rose to her hands and knees, reversed unsteadily, was grasped by a hand and went backwards down another slope until she, too, was out of sight.

Spiro followed.

Monica was admiring the moustache and asking if Kelly had ever grown one. She had the brush and paste ready for the beard when they heard the scream. It was close. A woman. Then there was another cry but this one was more of a gurgle, as if the person were being choked. From the other side of the bushes — no, within the bushes and no more than a metre or two away — they heard a man grunt, then swear. Branches crackled and there was another scream and the woman was calling out: 'Magnus! Magnus!'

Kolvenbach rose from the bushes. He bared his teeth, like an animal ready for the kill, and turned and ran.

He was running to Laura. Kelly pushed past Monica and went after Kolvenbach, not knowing why he was running or where Laura was, but drawn by those terrible screams.

He could hear Monica calling.

From one of the gullies that scored the top of the Rock, a man emerged carrying Laura across his shoulders. He was wearing shorts and had legs of incredible width. Kelly stopped and watched in a kind of fascinated stupor. The man must have had amazing strength, he thought, because he was running. He stopped, put Laura down, struck her across the face and turned to face Kolvenbach. He was squat, as thick as a sumo wrestler and with a neck that spread from skull to shoulders, and arms that were almost as wide as his legs. Kelly was close enough to see that the man was smiling. Karate fashion, he extended his hands.

Kolvenbach stopped just short of the man and began to circle him. He lashed out with a foot. The short man caught it and tipped Kolvenbach on his back. Kolvenbach landed near Laura, got to his feet, wiped his hands and resumed circling. He was talking. 'Who are you, eh? Another of our mysterious visitors?'

The man continued to smile. He opened his arms, inviting Kolvenbach in. The South African rushed him. Each locked the other in a bear hug. With an enormous effort, Kolvenbach lifted the other man off the ground. Their heads clashed.

The man bit Kolvenbach's ear.

He bellowed, shaking the man savagely, and the two of them fell, still locked together in their murderous embrace. They rolled over and over until, legs flailing, they rolled into a gully.

Kelly ran to Laura. She was holding her head and crying and trying to sit up.

Behind him Monica was shouting, 'Kelly, no! Get away, get away!'

He pulled Laura to her feet. Monica joined them. She had both bags over her shoulders.

'Leave her,' she urged. 'Quickly. While those two are fighting. I've got your gear. Let's go.'

'They're trying to kill me,' Laura mumbled.

'And everyone's trying to get you killed, Kelly — including your dear wife,' Monica said, pulling him by the arm. He pushed her away.

Laura screamed. 'They've sent someone else to kill me.'

'For God's sake, shut her up,' Monica said, looking at the mob near the distant monument. A large group of Japanese was gathering there.

Out of sight in the hollow, a man let out a great cry of pain.

'Let's get out of here,' Kelly said and, arm locked through Laura's, began to lead her towards the summit.

'Kelly?' Laura held her head.

'I'll take you down. Don't worry.'

'What on earth are you doing?' Monica shouted. 'Are you trying to get yourself killed? Leave her. She'll give you away. She did before. Get yourself out of here.'

Kelly shook his head. 'I've got Laura. Can you carry the bags?'

'You'll never get off the Rock with her on your arm.'

'You go on then.' He reached for Monica and pulled her roughly past him. 'Move. Save your own neck.'

Monica stood in front of him, blocking his way. 'That's Kolvenbach down there. I don't know who the other man is but he doesn't look nice. For God's

440

sake, Kelly, don't you see that if you don't get out of here quickly, one of them's going to catch you, and you won't get away with that poisonous anchor around your neck.'

'A man tried to kill me,' Laura said, gripping Kelly's arm. 'He came to the airport and he was going to kill me.'

'She's delirious.'

'She's not.'

'He was a professional killer,' Laura said. 'He was going to make me take tablets. And now they've sent another man. He tried to choke me.'

'Shame he stopped.' Monica turned in despair. 'Kelly, even with just the moustache, you look different. People won't recognise you. Hurry down the Rock. I've got a bus waiting. You can get away.'

From the gully came a sharp cry and a terrible thud.

'Someone's getting killed,' Monica said. 'You'll be next.' She looked at Laura. 'Maybe both of you are on the list. I don't know.'

'You're right. We've got to go.' Kelly began to hurry towards the monument, dragging Laura with him. 'I know another way down. Give me my bag.' He held out his spare hand.

'There's no other way down.'

'Yes there is. No one uses it but there is.' Monica was alongside him and he took the bag and slung it over his shoulder. 'You go for your life down the normal path. Kolvenbach must have followed you up so he'll follow you down, if he can. Don't waste a moment. Just get down there and get clear.'

'Where will we meet?' She was jogging to keep up.

'Do you know Maggie Spring?'

'I'll find it.'

'It's on the other side to the climb. Meet us there.'

'Us?'

441

'I'm not leaving Laura up here.'

'Kelly, you are the world's greatest fool.'

'Probably. Can we have some water?'

Monica transferred the flask to his bag.

'It'll be hot and thirsty the way we're going.'

'You'll have plenty of time to talk.' She blinked savagely.

Laura's feet were dragging like a doll's and Kelly had to ease his pace. 'Look, Monica, I know she's been unfaithful, I know she's not coming back to me, I know she's played me for a fool.' He stopped to take a deep breath. 'But I love her and I can't just leave her up here. Not with that man after her.'

Monica went faster until she was a few paces ahead. 'I'll meet you at Maggie Spring then.'

'Good. And for heaven's sake, hurry. Take care.'

She reached back and fluttered her fingers but didn't look at him. 'You too. Don't fall off any cliffs.'

Wearily, Kolvenbach pushed himself to his feet. He felt his ear. The lobe was ripped and blood was pouring down his neck, soaking one side of his shirt. He took out his handkerchief and pressed it against the side of his face. He felt his ribs and took a deep breath. His right side hurt but he didn't think anything was broken. One elbow ached and the arm was numb. He couldn't move the fingers properly.

The other man was still unconscious.

Kolvenbach had been losing the fight. The other man was crushing him in that cruel bear hug but Kolvenbach had used his height to lift him off the ground and ram him back-first into the rock face. That was when he'd hurt his elbow. The impact had dazed the man — just for a few seconds but that was sufficient — and Kolvenbach had been able to pick him up with his good arm, turn him upside down and drive him head-first into the speckled and unyielding surface of Ayers Rock. Hunnicutt was getting away. Handkerchief pressed to his ear, Kolvenbach climbed out of the gully and, still dizzy and sore from the bone-crushing hold, staggered towards the summit.

Monica was already a couple of hundred metres ahead when Kelly and Laura reached the monument. Several bus-loads of tourists had arrived at the same time. Two of the groups were Japanese.

'I have to sit down,' Laura said.

'In a minute.'

'I'm thirsty.'

'I've got water. I'll give you a drink soon.'

'You're cruel, Kelly.'

'You've got to be quiet. He's coming.'

'Who?'

'The man.' He had seen the distant but distinctive figure of Kolvenbach cresting a ridge.

Laura was not looking. She began to shake.

'You'll be all right. Do exactly as I say.'

She smiled, not quite focusing on him. 'Why is it that, suddenly, every man is telling me what to do?' She touched her forehead. 'You sound like Magnus.'

'Great. I'm flattered.'

Several of the Japanese were taking group photographs. Kelly recognised his friend from Nagoya. 'Don't talk,' he said to Laura, and waved. The man peered at him uncertainly, then returned the greeting.

'Ah, my friend who is learning Japanese.' He seemed confused by the moustache.

'Would you do me a favour?'

'Most honoured to.'

'My wife needs to sit down.'

The man offered Laura his most concerned greeting. Kelly led her deep into the group, using his arm to clear a path. The man from Nagoya, uttering constant apologies, followed them.

'Sit down,' Kelly said when they were at the monument, and Laura sat on the stones, shielded by the tourists. He opened his bag and gave her the flask of water. He turned to his friend. 'Would you ask everyone to gather around?'

The man's already long face stretched. 'Gather a round?'

'Yes.' With his hand, Kelly described a circle. 'I would like to tell them about the history of Ayers Rock. Very interesting. Black man's history. White man's history. I am an expert on the subject.'

He could see Kolvenbach drawing closer. The big man had stopped, obviously searching for them and, just as obviously, not knowing where they had got to.

The man from Nagoya addressed his fellow tourists. Twittering interest, they formed a tight circle. Kelly bowed and the sea of faces lowered and rose like a wave sweeping into and out of a pool.

'Would you please translate for me?'

'Certainly.' Kelly's friend bowed. He had been asked to interpret, he announced, and there were sighs of appreciation.

'For hundreds of years,' Kelly began, his eyes on the approaching Kolvenbach, 'this was a sacred place for the black people.' Kelly lowered his head while the Japanese translated. 'They did not live here permanently, because there was so little game — animals to hunt — but at certain times of the year, they gathered around this rock to perform ceremonies and rituals of special significance.'

He bent down. Laura, wiping water from her lips, whispered, 'Kelly, you are so full of bullshit.'

He lifted his head. Kolvenbach was no more than fifty metres away. He looked terrible. One side of his shirt glistened with rich, fresh blood.

444

A few of the Japanese had seen Kolvenbach and were staring at him. Kelly turned the other way. 'The paintings you will see around the lower areas relate to these rituals, to their myths and beliefs.' Down with his head again.

'Where did you get that moustache?' Laura said.

She sounded drunk. The blow might have given her slight concussion, Kelly thought, putting his hand to her lips. 'Keep your head down. The man who is searching for you is about to walk past.'

'We are ready,' the Japanese said.

'The first white man to see Ayers Rock was Ernest Giles, the explorer. He observed it from the far shores of Lake Amadeus. Over there.' He pointed to the north. The Japanese swung that way and all stared at the bloodied Kolvenbach. He hesitated but then, confronted by sixty curious faces, hurried past them.

'Accident,' Kelly said, rising on his toes to enjoy the sight of the big man's back. 'It is very easy to fall on this slippery surface.' There was a chorus of agreement and murmurs of sympathy for the injured man. 'But back to the story. That was in 1872,' he said. Or was it 1873? He couldn't remember. Never mind, the Japanese were enthralled. This was on-site education. 'Giles had two companions and they were all on horseback. They could not cross the great salt lake. They were short of food and water. The horses were dying. Giles had to turn back.'

There were gasps of disappointment.

'On the way home, riding south along the Overland Telegraph Line...' There was some discussion among the Japanese about that, and then a flash of smiles as a confusing point was cleared up. '...On the way south, Giles met another explorer, William Christie Gosse, who was heading north and whose party was mounted on camels.'

There were chortles of amusement. As part of their tour, the Japanese had ridden camels in Alice Springs.

'Giles told Gosse about the big lake that had blocked his path. He told Gosse to come this way. Gosse did, and reached Ayers Rock. As a result, he is credited with its discovery.'

Kolvenbach was out of sight, hurrying through a gully.

When the translation was completed, Kelly bowed.

'That is all?'

'That is the story.'

He bowed. 'We are most grateful.' The group applauded.

'I am delighted to have added some small measure of interest to your journey.'

'Not small interest. Very much interest.' He put his arm around Kelly's shoulders. 'Very fine fellow. Next time, you can tell story in Japanese.'

The group dispersed, to prepare for the walk down. Kelly helped Laura to her feet.

'Was all that true?'

'More or less.'

'That bit about Giles telling the other man where to go?'

'True.'

She shook her head slowly. 'You're wasted in this century. You should have been a court jester. Making up stories. Talking nonstop. You'd have been in your element.'

'Thanks.' He took her elbow and set off at the tail of the Japanese group. 'Feeling strong?'

'Where are we going?'

'Down the hill.'

She looked behind them. 'Where's Magnus?'

'He's run on.'

'What do you mean?'

'He's gone. He's chasing someone.'

'He left me?

'Afraid so. It's a cruel world, Laura. Come on, or we won't be part of it for long.'

Catching a glimpse of Kolvenbach surging ahead and going faster as his strength returned, Kelly wondered how rapidly Monica was travelling. She had strong legs from her years of tracking down obscure birds' nests, so hopefully she was quick. He felt guilty and worried. He was using her to draw Kolvenbach away from them.

He looked back but there was no sign of the other man. A couple of tourists, a tall blond man and an equally tall and fair woman, both laden with slim packs, were wandering towards the trees.

Along the top of the Rock, the correct path was marked by a painted line to prevent people following false trails and ultimately having the incident recorded on a brass plate at the base of the Rock. At one point, the line ran near the top of the gorge above Maggie Spring. There, Kelly stopped. He led Laura away from the track to a smooth mound. 'Sit down.'

Her head was clearing. 'Are you tired?'

'This is where we change direction. We're heading this way.' His finger pointed down, to the smooth folds falling towards the water hole.

'You are crazy.'

'Remember that story about Gosse?'

She stared at him blankly.

'The explorer who named Ayers Rock... When he reached the Rock, he climbed it. He and an Afghan companion came up this way.'

She had her head down and let it roll from side to side. 'Kelly, if you give me another of your history lessons, I swear to God I'll push you over the edge.'

'I'm just telling you the story so that you know it's possible.'

447

'Have you ever done it?'

'No. Not yet.' He checked the marked track. There were no climbers near them. He pulled her up. 'Come on, while no one's looking.'

She let her feet slide along the rock. 'I am not going down there.'

'That man is still somewhere behind us.'

Her legs quivered like jelly. 'Oh Kelly, you bastard, I'm scared to death. Don't make me do it.'

'You make yourself do it.'

'How far is it down?'

'About a thousand feet. Come on.'

After half an hour, they rested in a low but wide cave which was cut into the wall like a nick in a log. It offered both flat space to lie on and shelter from searching eyes. They drank some water and gazed in silent fascination at the land far below. They couldn't see the water hole but the trees were tiny: blackened needles casting spider's-web shadows across the triangle of dry grass that led to Maggie Spring.

Since leaving the formal track, the surface had been steep and slippery and they had made much of the descent in a squatting position, leading with shuffling feet and using their hands and bottoms to steady themselves. In the worst places, Kelly had sent Laura in front. She held a strap from his bag and he followed, clutching the bag and acting as her anchor.

Below the cave, the slope became even steeper. They were descending into a broad vee whose walls narrowed and met in a blackened groove. The wild flow of plunging storm waters had cut the groove; succeeding trickles had left the stain.

Kelly broke the silence. 'We'll have to go higher.' He pointed to the right side of the vee, a vast wall whose scaly surface was a swirl of pinks and oranges and shimmered with heat from the full blast of the mid-morning sun. 'Up there's a ridge. It's not as steep.'

She didn't look. 'Is that the way your beloved Gosse went?'

'I don't know.'

'What do you mean, you don't know?' She raised her head until it touched the cave roof. 'Are you saying he could have gone down the other side?'

'I don't think so.'

'Great. We're climbing down the world's biggest rock and you don't know if we're going the right way or not.' She took off a shoe.

'What are you doing?'

'Taking my shoes off. I've got a blistered heel.'

'Gosse climbed without his shoes ...'

'Oh, shut up.'

'And he tore the skin off the soles of his feet. Leave them on. Make a pad out of a tissue.' He checked his watch. 'Ready to go?'

'No. Let me rest a bit longer. My head hurts.'

He squirmed closer. 'All right, let's have a little talk.'

'Jesus, what a place for Twenty Questions. Or is it True Confessions?' She wriggled into a new position. 'Okay, I'll start. Are you sleeping with that frowsy little tart in the dashing shade of brown?'

Kelly closed his eyes. 'I wanted to discuss other things.'

'I'll bet you did.'

'Laura, have you heard about Gerry?'

She stopped wriggling.

'He's had an accident. In his car.'

The Porsche? An alarm bell was ringing. To silence it, she summoned up all her irony and said, 'Are you going to tell me he's damaged his car and now the bet's off?'

'It's serious, Laura. Gerry's dead.'

She sunk to the floor of the cave. 'Gerry?'

'Yes.' Gently, he told her what he knew.

'It was an accident?' Her concern had leapt from Gerry Montague to the mysterious McCarthy and the diamonds and the Porsche.

'They say he was drunk. Very drunk. He died instantly. It was a big cliff.'

They were silent for a long time. On the far side of the valley, a hawk was soaring in the currents that rose up the sheer cliff face. Kelly watched. Majestic grey bird, flaring orange walls. If there were such a thing as reincarnation, he would like to come back as a hawk at Ayers Rock. He could soon be eligible . . .

Laura was over the shock. Now she was worried. Where had Gerry put the diamonds? And the cash he'd found and those papers that Magnus seemed so concerned about? Had he changed hiding places? Had the police found them? Was he running away? Vaguely, she heard Kelly saying he doubted the police story. Then he was asking her about the man who had tried to kill her.

'Who was he?' He reached out to tap her hand, jogging her into the present.

'Which one?'

'You said something about a man at the airport.'

She told him the story. She didn't add the part about dumping him in the bush.

'And that other man up there. You hadn't seen either of them before?'

'Never.'

'You've no idea who sent them?'

'None.'

'Or why?'

She snapped at him. 'For Christ's sake, Kelly, I don't know who or why. It's like some horror movie, only I'm part of it. If I knew what it was all about, I could handle it; but I have no idea. I just know

450

that two men have tried to kill me and for all I know, there might be more of them waiting for me down there.'

'Don't get hysterical.'

'Why not?' She leaned out to look down at the tiny trees and laughed, but she was shaking.

The hawk had soared past a great, mouth-shaped cave that dripped bituminous stains down the rock face. Kelly watched the bird turn with no more than a lazy flex of a wingtip.

He scratched at the sandy floor of their tiny cave. 'And now poor old Gerry's dead.'

She stiffened. 'My God. You think there's a connection?'

'Well, there are certainly people who want *me* dead. There are, apparently, people who want *you* dead. And Gerry *is* dead.'

'But who would want to kill me?'

Just 'me', Kelly noted, and felt sad. It was over between Laura and him and he'd accepted that, but the little reminders still wounded him. 'It could be whoever took the diamonds. Maybe he wants to get rid of us because we're all involved.'

'All?' She seemed startled. 'How?'

'I'm blamed for it, you're my wife, so some people probably think you're involved, and Gerry is — was — my partner so they think he was part of it too.' He shook his head. 'I don't know. Nothing adds up. And we're not going to solve anything sitting in a hole on the side of Ayers Rock.' He swung his feet over the edge until they touched the slope. 'Time to move.'

He helped her out, steadied her and set off for the ridge.

They were able to walk erect for a while, with him holding her hand and both shivering whenever a fragment of the rocky crust crumbled beneath their feet.

To reach the ridge that Kelly favoured, they had to climb. The rock surface glistened and they were forced onto their hands and knees. When they reached the ridge, they stopped, planting their arms and legs wide apart to give maximum support. Now they could see Maggie Spring. It was a tiny slick of water. Some tourists had gathered on the sand. Like mites, they moved and gathered in groups. Voices drifted up to them.

She had to take her mind off the terrifying drop. 'Do you know a man called McCarthy?'

Kelly, feeling giddy, was concentrating on his shoes; they were close and solid. 'Should I?'

'He's supposed to be an acquaintance of Gerry's.'

'Never heard of him. Where did you hear the name?'

She said from Kolvenbach, and Kelly grimaced. Kolvenbach had telephoned someone. She didn't mention Canberra.

Kelly shook his head. Was McCarthy connected with all this?

She lifted an arm to brush a strand of hair from her eyes. 'I was just surprised. I'd never heard the name.'

'Neither have I.' He shouldered his bag and, rising with great care, got to his feet. 'We should keep going.'

'I'm frightened, Kelly.'

'So am I. What's new? I've been terrified for the past week. Every day, I wake up scared, I go to sleep scared.'

'You look as though you've been enjoying it.'

'In a weird sort of way, I have. They say fear's addictive. Gives the system a real shake-up. Come on.' He extended his hand.

452

37

McCarthy had been watching from the drinks caravan. It was a good site. He'd already eaten one ice cream and drunk two orange juices and he could see virtually all of the climbers, the eager ones going up as well as the worn ones coming down, silhouetted all the way to the crest of the sloping ridge.

For several minutes, he had been watching the woman from the minibus descending the Rock. She had reached the last section of chain. She was moving quickly, holding her bag with one hand and the chain with the other, and continually overtaking groups. Right now she had to detour wide of the chain to avoid some people who were sitting like squatting dogs, laughing and calling out to each other but unable to move up or down.

The woman kept looking up the slope. McCarthy understood why. Kolvenbach was two or three hundred metres behind her and moving fast — faster than she was. McCarthy wished he had binoculars because there was something strange about the way the man moved. He was descending with a curious swinging motion, as though he had a sore hip or leg. It was more than a limp. He was hurt. Other people stared as he passed.

Moving slowly to avoid attracting attention, McCarthy walked to the coach parking area.

He sat on the wooden fence near the Murray's

Tours minibus. There was no sign of Spiro or of the Hunnicutt woman. This he didn't like because, with two of the characters in this little drama rapidly approaching, he had to make decisions based on nothing more than guesses. The best guess was that Spiro had caught Laura Hunnicutt and was bringing her down at a leisurely pace. Spiro would have to do that if he were to pretend that she'd hurt her ankle and fainted.

By why was Kolvenbach chasing the woman? And who the hell was she? Where did she fit into the story? He assumed Kolvenbach had let Laura Hunnicutt go — or been forced to — and was pursuing the woman from the minibus. McCarthy swore to himself. He liked his dilemmas to be neat, and this was messy. It would be too easy to make the wrong decision.

Kolvenbach was hurt. McCarthy saw the bloodstains, blew a few of his imaginary smoke rings and felt better. So Spiro had fought him and beaten him. And Kolvenbach was running to get clear. Then the doubts returned. What was Kolvenbach doing chasing the woman?

What to do? Watch Kolvenbach, see what he did, follow him? Or wait for Spiro? Spiro must have the Hunnicutt woman. He would wait.

They reached a slight mound where it was possible to get more grip, and Kelly, who was leading, stopped and waited for Laura to catch up. His palms were buffed and tender and the base of one thumb was bleeding. He felt like a monkey coming down on all fours but he didn't dare stand erect. For a skilled mountaineer, this wouldn't be a difficult descent. It was just one big slide — and that was the danger. If he slipped, nothing would stop him rolling all the way to the bottom and that was at least ninety metres down.

Off to the left and hidden from anyone at ground

454

level was a valley, a wide cleft in the rock, from which trees jutted through a mass of fractured boulders. Water seeped from the base of the boulders. Behind them, he reasoned, must be a natural dam which filled after rain and trickled water down the glassy slopes into Maggie Spring. So that was where much of Maggie's water came from. He hadn't know that. Gosse had. It was their secret. William Christie Gosse and Kelso Hunnicutt knew of a hidden dam high above Maggie Spring.

Laura reached him and let her knees press into his back, both to cause pain and to gain support. 'I cannot go on. My hands are bleeding, I've broken a fingernail and my pants will be worn through.'

He rested his head on his knees. 'You can always go back.'

'Fuck you, Kelly, and fuck whoever it was who climbed down here first.'

'Gosse. And an Afghan.'

'Yes, them.' She pressed her fingers into her scalp and let out a muffled but stagy scream. 'What am I doing here? You're to blame. You grabbed me, you dragged me out of Melbourne and you brought me on this nightmare.'

'True. Now shut up, because there are people down there and they'll hear you.'

'I don't care.'

'You should. If they spread the word that there are two people coming down the Rock on this side, your friend who's built like a dozen bulldogs might hear about it and come around to give you a special welcome.'

She growled into his back.

'Just save your breath,' he said wearily. 'It gets easier from now on.'

Monica reached the ground and, legs quivering from the strain of the rapid descent, tried to run to the

455

minibus. She had trouble opening the door. There was a knack to it and the man in the Alice Springs car yard had shown her but she'd forgotten it. By the time the hinged affair had swung in and then back, Kolvenbach was behind her.

'Get in.' He pushed her through the door. Automatically, she sat behind the wheel. He slumped into the seat nearest the door and let his head loll back.

'Where is he?' He had difficulty breathing. He kept a sodden crimson handkerchief pressed to his ear.

Monica had been frightened on the way down but that had passed. She was too tired to be scared; and now that she confronted the man, he seemed less fierce.

'You're a bit of a mess.'

'I said where is Hunnicutt?'

'I heard you. I don't know. What's wrong with your ear?'

He removed the handkerchief for a few seconds. She sucked in her breath. 'It's in two pieces.'

'He bit it.'

'Grown men,' she muttered and stood up.

'Where are you going?' He searched for the pistol in his bag but his hand shook.

'To get my first-aid kit. I'll put a bandage on it.' In passing, she prodded his shoulder. 'And do you think you could take off that shirt? This bus is new and you're putting dirty marks all over the seat.'

He tried to seize her hand but she had gone. 'Forget the bandage,' he called out. 'Come back here.'

'In a minute. Do you feel like a drink of something? I've got beer, lemonade or water.'

He pushed himself out of the seat but now that he had stopped moving he was feeling bad; his arm ached, his side hurt and his head throbbed. He'd

456

lost a lot of blood. He faced her, having to bend to avoid the roof. 'What are you up to?'

'I'm trying to help you.' She jabbed a finger at him. 'Look, if you haven't got the energy to take off that terrible shirt, then leave it on. Just sit down and stop talking.'

He tried to move forward but became dizzy and fell into the nearest seat.

'That's two you've dirtied.'

Weakly, he waved a hand. 'If you're going to put a bandage on me, at least drive away from here first.'

'Why?'

'Because that man who almost bit off my ear...' he paused to take a breath '... may be following... or he may have someone down here... waiting for him.'

Her eyes widened in alarm. 'Yes. Of course.' She hurried towards the front and handed him a bandage. 'Here, use this until I can get something better.' She took his soaked handkerchief between thumb and forefinger and dropped it in the footwell, then struggled to shut the door. She peered out. There was no sign of the squat man. No one seemed particularly interested in them, although a fat man dressed in a white shirt and business trousers was facing their way. He seemed harmless.

'Anywhere special you'd like to go?' she said, starting the engine.

'Just get away from here.' One after the other, his lids closed over eyes that were glossy with pain.

McCarthy watched them leave. They were friends. Kolvenbach wasn't chasing her, they'd been hurrying to reach the bus. Running from Spiro.

He ambled towards the drinks caravan to buy another ice cream and to wait for his man and the Hunnicutt woman.

Mary Calibrano decided to go to Police Headquarters to check for herself. It was possible that the man on the phone had made a mistake. There might be a Superintendent Wilson in some special department and the man she'd spoken to might not have known that, or he might have meant there was no Wilson at Russell Street.

She was ushered into the office of a senior man with the patient look of someone who was sixty-four years and nine months of age, and who longed for the next three months to pass so he could go fishing. He had a suitably square policeman's face, wiry grey hair and creases that lined his cheeks like tribal initiation scars.

His name was Ulverstone. They shook hands. No, there was not a Superintendent Wilson in the Victorian police force but he was most interested in her story. The impersonation of a police officer was a most serious offence. He ordered coffee.

She had thought, she said, that Mr Wilson might have been one of the detectives who'd taken over Gerry Montague's apartment. Ulverstone tapped his teeth with the end of a pencil. He made a phone call.

No detectives had been in Mr Montague's apartment. How long had the men been there? Had Mr Montague described them? Had she ever seen them?

All she knew was that Gerry had seemed frightened of them. He had even left his own apartment and gone to stay in a city hotel; two hotels, in fact. She told him of the phone calls from the Regent and the Hyatt.

He made some notes and asked would she mind if another detective joined them. He rang for a Detective Mallowes.

Mallowes was dark, with the sort of chin that constantly needs shaving. He sat to one side and said little.

'How well did Mr Montague know Harald

Kolvenbach?' Ulverstone asked.

'Reasonably well. He called in to the office several times to discuss a film. The second Mr Kolvenbach, the good-looking one, called in after the murder. I didn't know he was a brother... not at first.'

Mallowes handed Ulverstone a file and he checked inside. 'That was Magnus Kolvenbach?'

'I don't know his first name.'

'So Mr Montague knew both the Kolvenbach brothers.'

'He'd met them, yes.'

Did Hunnicutt know the two brothers? No. Only the older one.

Was she aware that Magnus Kolvenbach had gone to central Australia and had conducted his own search for Kelso Hunnicutt?

No. She was shocked.

'We understand Magnus Kolvenbach is at Ayers Rock at the moment.' Ulverstone glanced at Mallowes whose eyes flickered confirmation. 'He has his own aircraft. He was at Innamincka when Hunnicutt was there, in Alice Springs when Hunnicutt was believed to be in the region, and now he's at Ayers Rock. Miss Calibrano, do you happen to know if Mr Hunnicutt is at Ayers Rock at this moment?'

She was so surprised at the revelations about Magnus Kolvenbach that there was no need to feign ignorance. Face blank, she shook her head.

Ulverstone locked his fingers and leaned across the desk. How close were Hunnicutt and Montague? They were good friends. They saw a lot of each other. Montague had been greatly distressed by the accusations against Hunnicutt. He was very upset.

Quite so. Did Montague know where Kolvenbach lived? Possibly; she was guarded. They'd had some meetings after work. Gerry might have gone to his home.

Ulverstone leaned back and let his fingers run

459

down the deep folds in his cheeks. A few things about the Kolvenbach case had been worrying them, he said, and Mallowes' head bobbed in agreement. 'Tell me,' he said in the confidential tone a fisherman might use to find the best place to catch bream, 'was Kelso Hunnicutt a particularly clumsy person?'

She sat up straight, braced to defend Kelly. 'Not at all.'

Mallowes said, 'In what way?'

She twisted to face him. 'In every way. He doesn't stumble over things, he doesn't drop things. He's neat. In fact, as far as work's concerned, he's meticulous. He's a wonderful cameraman. Very artistic and very easy on his equipment. Some cameramen are always scratching filters or getting sand inside the magazine but Kelly can come back from the bush and you'd swear his gear had never been out of the city.' She faced Ulverstone and adjusted the hem of her skirt. 'Kelly is not a clumsy man. Anything but. Why do you ask?'

'Whoever killed Kolvenbach was incredibly ham-fisted. He left a trail a blind man could have followed.'

'That worries us,' Mallowes added.

'People who commit robbery on a grand scale, as in this case, and then murder the victim, usually go to extreme lengths to make sure no one knows who did it.' Ulverstone played with the pencil. 'But we found traces of Hunnicutt's jacket on bushes outside the house. We found the imprint of Hunnicutt's shoes in a garden bed. We found one of his business cards near the body. We found his rifle. We found it very easily. And in Hunnicutt's house, we found the muddy shoes and the torn jacket. And, of course, we found that he'd disappeared. Miss Calibrano, do you know why he disappeared?'

She was blinking rapidly, trying to keep up with their thinking. 'No.'

'We found minute traces of blood and human skin at the murder scene. On one of the bushes, for instance.' Ulverstone was now speaking slowly, letting each phrase settle before it was pushed aside by the next. 'When Mr Montague was killed the other night, we took samples... blood and skin from the body of the deceased.' He leaned back in his chair and he no longer seemed an old man impatient to go fishing; he had the look of an astute lawyer who could bustle you into giving answers you didn't mean. 'The samples matched, Miss Calibrano.'

'I don't understand.'

'Those minute samples of skin and blood we found at Harald Kolvenbach's house were from Gerry Montague.'

Both men were silent but Ulverstone's breath rasped like a man who smoked excessively. Automatically, her breathing slowed to his pace. 'Are you saying that Gerry killed Mr Kolvenbach?'

'We're saying he was there.'

Mallowes leaned forward. 'Do you know where Mr Hunnicutt is?'

She'd caused Kelly terrible problems by helping the police before — or helping someone she thought was a policeman. Not being sure what to do, she shook her head.

'We really do want to talk to him,' Ulverstone said. The lawyer was gone, the folksy fisherman was back. 'There are some huge gaps in this case. Things that don't make sense. A long talk to Mr Hunnicutt might clear up a lot of the confusion.'

'Do you think he might try to get in touch with you?' Mallowes edged forward, noisily scraping his chair across the wooden floor.

'I don't know.'

'If he does, please ask him to ring either Detective Mallowes or myself.' Ulverstone handed her a card. 'There are day and night numbers written on the

461

back. You will ask him to call?'

She nodded. 'If he does ring. Of course.'

Mary caught a taxi back to the office and rang the Sheraton at Yulara. Mr Tate was not in his room. He had been due to book out that morning. No, he had not been seen.

The ear must be stitched or he'd risk losing it, Monica said, but finished taping the bandage around Kolvenbach's head. He also had bad bruising on his back and two crescent-shaped cuts on his neck. Another bite. The other man fought like an animal.

They were parked on the eastern side of the Rock. The billowing walls had turned a bland greyish brown and the great caves and pockmarked flanks, so spectacular at dawn and dusk, gave it the look of a decayed tooth. The middle of the day did not present Ayers Rock in its most flattering light.

A few cars and coaches had passed. None stopped.

Monica straddled the driver's seat so she could face Kolvenbach. 'Well, I'm your prisoner. What are you going to do with me?'

He touched the bandage. 'First, thank you.'

'You're welcome.'

'Who are you?'

'Monica Tate. Artist.'

'What are you doing with Hunnicutt?'

'I met him, accidentally, when I was camped on the Bulloo River. That's in western Queensland.'

'Accidentally?'

'Sure. I'd been there for a few days. He just arrived one night. He didn't know I was there. He camped right on the spot where I was going to take some photographs. I woke him up in the morning and asked him to move.'

'Photographs? You said you were an artist.'

'I take photographs of the birds. They help me with my paintings.'

'You didn't arrange to meet him there?'

'I'd never heard of the man. I didn't know the police were looking for him.'

He closed his eyes and using his fingers, gently stretched the skin across his cheekbones.

'You still don't look too good.'

He opened one eye. 'Why are you helping him, this man you'd never met before he intruded on your campsite?'

'Because I believe him.'

'And what does he tell you?'

'That he didn't kill your brother.'

He gave a little snort of disbelief. 'Of course he would say that. But he told me he has the diamonds and some other things and they are buried in his Toyota.' He took a deep breath and opened his eyes. 'Did you see him bury them?'

'No. Look, he hasn't had time to bury a car. He's never had the diamonds.'

'You're either his accomplice or a very gullible woman.'

'I'm neither.' She was beginning to feel nervous once again. This was the man who had been shooting at Kelly and he was frighteningly big; weakened or not, he was still powerful enough to break her neck if he felt like it. But he seemed the sort of man who would listen to a reasoned argument. 'I think I'm a good judge of people and I like Kelly. I think he's been telling me the truth.'

He dismissed that piece of female nonsense with a minute wave of his hand.

'Also,' she added quickly, recognising the arrogance of the gesture, 'I've seen what he's got with him. People said he had explosives and a machine gun. I haven't seen so much as a popgun. And there hasn't been a trace of diamonds.'

'He would have them hidden.'

'Where? And don't tell me you believe that nonsense about them being buried with the car.'

He tilted his head. Maybe, maybe not.

'Look, if you'd stolen millions of dollars' worth of diamonds you'd keep them next to you, right?'

His eyes held no clue to what he was thinking. He'd be a great card player, she thought, and said, 'I've lived and slept with this man for a few days.' She stopped, blushing. 'I don't mean I've slept with him. I mean I've been with him, night and day. He hasn't got any little bag tied around his neck. He doesn't take things to bed with him at night. I've seen him wash. I've seen him crawl out of his sleeping bag. He's got nothing.' Her arm swept towards the back of the bus where all their gear was stacked. 'Everything he's been carrying around is in those boxes and drums.'

'And you've looked inside?'

'I've seen everything. Tools, food, fuel, maps.'

'He had a bag on top of the Rock.'

'And that had his toothbrush, razor and a change of clothing. I bought the clothes. I packed the bag for him.'

'If Hunnicutt didn't shoot my brother and if he didn't steal the diamonds and the other things, why is he running away?' He leaned back, certain he had posed the unanswerable question.

'It started because of a silly bet.'

The eyes thinned to dark slits. The expression said he was prepared for a lie.

'It's true. He made a stupid bet with a friend.'

'Who was the friend?'

'Someone called Gerry. His business partner.'

The eyes widened abruptly. 'Gerry Montague?'

'Do you know him?'

'We met.'

'Well, I've never met this Gerry but I don't trust him. It seems to me that everything he's done has only made life more difficult for Kelly. He's caused all the trouble.' She shuffled her feet on the floor, nervous because she wasn't sure if she was convincing Kolvenbach or not. 'At least, that's how I see it.'

'You said there was a bet.'

She told him the story.

'But that is crazy.'

'Have you ever met Kelly — I mean, apart from the times you've tried to kill him? That bet is just the sort of crazy thing that would appeal to him. And he was drunk at the time.' She waved her hands excitedly, anxious to make the next point. 'There's a little boy in him that still wants to play games and that's what he thought he was doing. Setting off on a great big game of hide-and-seek. And, of course, the stakes were high. His car against Gerry's car. What a lark.' She sniffed. 'Of course it would appeal to him. You should get to know him. He's a bit crazy, but nice.' She bent towards him. 'And he really liked your brother.'

Kolvenbach examined his hands. 'How do you know?'

'He told me. Several times. He was really upset at what happened. He said he was such a nice guy.'

Kolvenbach touched the bite marks on his neck. 'When did this bet start? What time did he leave on his journey?'

She had to think. 'He said midnight. The bet applied for seven days, so they started at twelve midnight. Kelly's like that. Very precise about minor things.'

'And he left his home at that time?'

'Yes.' She puffed out her cheeks. 'Then he went to Carlton — that's a suburb of Melbourne — and picked up that amazing wife of his.'

Kolvenbach noted the 'amazing'. But he wanted to be certain about the chronology of happenings on the night his brother died. 'So he left his home precisely at midnight...'

'Farewelled by Gerry Montague.'

'Montague was at his house?'

'To make sure Kelly didn't cheat, that he left exactly on time. Then, on an impulse, Kelly went to Carlton and grabbed his wife.'

'He really did tie her with a rope and carry her off?'

'That's what he said.'

She'd told him the same thing. 'And this was about one o'clock in the morning?'

She spread her hands. About that.

'Do you know when my brother was killed?'

'I've no idea.'

'The police believe Harald was shot some time between one and four in the morning.'

'Which means...'

He compressed his lips. '...That if Hunnicutt really did leave at midnight, drive to Carlton and seize his wife, he couldn't have killed my brother.'

She crossed her arms over the back of the seat. 'I think this Gerry Montague set up the whole thing. I mean, it's all too convenient. He goads Kelly into a bet, a challenge he knows he can't resist, persuades him to leave town for a week. And then...'

'Did you know Montague was dead?'

She slumped backwards. 'When?'

He gave her the barest details and then asked if Hunnicutt had ever discussed a man named McCarthy. He hadn't.

Kolvenbach's gaze darted around the bus. He was unsettled, anxious to be somewhere else. 'I might have been chasing the wrong man,' he said, speaking to the ceiling. 'I might have been set up, tricked into following a false trail.' Again, the bright eyes became dark slits. 'Do you know where he is?'

'Maybe.'

He clenched his fist. 'Don't start playing with me.'

'And don't you start threatening me.'

'Or?'

She grinned. 'Or I'll take my bandage back.'

He pushed his head against the headrest. 'Why should I believe these things you've been telling me?'

'Because I think it's the truth and you know it makes sense. You've been chasing the wrong person.' She got up and sat in the seat beside him. 'Look, I'm not going to tell you where Kelly may or may not be until I'm sure you're not going to harm him.'

He held his head. 'I've been hunting the man I thought killed my brother. I thought he had taken papers that were of very great importance.'

'And diamonds.'

He waved a hand, dismissing them. 'Yes, but not as important. Insurance. You know.'

'But the papers are important?'

One eye studied her through a gap in his fingers. 'You cannot imagine how important they are to me.'

She leaned across the aisle to feel his forehead. 'You're burning.'

'I'll be all right.' He pushed her hand away. 'I would like to talk to Hunnicutt.'

'You won't hurt him? You'll let him go?'

He took a deep breath. 'You have my word.'

She hesitated. 'True?'

'I told you.' He gritted his teeth in pain. 'I've given my word.'

She stretched her lips, scratched her nose, then decided. 'Fair enough,' she said, and went to the back of the bus. She returned with a blanket. 'Here. Take off that shirt and put this round your shoulders. You can't go around looking like you've just been mauled by the Creature from the Black Lagoon.'

She had to help him remove the shirt. Then she restarted the motor and set off for the other side of the Rock and Maggie Spring.

467

McCarthy was anxious to check other parts of the Rock. The great monolith was more than eight kilometres around the base, but the road was good and he had calculated that he could do a lap in less time than it took someone to descend the slope. He'd used his watch to time several groups from the moment they came into view until they reached the ground, and he reckoned he could drive off when someone first topped the crest and be back by the time they'd reached the last section of chain.

He was growing more agitated over the non-appearance of Spiro and Laura Hunnicutt, and the fact that he had let Kolvenbach and the woman drive away. He felt foolish, stranded like the proverbial shag on a rock. He checked to make sure Spiro was not in sight, got in his rented car and set off to do a circuit of the Rock.

Both his hands were bleeding by the time Kelly reached the bottom. Laura was limping and whimpering, refusing to let him hold her hand. She had torn her pants. They climbed down through the fallen rocks and caves where Kelly had spent the night. He told her to stay there.

'Why?'

'Because I want to make sure there's no one waiting for us. That man was after you, right? Not me.'

She was angry because what he said made sense. She hated it when Kelly made sense. He left her the water.

'The road's not far to the right so keep out of sight,' he said. 'I told Monica I'd meet her at Maggie Spring. If she's here, she'll be at the pool. It'll take me a few minutes to get there, a few more to get back. Don't move. You'll be safe.'

'Going to meet your little girlfriend?'

'Just wait here. I'll be back.'

'You look ridiculous with a moustache.'

'I know.'

'You're a bastard, Kelly, and I hate you. That was the most terrifying thing I've ever done.'

He gave a backhanded wave and started to pick his way down through the boulders.

Monica was sitting on the sand at one end of the pool. She stood up, dusting her hands and smiling when she saw Kelly approaching. 'You look great in a moustache,' she said, and taking him by the arm, led him well away from the path.

'I have a surprise for you. It is a very big surprise and you must promise you won't be angry. I think you will, but, believe me, it's for the best.'

He stopped and tugged at her shirt sleeve. 'What are you talking about?'

'Over there.' She pointed to a bush where Magnus Kolvenbach was sitting.

He started to run but Monica grabbed him. 'Stop. It's all right.'

Kolvenbach stood but made no attempt to follow. He wore no shirt; just a blanket that was draped across his shoulders.

'Please, Kelly. I've had a long talk to him. He believes your story.'

It took her another minute to persuade Kelly to approach Kolvenbach. They stood apart like wary animals.

'She told me about the bet,' Kolvenbach said. 'Now, you tell me exactly what happened. With precise times.' He lifted his good arm and pointed at Monica. 'And you don't interrupt. I want no prompting.'

Kelly told him the story. Kolvenbach asked many questions. At the end, Kolvenbach said simply, 'It seems I've been tricked'.

'We both have.'

Monica spoke for the first time. 'I think Gerry Montague was involved.'

'I did not like the man,' Kolvenbach said and Monica nodded in accord. 'It seems he has become involved with a man called McCarthy, who is a private investigator. He has a reputation for being a rough operator. Do you know him?'

'No.' Kelly frowned. 'Nor can I believe Gerry would do anything like that.'

'There are none so blind as lovers and close friends,' Kolvenbach said and touched his ear, which was throbbing.

'So what do we do now?' Kelly said, not liking what he was implying.

'Get our friend to a doctor,' Monica said.

'We must get back to Melbourne,' Kolvenbach said. 'While we cats have been away, the mice have been playing.'

'And who are they?'

'I have some ideas.' Montague had been silenced; he was certain of that. He was also convinced that the anonymous blackmailer who had telephoned Lister was the mysterious McCarthy. Lister and McCarthy — they were the two who could have had Montague killed. Only McCarthy, however, would have the papers. McCarthy was the man he had to find and McCarthy was in Melbourne.

Only then did Kelly remember that Laura was waiting, hidden among the boulders near the entrance to Maggie Spring.

She waited ten minutes, then twenty. Kelly had abandoned her. He had met that strange woman of his and she'd refused to let him come back for her. To hell with him. To hell with them both. She got to her feet and found her way to the bottom. Near a cave whose walls and roof were a jumble of ancient paintings, she passed a group of tourists who were intrigued by a woman wearing torn pants and carrying a pair of shoes, emerging from behind

470

the *Prohibited Area* sign. Laura ignored them. She turned right, along the track that led to the road.

McCarthy was on his second lap of the Rock. He had stopped briefly at all the vantage points and was approaching the broad valley leading into Maggie Spring when he saw Laura through the trees. She was limping. He stopped short of the parking zone to see if anyone was with her. A mob of tourists, hurrying after their guide, had just gone the other way, towards the pool. She was on her own. She held a shoe in each hand and wore an expression that could have been misery or anger or both.

McCarthy drove up to the parking area and stopped near the point where she would emerge from the track. He got out.

'Wonderful sight.'

Her eyes held no suggestion of interest. He had that effect on people. They overlooked him. It had been a useful attribute during his police career.

She said, 'Yes', and looked down the road.

'Do you have to walk far to see the spring?' He was the classic tourist: amazed for the first few hours, bored in the middle of the day, exhausted by evening.

'I don't know.' She held up her shoes. 'My feet hurt.'

He gave her his grandfather smile. 'Mine too. I've had enough. I'm going back to the pub to sit down and have a cold beer.'

He saw the flash of interest.

'Are you waiting for someone?'

'I was. He seems to have forgotten me.'

'May I?' Gallantly, he swung an arm towards the car. 'I'm going to the Sheraton.'

She smiled, an immediate problem solved. 'So am I.'

He opened the door and, with relief, she sat down. She longed for a cold drink, a bath and a change of clothes.

He noticed her roughened hands. 'Oh, you've hurt yourself.'

'I fell. I was trying to climb the Rock.'

'Brave girl. I didn't even put a foot on it. I know my limitations.' He drove off. 'Are you one of those people who are going to rush dutifully back to see the sunset?'

'Definitely not.' She felt comfortable with this man. He was inane, and that was the maximum intellectual level she could handle at the moment. She needed to think but she was too exhausted.

'Good for you. Neither am I. I'm going to get clean, get drunk, have a good meal and go to bed.' He paused and laughed. 'I might skip the meal.'

She leaned back in the seat. 'I've had a day like you wouldn't believe.'

'Really? You must tell me about it. Say,' he said, as though suddenly struck by an idea, 'would you let me buy you a drink?'

She laughed, thinking of Kelly and his khaki girlfriend, who were probably hiding in one of the caves. 'Only one?'

On the other side of the Rock, a team of medics was working its way down the slope. They were carrying a stretcher bearing an unconscious man; they suspected he had a fractured skull. The man had apparently been climbing on his own and had fallen in one of the gullies east of the summit. A Norwegian couple had discovered him. He was a short man but exceptionally heavy and the medics were exhausted by the time they reached the ambulance waiting at the bottom.

38

It was not the time of the day to photograph or even admire the Rock but McCarthy swung the car into the parking area that gave most visitors their first view of the northern walls. Nervously, Laura ran her fingers along the seat belt. 'Why have we stopped?'

McCarthy prodded one cheek with a finger. 'I keep getting the feeling I've seen you before.'

'I don't think so.'

He did two things. He pressed the master button on the central locking system and he reached over the seat for his briefcase. From it he extracted a glossy ten-by-eight photograph. He showed it to her and, recognising herself, she tried frantically to open the door.

'What name did you use when you were modelling? Was it Laura Hunnicutt?'

She gave up the struggle to open the door. 'Who are you?'

'A friend of Gerry's.' With reverence, he put the photograph back in the briefcase. 'I knew him well. You did too, I believe. He's dead now, of course.' He paused to let fear take greater hold. 'He told me of the arrangement you two had. I know all about your part in the Kolvenbach affair.' His face crinkled into a maze of amiable lines. 'A great talker, our friend Gerry, wasn't he?'

McCarthy had questioned many women. He had no need to use force on this one. She was frightened and, if what Montague had told him was true, she'd been frightened from the beginning. A little pressure — innuendo of the right kind — was all that was needed to make her tell him where the missing papers were.

In his police days, McCarthy had been more than just a rough cop. When questioning certain people, he knew when to shut up and let silence do its work. So he smiled knowingly at Laura Hunnicutt and let her wonder how much he really knew, allowing time for the corrosive accumulation of doubt to make her decide he knew everything.

He believed he knew most of the story. Hunnicutt had shot Kolvenbach, panicked and given the diamonds to his wife for safekeeping. She, not knowing what to do with them, had passed them on to Montague, her husband's best friend, the only person she trusted at such a time.

'Mrs Hunnicutt, I want you to understand that I have no intention of handing you over to the police. I'm not interested in truth, justice and the American way.' Again, he produced the grandfather smile. 'I think you know what I'm interested in. You know what I want.'

'Are you the man McCarthy?' she whispered.

'Yes.' He beamed and she was sorry she'd said the name because his eyes gleamed like a snake's. 'How clever of you.' And then, in a hiss, 'Where did you hear my name?'

'From several people.' She lifted her chin.

'Oh dear.' He turned, as if confiding to the distant Rock. 'The lady's becoming bold. That's unfortunate.'

Both her hands gripped the seat belt, which she held in front of her like a protective shield. 'What do you want from me?'

'Nothing more than cooperation. Information.'

'Are you after the diamonds?'

'I have them, thank you.' The eyes almost disappeared beneath folds of satisfaction. 'Do you know where he hid them? In the refrigerator.' He laughed. 'A lot of fun, Gerry.'

But a weak bastard. He'd talked, implicated her and lost them the diamonds. What about the cash? Gerry had said there was more than 100,000 in US dollars. The cash wouldn't fit in the freezer. Had Gerry hidden the money somewhere or taken it with him in the Porsche? Her mind was starting to operate and at this point, Laura, who had thought herself dead, realised she could bargain her way back to life. Maybe even outwit this man.

'Have you sent men to try and kill me?'

'Yes,' he said brightly.

'But now you don't want to kill me. Now you want information.'

'Things change rapidly, don't they? I find that one of the most fascinating aspects of life.'

'So you've already got the diamonds.' She managed a matter-of-fact voice. 'What else do you want? Money? Is that what this is all about?'

He locked his fingers. 'I do appreciate people who don't waste time with silly denials. Good. Let's hope we can do business.'

'Well?'

'As you know, the safe contained diamonds, cash and papers. Very important papers.'

Papers? There were millions of dollars in diamonds and a fortune in cash, and both Magnus and this man were worried about papers.

'I need to know where those papers are,' McCarthy said. 'You know. You'll tell me.'

She squared her shoulders and faced him. 'What sort of deal are we talking about?'

He clapped his hands in delight. 'Dear lady, what

a pleasure it'll be to do business with you. Do you know where they are?'

'Yes.'

'And you'll take me there?'

'If the deal's satisfactory.'

'I'm sure we can come to an arrangement,' he said. 'How about you showing me if I promise to spare you your life?'

She returned his stare. 'Life without money is no fun.'

'My sentiments exactly.' He shook his head. 'Oh, lovely lady, where have you been all my life?' He restarted the motor. 'Should we continue this discussion over drinks?'

She displayed her scratched hands. 'I'd like to wash first and change clothes.'

'Then it's your room and I'll order drinks.'

And if Magnus is there, he'll kill you, she thought, and settled back in the seat.

'I will find her,' Kolvenbach said, when finally they left the Maggie Spring gorge. 'She has probably stormed off and got a lift back to town with someone. She is a wilful woman. Very headstrong.'

'I know what she's like, thank you,' Kelly said. 'She *is* my wife.'

Kolvenbach raised his good hand in a placatory gesture. 'What I am saying is that you two should be off as quickly as possible. The longer you stay, the greater the chance you will be recognised.'

'I'm going to put a beard on him,' Monica said. She'd taken a liking to Kolvenbach. He was direct.

The big man fished in his bag and took out a small folder. It contained two of the driver's licences he had taken from Harry the Hatchet. He handed one to Kelly.

'Here. You are now Allan Wilkinson of Figtree Pocket, Queensland.'

Kelly examined the licence. 'Where did you get that?'

'From someone who no longer has need of it. Don't worry. It's a good fake.'

'But it's not my picture on the licence.'

'By the time your friend adds a beard to your face, no one will know the difference. You will not pass a roadblock with a licence that says Kelso Hunnicutt. You should have no trouble with one that says Allan Wilkinson.'

They arranged to meet in Melbourne, where they would try to track down McCarthy.

Reluctantly, almost churlishly, Kelly asked, 'And you'll bring Laura back with you in that plane of yours?'

'I will.' Again the hand was raised in a vow. 'She means nothing to me but I will protect her. I promise you that.'

Kelly nodded and walked towards the minibus. It was the first time he'd seen it and he stopped when he could read the signs. 'Where did you get that?' he asked Monica.

'In Alice Springs. This nice man in the used-car yard offered me a deal I couldn't refuse.'

'What do you need a bus for?'

She jabbed him in the ribs. 'To get you through police roadblocks. And to use myself, whenever and if ever I get back to a normal life. It'll be better than the old truck.'

'How many kilometres has it done?'

'Oh, shut up.' She opened the door, doing it more skilfully this time. 'I know I should be polite to the passengers and you're the only one I've got, but would you just get in and stop complaining. We've got a long way to go.'

They drove Kolvenbach to his car and then set off for Melbourne.

'I know some good tracks,' Kelly shouted from his seat halfway down the bus.

'The police know you by now. They'll be watching all the tracks and taking it easy on the highways. We're going straight down the main road. That's very un-Hunnicutt.' She reached down and jiggled the bag. 'We'll stop down the road where it's quiet and I'll put the beard on.'

He stretched his legs across the aisle.

'Take your feet off the seats,' she said. 'And why don't you make yourself useful and get me a beer?' He got up, laughing because he was pleased to be away from Kolvenbach and to be with Monica. They headed towards Yulara and the highway back to the east.

Laura had expected Kolvenbach to be inside and entered the room with great trepidation. She'd seen the man in action and was ready to move to one side, to press herself against the wall and get out of the way. Magnus would hear her call for help, leap off the bed or out of the bathroom or wherever he was, and crush McCarthy in one wild, irresistible charge.

The room was empty. It was just as they'd left it, in the cold, dark and coffee-starved hours before dawn.

She took some fresh clothes, went to the bathroom and locked the door.

McCarthy rang room service and ordered toasted sandwiches and a large pot of coffee. He went to the mini bar and the refrigerator and made her a gin and tonic and poured himself a cold beer.

McCarthy waited for the thudding spray of the shower before picking up the phone again. He made two phone calls. The first was to the airport, the second to the Yulara police. He told the policeman that he and his wife were worried about an acquaintance of theirs. The man had gone to climb the Rock earlier that day and they hadn't seen or heard from him since. McCarthy described Spiro.

Gravely, the policeman said the friend was possibly a man who had met with an accident. The man had been carried off the Rock by a team of medics and was being transferred by air ambulance to Alice Springs Hospital. He might have fractured his skull. He had not regained consciousness.

One to Kolvenbach. Thoughtfully, McCarthy sipped his beer. He knew this was the South African's room but he was not worried. If Kolvenbach came back while he was there, he would merely introduce himself as the Good Samaritan who had found Kolvenbach's 'wife' in distress near Maggie Spring and driven her to the hotel. They would shake hands and he would leave.

It was worth waiting, risking Kolvenbach's return, to make a deal with the woman. She was smart and tough; he was impressed. And a little puzzled, too, because she didn't seem like a woman who would panic and hand over a few million dollars' worth of diamonds to a loose creature like Gerry Montague.

The coffee and sandwiches arrived just before she emerged from the bathroom.

They talked. McCarthy was concise. The papers were in Melbourne? Then they should fly there as quickly as possible. There was a jet out of Yulara that afternoon. It connected with a flight to Melbourne via Adelaide. He had already made bookings for two.

'I'm travelling with...' She hesitated.

'You have been. I think it wiser that we travel together from now on. Then I can watch you and you can watch me.' She seemed uncertain. 'If you want to stay here and fly on down with your big boyfriend, fine, but first you tell me where to find the papers and I'll go and get them on my own.'

'And if I don't want to tell you?'

He smiled blandly. 'You'll tell me.'

'What's the deal?'

'You take me to the papers. Half of what they're worth goes to you and believe me, lovely lady, they're worth a lot.'

'And the diamonds?'

'What a gal. Such a mercenary.' He chuckled. 'I love you. A million for you, the rest for me. That's a good deal. Accept.'

Just show me where they are, she thought, and I'll think of a way to get them all back. You might be smart, McCarthy, but you're crass. She said, 'Agreed,' and packed quickly, gulping down her drink and nibbling a sandwich. While she wrote a note to Kolvenbach, she sipped her coffee.

You work better on your own, she wrote. *Thanks for the protection and everything else. Good luck. Catch Kelly for me.*

'Ready?' McCarthy said and held the door open for her. He left the hotel first to make sure Kolvenbach was not in sight. He wasn't and they drove to the airport.

Kolvenbach reached the hotel ten minutes after they left. He found the note and made immediate plans to fly to Melbourne.

Detective Mallowes called into Ulverstone's office. There had been no reported sighting of Hunnicutt at Ayers Rock, or anywhere else, for several days. The man seemed to have disappeared. However, Magnus Kolvenbach had just lodged a flight plan that would take him directly from Yulara to Melbourne.

'Didn't one of our last reports suggest that Kolvenbach was merely touring around now?' Ulverstone said. 'He hasn't interfered with the police search since that incident in the far north of South Australia. He could just be returning to Melbourne.'

Mallowes paused deferentially, to indicate that

the offering had been worthwhile. 'He also told the police at Alice Springs that he was on his way to visit his diamond mine in the Kimberleys. And now, out of the blue, he's flying south.'

'Because?'

'Possibly because our man, too, is heading south. I think Kolvenbach knows more than we do. I think Hunnicutt's coming home, or is already well on his way, and Kolvenbach's flying down here to intercept him or to wait for him.'

Ulverstone buried a fingertip in the fold of his cheek. 'I think we should have a chat to Mr Kolvenbach when he lands here.'

'If I may suggest, sir, why don't we leave him to his own devices and follow him? Let him think we've lost interest.'

'I'd dearly like to have a long talk with Hunnicutt,' Ulverstone mused.

'I've a feeling that Kolvenbach will lead us to him.'

39

Kolvenbach flew to Melbourne and had his ear stitched at an all-night medical clinic. His head throbbed throughout the long flight, as he knew it would, but he also knew it would be simpler to explain an injury like a torn ear to a doctor in a big city rather than to the doctor at Yulara. He had no idea what had happened to the man he had fought but it was a reasonable guess that some-one who'd been pile-driven head-first into rock would have needed medical attention. He had no wish to be treated by the same doctor. A curious person might imagine some link in the injuries and ask questions.

The Melbourne doctor was interested, but only in the challenge posed by attempting to sew the almost severed piece to the stub of the ear. He was a craftsman, not a busybody. Kolvenbach's story was that he had been set on by a pack of louts. He had fought them off. No, the police were not involved. Nothing had been stolen.

The doctor took great care to be neat and gentle and paused frequently to admire his needlework. The scar would be partly hidden by the natural fold of the ear, he said and, with a hairdresser's flair, used a mirror to show his patient how well he had put the halves together.

Filled with serums to protect him from various

noxious possibilities, Kolvenbach went to his brother's house.

He rang Lister in Canberra.

The blackmailer had called again. Lister had demanded proof that the caller had the papers in his possession, but had heard nothing since. He assumed the caller was McCarthy. Only a hunch. He had no proof. In fact, he added with a sardonic chuckle, he had no McCarthy. The man had disappeared.

'You don't know where he is?'

'Not a clue.'

'How long has he been missing?'

'A day or two.' He breathed heavily and painfully, and Kolvenbach had an image of a man with skin like wrapping paper, a sunken chest and a cigarette perpetually in his left hand — a man in the early stages of emphysema. He'd never met Lister. All the negotiating had been done by his brother. 'Now that you're back from your paper chase across half of the bloody country,' Lister was saying, 'you might be able to do something useful and try and track McCarthy down.'

Something useful? Kolvenbach's nostrils flared like a horse feeling the spurs for the first time. Again, he wished Harald had kept away from this man but his brother was naive in some matters. He could imagine the conversation: 'You just leave this to me, Harald ... I'll negotiate with these blacks and you pay a modest fee ... You won't get approval without my help... It's the way we get things done in this part of the world.' Sure. And now McCarthy or someone was applying the screws and the whole project and his family's reputation was in jeopardy.

'And, Magnus' (Lister never called him by his first name; the tone was of a grown man to a little boy), 'forget Hunnicutt and concentrate on McCarthy. We've got to find this bastard before he nails our balls to the back door. If I find him, I intend to have him put away. I expect you to do the same.'

Slowly, Kolvenbach said, 'Put away where?'

'Don't be coy. You know what I mean. Got to go. Oh, and welcome back to the big smoke. Maybe you'll have more luck in the city than you had in the bush.' He hung up.

Kolvenbach was so angry and tired and sore that he had trouble sleeping. When he stopped worrying about Lister, he thought about Laura. They were scrambled thoughts, littered with fragments of old conversations. Alice Springs: she had rung Montague. No one else. Not her sister, who was allegedly so worried about her.

'Gerry was going to meet me at the airport.'

He got up, lit a cigarette and walked into the room where his brother had been shot.

And in the plane, when they were flying into Queensland. Montague? Yes, she knew him, but only vaguely. They had little contact with each other. She knew nothing of the business. She was lying, of course, with the polish of a person practised at the art. He became agitated, finding odd pieces falling into matched slots.

Kolvenbach sat in Harald's favourite chair and stretched out. His feet brushed the carpet near the spot where his brother had died. *Without a struggle.* Kolvenbach sat up. Harald was easily aroused, suspicious of strangers, immensely strong and fully capable of defending himself. That meant he had known his killer and welcomed him into the house. He had few acquaintances in Melbourne and fewer friends. He knew Hunnicutt and Montague. Hunnicutt was gone, off to win his bet, when Harald had been shot.

Montague?

Montague had been in town. He had farewelled

484

Hunnicutt at midnight, from Hunnicutt's house. A house that presumably contained Hunnicutt's sports jacket and shoes and rifle.

Kolvenbach got up and poured himself a drink.

Had Laura and Montague duped Hunnicutt? Persuaded him to take off on his game of hide-and-seek while they got on with the business of killing Harald, of emptying the safe and focusing the blame on the cooperative but innocent Hunnicutt?

She had the mind for such things. Montague would have killed his brother. Laura would have planned it.

Hunnicutt almost spoiled things for them by grabbing her and carrying her off with him. Montague had been left on his own. He wasn't smart — not like Laura was smart. He'd made mistakes, got involved with someone — McCarthy? — and been disposed of. Which was why Laura had rushed back to Melbourne. To straighten things out, retrieve the diamonds, get the papers.

Glass in hand, Kolvenbach paced the room.

But she had been frightened, genuinely frightened, of returning on her own. Had she met someone? A lap of the room and he decided. Yes, someone had either forced her to return or had been able to convince her she was safe in his company. That man had met her at Yulara, taken her to Melbourne.

No one could force her to fly with him. It was not possible to put a reluctant hostage on a commercial jet and travel all the way to Melbourne without arousing interest. Particularly someone as resourceful as Laura. No, she'd gone back willingly.

He stubbed his cigarette and swallowed his drink. He had to find Laura. She would know where the papers were.

And she had planned the murder of his brother.

Kelly tried to persuade her to take the southern road from Curtin Springs down to Mulga Park. He knew of a way across the Musgrave Ranges to the Ernabella Mission and Everard Park. From there, they could join the highway well to the south of the Northern Territory border.

Monica refused. The police had planes and helicopters, and if they saw anyone taking such an unlikely route they would investigate immediately. No, they would stick to the main road, where minibuses were expected to travel. Kelly scratched at his beard but could do little else. She was at the wheel, stubbornly locked on course.

They passed through two roadblocks. The first was at the intersection of the Petermann Road — the main route to and from Ayers Rock — and the Stuart Highway. The policeman was intrigued by a tourist vehicle with only one passenger.

'I only hold six at the best of times,' Monica said. 'And we're in a recession, or hadn't you government employees noticed?'

He was only interested in the men who were passing through and, ignoring her, he checked Kelly's identification. The policeman looked at the picture on the Queensland licence and, face twisted in doubt, studied the bearded countenance smiling at him.

'He told me he grew the beard to surprise his girlfriend,' Monica said before the policeman could speak. 'No wonder he's come on his own. She's left him.' She laughed unkindly and the man handed Kelly his licence and nodded sympathetically.

'You look better without it,' he said.

The second checkpoint was smaller and simpler. This policeman, irritated by two long days of jibes and jokes, saw the clearance sticker from the northern roadblock, glanced at the two faces and waved them on.

486

Kelly was insistent that they avoid Port Augusta. This was the crossroads of southern Australia, a town where the principal routes from Darwin and Perth linked with a road that fanned into highways leading to Adelaide, Melbourne and Sydney. Port Augusta would have a major checkpoint. The police there, he argued, could be enthusiastic to the point of being troublesome. So he persuaded Monica to take the Oodnadatta Track. It was an established route for tourist vehicles, so they would not arouse curiosity, and it led to the Flinders Ranges.

Once in the ranges, they turned left at Copley and took back tracks to Mingary, on the Barrier Highway near Broken Hill. They drove into the mining city and even dared to have a meal at the same roadhouse where Kelly and Laura had eaten twelve days earlier.

From Broken Hill, they followed Kelly's original route to Melbourne. They drove day and night. The journey from Ayers Rock took them two and a half days.

Kelly slept on the back verandah of Monica's old house in the mountains. When he woke, he rang Mary Calibrano. She was frantic. 'Where have you been?' It was the sort of accusation she used to level when he was late back from lunch.

She said she had been to Police Headquarters, convinced him the policemen were genuine, and told him of the skin and blood samples.

Ever since Gerry had been killed, he said bitterly, people had been trying to link his partner with the murder. They hadn't said such things when Gerry was alive.

She didn't know how to answer that but urged Kelly to telephone Ulverstone.

'You call him. Tell him I rang, don't tell him where I am — just say somewhere in country Victoria so

all those poor blokes on the roadblocks can go home
— but say that I'm prepared to meet him soon.
I'll tell him where and when.'

'I don't think he'll like that.'

'Tell him those are the conditions.'

He didn't leave a number. Mary hung up, thinking
Kelly sounded harder than before and that he must
have missed a lot of sleep and a great many meals.

She'd forgotten to tell him that Magnus Kolvenbach had called in. They'd had such an interesting
talk. The poor man; attacked by louts. The city
wasn't safe any more. He was, she thought, a very
attractive man, even wearing a bandage.

Kelly rang Kolvenbach. The South African seemed
pleased to hear from him. They should meet. He
had news. In the last two days, he had discovered
where Laura was staying.

Wasn't Laura with him? Kelly had presumed
Kolvenbach had found her, brought her back and
been keeping her at his house. Enough remained
of the spurned husband to have had the thought
gnawing at him.

No. He would explain. And he thought he had
found McCarthy. He asked Kelly to come to his
house immediately. 'You know where it is?' He spoke
without a hint of irony and Kelly promised to be
there within an hour and a half.

He no longer wore the beard or moustache; he
was sick of wearing it and his skin was still itchy
from the adhesive. But Monica was upset; three million people in Melbourne knew what a clean-shaven
Kelso Hunnicutt looked like but the bearded version
could move anywhere in anonymity. More than that,
he was her exclusive creation. Her own man.

'The police have found evidence that Gerry was
at Kolvenbach's house the night Harald was killed,'
he told Monica without any joy.

'I'm not surprised.'

'They want to talk to me.'

'They always have.' And then, to brighten him, 'But that's a hopeful sign. Are you going to see them?'

'Possibly. After I see Kolvenbach.'

She drove him there, not liking the assignment of delivering him to a man who would deliver him to his wife. On the way, she felt compelled to deliver a lecture. She told him how foolish he was to have trusted Montague, how the bet had been a ploy to get him out of the city and how he should keep clear of his wife. She knew she could be accused of being jealous, bitchy, or any other of the so-called female curses; but she didn't like Laura.

'I've seen her in action, remember? I've heard her tell the most outrageous stories about you. According to her, you tried to kill her. You fired at them, you cracked Kolvenbach on the back of the head, remember? It's not just a question of her not loving you, Kelly. She's out to get you. I don't know why, but she wants you destroyed.'

He didn't speak, other than to give directions to the Kolvenbach house.

They were in the room where Harald had been shot. Magnus Kolvenbach knew that and watched Hunnicutt through hunter's eyes: never leaving the man, noting every move, following every glance.

He offered them drinks. Both refused.

Finally he sat down.

'Harald was killed right where you are standing.'

Kelly shuffled to one side.

Kolvenbach scratched his chin, then settled into his brother's deep leather chair. He motioned for the others to sit down. 'You didn't kill him.'

Kelly looked at him in surprise. 'You've been testing me?'

'Yes.'

He glanced at Monica and laughed nervously. 'I thought we'd been through all that.'

'I'm a very cautious man. Cynical by nature but thorough and, I hope, fair.'

Kelly began to rise. 'Is that why we came here?'

Kolvenbach signalled for him to remain seated. He patted the bandage around his head. 'Despite the fact that my head hasn't been working too well, I've been doing a lot of thinking. I believe I now understand what happened here.' He waved an arm across the carpet and, sweep completed, let his wrist dangle over the armrest.

When he said no more, Kelly said, 'So what did happen?'

'Later. I'll tell you more when I'm sure.'

Monica, who had been chastened by Kelly's silence, said softly, 'I think there are times when you could be a very difficult man, Mr Kolvenbach'.

'Not could. I am, and for most of the time.'

'Thank God for a bastard who knows he's a bastard.'

Without smiling, he nodded acknowledgment, then turned to Kelly. 'I visited your office. Your secretary was most helpful. She gave me Montague's address. I went there. So did your wife.'

Kelly leaned forward. 'Laura was there?'

Kolvenbach allowed a sly smile to escape. 'After a week of frustration, a little good luck came my way. She was going into the apartment with a man. An older, fatter man. Most interesting, that.'

Again, he became silent and Kelly had to ask, 'What was most interesting?'

'I'd seen him before. At Ayers Rock. When I climbed down, following you...' his eyes swung briefly to Monica, '...I noticed this man at the bottom. I was studying the crowd, one by one. He was very interested in you. Did you not notice?'

She was embarrassed. 'I was watching you.'

'He was there. Now he is here. I would say he is the one who persuaded Laura to return to Melbourne with him. I believe he is McCarthy.' Awkwardly, leaning on one arm, he pushed himself from the chair. 'We should go.'

It was cold outside and flimsy puffs of mist encircled the street lamps. They went in Kolvenbach's car. On the way he told them more about Laura and the fat man. He had waited an hour for them to emerge from Montague's flat. They seemed agitated. He followed them to a small house in Fitzroy. Once, they left to visit a car wrecker's yard. It was locked. They spent some time peering through the chain-wire fence.

Kolvenbach searched for Kelly's eyes in the mirror. 'There was a Porsche inside. Or rather, what was left of a Porsche.'

Neither man spoke. Monica, who was in front, switched from one to the other, seeking a clue.

'Montague drove a Porsche,' Kolvenbach said.

'So where are we going?' Monica said, when it was obvious they were not driving to the small house in Fitzroy.

'To the wrecking yard.' Kolvenbach used his good arm to move the seat belt from his sore ribs. 'I thought we might park near there and wait. I have a feeling they're coming back.'

'A feeling?' Monica raised her hands and turned to Kelly for explanation, but he only shrugged. 'We're going to sit all night outside a junk yard? I spend a week playing hare to half the police hounds in Australia, bring you home safely and now, as a reward, I'm being treated to a night out at a junk yard?'

Kolvenbach slowed when they approached the yard. He drove past it once, pointing out the Porsche; it was in a dark corner, all bent panels and shattered glass covered with clods of soil. It was separated from the other wrecks by a rope barrier.

He continued around the block.

'It is possible Montague had something of value with him when he crashed. It would seem the police have not found it.'

'You're saying,' Monica said, 'that Laura and this fat man, McCarthy, are going to burgle a wrecked car?'

'I think they expect to find something.'

'What does McCarthy think he'll find in the Porsche?' Kelly said.

Monica pushed Kelly's shoulder. 'What's wrong with *Laura* thinking she'll find something or even taking this man to show him something?' She pushed him again. 'I wish you'd think clearly and stop trying to protect her.'

'Leave her alone, Monica.'

'Leave her alone, Monica,' she mimicked, lowering her voice to Kelly's level. They were on the far side of the block and approaching a few shops. 'Who'd like coffee and a hamburger?'

Kelly had forgotten he was hungry. 'Me.'

'I know, you'll have a hamburger with everything.' She touched Kolvenbach's arm. 'How about you?'

'Why not?'

'I suppose that means everything. How do you like your coffee?'

'Black.'

'Okay. Let me out. I'll buy dinner; you go on. I'll walk around.'

'I'll park just around the corner,' Kolvenbach said.

'Be careful,' Kelly said.

'My God, he cares for another woman.'

'I mean don't make a lot of noise when you come back to the car.'

'I feel better. Things are normal.' She raised a hand. 'Don't worry if I'm late. Get them to start the show without me.'

She waited until Kolvenbach's car had turned the corner before crossing the road to a phone booth.

McCarthy was nervous. Govorko was good but Spiro was better at this sort of work and Spiro was in hospital in Alice Springs. By the time he was released, McCarthy would be a rich man. Very rich. The thought of all those millions made him feel better. He checked the mirror. No sign of Govorko's car but that was all right. Govorko knew where McCarthy was going and he'd be well back, to make sure they weren't being followed. Even so, he used the phone. Yes, Govorko was there, two and a half blocks back. All clear.

'He's there', he announced. 'No one's following.'

Laura, who was holding the street directory and was concerned with where they were going, not what was behind them, said, 'He was there and no one was following two minutes ago'.

'In this business, it pays to check.' McCarthy replaced the phone but his fingers lingered to tap a nervous beat. 'Are you sure you know where to look in the car?' He'd asked the same question several times.

'Exactly. I might need help to get to it. It depends on the damage.'

'But you know?'

'Oh for heaven's sake, relax, McCarthy.'

'Montague told you?'

'I saw.'

'You two must have been close.'

'Just this once.'

'You're cute.'

'You're nervous and it's making me nervous.'

'Not you. You've got nerves of ice, lady.'

'Thank you. Next turn left. This is it.'

McCarthy turned, slowed and scanned the street. There were a few parked cars. No pedestrians. Slowing even more, he passed the yard. It was lit by a single bulb which shone above the door of a small shed. One group of wrecks, stacked near the fence like metallic sandwiches, glinted with grotesque reflections. The mangled Porsche was in shadow. They saw a dog, a German Shepherd lying under the light, lift its head at the sound of the car.

McCarthy stopped beyond the yard and picked up the phone. 'We've reached it,' he told Govorko. 'It seems okay but do a pass and make sure everything's clear.'

Govorko acknowledged, drove past McCarthy's Falcon and did a slow lap of the block. He re-entered the road and parked about fifty metres beyond the corner, where he had a good view of McCarthy's car and the wrecking yard.

'Nothing.' He lowered his seat.

They were parked on the other side of the road. Kelly was sprawled across the back seat with one eye level with the window. 'That man in the Commodore is either with them or watching them.' Kolvenbach, compressed into the driver's seat, began to lift his head, but Kelly stopped him. 'He's looking around. He's tilted back the seat but I can still see him.'

Up the road McCarthy got out of his car, walked to the yard and stood at the fence. Snarling, the dog charged him. McCarthy tossed something through the wire and hurriedly returned to the car.

After a few minutes, Kelly saw the dog fall down. 'He's doped it.'

'Can I get up?' Kolvenbach's ribs were hurting.

'No. The man's still looking.'

Kolvenbach grumbled, disentangled his legs from beneath the steering wheel and stretched himself across both seats. Without bothering to ease into the topic, he said, 'You are foolish to think your wife will come back to you'.

The man in the Commodore had twisted to check their side of the street and Kelly lowered his head. 'Really?'

'Yes. I've had some time to study her and I feel I can say she has no intention of returning to you. Or to any man. In fact, I can't imagine a woman like that being married to any man. She's very... strong... amazingly self-contained. She's quite ruthless, you know.'

'Is she?' Kelly's voice was flat. First Monica, now Kolvenbach. The difference was that Kolvenbach had probably been sleeping with Laura.

'When I was hunting you, thinking you had murdered my brother, I told her I might have to kill you. That was if you resisted, or threatened me. Do you understand?'

'Sure.' Perfectly all right to kill me, he thought, as long as you believed you were doing the right thing. No hard feelings.

'She didn't mind.'

He lifted his head to check. The other man had sunk out of sight. 'Mind what?'

'Mind the thought of me shooting you.'

What bullshit. 'Is that so?'

'And later, when McCarthy or someone had sent a man up to Alice Springs to kill Laura, and I had managed to overpower him, she quite seriously asked me if I intended to kill him.' He shifted in the seat and Kelly felt the vehicle rock.

'Don't move.'

'Sorry. I am very uncomfortable.'

'Well, put up with it.'

Kolvenbach laid one arm across his chest, to soothe the sore ribs. 'She said it in such a way that it sounded like a suggestion, not a question. Do you understand?'

'Very clearly.'

The big man grunted, lecture finished, summary about to begin. 'So I would forget her. I think you're probably a nice man. You should get away from her while you're still in one piece.'

Kelly saw McCarthy get out of the car and cautiously approach the fence. 'He's going to see if the dog's asleep.'

'And is it?'

'Well and truly.' He raised his head until he could peer through the rear window. 'I'm frightened that Monica's going to come breezing around the corner and give us away.' He slid out of sight. 'We should never have let her go.'

'You were the one who was hungry. Anyhow, she's better out of the car.' Kolvenbach risked a glance through the windscreen. 'We should do something before she gets back.'

'Not yet.' McCarthy was walking back to the car. Settling into a position where he could observe him and yet be hidden from the man in the other car, Kelly said, 'Do you mind if I ask you a question?'

'People who say that always mean an awkward question. Go ahead.'

'Why are these papers so important?'

Kolvenbach made a soft, rumbling sound. 'How well did you know Harald?'

'Reasonably well. It was a business arrangement. We'd had a few meetings, a few meals together. I liked him. I think he liked me.'

'He was a very direct man but naive in some areas. He was impatient with complex issues, with things that wasted his time, with matters that required finesse or the untangling of red tape. He liked other people to handle such things. He disliked politicians and bureaucrats. Didn't know how to deal with them. There was one man in Canberra, a very senior politician, who was involved in the granting of permission for the project. There is the question of Aboriginal land, you see. Very complex. Baffling to an outsider. Harald was persuaded that some gifts and a bit of cash would smooth matters.'

'Bribes?'

'That is what people would call them. He was told it was the natural way of doing things. Inevitably, things developed and the bribes got bigger. The biggest bribe of all was required by the man in Canberra.'

'And all this is in the papers?'

'There are letters. Unhappily, there are also notes. Harald made notes of every transaction.'

'And if the wrong people found these papers, they would cause you, er, great embarrassment.'

'It could mean the end of the mining project, with the loss of millions of dollars. Disgrace. Gaol.'

'You'd go to gaol?'

'Probably. And the man in Canberra.'

'But you weren't involved.'

'The company was.'

Kelly saw Laura and hushed Kolvenbach into silence. 'They're both out of the car,' he whispered.

McCarthy had injected enough drops into the meat to put the German Shepherd out of action for twelve hours but he still approached the fence with caution. He was frightened of dogs. Most people were, which is why big dogs were so common in new-car yards, used-car yards and graveyards like this.

He used bolt-cutters to slice through the chain, and opened the gate. Laura followed. They went to the Porsche.

She held her breath, not knowing what they

might find when they were close enough to smell the oil and acid, to touch the scraped paint and look inside. She bent to look and breathed again. There were no ghastly pools of dried blood, no leftovers from the last hideous moments of the man who had been strapped behind the wheel. Gerry's Porsche was a shadowy mass of painted, plated, moulded, stitched, broken things.

She made a small laughing sound. 'Kelly went through all that to win this car.'

'Life's like that, lovely lady. Yesterday's treasure is today's junk.' McCarthy put down the tools he had been carrying and produced a torch. 'Now, where's the hiding place?'

She led him to the back. The crash had bent the engine cover and ripped one end off the vast spoiler and, for a moment, she was concerned that the special enclosure might have been crushed or torn away. But the flat six-cylinder engine seemed to be intact. Certainly, she could see the air filter.

'In there.' She pointed. 'Gerry modified it to make it half filter, half receptacle. It was his second hiding place.'

McCarthy pushed past her and flashed the torch into the engine bay. It was covered in oil and mud. 'In the filter?'

'Yes. You have to take it apart.'

'Our friend Gerry was a great one for hiding things in strange places.' He chose a spanner. 'Either the cold of a freezer or the heat of an engine. Very resourceful.'

'He liked the unusual.' She reached into her purse.

Despite his aching side, his damaged arm and the bandaged ear, Kolvenbach was keen to move. The man in the Commodore was the problem. 'We will have to remove him. I will take care of it.' He reached up to ensure the interior light switch was in the off position. 'Is he looking this way?'

Kelly peeked. 'Christ. He's getting out of the car.'

'And doing what?'

Kelly smothered a laugh. 'He's having a piss. He's got his back to us.'

'Perfect.' Kolvenbach opened his door and slid to the footpath. Kelly followed. He was anxious to be out of the car, to find out what McCarthy was up to and discover why Laura was with him.

Bent double, Kolvenbach glided across the road, withdrew his large pistol from a trouser pocket and was waiting when Govorko zipped his fly and turned.

He aimed the pistol at Govorko's belly. 'Hands up. No noise.' His lips spread in a mirthless grin. 'I'm sure you know the rules.'

Kelly was behind him. 'I might have a look at what's going on in the yard.'

'Just a look. I'll be with you in a minute.'

McCarthy had great difficulty prising apart the air-filter casing. He found no filter element; instead, the case was divided in two, with one half clear to suck in air and the other blanked off and lined with a heavy plastic. Tucked inside was a large, folded envelope.

'The papers,' he breathed and stopped. A small but cold ring of metal was touching the back of his ear.

'Pass them to me.' Laura held the small assassin's pistol Kolvenbach had given her in Alice Springs.

'This is most foolish of you,' McCarthy said but, without turning, handed her the envelope.

'Don't you be foolish and try something. This gun is small but very effective at this range. Now, I'm backing away to see what we've found. Don't move.'

He attempted a laugh. 'Believe me, lovely lady, I won't.' McCarthy was trying to picture the scene behind him: she would have the pistol in one hand, the envelope in the other. She would use both hands to open the glued flap and for a brief period, the gun would be pointing up; her attention would be focused on the papers. The .38 pistol he had intended using on her later that night was under his armpit. He was not quick but he could draw it and fire in, say, two seconds. How fast would she be? Facing him, gun in hand . . . maybe one to one and a half seconds.

He decided to wait until he had turned and could see her. He had passed the age of taking uncalculated risks and was now cruising through the age of cunning. He should keep her talking.

'What happened to our agreement?'

'It's being renegotiated.' She opened the envelope. There were two bundles, each held by a spring clip. She turned so that the light from the shed illuminated the papers.

'What have you found?'

'Papers. Be quiet.'

One lot were notes in Gerry's handwriting. She put them back in the envelope. The others were the ones they were after: a mixture of sheets bearing strange names and sums of money and a few typed pages.

'Well, we've found what we were looking for,' she said and raised the pistol, aiming at the back of McCarthy's head.

'No!'

It was Kelly.

She spun towards him but he was so close he knocked the gun from her hand.

McCarthy, as cumbersome as a great turtle and wheezing from the constraints of bending beneath the mangled engine cover, advanced on Kelly. He raised the torch like a club.

Kelly hit him and McCarthy stumbled backwards into the wreckage of Gerry Montague's Porsche.

'Quick.' Kelly grabbed Laura. 'Get out of here.'

She tried to hit him with the papers and he pulled them from her. She pummelled him with both fists.

'What are you doing? I know where he's got the diamonds.'

'Laura, for God's sake get out of here.'

'We can share. I know where they are. Don't you understand?'

He pushed her away. 'I don't know what you've done, but try to get away, please. Before it's too late.'

'Give me those.' She snatched at the papers.

Bright lights flooded the yard. Suddenly, there were men near them, lithe, sinister men in dark outfits and blackened faces. Some rose from the fence. One stepped from the shed. All were armed.

Kelly swung away from them, out of the glare of the lights. He had the envelope in one hand, the sheets of paper in the other.

When he turned to face them again, Kolvenbach and Govorko were at the gate, surrounded by men. McCarthy was being hauled from the wreckage of the Porsche.

Laura was near him. 'I hate you, Kelly. I want you to know that. You're so weak.'

Mallowes came forward and stopped in front of McCarthy. 'Hello, George, fancy seeing you here.'

'Ben.' McCarthy made a show of being delighted. 'Thank heavens for a friendly face. What a night.' He brushed his clothes. 'I've been following this little lady for some time. She led me here. There was a secret hiding place in the car.' His face bloomed into bright flushes of incredulity. 'In the motor. They had built this hiding place in the motor. She went straight to it. Fantastic. I think I've solved the case.'

He was walking towards the gate, constantly brushing his clothes; a man about to say goodbye and go home. Mallowes, walking with him, had not returned the smile.

'What are you doing here, George?'

'I told you. Following her. I've been doing it for days. All because I was a good friend of Gerry Montague.' He was pumping out sentences. 'I don't know how to say this but I discovered that the two of them were involved in the Kolvenbach case — you know the big diamond robbery and the murder a week or so ago?'

'Montague and Mrs Hunnicutt were involved?'

'Yes.' He had grease on the cuff of his pants and bent, worrying over it.

'Okay.' Mallowes nodded to one of the special policemen. 'Take Mr McCarthy back to Russell Street. I think we'll have a nice long talk a little later.'

'Ben!' McCarthy was led away.

Mallowes walked slowly across the yard to where Kelly was standing. 'You're Kelso Hunnicutt?'

The end of the game. The end of everything. He felt deflated, incredibly weak. 'Yes.'

Mallowes took his elbow. 'You've no idea how much we've been looking forward to catching up with you.'

The street was wreathed in mist and Monica, waiting outside the car, had folded her arms against the cold and was restlessly crossing and uncrossing her feet. The box with the coffee and hamburgers was somewhere on the footpath, where the policeman in the blue cap and blue overalls had told her to put it. Everything would be cold and the shop would be closed. A few people had gathered to watch. A man who had been walking a pair of terriers sidled up to her. 'What's going on? Any idea?'

'I think someone broke into the car yard.'

The man peered at the bent and crushed relics.

'I didn't think times were that tough,' he said and resumed his walk.

Inside the car, Mallowes and Kelly were each squeezed into a corner of the back seat. Kelly handed the detective the envelope.

'That's what they were after?' Mallowes turned the envelope in his hands. He played with the opened flap. 'Must be interesting.'

'Apparently. I interrupted when I thought there was going to be a shooting.'

'We saw.' He glanced at his watch. 'Well, what say we bring Miss Tate inside and we all go to a place where it's a bit warmer.'

Ulverstone ordered four coffees. Monica was in the corner, still shivering from the cold. 'Miss Tate had the presence of mind to ring me. Apparently you'd mentioned my name?'

Kelly glanced at Monica. He was numb. The time for thanks or accusations had yet to arrive.

'She was concerned for your safety. She thought, quite reasonably, and I would say accurately, that you were putting yourself at considerable risk. However, we had a fair idea of what was going on and we already had some of our special forces in place in the yard.'

'How?'

'We'd been following Mr Kolvenbach for some time. Not that he was necessarily under suspicion but my colleague, Detective Mallowes, had deduced that Mr Kolvenbach seemed to have greater knowledge of your whereabouts than we did. We followed Kolvenbach so that he might lead us to you. Instead, or perhaps I should say, additionally, he led us to George McCarthy and your wife.' Ulverstone stroked his cheek. 'A most unusual combination. They led both Mr Kolvenbach and us to that wrecker's yard where Montague's Porsche was kept.'

He drank some coffee but never took his eyes from Kelly. 'Do you know what was in those papers you gave us?'

Kelly shook his head.

'Notes made by your former partner, Mr Montague. They were most comprehensive. They appear to implicate both himself and, I'm sorry to say, your wife in the murder of Harald Kolvenbach.'

Kelly lowered his head. Monica was looking at him, he knew. He closed his eyes. He wanted to be alone, to lie down, to shut off his thoughts, to sleep.

'Some of my people are presently questioning Mrs Hunnicutt. There's a very strong possibility that we'll be laying charges against her in the morning.'

Kelly looked up.

'They may be most serious charges, Mr Hunnicutt.'

Monica coughed discreetly. 'Can Kelly go home?'

Ulverstone glanced at Mallowes, whose eyes flickered. 'Why not?' He bent his head, to meet Kelly's lowered eyes. 'We could reach you tomorrow? I'm sure there are more questions that some bright detective on my staff will think up.'

'Of course.'

'He's staying at my place,' Monica said. 'I live near Warburton.'

Kelly shook his head. 'No. I'll be going home.' He glanced at Monica and smiled. 'Thanks. I'd rather go home. I'll be okay.'

'You led us quite a chase, Mr Hunnicutt.' Ulverstone rose and sat on the corner of his desk. He gave a brief but conspiratorial smile. 'I rather like travelling in the bush myself. I'm a keen angler, you see. Rivers and dams. Perch, cod, trout. Wonderful fish.' Eyes glowing with secret visions, he held out his hand. Kelly shook it. 'One day, Mr Hunnicutt, we must get together and have a long chat. I'd like to know where you've been. You might know some good, secluded spots.'

Monica laughed. 'You'll need a long time. He'll not only tell you where he went but the history of the place.'

Kolvenbach was outside. He was on a small chair and looked huge: a circus bear on a stool. He got up, shook hands with Mallowes and assured him he could be reached at the number he'd given them. Gloomily, he led Monica and Kelly to his car.

'So you're off the hook?'

'Yes.'

'Good. There is justice after all.' He shook Kelly's hand, tried to smile and then grew sombre. 'And they've read the papers?'

'They've been examining them very carefully.'

Monica said, 'They're talking of laying charges against Laura'.

'I'm not surprised.' He touched Kelly's shoulder. 'I'm sorry. I know how you feel but it is the way it must be. I had a feeling about her.' They reached the car and he unlocked the door. He sighed, spreading mist across the roof. 'I am a great hunter. I didn't catch you, I didn't get the papers. Both my quarries eluded me. Now the police have the papers and, tomorrow, I can expect the beginning of an inquisition that will lead to very unpleasant things.'

They got in the car. While Kolvenbach was buckling his seat belt, Kelly unbuttoned his shirt. He handed Kolvenbach a sheaf of papers.

'There were two lots of papers in the envelope. I gave the police one batch that I thought didn't matter. These are yours.'

Mouth open, Kolvenbach took them.

'I haven't read them,' Kelly said. 'I don't want to. Why don't you take us back to your place, make some coffee and use those papers to light a nice, warm fire?'

It was two weeks before Kelly saw Monica again. She called at his house; they had arranged to have lunch at a Chinese restaurant in Little Bourke Street. She had painted the minibus. It was now a dark bush green but both sides were covered with paintings of exotic birds.

'You've been busy.'

'Do you like it?'

'It's unusual.' He walked around the bus. 'Won't it frighten the birds?'

'Birds do not get frightened by pictures of birds.' She nudged him in the ribs. 'I took it to my mechanic. He says it was a good buy.'

'Great.'

'All it needed was a little motor.'

'You mean a short motor?'

'That's it. He put in a short motor.'

'You needed a new engine?'

'Not me. The bus. He says it will need running in.'

They were finishing lunch. Kelly reached across the table and touched the back of her hand. 'Have I ever thanked you properly for what you've done for me?'

'No.'

'Thank you.'

'You're welcome. Why don't you pay for lunch and we'll say we're all square?' She used the napkin to wipe some chili crab from her lips. 'What are you going to do now? You need to get away for a while.'

'I've been away.'

'You know what I mean. You should have a break.' Kelly's return to Melbourne and the charges against Laura Hunnicutt and George McCarthy had been major stories. Television crews had even camped outside his house for days.

'Well, I have a good Landcruiser hidden on the bank of a creek up in western Queensland. I should go back and get it before it rains and there's a flood.' He thought for a moment. 'And I should go and speak to a character at the opal fields near there and tell him where he can find his wagon. And I should go back to Innamincka station and find their motorbike for them.'

'You're going to be busy.' She used the finger bowl again. 'So am I. I haven't got nearly enough paintings for this exhibition of mine and now I'm behind schedule.'

'So what will you do?'

'Go back. Do more paintings.'

'To Queensland?'

'I was thinking of going somewhere near Cunnamulla, actually.' She folded her napkin and slowly raised her eyes. They were bright with challenge. 'Could I interest you in a lift?'

He hesitated. 'Do I have to wear a beard?'

'Not this time.' The eyes grew brighter. 'It'd be a good chance for us to plan your next couple of films. I've got some ideas...'

EPILOGUE

A few months later, Kolvenbach's Kimberley diamond project was officially opened. The site was magnificent: a clearing in the middle of a ring of mauve mountains with distant stands of baobab trees providing bulbous splashes of white. Seats were arranged on a levelled patch of red earth and the official stand was bedecked with national and Aboriginal flags, and rosettes and streamers of red, white and blue. The principal guest, who delivered an eloquent speech in praise of the pioneering work done by, and the cooperative spirit shown by both the mine management and the Aboriginal elders, was the Minister for Aboriginal Affairs, the Honourable Rob Lister.